# OTHER CARRIERS

Manuel Antonio Rodríguez (age 5)

Juan Ortiz (age 11)

Cándido de los Santos (age 4)

José Fragoso

Luis Blanco (age 2)

Ignacio de Jesús Aroche (age 11)

Juan Bautista Madera (age 13)

Bartolomé Díaz (age 8)

Andrés Díaz (age 10)

Josef Toribio Balsa (age 7)

Josef Celestino Nañez (age 8)

Doña María Bustamente's son (age 10)
  and two slave girls (ages 6 and 8)

Ten soldiers from regiment in
  Veracruz to Mexico City

Governor Castro's two daughters

Dr. Francisco Oller's sons

Twenty-eight children waiting at
  Puerto Cabello, Venezuela

Juan Valiente's daughter (age 18 months)

Miguel José Romero, drummer boy
  of Cuban regiment

Three slave girls sold by Lorenzo Vidat

María Desideria Castillo (age 4)

Máxima Esparza (age 4)

Apolinario Pardo (age 5)

Toribio Lorenzana (age 6)

Juan Francisco Morales (age 6)

José Antonio Lagunas

José Ricardo Vello

Five musicians from Veracruz
  to Campeche:
    José Velasco
    Mateo Vargas
    Matías Gonzales
    José Carmona
    Ignacio de la Torre

José Marcelino Ferroz

Juan Nepomuceno Marnz

José Luiz Gonzala

Juan Bautista Cuenca

Apolinario Saranyo

Mateo Mora

Fernando Cheuca (age 10)

Juan Bautista Cheuca (age 7-8
  months)

Francisco del Patrocinio (age 10)

Three boys from Manila to Macao

One Chinese boy from Macao
  to Canton

# SAVING THE WORLD

# SAVING
# THE
# WORLD

A NOVEL

Julia Alvarez

*A Shannon Ravenel Book*

ALGONQUIN BOOKS OF CHAPEL HILL 2006

ℝ  *A Shannon Ravenel Book*

Published by
ALGONQUIN BOOKS OF CHAPEL HILL
Post Office Box 2225
Chapel Hill, NC 27515-2225

a division of
WORKMAN PUBLISHING
708 Broadway
New York, New York 10003

Excerpt from "Voices from Lemnos" from *Opened Ground: Selected Poems
1966–1996* by Seamus Heaney. Copyright © 1998 by Seamus Heaney.
Reprinted by permission of Farrar, Straus and Giroux, LLC.

Excerpt from "The Turn of the Century" from *Miracle Fair* by Wisława
Szymborska, translated by Joanna Trzeciak. Copyright © 2001 by Joanna
Trzeciak. Used by permission of W. W. Norton & Company, Inc.

This is a work of fiction. While, as in all fiction, the literary perceptions and
insights are based on experience, all names, characters, places, and incidents are
either products of the author's imagination or are used fictitiously.

Library of Congress Cataloging-in-Publication Data
Alvarez, Julia.
    Saving the world : a novel / Julia Alvarez.—1st ed.
        p. cm.
    "A Shannon Ravenel book."
    ISBN-13: 978-1-56512-510-0
    ISBN-10: 1-56512-510-X
    1. Married women—Fiction.   2. Middle aged women—Fiction.
  3. AIDS (Disease)—Patients—Fiction.   4. AIDS (Disease)—Patients—
  Family relationships—Fiction.   5. Expedición Marítima de la Vacuna
  (1803–1810)—Fiction.   6. Balmis, Francisco Xavier de—Fiction.
  7. Vaccination—Fiction.   8. Smallpox—Fiction.   I. Title.
  PS3551.L845S28 2006
  813'.54—dc22                                          2005053064

10 9 8 7 6 5 4 3 2 1
First Edition

FOR BILL

*believer*

After such knowledge, what forgiveness? Think now
History has many cunning passages, contrived corridors
And issues, deceives with whispering ambitions,
Guides us by vanities . . .

                 Think
Neither fear nor courage saves us. Unnatural vices
Are fathered by our heroism. Virtues
Are forced upon us by our impudent crimes.
These tears are shaken from the wrath-bearing tree.

T. S. Eliot
from "Gerontion"

History says, *Don't hope
On this side of the grave.*
But then, once in a lifetime
The longed-for tidal wave
Of justice can rise up,
And hope and history rhyme.

Seamus Heaney
from "Voices from Lemnos"

The child carriers are all but forgotten, but their humble if wholly unrewarded efforts deserve a place in human recollection.

Sherbourne F. Cook
from "Francisco Xavier Balmis and the Introduction
of Vaccination in Latin America"

# SAVING THE WORLD

# 1

In the fall of her fiftieth year, Alma finds herself lost in a dark mood she can't seem to shake. It's late September; she has actually not turned fifty yet, but she has already given that out as her age, hoping to get the fanfare and menopause jokes over and done with. It's not her own mortality that weighs heavily on her. In fact, it makes her sad when she reads that women of her profile (active, slender, vegetarian, married) will probably live—if they take care of themselves—to ninety and beyond.

She should probably feel glad that her glass of time is half full. But instead she wonders who might be alive in her dotage whom she would care to be with? Richard, her husband, overworked and project-driven, will probably not live that long; Tera, her best friend, over-weight and full of political-activist rage, will likely die before Alma does; her saintly neighbor Helen, already in her seventies, fat chance she'll stick around. Day after day, Alma feels that peppery anxious feeling that she has truly lost her way.

Earlier this year, she went to see the local, small-town psychiatrist, a very short man with an oversized face that reminded her of the post-deaf Beethoven. She explained that she felt as if a whirling darkness were descending on her, like dirty water going down a drain or that flock of birds in the film by Hitchcock.

The doctor, who'd been jotting down her explanation, had looked up. He was so young; he probably hadn't seen the film. "What kind of birds?" he had asked.

At least he is being thorough, Alma thought.

He asked a lot of questions, referring to what seemed a long list on a clipboard—about whether Alma had fantasies of killing herself, whether she had a gun in the house (Richard did keep an old shotgun down in the basement, which he would occasionally use on the raccoons and groundhogs that invaded his garden), whether there had been any untoward events in their family.

Alma tried to be accurate and provide him with the information requested. She was baffled by this dark mood but still trusting that medical science in the guise of Dr. Payne (incredibly, that was his name) could help her get back to her old self.

But after months go by and one after another of the antidepressants Dr. Payne prescribes fail by her lights—she is "better" but numb all the time; she sleeps well but can no longer smell the paperwhites Richard brings her; nothing truly upsets her, even when her agent, Lavinia, sends her an ultimatum letter about Alma's overdue novel. (She is going on her third year overdue.)

One afternoon when she is trying to rouse herself into some wifely attractiveness before Richard gets home, she goes into their bathroom, opens the cabinet and collects all the prescription bottles she has accumulated over the last months of treatment, and for some reason, rather than flush them down the toilet, she puts on her coat and walks to the back of their property near the tree line. She scoops a small hole in the ground with her boot and pours the contents of these vials inside—no doubt hundreds of dollars worth—then kicks some dirt over it. She is concerned that deer or raccoons or groundhogs will find this trove and drug themselves into a stupor and thus become easy targets for anyone with a shotgun, perhaps Richard himself. In these small ways Alma finds she can still trust herself. She rolls a heavy boulder over the spot, circles it with the upended emptied bottles wedged into the earth (the ground has not yet frozen), and then waits, for it seems some ceremony should close this moment. But she can think of nothing, so she merely stands there for a few more minutes before the dusk and cold draw her back indoors.

She tells no one, not Richard, not Tera, whose impatience with Alma's persisting sadness Alma can hear in her friend's voice. As always, Tera is involved in one or another of her causes—antiwar, antimines, antisomething—and any confession on Alma's part will bring on an invitation to join Tera on the front lines. But Alma knows she can't treat this thing with peace rallies and political work. So, no, she does not tell Tera either. (Another sign that her instincts are still trustworthy: she knows who to talk to, mostly who not to talk to.) Most definitely, Tera won't approve. *We're all so goddamn lucky*: hers is one of the voices lodged in Alma's head. *Depression is nothing but a first-world dis-ease* (she parcels out the word that way). Tera has been Alma's best friend since Alma ended up in this rural state two decades ago, still young enough to be thought of as a waif, not a lost soul. Now Alma is older, and as her sense of detachment grows, she watches Tera go about her campaigning, her picketing, her trips down to Washington with her live-in companion, Paul, to protest any number of atrocities that Tera somehow always finds out about; e-mail has proliferated her sources of horror. Alma watches Tera the way she would a movie, a good movie, but one she has seen several times already and that, therefore, leaves her slightly bored.

Alma pretends to Richard that she is still taking her antidepressants, but she goes about her own way. She writes Lavinia back and tells her an outright lie, that the novel is done and she is merely going through it one last time. She is still making an effort to maintain her old life, covering for herself, as if she is setting up mock models in one or another room, Alma cooking, Alma going to bed, Alma writing a letter, Alma writing a novel—displays people can look at through a lit up window—but meanwhile she has slipped out the back door with no idea where she is going except somewhere far from this place.

She has every intention of returning—that, in part, is the reason for her secrecy. But she has no story yet to lead her out of her dark mood and restore her to the life that, she has to agree with Tera, she's damn lucky to be living.

ABOUT TWO WEEKS LATER, Alma is standing by the window on the landing looking out at the place where she buried her pills. She has not revisited the spot since. There have been a couple of what the weatherman calls snow showers, dusting and disguising the ground, so she isn't even sure that the mound she is looking at is *her* boulder.

Again, it's that time of afternoon when even in happy periods of her life, Alma often feels a heaviness of heart. In fact, she once read an article in a woman's magazine about how this time of day, dusk, was the most often cited as the nadir of mood swings. She is standing at the window, not having had lunch yet or, more accurately, not remembering if she has had lunch yet, when she sees a man coming up out of the woods. Without a coat, that's what she notices first, wearing only one layer, as people up here like to say. She would be adding what she later learns if she says that this stranger's hair is longish, that the shirt is a worn plaid, that he is attractive in a mildly disturbing way. The man is walking up from the line of trees that separate their own from Helen's property. Pin oaks, Richard has told her, the last trees to let go their leaves. In fact, they still have their brown, withered foliage—why Alma might not have seen the man right off.

She thinks of calling Helen but then thinks again about the wisdom of worrying an old, near-blind woman, alone in a run-down farmhouse, relying on a walker to get around. Besides, this man isn't doing something wrong, he isn't carrying a gun or a chain saw. But the fact that he isn't wearing a coat strikes her for some reason as suspicious. He walks with large, easy strides—in good shape, every once in a while stopping, looking around, finally spotting the house. Alma steps back to one side of the window before he can see her and watches as he climbs up the slight rise toward the house. He is still a distance away—they have ten acres, "more or less," surprisingly a legal phrase in the local registries. It crosses her mind to check that the doors are locked, but the man has stopped—and this is the curious thing—at that mound, though she can't swear it's *the* mound, but she has herself believing it is. He has taken on the pose of discoverers or explorers in statues: one foot on that boulder as he looks around, reviewing the house, the surrounding pasture, Richard's garden, the pond with the raft already pulled out of the water and resting on four wooden blocks. Then the man turns, facing the woods, assessing, assessing Alma doesn't know what.

She stands there, waiting, annoyed at the ringing phone. For some reason the answering machine has not kicked in with Richard's curt welcome and instructions. Finally, when it seems that the ringing won't ever quit and the man has indeed turned to stone, she races down the rest of the stairs. Her intention is to get the portable and hurry on back to her lookout on the landing.

"IS THIS MRS. HUEBNER?" a woman's voice asks when Alma picks up.

Alma considers correcting her. But the woman has pronounced Richard's last name correctly, so Alma assumes the caller is someone he knows, perhaps a childhood friend from Indiana. "This is Richard Huebner's wife. Can I help you?"

"Okay," the woman says as if that's all she called to settle.

"Can I help you?" Alma asks again. Why doesn't she just hang up? The caller is obviously no one she knows. But she can't not respond. Years ago, she briefly dated a man who accused her of having a "victim personality." You make eye contact in subways, he explained. You stop when someone scruffy says, You gotta a minute? Good for me, Alma thought. But the man meant it as a criticism. As a reason for breaking up with her.

"Are you alone?" the woman wants to know.

By this time, Alma has made it back to the landing. The stranger is gone. "Who is this?" she asks. The woman now has Alma's complete attention. Of course, Alma is alone. Richard is at the office, meeting day today, two hours at least before she'll hear the garage door coming up under the floor where she has her study. "What is this about?"

"I'll tell you, I'll tell you," the woman snaps back. "It's not easy for me either, you know."

What can it be? Alma's mind begins racing around, inventing ways her life will soon be destroyed. She supposes that even a determined runaway will turn back if she looks over her shoulder and her house is on fire. Unless she has set that fire herself, of course. Alma feels a pang of guilt, as if she has brought on whatever losses are coming, even though she never intended anything to change. Her present state of mind is baffling and private. She doesn't want to lose Richard over it.

"I'm an old girlfriend of Dick's."

Richard, she almost interrupts the woman. Before Alma came into his life, Richard had been known as Dick among his family and circle of friends. From early on in their romance, Alma hated calling him Dick, a name she associated with the punch lines of stupid party jokes. Richard himself admitted that he disliked the nickname but didn't want to make an issue of changing it. Alma began referring to him as Richard to their family and friends, and slowly most everyone followed suit. It's one of the little changes she has brought about in his life that she prides herself on. This woman obviously knew Dick before his life with Alma transformed him into Richard.

"'Course he's going to tell you he doesn't know me." The woman could be laughing, could be clearing her throat. "They never know you, do they, after they get what they want."

Alma lets out a sigh of impatience. She wants her guillotine sharp and quick. Actually, Alma is hoping to be spared. In part, she doesn't want to be distracted from her present state, from the possibility of coming through to the other side of her dark mood. *Please*, she addresses Richard retrospectively. *Don't have done anything stupid, please.* A tryst during the company's last overnight retreat? A reunion with an old girlfriend when he flew back to Indiana for the funeral of a favorite uncle? Recently, he brought home a cell phone. Richard, who dislikes the whole idea of cell phones ("I don't want to be reachable every moment of my day"), now has his own private, portable number, courtesy of Help International, in case one of his on-site people needs to get hold of him. But mostly, Richard uses it to call home so Alma can read him the grocery list he has forgotten on the kitchen counter or to tell her he is stuck in traffic on Storrow Drive on his way home from his Boston meeting or to ask her how she is feeling, if she has made any progress in the novel he, too, thinks she is almost done writing.

Maybe Richard is also using this private line to get in touch with other women.

"I have some bad news," the woman is saying. "I'm calling everybody."

Alma is sure now. The woman has some communicable disease. But Alma can't really see how this applies to Richard. Her present mood notwithstanding, they have been basically happily, monogamously married for more than the requisite years you can carry these infections around with you. All those adverbs (*basically, happily, monogamously*) suddenly sound suspiciously assertive, defending themselves against the onslaught of *Are you sure?*

"Where are you calling from?" If Alma can place the woman, it might be easier to dismiss her.

"I've been so sick." The woman goes on, ignoring the question, as if she has to get through what she has called to report. "I just found out and so I'm going through my book to warn everyone." A *book* to go through? What does the woman run, a service? How many calls has she made already? Is Richard the first?

"What exactly is it you have?" Alma asks the woman, trying to inject concern in her voice. It's a strategy from her old hitchhiking days when some driver would suddenly turn weird or aggressive. Alma would start gabbing, asking questions, pretending to great interest as if being a nice person might keep her from being raped and murdered.

"I've got AIDS," the woman pronounces the word importantly. Like a trophy.

Of course, Alma is thinking. What other epidemic do people worry about in this part of the world? Elsewhere, along with AIDS, there are other plagues brewing, in terrorist bunkers, in open-door clinics with dirt floors, flies buzzing over wasted faces, diseases long since banished from the richer-world neighborhoods—Tera knows all about them. Alma has been researching the subject, specifically the smallpox epidemic, Balmis and his vaccine expedition around the world with little boys. She doesn't know why, but in her present mood, it's the one story that seems to engage her, as if through it she might discover where it is she is going.

"I'm calling all the wives," the woman is explaining. "I just know how men are. They're not going to tell you."

Alma has had enough. "Look here," she tells the woman. "I don't know who you are, but I know who my husband is, and he shares everything with me, okay? Everything. And for another thing, his past relationships do not concern me. If you want to talk to him, you have our number, you can call tonight." She is about to hang up, glad she has conquered her pettiness and mistrust, but the image lurks before her, Bill Clinton, Monica Lewinsky, the president having oral sex in the Oval Office while heads of state wait in the anteroom. Then there are Alma's cousins back in the Dominican Republic, fading beauties having their hair colored and their faces lifted, joining Bible study groups led by young, attractive Jesuit men from Spain, while their cocksure, cologne-scented husbands go off to their mistresses in designer guayaberas. Alma wavers, wanting and not wanting to know more.

"I know what you must think . . ." The woman's voice trembles. "But I'm not some whore. I'm just calling everyone to be sure."

Whore? How old-fashioned the word sounds. There are no whores in the USA anymore, Alma feels like saying. Everyone has a new name now. Flight attendant, waste disposal engineer, sex worker. And what does it mean that the woman is *calling everyone to be sure*? To be sure of what?

"AIDS is just the last stage," the woman goes on. She sounds tired, worn out with trying to reconstruct all that some health professional has told her. "I've probably been HIV for some time. But I don't have no health insurance. So I didn't know myself till I got real sick."

It's only now that Alma notices the woman's bad grammar. Oddly, it makes her feel safer. Richard wouldn't risk their happiness for someone who can't talk right, would he? Like a lot of former farm boys, Richard can be a snob about certain things. Then, too, the woman might not be smart enough to have gotten the details right. Maybe she had sex with Richard years ago. HIV doesn't lie dormant that long. Or does it? Alma knows so little about it—a pamphlet she read while waiting for her flu shot at the hospital. She actually knows more about Balmis and smallpox than about her own millennium's epidemic.

But this is irrelevant: Richard has told her about everyone he has slept with, and among the modest handful there are no quick affairs, ladies who might later call up with bad news. Alma recalls their first days as lovers (she was thirty-nine; Richard, forty-seven), the thrilling sense that even as middle-agers they could still be the principals in a love story: the long, housebound days on weekends the boys were with their mother, the rumpled sheets, the life stories they shared, the lights of the little town beyond the window, snow beginning to fall. "Okay," Alma says finally, as if granting the woman some point. "Just tell me, when did you and Richard get together?"

"Please don't get mad at me, Mrs. Huebner."

"My name is not Mrs. Huebner," Alma says, her voice rising again. "I'm Fulana de Tal." Her professional name, necessary camouflage upon family request. "It sounds too much like a title," Lavinia had objected, finally relenting when Alma explained that *fulana de tal* actually meant a nobody, a so-and-so.

"What?"

"Fulana de Tal," Alma repeats. She doesn't try to Americanize the pronunciation. This woman will probably assume that Richard found her during one of his third-world consultancy trips and brought her back to be the good wife it is now difficult to find in this country.

"You don't give a shit, do you? As long as you're safe." The woman's voice has turned nasty. "I hope you get exactly what you deserve! Go to hell!"

"Wait! Please!" Alma is the one pleading now. She wants the woman to take back her curse. But the woman has hung up her end.

Alma is still at her post at the window. She looks out as if she might spot the woman racing across the back pasture toward Helen's house. She thinks of the stranger she saw earlier. It's as if in her gloominess she has mistakenly wandered into some twilight zone, among the bruised and broken with no way to defend herself from their intrusion or ill will. This woman's curse is an infection she won't be able to shake off.

Only, Richard—loving him, being loved by him, if he hasn't already betrayed her— might save her.

SHE WANTS TO CALL Richard and hear him deny everything. But it's Thursday afternoon, when HI holds its weekly company meeting, reports from the different project managers: What's happening with the water-system project in the West Bank? Is the financing application for the Haitian reforest-a-mountain proposal finished? Did we get back the estimates and feasibility studies from the microloan coffee cooperative in Bolivia?

Whenever Richard talks about these meetings, Alma imagines all the men in the company standing over a large table map, dividing up the world. Always it's the men she imagines—though a few women do work as coordinators and project managers. And though Alma knows that Help International represents the good guys, many of them former Peace Corp volunteers, corporate Robin Hoods funneling funds from the rich and powerful in the first world to improve the lives of the poorest of the poor, their talk at these gatherings, at least as reported by Richard, sounds to her like four-star generals plotting in the back rooms of the Pentagon. Sometimes Alma wonders how much difference—besides content—there is between these types of men.

"A world of difference," Tera would say. Bossy and big-hearted, Alma's best friend is a force of nature. Just who Alma needs to talk to right now. Any number of times in the past, Tera has been the emotional equivalent of God reaching down toward Adam's lifted forefinger on the ceiling of the Sistine Chapel. Tera has breathed grit into Alma.

The phone rings and rings. Unlike everyone else Alma knows, Tera refuses to get an answering machine and buy into the impersonality of the first world. Dear Tera, everything is a political struggle. But Alma has learned to get beyond this first string of her friend's defense. She has come to realize that this is Tera's way of girding her loins, so to speak, making her poverty mean something. Tera actually survives on less than twenty grand a year and no health insurance, teaching as an adjunct at the local state college. She also conducts weekend journal-writing workshops in which a half-dozen or so women participants uncover horrible pasts and buried terrors. One time, as the guest writer, Alma sat through three hours of a sharing session. It was awful.

"Hey!" Tera sounds breathless. She needs to lose some of that extra weight. How to approach the topic again and not have it turn into the evil forces of anorexia attacking the organic, expansive shape of the female body. "I was outside," she explains. Tera is an incredible gardener—a passion she shares with Richard, although usually it takes the form of competition: who is still harvesting kale in November, who has the first tomatoes. "They're predicting a big frost tonight. Paul, don't bring that in here!" Tera's companion, Paul Vendler, is a tall, docile Quaker, whom Tera has been living with for way longer than anyone they know has been married. Needless to say, Tera does not believe in marriage. "Just set it in the mudroom for now."

It always annoys Alma: Tera's stereo conversations with her and Paul. Today especially, Alma wants her friend's undivided attention. "Tera, I just had this upsetting phone call," Alma blurts out.

"What happened? Hold on," she adds before Alma can even begin. "Shut the door, Paul. I can't hear a damn thing." It's Tera's own fault. She refuses to update the vintage rotary bolted to the wall of the kitchen, the receiver cord so short there is no way to migrate away from noise. Alma once tried to pass on her old portable (marriage with Richard doubled, and in some cases tripled, their cache of certain items: four alarm clocks; five assorted wine bottle openers; six phones, including two portables). But Tera refused the gift. "Ours works fine. But I'll take it for the battered women's shelter." Alma has not told Tera about the cell phone—afraid Richard and she will be consigned to that corrupt circle of consumer hell Tera reserves for people who replace things that aren't broken.

"Tera? Are you still there?" There is an absent sound on the other end. Tera must have given up on Paul and gone off to shut the door herself.

"Sorry," Tera says coming back. "Go on."

Alma has already decided she won't bring up her dark mood. She doesn't want a reminder about how lucky they all are. Right now, what Alma wants is Band-Aid reassurance, someone reminding her that her fears and doubts are unfounded.

"Have you talked to Richard?" Tera asks when Alma finishes her account.

"He's at a meeting. And I just couldn't concentrate on anything. I had to talk to someone." *Someone* doesn't sound like an adequate category for her best friend. "I wanted to talk to you."

"I wish you weren't so far away." Tera sighs. When they lived in the same town, they met almost every day for a walk and talk. Presence is important to Tera. It's one of her articles of faith: being there. Maybe that's why she has let herself get so large. More of her bearing witness, marching on a picket line, being there.

"Here's what I would do," Tera says in a voice so strong and sure, Alma feels as if her friend's capacious arms are pouring out of the receiver and wrapping themselves around her. Although they are the same age, Alma often thinks of Tera as older, wiser. "First, you absolutely need to talk to Richard before you get worked up. It sounds to me like this poor, lonely woman got diagnosed with this horrible disease and got piss-poor medical information and counseling and went home and took out her old address book and started calling everyone she even shook hands with or lusted after in high school. Seriously, the health care in this country is just the pits—"

"Like you say, it's probably nothing," Alma puts in, nipping Tera's rant in the bud. If Tera gets started on the Big Issues of the World, Alma's petty problems won't stand a chance. "It's just, oh, you know how down I've been, Tera. And this call just reminds me how everything can come tumbling down."

"You said it," Tera agrees. But instead of pursuing any number of corroborating horrors, Tera stays with Alma. Perhaps she senses the desperation in Alma's voice. "Hang in there. It'll pass, really. And you got me, babe, like the song says. Are you taking your Saint-John's-wort?"

Just the name makes Alma cringe. Unlike Tera, Alma doesn't believe in all those expensive, alternative tins and jars at the co-op. But it's more than that. She doesn't want to take Saint-John's-wort; she doesn't want to be on antidepressants; she has stopped going to Dr. Payne. There has to be a place left in modern life for a crisis of the soul, a dark night that doesn't have a chemical solution.

"I'll tell you what," Tera offers. "I'm going to drive down and stay with you till Richard comes home. I'll give you a back rub, make you some lemongrass tea, whatever you want. I just want you to know you're not alone."

"Oh, Tera." Alma feels a surge of guilty love toward her dear, generous friend, whom she so readily lets slip into caricature in her head. "I'm fine. Really." Richard will be home soon enough. It's probably best if Tera isn't here. Richard and Tera, well, they have to work at being friends. Tera's high-horse antiestablishment takes on everything offends Richard's bottom-line, heartland faith in the United States of America, the Golden Rule, and not biting the hand that feeds you. But Alma suspects that it has less to do with conflicting ideologies than with the fact that they both want to boss her around, though both are succeeding less and less these days.

"Richard doesn't have to know. I'll park on the back road. When we hear his pickup, I'll go out the back way and hike across the pasture."

Just the thought of her baggy-panted friend hiking across the back pasture, bumping into her Paul Bunyan peeping Tom, makes Alma laugh. "Ay, Tera, what would I do without you? I'm okay, really. Just promise that if Richard and I break up . . ." She doesn't know what to ask Tera to do or be in that eventuality. "You'll marry me, okay?" They've played this way for years. Holding hands walking down streets. Long, passionate hugs when they part or meet. Wannabe lezzes, their gay-couple friends, Marion and Brier, call them. In fact, when Richard and Alma first starting going out and he met Tera, he assumed that at some time in the past they had been lovers.

"I don't believe in marriage, remember?" Tera reminds her. "And don't talk horseshit. You and Richard are not going to break up."

"But if we do—"

"If you do, you move in with us. We fix up the shed as your study. We take turns cooking meals from the garden. We carpool, save on gas. We'll have a great life all together."

It's scary the way it sounds so doable. This isn't the reassurance she needs. "Well, like you said," Alma reminds them both, "this woman was probably just calling everyone in the phone book. Oh, Tera. I don't know why I've let this get to me. I mean I know Richard really loves me. We have a good life. I'm a lucky person."

There's a worrisome pause. "Of course, Richard loves you," Tera agrees. "I love you. Lots of people love you." It sounds like Tera is conjugating a verb that has always given Alma trouble, in English and in Spanish.

AFTER HANGING UP WITH Tera, Alma heads for her study. She'll try to squeeze a few hours of work out of this wasted day. Will and discipline have gotten her out of old lives and bad habits before; that's what she'll try for. Keep at it, and one day she'll look up and the dark wood will be a flourishing garden, kale in November, tomatoes in mid-January.

All morning, she has taken notes, answered e-mails, called a catalog company, pretending to be her mother. The wrong size cotton briefs have been sent, and her mother has called Alma to correct the mistake. Poor Mamasita is no longer able to negotiate her way through the automated mazes of customer service, much less rectify mistakes when an impertinent, young voice finally answers at the other end. There went Alma's morning. Then the intruder in the back pasture, followed by the woman's weird phone call have thrown her off completely.

It will make her feel good if she succeeds in getting herself back on track. A sign that at this mature stage of life, Alma can count on inner resources. Shouldn't she have deep ones by now, on the eve of fifty? Oil fields of inner resources to tap?

The file marked BALMIS is still on top of her desk, pages and pages of notes from the dull, dusty tome she borrowed from the university library, using Tera's card. Francisco Xavier Balmis was no spring chicken when he embarked on his smallpox expedition from the Galician port city of La Coruña in 1803, Alma's age exactly. He had already been to the New World four times, stints at a military hospital in Mexico City as a young man. But this time his plans were to continue around the world, from Mexico to the Philippines and on to China, with his boat-load of orphans, and then round Cape of Good Hope to St. Helena and home—a trip that would take almost three years to complete. His poor wife! *Josefa Mataseco, dates unavailable. Marriage, childless.* All of this Alma has learned from her e-mail correspondence with the historian in Spain who tends the Web site. There is a Web site on Balmis! A Web site on everyone.

Alma's mind wanders. What would it be like to live without Richard? It's not a new question. She has been bracing herself, ever since they lost both Richard's parents within months of each other almost two years ago now. Her own have moved to Miami, close enough to "home" to be flown back to the island easily for their last days, as they have instructed. Mamasita and Papote—sweet, slightly buffoon-ish names, courtesy of the grandkids—are now tottering on the edge of their graves, reaching out for Alma's hand. "I can't see anymore from my left eye. No, it's not a cataract. The doctor says there's nothing to do about it. Eat spinach. Can you imagine, I'm paying this doctor una fortuna and he tells me to eat spinach! Papote? You know how he is: Today he asked me if he had children. Yesterday he was quoting Dante. In and out. His blood pressure is up. Of course, I'm worried about his diabetes. He hasn't had a bowel movement in days. So, how are you?"

The losses that lie ahead . . . Alma is not looking forward to this next stage of her life. "Don't dwell on the inevitable," Helen often counsels as she creeps around her drafty kitchen, preparing their tea, Alma's visit the day's event. But like the proverbial child told not to spill her glass of milk, that's all Alma can think about. Maybe if she had had

children, she'd throw her gaze over her shoulder, see the next generation coming up and feel heartened. Having stepsons doesn't help,
though she tries to pretend that it does. David and Ben and Sam are
not her babies; she never pored over their little bodies, nuzzling and
grooming them; and it's that primal, animal comfort that is called for,
the creature surrounded by what it has spawned. She is proud of
them, her handsome, good-hearted stepsons, but she can't get over
their size, their big jaws, their flushed faces when she fusses over them
too much in front of their fancy New York City girlfriends.

"Nothing in the world like having children," her mother, who never
seemed to enjoy having her own, would lecture Alma over the phone
during the early years of her marriage. But Alma was never swayed.
Not much of her mother's advice ever worked Stateside anyway. Besides, a new husband and three young stepsons were challenge
enough. By then, Alma's first novel had been published, and she was
in the thick of a family fallout. The idea of generating more family was
terrifying.

Cosas de la vida, cosas de la vida . . . You look up one day, and the
adults of your childhood are gone, and the big questions you still
haven't answered come flooding into your head at three o'clock in the
morning. Who to turn to for answers? Alma wonders, remembering
the lines in a poem she recently read and copied in her journal:

> How to live—someone asked me in a letter,
> someone I had wanted
> to ask the same thing.

Her writing woes, though absorbing, are minor when compared with
the winds of time blowing right in their faces as the windrow of parents goes down.

Losing Richard is what she has been bracing herself for. A fatal
heart attack; a car accident, the body she loves strewn across the pave-
ment like so much roadkill. For a while, after the deaths of his parents,
Alma readied herself. She bought a small, spiral notebook and tailed
him for days, writing down instructions on how to do all the things in

the house that Richard always took care of, mysteries to her: hooking up the generator if the electricity failed, refilling the water softener, programming the thermostats. When she asked him to teach her how to plow the driveway, Richard said, "What on earth do you want to know all this for?"

"So I can live without you," Alma admitted grimly. Richard's eyes filled. "Oh, Alma, have a little faith." But he went ahead and taught her to plow the driveway, though her terror of driving through drifting snow convinced her that she would probably die of a heart attack if she tried to do this herself.

After this afternoon's phone call, Richard's loss, which Alma has always imagined as tragic and terminal, is now transformed into something tawdry: betrayal and divorce. I'll kill him! she thinks, smiling in spite of herself at the irony of causing the very loss she dreads. They have already had the infidelity conversation. "I'm not Hillary Clinton," Alma has told him. "I'm too insecure. I wouldn't like the person I'd become if I were married to a man I couldn't trust." Richard let out a deep, convincing sigh. "When are you going to get it through your head that I adore you?"

It's probably what Francisco Balmis told Josefa on the eve of his departure. Did she believe him? Did she look over the final registry of the members of the expedition—a list the Spanish historian sent Alma via e-mail—and ask, So what about this Isabel? Alma's own eye was caught by this little detail. Accompanying Balmis were six attendants, twenty-two boys, the ship's crew, and—unheard of on an expedition of this sort—a woman, Isabel Sendales y Gómez—or López Gandalla or Sendalla y López. ("Of her surname we cannot be certain," the Web historian noted.) Not only had the rectoress of the orphanage granted Don Francisco the little boys he asked for, but she had joined his mission herself! On the darkest days, when nothing else seems to interest her, Alma finds herself thinking about this crazed, visionary man, crossing the ocean with twenty-two little boys all under the age of nine, and the mysterious rectoress about whom nothing is known for certain but her first name.

It surprises Alma—being drawn to these historical figures. She never did very well in history when she was in school. Particularly as a child, reading about a watershed episode or a battle or an important discovery made her anxious: as if she were watching a scene of impending disaster she could do nothing to change. That Portuguese captain was going to buy that first cargo of slaves and start a shameful commerce that would lead to revolts, divided families, tragic lives, civil war, the Watts riots, the murder of Malcom X, Martin Luther King, on and on—a whole juggernaut of results to be dealt with in later chapters. Alma wanted to go back and yell, *Stop! You don't know the half of what you're getting us all into, a hemisphere soaked in the blood of innocent people!*

Maybe what intrigues her about the historical Balmis is that she doesn't know if she would have tried to stop him. Sure, poor orphans were used as visionary fodder, but the world was saved, sort of; massive epidemics prevented; the boys were given an opportunity to go somewhere where they could reinvent themselves and not always be bastard kids from La Casa de Expósitos. And so instead of feeling anxious or dreaming of intervening, Alma wants to go along with Isabel on the Balmis expedition.

Alma stumbled on this story as she was writing the sequel to her second novel: a multigenerational saga of a Latino family, something weighty to make up for the six-going-on-seven years since she published her last novel. Midway through part 1 (the eighteenth century), Alma realized she didn't care for these people; she was tired of their self-conscious ethnicity, their predictable conflicts. But what to do? The novel was bought! The signing advance spent. Her original editor, sweet Dorie, has been retired to an imprint focusing on memoirs by people who have worked for or are related to the famous: Lady Di's maid, Elvis's manager, William Faulkner's second cousin. A young, very hot editor has replaced her, Vanessa Von Leyden, Veevee as she is known in the book world. Alma has not met Veevee, but they have spoken twice: once, when Veevee called to introduce herself, and then when Veevee called again to introduce herself, no doubt having forgotten to check Alma's name off her master list. Often, in glossy magazines she peruses on grocery lines or in waiting rooms, Alma sees photos of Veevee, attending literary dos, handing over prizes, looking more like a model than someone who reads, much less edits, books. Maybe publishers have to do a certain amount of schmoozing these days of dwindling readership, midlist titles spiraling down toward the bottom line, corporate owners for whom books are commodities to be marketed as if they're so many barrels of crude oil or cases of wine. Pressure is on poor Veevee, on Lavinia.

"Veevee called," Lavinia sometimes mentions. "She wants a guesstimate."

*Guesstimate*? What is happening to the English language down in New York City? How to trust an editor who talks like this. "I can't talk about it," Alma tells Lavinia, as if it's some Latina superstition she has to observe, a mystical circle of silencio around the writing. Finally, Lavinia has backed off. Periodically, she forwards a gushing e-mail from a young fan or a note from an editor praising Alma's work, adding: *See, you have lots of loving, devoted readers eager for the next one*, as if she, too, suspects the truth: Alma has lost faith, caving in to that old self-doubt that's gonna get her in the end unless she taps into those oil wells of faith.

Alma's disenchantment with the book-biz world has been growing over the years: the marketing strategies; the glamour shots; the prepub creation of buzz, as the publicity departments call it; the clubiness of the blurbing; and, then, the panels in which one of every flavor minority is asked to respond to some questionable theme: Coloring the Canon; The Future of the American Novel; Politics and the Postcolonial Writer. And although Alma feels that it's a far piece from what she set out to do as a writer, she has participated in it, convinced that—as Lavinia constantly reminds her—she's damn lucky to be asked.

What finally sealed her silence was that mean-spirited article in a small alternative journal, an article that would have been otherwise ignored but was picked up by the mainstream media eager to report on mudslinging among the minorities. It had come about because of her name, that ridiculous name Alma adopted years back out of frustration and hurt at her family's censorship. Mario González-Echavarriga, the patrón of Latino critics, deconstructed Alma, as Tera liked to put it. *Fulana de Tal is nothing but a Machiavellian user of identity. Her ridiculous pen name is an irresponsible attempt to undermine the serious political writing by voices long kept silent. Does this writer consider her ethnicity a joke?*

It went on and on like this for three pages, two columns a page, quoting, or rather misquoting her remarks in feature articles that always—it's the lay of the land in journalism—got some detail wrong: her father had led a revolution (Papote fled the dictatorship); her grandmother was Haitian (Alma's great-great-grandmother had been a Frenchwoman back when the whole island belonged to France). The critic made the biggest deal out of the fact that Fulana de Tal would not let herself be openly photographed, that her picture on her book jacket showed a chiaroscuro face in the shadows, which, of course, made her look brown—which, he went on to suggest, was her point: to pass herself off as a woman of color.

How could someone get her so convincingly wrong? True, a jacket photo for an author attempting to preserve a measure of anonymity was tricky. Alma tried to beg off, but her editor insisted. In this tough publishing world, it was just too hard to sell a first novel by a writer who required total anonymity. You had to have a story to go with your stories.

Then, too, what was the harm? "Who has to know?" Lavinia argued. Alma could publish and tour as Fulana de Tal. "It's not like in this huge country anyone's going to recognize you." Spanish speakers would understand that Fulana de Tal wasn't a real name. So? In a population, which included a sizable number of illegal aliens, using a false name was, if anything, emblematic of the Latino condition in the USA, a solidarity gesture. And so it was received, until Mario González-Echavarriga came along.

Alma caved in to these arguments, too afraid to lose the big break she had so wanted and the livelihood she needed. At first, it was some-

thing of a game, and it had worked to her advantage. The secrecy surrounding who she really was created that buzz around her novels,
which did indeed help them sell. After the season of publication, the
buzz died down, her second novel went out of print, her first survived
through course adoptions, a popular multicultural chaser to the clas-
sics *Huck Finn, The Great Gatsby, Great Expectations,* her literary importance never big enough to warrant a newspaper sending out an
investigative reporter to hunt down the true identity of some flash-in-
the-pan autora.

During Q&A sessions after readings, the question, of course, always
came up. Why couldn't Alma use her real name? And she was frank,
explaining how her family had requested that she not use "their"
name; how, yes, she resented their petty reasons—their fear of social
embarrassment (Latina girls enjoying sex before marriage; enjoying
sex period; having breakdowns, divorcing—just like spoiled gringa
girls)—but she also understood their terror, the deep scars after years
in a dictatorship, the possibility they cited of political repercussions to
the extended familia who had stayed back home. Alma considered an
Americanized name, but her publisher vetoed that idea. A Latino
name was just too attractive a draw these days. Besides if an Anglo author wrote about a Latino family in today's charged multicultural climate, she would be raked over the hottest of PC coals, accused of
co-opting and colonizing nuestra historia.

"Why write?" a disheartened reader sometimes asked after hearing
Alma's story.

"It's not a choice," Alma would counter. Though with the years, she
began to wonder. So much staked on one passion. Monocultures always got in trouble; that much she has learned from Richard.

"Well, I think it's great we finally have Latino authors out there in
the mainstream!" some defender would exclaim, inciting a round of
applause.

Of course, Alma knew better. "Part of setting down roots in the field
of literature is finding there are worms in the soil," she reminded the
audience. She had stolen that remark from Helen, who had been

speaking about life in general and who, of course, found the good in this: worms enrich the soil; problems build character. When Alma was younger, she believed that people who were optimistic were just not as smart as pessimists. Now she sees the blessing and intelligence of Helen's resiliently cheerful point of view.

"That was awesome! Do you do that everywhere?" the events manager in a small bookstore in Chicago asked Alma during her last book tour. And it was then that Alma realized that although she'd been flooded with sincerity each time, any repetition of such moments condemned them to staginess and inauthenticity. She began to dislike her whole persona, to believe that writing under her pseudonym was actually bad luck. FULANA DE TAL IS DEAD, she titled the e-mail she sent Lavinia, cc'ing Vanessa and getting an instant *Out of the office; please contact my assistant* reply. (Was Veevee ever in her office? Did she actually edit manuscripts or did her assistant do all the in-office work for her?) Now that Papote's memory was foggy and Mamasita was unable to read with her bad eyes and perpetual agitation, Alma could safely write under her own name. What was the story she would tell openly as herself? What freedom would be gained with the loss of Fulana de Tal? Before Alma could even begin to answer these questions and rekindle some new spark of faith in herself, Mario González-Echavarriga's article appeared, pounding the last nails into the coffin in which Fulana de Tal lay.

"But that's what you wanted, right?" Lavinia argued. "And this negative publicity can only help! You'll sell more books than ever with the next one, believe me! We'll put the old, veiled picture on the cover and then a new full-face close-up in back. Maybe we can get Annie Leibovitz to do a new photo."

It was the first time ever that Alma hung up on someone. Even today with the disturbing caller, her manners had too strong a hold on her temper. But Lavinia's turning this attack into a marketing opportunity made Alma suddenly feel that in fact she deserved to be taken to task for letting herself become an ethnic performing monkey. She resented the assumption that her writing was nothing but a game of

hide-and-seek with her readers. So that's what Lavinia thought of her
work!

Maybe that is why Alma is fleeing to the nineteenth century. Why
Balmis's project intrigues her. The man wanted to do something truly
good—save the world from a deadly disease, a spreading epidemic.
But his means were questionable, using orphans as carriers of his vaccine! Did Balmis feel the least bit troubled? How had he talked the
rectoress, whose job it was to protect those kids, into going along with
him? She had been intrigued by him, no doubt about it. Alma studies
the only image she has been able to find of the man, a photo of a bust
on his Web site: the face a little too stern (there is something about
busts—severed heads, after all—that make faces grimmer), the jaw
too set, the carved, pupil-less eyes blank as if they are blind or gazing
far away. But there is a redeeming softness around the mouth, human-
izing the man, making him someone Alma, too, is tempted to find out
more about.

# I

SEPTEMBER 1803

IT WAS THE FEAST DAY of the twin brothers Cosme and Damián, patron saints of doctors, and our day to deworm the boys.

Once a year, by recommendation of the doctors at the charity hospital next door, we made our brew of rhubarb and calomel, mixed with plenty of molasses, and dosed all our boys upon waking. By midday, most of them had spent time on the chamber pots we had placed in the yard so as to keep the stench out of doors.

There they were squatting on their pots against the back wall. They had stepped out of their soiled tunics, and a big cauldron of soaking clothes was already setting on a low fire by the kitchen door. Nati was stirring, the white kerchief tied around her head making her look like a bandaged patient who had wandered over from next door. Every once in a while she caught my eye, and I guessed the thought going through her head. Where were our fine lady volunteers who came to earn indulgences and show off their good deeds when we needed them?

Little Pascual was holding on to my skirts, nagging that he was hungry. "No, you cannot have something to eat until supper!" I snapped at him. Where had my patience gone? Why had God spawned so many creatures into the world and left them for me to take care of?

Across the yard, several boys were calling for me to come see an enormous worm.

I turned away into the house, leaving Nati to tend to them.

IN MY ROOM, I lay down on my cot and closed my eyes. Imagine, I told myself, another place, another time . . .

But today, as with many days recently, my old stratagem would not work. I could not envision any other life for myself than the present one. Twelve years I had been cloistered in this orphanage or working at the hospital next door; before that, six years tending to the sick in their own homes. A lifetime inured among the sick and suffering.

Each of the sixty-two boys presently under our roof was like a stone closing up the doorway out. Why had we admitted so many? We hardly had room for fifty! But with the bad harvests of the last few years, fewer and fewer families wanted to take in another mouth to feed. And yet the same bad harvests only seemed to increase the number of bastard children abandoned at the hospital or at our very door.

Our benefactress had noticed the change in me.

"You are worn out, Isabel," Doña Teresa noted. "You need to take a fortnight away from your labors. Even our Lord . . ." *Rested on the seventh day.* I knew all her homilies by now.

As I lay there, my hand wandered as it often did to my face, exploring the rough skin, the misshapen nostrils. It was a perverse desire to pick at the wound, and each time, as if for the first time, I felt shock at not finding the face I had had before the smallpox. I had been spared, one of the lucky ones — so I was told by those who had not lost everything: mother and father and sister to the smallpox. And not just past but future loves! Was I to go down to my grave, having spent my allotment of time, without ever having known a man's love, ever given birth to a child from my own loins?

"A man would not bring the solace you dream of, believe me," Nati had told me. We were the same age, though Nati had two strapping sons to show for her ripe years. Her husband, "the father of the boys," as she preferred to call him so as to distance herself as much as she could from him, had disappeared when the boys were young, which was just as well. Whenever I lamented my single state, Nati would console me with discouraging tales of her marriage.

I felt the tears seep out from under my closed eyes. What, then, did one live for?

Imagine! I told myself now more desperately, another time, another place. My black dress and veil shed, my skin scarred or not scarred, no matter. It was the future, the world without me. Someone would come upon my story, all that was left of me, a story. Isabel, a good woman, the rectoress of an orphanage. Who would guess my desperation, my desire to break out of the life I was living?

In the yard, I could hear the boys shouting. Some rowdy game was afoot I was glad not to be there to put a stop to, but I had left poor Nati in the lurch. She was my right hand, the only one besides myself who knew how to read and write.

"That's enough, boys!" Nati was shouting. I could tell from her voice that she, too, was at her wit's end. I lifted myself from the bed to remedy what I could, stop a fight, stroke a sick boy's forehead, make a promise I could keep.

THAT EVENING, I WAS in the chapel, setting up for evensong. The day was finally done. The boys were cleaned up, and after prayers their only meal today awaited them. The halls and dormitories had been cleansed; we had borrowed Father Ignacio's censer from the chapel and waved aromatic smoke in every room. The place smelled of High Mass and just the faintest scent of what it was masking, the stench of human waste.

"Doña Isabel! Doña Isabel!" the boys were calling for me.

I heard the sound of running down the corridor. I sighed, gathering patience for the scolding I anticipated having to deliver.

Given the hour, I wagered the boys had probably spotted Doña Teresa's carriage through the windows and were racing to give me the news. Our benefactress often stopped by in the evening on her way home from some outing or other. "I hate going home to that empty house," she often declared. Doña Teresa had her own heavy losses to bear: her husband, Don Manuel, had been gored by a bull when, drunk and boasting, he had wandered into the ring at a bullfight. "How many times didn't I tell him it was a savage sport," she told me many times. Soon thereafter, her sole child fell ill with the smallpox, perishing in this very house—a boy not yet nine. "Why I am drawn to our dear boys," Doña Teresa had explained.

Her tragedy had indeed been the salvation of orphan boys, over a thousand harbored in La Casa de Expósitos, since it opened almost a dozen years ago. Our earliest residents, who had since grown to manhood, sometimes returned, bringing a young wife or newborn child for us to see. More often we heard of them conscripted into the navy, being buried at sea. The poor and helpless were all too often the fodder for the wars of our kings. But that was Doña Teresa's homily.

I sat myself down heavily in a pew and waited for the boys to run in with the news that Doña Teresa had arrived.

Almost as if this were a signal, the flock of darkness I had fought off all day descended, their wings beating in my ears, their black-feathered softness snuffing out the spark of my will. This would not do. This would not do. I reached in my pocket, absently, and felt for the rosary I had taken to carrying with me for solace. *Hail Mary, full of grace.* What grace would come to such as me? I fingered the beads as if they were magic, then pulled hard at the string until it snapped and the black beads spilled upon my lap.

The boys were now just down the hall, calling out for me.

I sighed and gathered the beads, putting them back in the pocket of my dress. Tonight, after the boys were asleep, I would string them back together by candlelight and then use them to pray for forgiveness and peace.

WHEN I CAME TO the door, the group of a dozen or so boys caught sight of me and braked to a stop. They knew the rules. "A visitor in the front parlor!" they announced as if this news somehow excused their shouting and running at full speed indoors. I would have corrected them, but the look on their faces stopped me. It was a look I knew well, excitement qualified by apprehension, the younger showing more excitement, unsuspecting as they still were of what the world was likely to bring them. A visitor could mean good news: someone in search of a foundling to raise, a childless couple or the more questionable lone man looking for a boy to do his work. Maybe by nightfall one of them would have a new family. This thought was running through their heads, to be sure.

"A man in a uniform," Cándido offered, his eyes widening, impressed.

A man was a further novelty in this world of children and the women who cared for them. As for the uniform, that was not unusual in our garrison city with its busy port, though a uniformed man's presence in a foundling house was somewhat puzzling.

"Did he state his business?" I asked, looking from one to the other. Despite their excitement, they seemed pale, weary, too. It had been a long day for them as well, I reminded myself.

"He didn't say." Cándido had become the spokesman. "He asked us if we wanted to serve our king!"

My heart sunk. Could the army now be drafting boys? For the first time in years we were not at war with England or France. But since May the two powers had been at war with each other, our neutrality doubted by both. "And so we are arming ourselves in preparation for going to war to prove our neutrality!" Doña Teresa had remonstrated, shaking her head, as if the king were sitting before her, ready to be improved. "Are you sure the visitor did not make mention of his business?" I asked again, trying to control the worry in my voice. The boys picked up my moods the way a pail of milk picked up odors. "Did he give a name?"

The boys had sensed my worry. Apprehension now had the upper hand on every face.

"His name is . . . is . . . F-F-Federico." Andrés, the older of the Naya boys, had a bad stutter. As he spoke, I cast a warning eye about, lest any make matters worse by taunting him.

"His name is not F-F-Federico!" Francisco mocked, having just joined us. No doubt he had stayed behind with our visitor, hoping for some advantage that could only be given to one. He was a big boy and a bully. One of the ones I had to struggle to love. "His name is also Francisco," he boasted. He would remember that.

"*Don* Francisco," I corrected. A courtesy owed to any man, no less one sent by the king. "Please tell Nati to attend to our visitor. Do so quietly," I added, expecting a noisy stampede to the kitchen.

Francisco shook his head. "The gentleman said he had orders to speak to the rectoress, Doña Isabel Sendales de Gómez," he rattled off my full name.

"Sendales *y* Gómez," I corrected. Was the fresh boy taunting me? *De* would only come to me by marriage. I had been teaching the boys about names. But why should they remember? They who often came to us with no names.

My old discomfort rose up, a peppery nervous feeling I knew well. Rarely did I attend to outside visitors. Occasionally, a dignitary or a bishop had to be greeted or an official required a report by the rectoress. Almost always, these visitors were accompanied by Doña Teresa, who would have forewarned them about the rectoress's strange habit. "Is Doña Teresa with our visitor?"

"No!" the boys chorused. "He came from the king," they repeated.

"He said he wanted a p-p-private audience with our rectoress," Andrés explained, blinking as if the stutter were afflicting his eyes as well. I eyed Francisco. *Don't you dare.*

There was no help for it but to go to the front room and attend to our visitor. "Boys," I ordered, "I want each and every one of you to ready yourselves for prayers." Groans. "Afterwards we will have our supper." I herded them down the corridor, stopping at my chamber door. "Go on. I'll be there soon."

"Are you going to cover yourself?" Francisco asked, calling attention to my vanity. I had caught him making faces behind my back, something rare in my boys. To most, I was the first face that had hung over their cribs and loved them into boyhood. But Francisco had come to us late; a drunk uncle had used and abused the boy, beating him within an inch of his life, which was why the boy had ended up at the hospital next door, miraculously recovering and becoming our charge. He had already been toughened by the hard ways of the world. "You are to help the younger ones get ready," I reminded him, ignoring his question altogether.

I watched for a few seconds as the boys strode away, then slipped into my room. Quickly, for I had kept my visitor waiting long enough, I removed my apron and shook out the folds of my skirt. I felt the heaviness on one side—the beads! I scooped them out and lay them on my bed to take care of later. As I did so, I heard a noise, too purposeful to be our cat, Misha, or the supper Misha would be after at this hour. I lifted the side of the coverlet and peered under the bed.

For shame! To use the most unfortunate and helpless of beings—orphan children—as subjects for this most questionable enterprise. The man was mad. I would not allow it, even if a king called for it! And to think I had been almost swept into agreement by this stranger's intensity. Satan, too, was a master of persuasion, so Father Ignacio had reminded me. Looking up, I spied the angel Gabriel descending from the court of heaven with his cruel annunciation. Was there no mercy in the world?

Our visitor raised a quizzical eyebrow, as if sensing my disapproval. "I can assure you no harm will come to the carriers. I would infect my own child were I fortunate enough to have one."

I had almost succeeded in shutting out his arguments, but this last remark was a foot in the door. He, too, had no issue. Perhaps he, too, was alone in the world? *It is difficult to lose those dear to us,* he had said. He, too, had devoted himself to the service of others to forget an enormous loss.

"You will need to talk to our benefactress, Doña Teresa Gallego de Marcos," I said hurriedly, for I was feeling unequal to judge the arguments of this intense man. Doña Teresa was no friend of our king. She would not give in easily to this questionable request.

"Out of courtesy, I will speak to your benefactress, of course. But this is the king's order," he reminded me. He picked up a scroll that lay beside his hat and reached across the table with it.

As if it were the smallpox itself, I would not touch it. "I trust your word," I said, refusing the proffered document. Rather he think I could not read than that I was defying a messenger of the king. "I can do nothing for you, Don Francisco. I am only the rectoress. I serve. I follow orders." Each additional excuse was an admission that I was having difficulty refusing him.

"I, too, only serve," he observed quietly. "It is why we are all here," he added. He had lowered his voice again as if this were a secret we shared, this understanding that we were here on this earth for a nobler purpose than to be feverish little clods full of ailments and grievances. Indeed, our true joy lay in allowing ourselves to be used for a mighty purpose. His words reminded me of what I had forgotten, dulled by habit, preoccupied by the dark flock of my own sorrows.

"What part is it you find most questionable, Doña Isabel?" He was asking *me*. What do my objections have to do with it? I thought of asking.

He must have sensed my timidity, for he went on. "Using these unfortunate boys, is that how you think of it?"

"If I do not protect them, then who will?" I had tried to keep passion from my voice, but I had failed.

Our visitor nodded in vigorous agreement. "The king himself will protect them, Doña Isabel! These children will become his special charge." Don Francisco broke the seal and unrolled the scroll, scanning it for the appropriate passage. "These boys will be taken care of, fed, clothed, educated."

"We are already providing all those services," I reminded him.

"But hand to mouth, day by day, always worrying about where the next funds will come from. I know how our charitable institutions are run. I myself have directed several hospitals here and in New Spain. The king is making these boys his special charge, as if they were his own sons!"

"At what cost to them?" I said sharply. "*If* they survive being infected—"

Our visitor shook his head, smiling at my ignorance. "You don't understand—"

"Oh, but I do understand!" In one quick motion, I lifted my mantilla and let it fall to my shoulders. I had thought to shock him but instead tears started in my eyes. Surely, he had imagined a different face from the grotesque one that now stared back at him.

But his own face betrayed no disgust or aversion. He was, after all, a man of science, interested in specimens. "I can understand why you would fear for your charges," he said quietly, rolling up the scroll as if admitting surrender.

The tenderness in his voice touched me. He understood. I bowed my head, fighting tears.

He was silent a moment. When he began speaking again, his voice was less insistent, as if he knew to tread gently on ground where many losses lay buried.

"Yours is precisely the fate we would be sparing so many from suffering. Four times I have traveled to New Spain, and each time I have seen suffering beyond my capacity to describe." He bowed his head, as if now, he, too, struggled for self-control. "Entire villages. Whole populations deci-mated. The afflicted tearing down their own houses on top of themselves, their homes becoming their sepulchers." His eyes glazed over. "You cannot imagine how powerless one feels. I am, after all, a doctor, my purpose is to heal."

My own losses seemed dwarfed by this dismal picture of universal misery.

"The natives in America have been especially susceptible, suffering a more virulent form of the smallpox than we."

Mamá, Papá, my sister were dead. Was that not virulence enough?

"The lucky ones who survive are so disfigured by the profound marks of the eruption, they horrify all who see them."

I, too, had seen those looks on faces. I, too, was one of those lucky ones.

"Hell will hold no surprises for me . . ." His voice trailed off.

He would hardly be going there! A man so touched by the misfortunes of others. Already, in my own mind, I was defending him.

He had been gazing absently at my face, but I saw him slowly return from the hell he had been describing. "Yours, Doña Isabel, if you will per-mit me to say so, yours was a kind pox."

A kind pox? Incredulity must have shown on my features.

He was examining me now. I reached for my veil to cover myself, but when he lifted a hand as if to prevent me, I allowed the mantilla to drop back on my shoulders. "Your face was marked, not marred, Doña Isabel. Of course, any blemish on a handsome face saddens us. But consider this. Time would have accomplished over the course of the years what the smallpox razed in a fortnight. You were spared the slower loss."

"I see you are not just a surgeon but a philosopher!" I had to smile, in spite of myself. But I could tell by his sober look that he had not intended any humor.

"The consolations of philosophy are numerous," he admitted, sighing. "But our losses must first be felt in the flesh. And I am imposing on you in a sad time, I can see." He gestured toward my dark dress. "Perhaps I should return in the morrow?"

I had already exposed my face, why not my true condition? "You are not imposing, Don Francisco," I assured him. "I lost my parents and sisters twenty years ago in the great epidemic. Thousands upon thousands perished here in Galicia." He nodded. Of course, he would know of that epidemic. "These"—I indicated my dress, lifting my mantilla slightly and rearranging it on my shoulders—"well, we have a boy here, also by the name of Francisco, who has helped me see that these are marks of my vanity, under the guise of courtesy to others."

"You are too harsh a judge, no doubt." His smile was kind. He could see the better facets of my nature behind the harsh mask I was holding up before him.

"Doña Isabel?" It was Nati in the doorway. She looked from one to the other, no doubt surprised to find me unveiled before company. "Shall we start without you?"

"Please, Nati."

She lingered a moment, no doubt trying to piece a story together. A visitor in uniform. An older man. Old enough to know better than to philander in our port city, getting some young lady in trouble. For shame. No doubt he was now in a pickle, or the young lady was, and he had come to make arrangements. Her face hardened in judgment. She cast me a look as she turned to go. *What did I tell you about men, scoundrels all of them!*

Alone again, Don Francisco explained how the vaccination would work. The carriers would not suffer any ill effects. A mere vesicle, perhaps a slight discomfort or feverish feeling. "Small price when one thinks of the salvation they will be bringing to the whole world. Yes, the whole world!" It seemed the expedition would not stop in the Americas but proceed across Mexico by land, from Veracruz to Acapulco, then on to the Philippines and China, round the cape of Africa and back to Spain. The names—New Spain, the Philippines, China, Africa—were ones I had taught the boys as I turned the globe stroking the places we would never go.

"And, of course, by being carriers, the boys will be spared the smallpox themselves. Immunity," he called it. "They will be bringing a bodily salvation, which will no doubt open the way to a larger salvation and conversion to the true faith." As he spoke, Don Francisco's eyes, and my own following his, were drawn up to the tapestry that hung like a presence in the room. In the growing darkness only the gilded touches were visible, the halo on the angel, the illuminated Virgin, and riding down a shaft of light, a tiny glowing being which was now transformed in my sight into the smallpox vaccine descending to save mankind. We had been looking to God, but salvation had issued from our own reasoning minds.

Oh sacrilege! I shook myself. Was this Don Francisco a servant of a higher purpose, as he called himself, or a minion of the Evil One? Had my rosary been in my pocket, I might have been tempted to thrust it in front of this stranger. Father Ignacio had advised I do this whenever I felt the Evil One lurking.

"You seem in shock, Doña Isabel?" His voice had a touch of amusement.

"It is a lot to learn in one afternoon," I admitted.

"Would that all my students and listeners were as receptive and intelligent as you."

Our Francisco had correctly named me. Vanity was alive and well in the rectoress. I ached for more of his good opinion. "You will not find Doña Teresa an easy person to speak with," I warned him.

"This *is* an order from His Majesty," he repeated.

"That might not get you a long way with our benefactress," I hinted. Doñā Teresa had powerful allies, who agreed with her opinions. The king indulged them, too afraid of alienating the nobility and leaving himself wide open to the rabble's revolution as his cousin had done over in France, losing his royal head in the bargain. I could already hear Doña Teresa's objections. She would not submit her orphan boys to some experiment that a silly cuckold king had no doubt been talked into by his vixen wife and her lover, that shameless tramp of a prime minister. "Indeed, Don Francisco, perhaps you should not mention that this is a *royal* decree." Another secret between us.

Our visitor cocked his head, studying me. A small smile touched his lips. "I see," he said at last. "But who shall I say sent me?"

"Did you not say His Holiness had blessed the procedure?" This was most unsettling! To be devising a stratagem to sway my benefactress—and with a stranger, no less! But I confess that what I felt was a sensation of pleasurable surrender to whatever good or bad angel was leading me on.

Our visitor was nodding. "Perhaps, Doña Isabel, it would be better if you could speak with your benefactress . . . in preparation." He hesitated as if in acknowledgment that he was sending me first into the lion's den.

In the silence that followed, we could hear the boys singing the Ave Maria. Far off, the cook and porter were setting the long tables. I could hear the clatter of bowls, the clang of spoons. The meals, the prayers, the lessons, the globe spinning under my fingers: Africa, China, Mexico. Every day the same. The small round of my daily life tightened like a noose about my neck. Again, I felt I could not breathe.

Don Francisco was waiting.

"I will speak with her." My voice was firm, but my heart was a wild bird trapped in the small, empty room of my life. "I will explain everything and prepare her for your interview."

Even in the dim light that fell from the tall windows, I could see the worry lines on his brow relax. "I would be most grateful," he began.

"But I will ask for a favor back."

Again, he cocked his head, bemused, waiting.

As he had been speaking, the idea had taken hold inside me. Later, I would tell Doña Teresa that it was Don Francisco who requested this. But I was the one who asked this favor of Don Francisco. I wanted to be a part of the noble purpose he had described. "You must take me with you," I said.

He did not immediately answer me. It was difficult to read his face in the dark room. I waited, I could feel the perspiration on my face, under my arms, between my breasts. My whole body seemed to be weeping—with joy or sorrow, I could not tell. I had chosen to change my life. Was this even possible? Perhaps only God in his wisdom had the power to do so, sending down his messenger with a divine invitation.

"It is not the custom for a woman to accompany these expeditions," he said finally.

"Someone must take care of the boys." I, now, was the one persuading.

"I have been assigned three assistants, three nurses, three practitioners, men all of them, to be sure—"

"And these boys need a woman's touch." I finished his sentence. My boldness had indeed grown in the course of our interview. "It will go a long way to convincing Doña Teresa to say the rectoress will go with our boys."

"I see," he said again. "The boys will need a woman's touch," he repeated, as if he had just thought up this idea himself. There was a smile in his voice. Already we were working together to save the world by removing whatever impediment Doña Teresa might put in our way.

Before he departed, Don Francisco asked that I begin sorting the boys; all those who had suffered the smallpox or been exposed to it must be weeded out. If there was the slightest doubt, the boy must be eliminated. One or two wrong choices and the expedition could be imperiled. He had calculated that exactly twenty-two carriers would be needed to cross the ocean and provide for a first round of vaccinations once we reached land. Two must be vaccinated at a time lest the vaccine not take in one or the other and the precious cure be lost. In the colonies, we would pick up new orphans for the rest of the journey. In my excitement, I did not think to ask how the boys were to be conveyed back to Spain so that his Royal Highness could keep his promise of raising them like his own sons.

"I have known many of these boys since birth," I assured him. "I can answer for any illnesses they have had."

"Excellent!" In his voice, I heard my own excitement. He had already begun his preparations, ordering supplies and equipment. Five hundred copies of his translation of Moreau's treatise on the vaccine were being printed up to distribute around the world. It was through Moreau that Don Francisco had found out about Dr. Jenner's experiments. He held up the copy he had brought for me.

I took the book in my hands. I had never owned one. "I am honored," I thanked him, glad for the opportunity to show that I, indeed, could read. I could see by the flush on his face that it had been the correct thing to say.

The ship was now the issue, he went on. It was proving difficult to procure one. A frigate had been offered but needed repairs. With each detail the voyage seemed more and more imminent. We would set sail in a month across the seas in answer to those crying voices.

"Our undertaking shall be remembered by future generations," he concluded.

*Our* undertaking.

"We shall save the world, Doña Isabel." His voice had taken on a hesitancy. Perhaps a doubt had assailed him. "At least we shall try."

"We will," I assured him. We were at the door.

"I am most grateful." He took my hand, pressing it warmly. I wished again that I had worn my gloves.

"Tomorrow, I shall send over a list of what the boys will need. At present, I am staying at the Charity Hospital next door if you should need me," he added, putting on his hat. It fitted him handsomely. His face was in shadow.

I lifted my mantilla to cover my own face as was my habit when I escorted someone out, in courtesy to some passerby on the street, or out of vanity, as my other Francisco would have it. I would soon be rid of the boy, his judgments and bullying. A moment later, I felt ashamed. Who would love this boy if I did not? But he could not come along; he had only been with us a year. I could not account for his past exposure to the smallpox. But what then of Benito? I could not account for him either. No matter. I would not leave him behind. That would be my secret.

"You must learn not to cover yourself, Doña Isabel," Don Francisco was saying. "Those scars will fade even further with exposure to the sun and salt air. Though a pocked face would serve our mission better. A convincing warning to those who might resist us."

His words were a needle in my heart. Had his earlier compliment been only a ploy to win my agreement? *A face marked but not marred.* His very words. We would save the world together, but my role was to serve as a cautionary figure!

I was glad I had covered myself so that he could not see the tears starting in my eyes again. I had been chastened, reminded that I was to serve a noble purpose, not feed my vanity and self-pity! There was a blessed future before me. I would devote myself to our mission. I would become worthy of Don Francisco's expedition.

Later that night, after the boys were asleep, I knelt down by my bed, trying to pray. "Let it be according to thy word," I pleaded. But it was not our Lord nor the angel Gabriel nor even the Virgin I was addressing, but Don

Francisco himself. I had given him my word. I would talk to Doña Teresa. I would convince her. The boys would be in my charge. And Nati was more than capable of directing La Casa until I came back . . . if I came back.

In the time before I blew out the candle, I gave myself the task I had set aside for this night. I found a piece of string and strung together the beads I had left on my bed. At the last, however, instead of attaching the crucifix, I took the strung beads and tied them around my neck. For the first time since my illness, I wished I had a mirror so I could see how the rectoress of a foundling house might look to a surgeon from the royal court, director of a noble expedition. Later in the dark, I went over and over our interview, touching the beads as if they were memory aids, recollecting what he had said, what I had replied, the fever in his eyes, the softness around his mouth. All night, I tossed and turned as if I were already on board that ship bound for a new life.

# 2

Alma is surprised when she hears the pickup coming down the driveway. She glances at the clock. She has been at it for two hours, reading and writing notes in her journal, notes that end up as full-fledged scenes and conversations leading her further into Balmis's story.

As the garage door rumbles open, the floor shakes under her feet—Richard is home! Quite the metaphor, she thinks. Quickly, she puts her journal away, glancing around as if to remember this moment in case it proves to be memorable: the moment before everything changed for the worse. *Please,* she pleads to all the things in her room: posters of some of her book covers; maps of the island; the homeland flag draped over her computer; her collection of virgencitas—as if these objects could guarantee her safety in the world. She closes the door and hurries down the stairs.

"Wow!" Richard's face lights up as he steps through the garage door and finds her waiting for him on the other side. "A personal greeting!"

Alma feels a pang. Has it been that long? Usually, she calls down, "I'll be right there." But by the time she turns off the computer, puts her work away, and makes her way downstairs, ten, fifteen minutes have elapsed, and the zing is gone from her greeting.

"Hey," she says, pressing herself into him, not wanting, for the moment, to be a separate person, a person he could betray or discard.

He folds his arms around her, laughing into her hair, but after a moment, when Alma doesn't pull away, he grows still. "What's the matter?" he finally asks. Sometimes he surprises her. Alma will think that Richard has checked out, gone to that fantasyland where—if the talk shows and those old misogynist Thurber cartoons are to be believed— husbands in long-term marriages go, but let Alma change one little thing in Richard's routines, put his running shoes somewhere else, use a different cup for his coffee, and he notices. "Something happen today?"

Alma had planned to tell him everything right off, but she finds herself delaying the moment. First, let him be reminded of what a good life they have together: a drink before supper, maybe supper out, maybe sex. It's as if this new savvy self has splintered off, the smart wife who plays her cards right, uses magazine-article ploys to keep her man happy. (*Dress up in something sexy; invite him for a date in bed.*) "I'm fine," Alma murmurs into his chest. "Why not? I have a wonderful husband." She pulls back to look him in the eye. Maybe saying it will be like holding a crucifix up to Dracula in the old movies. If Richard is not truly a wonderful husband, he will turn into a puff of smoke in her arms. "Right?"

He is looking at her quizzically, not totally convinced by this new lite version of his moody wife, then nods. How hard the last few years have been for Richard: losing both parents, sinking into depression (even if he refuses to call it that); then, finally, in the last few months beginning to rally, only to have his wife lag behind, a gloomy reminder. She takes his hand and leads him up the short flight of stairs to the main room, invites him to sit while she fixes his drink—wishing she didn't always forget what goes into a martini—then pours her own pedestrian glass of whatever wine is already open.

"A toast," he says when she sits down. "To new adventures." He winks before drinking.

Suddenly, Alma realizes that she's not the only one with a secret to report. The last time Richard came home with that sheepish smile and a toast to adventure, he had just bought a boat. He had gotten it for next to nothing from a colleague leaving for Ethiopia.

"But you don't know how to swim," Alma had reminded him. On their first date, Richard had confessed that his dreaded way of dying was by drowning. He hated even watching pirate movies. Now he was going to sail the seas?

"Not the seas, just the lake." He had grinned, pleased with himself. "And it's a motorboat, not a tall ship."

Alma had gone along with it, why not. Let him enjoy being a boat owner. Better that than a mistress, she'd thought, a thought that now glides across her consciousness like some evasive and deadly microbe on a slide.

"So, what's up?" She studies his face, the heightened color in his cheeks. She has always loved how coloring betrays him. Unlike many Americans whose faces seem so deadpan when compared with Latin faces, Richard's is . . . not exactly expressive but transparent. Alma has always believed she can see right through him.

"Okay, here's the deal. If you agree, only if you agree—and I told Emerson I had to run it by you—we can go live in the DR for a while! Wait, wait, don't say anything yet, let me finish. HI just got this really exciting contract to start a green center in the mountains. And Emerson's asked me to supervise the start-up. Five months max on site. That'll take us through the worst of winter. You won't have to plow the driveway," he teases. This is a gift he is offering her, a chance to return to her native land, to get away from everything she has been complaining about in his country.

"You've been saying that you really feel like you need to go back to recharge yourself. How you need some downtime to just find out who you are anymore."

It sounds like her. Richard wouldn't invent talk like that. Alma sighs, speechless before this incontrovertible proof of her own petty self in full complaint.

"I thought you'd be excited." His face has fallen, the color draining.

"I am, I am. It's just that I'm working on my novel." Moving involves distraction, meeting new people, reinventing your self again.

"What do you mean? You can write anywhere." Why do people

always assume this? Why does Richard assume this? He should know better. Last summer in an effort to resuscitate her saga novel, she had painted her study bright salmon to bring the tropics to Vermont. Within a week, she painted the walls back to off-white because the new color was drowning out her characters. "Oh, Alma, don't you see? This is just the change you need." When Richard is so sure, he is the husband equivalent of those salmon walls, drowning out her qualms. "You could get away from all this." He waves his arms, meaning, she knows, the world of book biz, the faxes and phone calls, the plague of e-mail, Lavinia gently but firmly reminding her that the saga novel is overdue.

"We can easily fly to see your parents. It's closer to Miami from there than from here." Richard's voice has turned plaintive. He is running out of arguments, and she is still not convinced. "And David and Sam and Ben will love to visit. Do you realize they have *never* been to their stepmother's native country?" Alma doubts that this bothers her stepsons as much as it does Richard. "Oh, Alma, please think about it, please?"

Were she to think about it in her present state, the thought would get lost in the moody mazes of her mind, like Mamasita in the entrails of customer service. Too many ifs, ands, buts, and worse-case scenarios popping up. And Richard doesn't really want Alma to think about it. He wants her to say yes.

He leans forward, takes her wineglass, sets it down, then cups her face in his hands. Those strange blue eyes that will never seem totally real look softly down into hers. It always shocks her to find a mother's cherishing gaze on Richard's face. Something she never knew from her own mother, and which she never thought could come from a man. He kisses each eye closed, then tenderly kisses her mouth. Maybe he, too, has been reading the glossy magazines at the dentist's office. "How to Make Your Wife Happy." "How to Get Her to Say Yes to Your Fantasies."

Richard gives her the specifics. "HI's been selected by this company, Swan, to help them with a sustainable project in the central mountains of the Dominican Republic. "It's totally off the grid," Richard says excitedly, as if not being able to run a hair dryer or toast a bagel were attractive features of the assignment. "No electricity. Solar panels and wind power." He anticipates her objections. "Enough to work a pump and lights and a few other necessaries. I mean, no one, not Lavinia, not Mario Whateverhisnameis, could get to you there."

Alma wishes Richard had not brought up her nemesis. Still, it does cross her mind that this would be a chance to prove how authentically Latina she is: up on a mountainside working with poor campesinos. How to live your life as a reaction to other people's projections on you. Alma shudders. It sounds like childhood all over again.

"It's a chance to save those mountains and communities," Richard goes on. HI will be working with a cooperative of campesinos in establishing the first eco-agricultural center in the country. "Swan's already opened a clinic there, up and running. It's a happening place. A real chance to make a difference." In addition to its ongoing team of consultants, HI will provide on-site management for the first phase of the green center. "That's where I come in," Richard adds. These projects always sound so good. Like descriptions of apartments in rental ads: *French doors,* which end up being tacky sliding panels that let in the wind midwinter; *quaint alcove off kitchen,* which means a closet has been converted into an extra room you will be charged for.

"Why doesn't HI hire a Dominican manager? Use local talent?"

Richard is nodding so vigorously that even though he hasn't spoken a word, Alma feels interrupted. Of course, he agrees with her! He was the one who introduced her to this whole eco-agri-social-justice-sustainable green movement, which is the raison d'être of HI. Before Richard, Alma always thought of conservationists as a fringe group who had never fully recovered from having gone to summer camp as kids.

"You're absolutely right!" Richard concludes when Alma falls silent. "That's exactly what HI suggested. But remember, this kind of eco-management is a new concept. It needs to be modeled. That's why there'll be a local intern . . . and then me."

He has already in effect chosen this mission. For Alma to try to dissuade him would be to put a pinprick in his balloon. To shipwreck his expedition. He has to go and play out his dream. Who would he become if she cuts off his wings? Who would she have to be to do such a thing?

"When you say 'off the grid,' how off the grid do you mean—a hut, a dirt floor?" She has seen poverty back home and it is not a pretty thing. "How about medical care? What if you get AIDS?"

The look of incredulity on Richard's face almost makes her laugh out loud with relief. He could not be that good an actor.

"Why would I get AIDS? You mean from being in a third-world country?" He makes quote marks with his fingers. It is a term he disliked even before he met her. One of the things Alma found attractive about him on their first date.

"Come on, I'm not that stupid. It is my country, you know." She feels a competitive need to remind him of her authority over all things Dominican. True, he knows many more facts about her native land and can answer dinner-party questions about the size of the population, the gross national product, the amount of aid flowing into the country. But she has got the language and the intuitive feel for how that world works. If he ends up on a desolate mountain farm, surrounded by campesinos, he will need her help, for sure.

"So why would I get AIDS?"

She can feel his gaze trawling her face for an answer. "I had this weird call today," she begins, then blurts it all out: the woman's accusation, the curse at the end.

"When was this? Did you get her name? How did she say she knew me?" Richard is cross-examining her, as if she were the guilty party.

Suddenly, Alma is aware of how ungrounded her suspicions will seem with so few details to back them up. She remembers reading an article about magical realism, the writer saying that the only way to convince a reader that there are elephants flying in the sky is to use details, to say that there are seventeen elephants with garlands of yellow flowers flying in the sky. Why didn't she even think of asking the woman's name, especially since the whole issue of names had come up? "She called me Mrs. Huebner. She pronounced it right."

Richard has been heading toward the phone, as if to confront the caller, but now he turns to confront her. "You're not telling me you believe this, are you?"

After a slight pause, Alma shakes her head.

"Good." He has to have noticed her hesitation, but he is letting it pass. He doesn't want to risk not going on this DR project. Knowing Emerson, owner and director of a highly successful green consultancy company, international troubleshooter par excellence, who doesn't suffer hesitation and delay easily, Richard probably has until tomorrow morning to make a decision. A bad fight could ruin it all. "Did you call anyone else?" Richard asks, picking up the phone and punching in some numbers.

"Why?" And then Alma remembers Helen's telling her about a way to call back a missed call, a feature Helen often uses as she can't get to the ringing phone fast enough on her walker. Richard will be annoyed if he knows that she called Tera. He does not like Alma sharing their personal problems with a best friend who will influence her thinking. She shakes her head, then nods.

But Richard is already barking into the receiver. "Hello? Who is this? Paul? Paul Vendler? Oh, Paul, I'm sorry, I was just checking something on our phone." Richard turns and gives Alma a withering look, all the more unpleasant for the discrepancy of his pleasant tone of voice. "We're fine, fine. Sorry to bother you. Things okay? Good, good. Same here. Sure will. Hi to Tera."

Richard puts the receiver back slowly and stands with his head bowed, as if he were praying over it. He is not one to lose his temper in any way that would register on the Latina telenovela scale Alma is familiar with. But after a decade together, she can read anger in the tight jaw, the big ears that seem to darken and perk up, the thin line of his mouth stretched tight when he finally lifts his head. Maybe he will risk a fight tonight after all. Then stomp off in a huff for five months to the Dominican highlands.

"I tried to tell you that I had made a call," she says lamely, not sure which of her sins he is finding most unpardonable: her talking to Tera, her equivocating about it, her mistrusting his fidelity, her not being overjoyed about his virtual acceptance of an assignment that holds her over a barrel: either she must desert her work or be parted from him for almost half a year.

"When are you going to get it through your head that I adore you?" he says finally.

Alma feels suddenly weepy with gratitude. Her wonderful, faithful, deserving compañero! Of course, he should go where his joy and passion lie, and Alma must not interfere.

Richard comes to her, puts his hands on her shoulders. That cherishing look is in his eyes again. "I have never, ever, been unfaithful to you, even for one moment." The repetition reminds Alma of their wedding ceremony. Richard's favorite uncle, Dwight, an older, bald, Lutheran minister version of Richard, had flown out from Indiana to marry them. Uncle Dwight had asked if she, Alma de Jesús Rodríguez (a name his Midwestern mouth found hard to negotiate), took Richard Huebner to be her lawful, wedded husband, detailing each vow in a loud, slow voice as if Alma might not fully understand English.

"I do," Alma had said quietly. After two decades of rootlessness and many true loves later, she had no idea what it meant to say forever to anyone about anything. And any exuberance would have been tempered by the thought of her stepsons, brave boys standing by their father, his three best men, a clean, scrubbed look about them, their blond hair still wet and showing comb marks. How could they be happy at a ceremony that marked the end of their original family?

"Let's play it low-key," she had told Richard as they planned the wedding, which was, of course, the way Huebners did things anyhow, she was discovering. It was her family she had to control: her dramatic, emoting sisters and cousins; the showy displays of nuestra cultura; merengues and boleros on a boom box; the lavish spread of spicy, tasty food brought to Vermont over distances; everyone talking too loudly, kissing and hugging too much, reminding the boys they were now familia and had to learn Spanish. Poor guys. No wonder they hadn't pushed to visit their stepmother's native country afterward.

"About this offer of Emerson's," Richard reminds her. Alma has always admired Richard's ability to stay focused on his goals. How he can draw up a five-year plan and a ten-year plan for their lives, everything prioritized. "Now you write up yours," he has urged her. And Alma has sat at the table, feeling muddled as to where to start, the same pressure she feels at New Year's when she tries to come up with resolutions. Finally, she is more of a fatalist about life than Richard. What will be won't be anything she has any control over. Why even tempt the fates by revealing what would hurt most for them to deny her.

When the phone rings, they both jump, startled by its intrusion. "Let the machine get it," Richard suggests.

Alma nods, but as the ringing continues, she remembers that the machine did not kick in this afternoon. "Something's wrong with it," she tells Richard now. The power outage last night probably tripped the mechanism and it has to be reset. "It's okay," Richard says, shrugging off the caller. "They'll call back later." But he, too, tenses each time another ring comes. Fifteen rings, a lot of persistence there.

"Your mother," Richard guesses. It's true that Alma's mother will let the phone ring and ring as if her call, like a baby's cry, will be taken seriously and attended to if she persists. But Alma has already spoken to her mother today about the underwear order. This must be the AIDS woman calling back. She wishes now that Richard had answered it. His transparent face would have told all. Instantly, she feels bad at how easily she loses faith. She burrows into his chest, as if trying to get away from herself again.

"Hey." Richard is pulling at her gently. "So what do you think?"

Just make believe I'm not here, Alma is thinking. Just carry me strapped to your chest wherever you go. She listens to the beating of his heart, steady and strong, a blacksmith's hammer decisively hitting the anvil.

"You okay?"

Alma nods into his chest. When did this happen? When did she lose the independent warrior woman of her twenties and thirties, the writer who loved solitude? She has become domesticated, a Mrs. Huebner, like the woman caller said. "Richard love," she might as well come clean. "Have you ever like totally wanted to just let go of everything, shed it all, and find out what's left?"

He looks down at her, one eyebrow raised, no doubt wondering what troublesome maze this non sequitur might lead him into. "Sure," he says finally. "Why do you think this project is so appealing to me? I'm always writing and talking and consulting about this stuff. This is hands-on. I get to do it myself for once, you know?"

Alma nods, feeling suddenly saddened by his noble reply. This is Richard's only life, too. Why should he be a minor character in hers? "Let's go upstairs," she suggests, wishing it were sex she wanted, not just a legitimate way to disappear.

"Wow," Richard says for the second time tonight, a word from his Indiana boyhood, one he reverts to whenever slightly embarrassed by an indulgence he doesn't feel he has earned. He looks unsure. He has come home to a different wife than he is used to. Alma, too, is perplexed. A self is splintering off, not the smart-cookie, magazine wife, playing her cards right, but a woman from some other story than the one Richard and she are living in together.

"You don't want to talk over our plans first?" Richard is asking.

Alma shakes her head, watching as he downs his drink. "I've already made up my mind."

His head jerks up, surprised. "Oh?" He hesitates. "What . . . did you decide?"

"I think you should go. I think I should stay—"

"No way. I'm not going without you!" Richard shakes his head adamantly. But something in his tone, in the way his face shone after Alma said he should go, tells her he can be convinced. It makes her sad knowing how easily she can talk him into leaving her.

Alma gives him her reasons. She will be able to totally focus and finish her novel. He will be able to concentrate on his project without worrying about her. This will be a test of their love. After ten years, they should be able to survive the deep and separate dive into their individual passions. "Remember that quote I used to have on our fridge?" she reminds him. "What Rilke said: 'Love is two solitudes that protect, something something, and salute each other.'" She can never remember the middle verb.

He winces. "I never liked that quote. It sounds painful. Besides, I know I can survive a separation, just that it won't be much fun. So why do it?"

She does not want to sound like the Puritan in the family, though for a long time, Alma has suspected that she, from the culture of flamboyance and excess, is much more willing than Richard to don sackcloth and talcum-powder herself with ashes. "Sometimes we have to do stuff that isn't easy."

He sighs, as if he knows what's coming: how writing is hard work, the fascination of what's difficult, and so on. But it's not that, even if it's the reason she gave him for staying. She wants to find out who she is anymore without him, to follow the vague, shadowy woman she has been avoiding and see where she might be going. Of course, if Alma breathes a word of this to Richard, he will think that she is falling apart, that he has to stay and take care of her.

"Well," Richard wavers. "I guess it could work. We could see each other a couple of times at least. I'm going to have to come up and check in with the main office and my other projects. You can come down like in the middle or something? Also, we can meet in Miami for Christmas with your parents."

Alma feels just as she did when Tera outlined their post-Richard life together, amazed and depressed by how doable it sounds, surviving any loss, becoming someone else.

"I'll miss you so much," Richard adds, but his face is flushed with excitement, his eyes already dreaming of the deforested mountainsides of the Dominican Republic he will green up. Alma is the one who's bracing herself, as if she is getting ready for major surgery, the removal of Richard from her heart, a delicate excision she is not sure she will survive.

"Here we are talking first," he reminds her, grinning. "I like your original plan about going upstairs."

She lets him lead her by the hand, as if he were wheeling her down the corridor to the OR. As if he were leaving tomorrow, forever. The woman's call had been a sign of a big change after all. Her curse is already hard at work.

As they go by it, Alma glances over at the answering machine. A signal is flashing on the narrow panel. Only Richard knows how to clear and reset the recording. Another set of instructions she will have to write down in her spiral notebook.

"Shall we clear it?" she asks. Richard shakes his head. "Later." He is a man intent on his goal now. Alma follows, slowly climbing the stairs, as if having sex will be that conclusive handshake finalizing their new plan. The odd thing is that until the last minute, she thought she would accompany him. But then *she* appeared, beckoning from the edges. *A woman yearning for the larger version of herself* is how Alma would describe her, if this woman were one of her characters.

The phone rings again while they are making love. "Damn! I should've taken it off the hook," Richard sighs, when the rings go on and on. They wait it out, as they did the first time, but the interruption breaks the mood. "Don't worry about it," Richard says. "It's fun just being in bed with you." Alma doesn't for a moment believe him, but she has come to appreciate these small courtesies, which in her younger, woman-warrior years, she would have dismissed as BS. Now she sees that they, not passion, are what keep a marriage oiled and running smoothly.

Later, before they sit down to supper, Alma resets the machine as Richard talks her through the steps. For the first time since they got it, it's her voice on the recording. "Hi, this is the number for Alma Rodríguez and Richard Huebner. Sorry we can't come to the phone right now . . ." On and on, the message unfolds chattily, as opposed to

Richard's curt "You've reached 388-4343. Leave us a message." "It's friendlier," Alma protests when Richard rolls his eyes.

They've just begun eating when the phone starts ringing again. They wait, sighing with relief when Alma's voice comes on. "I wonder who it's going to be?" Richard lowers his voice, as if the person were in the next room, ready to make an entrance. "I bet—"

"Hey!" the voice begins after a brief hesitation. "I expected Richard. Did you kick him out or what? Just joking!" It's Tera, static crackles and all, calling from her antique phone. "Anyhow, I was just listening to the local news. And you will not believe it: there was a report about this woman who's been calling people all over the county. Hannah . . . Something. What was her name? Paul, what was that Hannah woman's last name? Hannah McSomething. Anyhow, this woman always asks for the wives and pretends she has AIDS and has slept with their husbands. She claims she's part of some weird ethical terrorist group trying to save the world. Well, it turns out this poor woman is mentally ill and had been getting treatment, but with the cuts on spending the counseling center terminated her care. I tell you, we can bomb other countries, we can let people go homeless—" Tera is abruptly cut off. There is a three-minute maximum on messages.

Alma can feel Richard's eyes on her. She can guess the look on his face: a mixture of I told you so and something else, a new look he has been giving her these days when she has been so sad. A look of helplessness, as if he is no longer sure he can save her from that part of herself he hoped would disappear with love.

"See," Richard says softly. There is no righteousness in his voice. "You have nothing to worry about."

"I know," Alma says, giving him a small, chastened smile. Of course, he is right. What was that quote she used to quote to him? *We are saved not because we are worthy; we are saved because we are loved.* She is lucky to have his love. This crazy woman is a warning of what can happen when you wander off from the safe, gated neighborhoods of the human heart, out where the winds of mortality blow hard.

"I wonder why she flipped?" Alma wonders out loud.

Richard shrugs. "Life. Some people can't take it."

All through supper and as Alma does the dishes, she ponders Richard's words as he sits at the table, making notes on the margins of the project report he has brought home. Why can't she just settle down to being his lucky, beloved wife, author of a couple of decent novels, a nice person to the people in her life? Why this periodic need to reinvent the world and herself along with it? Sure, it fuels the writing, but taking it literally is madness. She recalls a woman who wrote to her years back, inspired by a revolutionary character in one of Alma's novels. The woman had decided to go to Sandinista Nicaragua and be a human sandbag for peace on the northern border. Oh my God, what have I done? Alma had been alarmed. She wrote back, *It's fiction!* She never heard back from the woman, but for months Alma worried over every word she wrote. She had never before considered that a novel could have casualties.

Perhaps she will become a casualty of the novel that she has yet to write. When she is done, Richard will find the manuscript in a neat stack on the desk and below, on the floor, a pile of pencil shavings— a cartoon on a *New Yorker* back page, next to the ads for bow ties and expensive diamond animal pins.

But Alma could still decide to go with Richard on his mission to help her part of the world. Like Isabel, willing to follow Balmis around the world. What pluck it must have taken for this rectoress of an orphanage to cut her ties and risk her life and those of twenty-some little boys in the bargain! She must've felt a pang as each of her little charges climbed aboard that ship.

Some stronger pull than Alma feels kept Isabel from changing her mind that gusty November day. A steadfastness that evades Alma's pro/con mind, back and forth, endlessly for the weeks before Richard finally boards his flight to Newark and on to the Dominican Republic. Yes, no; yes, no—like a heartbeat, this time her very own.

# II

M Y HEART WAS POUNDING as my boys boarded the ship on that windy November day. What had I done? Each one of these innocents was on my conscience! Each one seemed all the more fragile and precious: Juan Antonio was coughing, his little nose running; Pascual wailed that he was hungry—who knew when the next meal was coming; even my little bully Francisco looked pale and frightened.

The herald read out each name as if it were a title, a trumpet blew, the bishop lifted his hand in blessing.

I dared not look up at the skies for consolation, for then I would have to see the ship before me, the men up in the rigging gawking at me, the gray open sea beyond the bay, preparing to batter us with its waves.

And so I fixed my eyes on her, the figurehead on the prow after whom the ship was named, María Pita. Centuries ago, she had defended La Coruña from the British invaders after her husband was slain. In old stories, people seemed braver than I could ever be. Yet it occurred to me that to all those looking on from the crowd on the dock, I seemed a courageous woman, standing with my little boys, letting them go, one by one, up the gangway—sheep to the slaughter or souls up Jacob's ladder toward a great reward.

They say that before one passes on to the Lord's judgment, one's whole life appears before one's view. I thought back over all my hard work in the last few months, and I admit I cared more what Don Francisco might think of me than how history or God might judge me. Perhaps all our noble deeds begin as the mustard seed of the parable, which bears a mighty tree.

Mine indeed was a tiny seed: subterfuge and selfishness; my little boys, God spare them, buying my freedom. How could any good come of such lowly beginnings?

My part in this grand moment had begun two months ago, the day after Don Francisco's visit. As the fly might fall in the spider's web, Doña Teresa had come calling.

It was a rainy Saturday morning, so I had not been expecting her. But our benefactress had been visiting a sick friend and, passing by on her way home, had dropped in to see her boys and deliver some grapes she had bought for them.

Before she was in the door, the boys had given her the report. A visitor had come from the king! All the cleverness I had spent devising a way to tell our benefactress about the expedition without alluding to its royal origin was for naught. I should have known better than to think a matter the children knew about could be kept secret.

Doña Teresa was scowling by the time I greeted her. "What's this I hear about the king sending a visitor here, Isabel?" she asked in place of a greeting back.

"Let me help you with your cape," I offered, delaying in order to figure out how best to respond.

She was stamping her muddy shoes on the carpet she had bestowed on us and so could soil at her pleasure without my correcting her as I would have my boys. "That cuckold king has done nothing for destitute children during his whole reign!" ("What is a cuckold?" the boys had asked the first time Doña Teresa had gone into one of her royal rants in their presence.) "Thank you, Isabel," she said, allowing me at last to remove her cape. "Now tell me what this is all about."

"We had an important visitor yesterday, yes," I said as I hung her cape on the post by the door. "He came with a special request for a mission approved by His Holiness."

SAVING THE WORLD 63

"Oh?" Doña Teresa's face suddenly softened. She was a pious woman. In the Roman Church she had found her substitute to the court in Madrid. The many battles she fought on its behalf—the church should not be forced to sell its properties in order to bail out the Royal Treasury; Rome, not Spain, should decide marriage cases; monasteries and convents should not pay additional taxes—distracted her from persisting in questions that could not be answered, questions that had haunted her after the death of her son. "What does the Holy Father require of us?"

I felt a surge of confidence. Perhaps this would not be a battle after all. "An expedition will be setting out from La Coruña in a few weeks," I began. I mentioned the director's name. "It was Don Francisco, who was here yesterday—"

"So, is it money he wants?" Doña Teresa was scowling again. She had an open, expressive face, and though it was unlikely one would not already know from looking at it, she also reported exactly what she was feeling. There always seemed to be this redundancy about her, why Nati found her trying. "Now, Isabel, you know very well I don't like to give money to individuals."

"No, Doña Teresa, I assure you Don Francisco was not asking for money." I took a deep breath. "He came here . . . asking for members to join an expedition to cure the world of smallpox." At the mention of this plague, Doña Teresa's face drained of color. She sat herself heavily down in one of her husband's uncomfortable chairs. She did not seem to notice her selection nor did she question the oddness of searching for expedition members in a home for orphan boys. Her mouth had dropped open. "Rid the world of smallpox? Is this possible?"

Clearly, she had not heard the hospital rumors about the English doctor. This was odd as Doña Teresa kept abreast of most gossip. *La gaceta,* especially, had proliferated her sources of scandals, strange tales, and memorable stories. "Are you quite sure, Isabel, this isn't another one of *his* cures?" she scowled again. King Carlos was known to dabble in the sciences and was often offering purgatives and palliatives to his nobles and foreign visitors. So *La gaceta* had reported.

"No, no, Doña Teresa. This cure is already established in Rome, France, Russia." I recounted what Don Francisco had told me, assuring her at crucial points where my own faith had faltered that science was handmaiden to religion. I outlined Dr. Jenner's experiment, omitting that he was English, explaining about the milkmaids, the cowpox, the epidemics raging in the colonies. But in order to get the vaccine across the ocean, live carriers were required, which is why Don Francisco had come to the foundling house. He was requesting twenty-two of our boys to carry the cowpox fluid across the sea.

"I see," Doña Teresa said with a deep nod. She was quiet a moment, gazing fondly at the boys who had been listening intently to the story. This was the first they knew of our visitor's request, for the fact that he had come from the king had eclipsed any further questions about the reason for his visit. "So, my little sailors," Doña Teresa inquired of them, "which of you wants to go on a big ship across the ocean?"

"Me!" they shouted and lunged toward Doña Teresa, almost toppling her over in her chair. She might have been the big ship herself they were ready to board.

"Boys!" I scolded. But I could tell our benefactress was enjoying herself. She came precisely to feel the sticky, needy warmth of their affection.

"You mean to say that you would leave your Doña Teresa all alone here in La Coruña?" She made a pouty face.

"I'll stay," Clemente offered, inciting a complete reversal. So much for the enlightened rule of the multitude, I thought, remembering how it was the rabble next door in France that had cut off their king's head. Or so I had read in one of the discarded *Gacetas* Doña Teresa had brought me.

Only Francisco held his course. From the beginning, that boy was determined to go. "Por favor, Doña Teresa, let me go." *Por favor?* I registered the change. The boy might still mend.

"That's enough now, boys," I quieted them. I should never have started this explanation with the boys afoot. But Doña Teresa's questions had met me at the door, forcing me into the conversation I had cleverly (and uselessly!) prepared for.

She was shaking her head at them now. "You must remember, my boys, that if His Holiness asks anything of us, we must obey. That way, we can all finally be together in heaven. We will all meet there, will we not?" The boys nodded solemnly.

Only your conniving rectoress might not be there, I thought.

Doña Teresa turned to me. She spoke in a lowered voice, as if the boys were incapable of hearing anything said in confidence in their presence.

"I worry only about these poor innocents. They have never been further than the Tower of Hercules. How can we be sure they will survive such a voyage? And when will they be sent back? What if they catch some other horrid disease? *La gaceta* reports that the Americans are full of illness." All the questions and qualms I had swept aside in my excitement swarmed round me. I had scooped out honey from the hive, tasted its sweetness, but now the worrisome bees were after me. My mind was full of unease.

Perhaps my face was as easy to read as hers, for Doña Teresa stopped abruptly. "Oh dear, Isabel, now I've got you doubting. Always, the Evil One tries to tarnish a noble deed with ignoble quandaries. I have known you these dozen years, and I know you would not endanger the welfare of boys you love so well."

My face burned with shame at her undeserved trust. "I myself will accompany them," I said, knowing my self-interest would be mistaken as self-sacrifice. "Don Francisco requested it," I added, not daring to look up for fear Doña Teresa would see the lie in my eyes. "Natividad can take over until my return," I proposed, anticipating a possible objection.

"Brave Isabel!" Doña Teresa was now smiling fondly at me.

I could not bear her praise. Any moment now, I would blurt out the truth. "Boys." I turned my attention to them. "Go tell Nati Doña Teresa is here, to put on the kettle. Go on now! A warm tea, Doña Teresa?" I offered. "You have gotten wet in this rain. You must not catch cold."

"In a bit, in a bit." She waved my offer away. She was still in the thrall of all she had heard, just as I had been. "To think, Isabel, that there might be a cure for the smallpox." Her pale eyes grew watery. "If only that discovery had come sooner! Consider how our own lives would have been so different."

I thought of my parents, my dear sister, and I felt that heaviness in my heart again. Perhaps, no matter how far I wandered, there would be no escaping it.

"Now, I'm making you sad, poor Isabel." Doña Teresa blew her nose into the kerchief she had removed from the pocket of her dress, a trumpet sound that made the boys at the door giggle, disclosing their misbehavior.

"Boys!" I chided. "What did I say? Go wash your hands for merienda!" Off they went, anticipating the snack of grapes that Doña Teresa's coachman had carried into the kitchen earlier. "You, too, Francisco." Reluctantly, the boy peeled himself away. But before disappearing down the corridor, he sounded his little trumpet one more time. "He came from the king—"

"Francisco!" I cut him off, but Doña Teresa had caught the one spark that could kindle her temper.

"What does that ridiculous cuckold have to do with this noble mission?" She was addressing not just me but the room itself, which had witnessed the interview with our visitor. She went on to provide the answer, sparing me another lie. "Let him try to take over this mission. Just let him! These are my boys, and I myself will help with the cost of their expenses."

I was torn between guilt at my means and delight with the results. Although Don Francisco had not asked, no doubt he would welcome additional monies for his expedition. *Excellent!* he would say. *You are a wonder, Doña Isabel. Provision as well as permission!*

Doña Teresa stood up slowly, a pained expression on her face, which turned to fond chuckles when she noticed the seat she had chosen. "That Don Manuel," she said, shaking her head. "We really should gift those chairs to the Royal Council!" (The council had recently voted to levy additional taxes on all church properties.) Then, gathering herself up, she hooked her arm in mine. "Let us go see to our boys' grapes." Doña Teresa enjoyed delivering her treats in person.

"By the way, Isabel," she said as we came apart at the narrow corridor that did not allow someone of her wide girth to go accompanied, "you are looking quite handsome. That necklace suits you!"

My hand flew to my throat. I had forgotten to remove my beads! My face was burning again, as I fell in behind her, thinking how easily we can change our lives if we desire to do so above all other things.

WITH DOÑA TERESA'S BLESSING, I began to select the twenty-two boys who would take part in the expedition.

Each one had to be checked thoroughly to be sure that he had never been exposed to the smallpox. Suddenly, relations began stepping forward, fathers and mothers and brothers who had never existed before, wet nurses who had given the breast to this or that infant boy, all of whom had heard that the chosen boys would become the king's special charges and so had come to claim their rightful compensation for letting His Majesty have *their* boys.

Once I had chosen the carriers, I began assembling what they would need from the list Don Francisco provided for me. Each boy was to have six shirts, a hat, three linen trousers and jackets, one woolen trouser and jacket; three kerchiefs for the neck, three for the nose; three pairs of shoes; one comb. So much to be bought, sewn, attended to!

The hours sped by; the days were over too quickly; September turned into October in a heartbeat; and then it was November, and we were still getting ready. A ship could not be found. Some of the instruments Don Francisco had ordered had not arrived. France and England were at war, and safe conduct for our expedition had to be sought from both countries; proof had to be presented that we were carrying boys, not munitions.

I was glad for these delays, for I had twenty-two wardrobes to assemble, not counting my own "trousseau," as Nati had begun referring to it. "For you are bound to get married over in New Spain." She was sure of it. I waved her off, though I admit, it pleased me to think that perhaps in America among so many survivors of the smallpox, my scarred face might blend in. A new Isabel would emerge in that new world!

"What man will take me with twenty-two boys in tow?" I challenged. Out of habit, I could not let myself hope.

Nati crossed her arms and regarded me. "You don't know the first thing about men, do you?"

"I have been raising them for a dozen years," I reminded her.

TODAY, FINALLY, THE HOUR of our departure had come. We assembled in the front parlor, each boy attired like a little prince. We were to parade down the crowded streets toward the docks, Don Francisco's idea. Our departure should be accompanied by fanfare. Ours was a noble venture, which all of La Coruña should know about. And it would hearten the members of the expedition to hear the cheers and see the waving crowds.

This was probably true for his assistants and nurses, who marched ahead, accompanied by our bishop and officials from the city council. But the children were too frightened to enjoy the added commotion, even the older ones who pretended confidence, and yes, *even* my thorn, Francisco, who had managed to talk his namesake into allowing him to come, swearing upon several holy objects that he had "never been near no pox." All the good-byes at the orphanage, the kisses and embraces lavished upon them, admonitions to be brave, not to fear the ocean with its great Leviathan or the savages who ate their own kind—my poor boys were beside themselves with terror. They clung to Nati and Doña Teresa, to bedposts and wall posts, to the boys who were staying. Only Benito seemed strangely calm, but, of course, he was clinging to me.

For the last few weeks on pleasant days, I had been bringing the selected group down to the dockyards to accustom them to the idea of going on a ship, crossing the ocean they knew only as a span of blue globe they could cover with their hands. A quiet stroll down to the docks and a climb aboard the ship with no ceremony would have been far better. But our director, of course, had the greater glory of our enterprise to consider and not the silly fears of little boys, fears stoked by the envy of those who were staying behind.

We must have looked a sight, dressed in the colors of Spain, the rectoress and her twenty-one boys! (At the last minute, Carlito had fallen ill and could not come along; a substitute boy I knew nothing about would be joining us on the ship.) Uniforms had again been Don Francisco's idea. "We will be marching into villages and settlements in the wilderness and our attire must create a sense of wonder. It will impress, believe me." Of course, I believed him. He had seen so much of the world, knew the hearts and minds of men and had ministered to their bodies. What did I know but my little round of duties, shut away in a foundling house for a dozen years? "And you, too, Doña Isabel, must wear our colors. You are now an official member of the expedition. The king has approved your appointment."

I, who had worn only black for so many years, was now dressed in crimson and gold! Nati was speechless. "I feel like a flag." I laughed nervously.

Nati shook her head. "You look like a lady. You will have to fight the men off with this." She handed me the farewell gift she had purchased at the seamen's bazaar, a hairpin with a pearl at one end for holding my veil in place. I did not have the heart to tell her that Don Francisco had ruled against my covering my face.

At last, the boys had calmed down, lining up, an older one with a younger one at each hand. Out we went into the street, past the post where Benito had been tied, past the hospital where most of them had been abandoned, past the Carmelite convent with its grates at the window, where I perceived the vague shadows of Sisters looking out upon this commotion. I dared not glance back to where a tearful Nati and Doña Teresa stood at our doorway, calling out reminders to me and the boys. One glimpse of what I was leaving behind, and I feared that my heart, if not my limbs, would turn to stone.

What on earth had I been thinking? My poor little boys, big-eyed, trying to be brave, were about to embark on a perilous journey! Eight of them, including my Benito, were no older than three—the younger the boy, the less likely he had ever been exposed to the smallpox. They still tottered on their land legs, still wet their bedding, though even some of the oldest had been doing so with the excitement of these last few days.

I suppose I, too, was in a state. Not since my illness as a young girl had I shown my naked face in public. To my surprise, no one turned away or curled a lip in disgust. Awe had blotted out any defects. The crowd cheered for the boys! They cheered for the rectoress! "See," I tried to rally my charges. "Everyone is so very proud of you." They looked about warily, as if they were unsure whether they were soon to be fed cake or fed to the Leviathan.

The *María Pita* loomed before us. Don Francisco had called it "a modest ship," a last-minute choice after the larger frigate he had contracted was delayed in repairs. One benefit of a smaller vessel was that it could enter the harbor and we were able to board right from the dock. I could not imagine the added trouble of a double embarkation: first onto a boat to take us out to sea, then up a rope ladder to the deck of a rolling ship, sails fluttering and filling with wind. My hands were full enough already! The boys were hanging back again, eyeing this floating house that squeaked and tilted as if one good stamp of the foot could break it apart. One thing was to have seen the ship from shore, another thing to climb on board and sail away until you could see land no more.

"What an adventure we will have!" I quickened my step to encourage them. Of course, they hurried along. I was the one bit of firm land in this sea of strangers. They dared not lose sight of me!

At our approach, a trumpet sounded. The dignitaries and other members of the expedition parted ranks. Don Francisco had already explained the protocol: we, the children and I, were to go up the gangway, as our names were called out to cheers and applause by all present. But first a herald read out the royal decree:

> *His Majesty, the King, considering the ravages caused by smallpox in his dominions, and being desirous of granting to his beloved vassals the aid dictated by humanity . . .*

A strong wind was blowing upon us—why we were leaving today, finally, having waited all week for the weathervanes on the housetops to swing back round to a favoring wind. The boys were getting chilled. Pascual was hungry; indeed, the little rascal was always hungry! Juan Antonio sniffled; he was bound to catch cold. Tintín and Bello, bundled in blankets, wailed in the arms of their nurses. Little did our king guess, as he dictated to scribes in a warm chamber, that the length of his decree might imperil the very mission he was decreeing. If our first carriers fell ill, would the vaccine lose its efficacy? "Soon, soon, my little princes," I promised the boys, hoping none would call me to account by asking, "But how soon?"

*Martín!* the herald finally barked out.

"Tintín," I murmured his nickname, flashing the teary-eyed little fellow an encouraging smile.

*Vicente María Sale y Bellido!*

Bello. A homely boy, despite his nickname.

No doubt, Tintín and Bello were being boarded first to get them out of harm's way right off. Three days ago, Don Francisco had vaccinated the two children with cowpox fluid from a carrier brought from Madrid. The vaccine had taken, and what a labor of Hercules that had been! The two toddlers had to be watched day and night lest they scratch their arms and destroy the vesicles that were beginning to form; nor were they to mix with the other carriers lest they vaccinate anyone accidentally and break the chain of transmission mid ocean. Of course, being toddlers, Tintín and Bello could not comprehend the caution we kept drumming into them. Their young age, which in one regard was a benefit, in another created quite a challenge. How was I going to manage on board without Nati to help me? I had commented on this to Don Francisco, who assured me that from the moment of vaccination, the task of caring for the two carriers would fall to the three expedition nurses. After the fluid had been successfully conveyed to the next pair, the immune carriers would fall back to me. He spoke as if we would be dealing with so many barrels of molasses or kegs of rum, not with lively little boys with troublesome minds of their own.

Tintín and Bello were carried up the gangway by their two nurses, kicking and screaming and reaching their little hands out to me. "Stop that!" Don Basilio Bolaños, the short, gruff nurse, snarled at little Tintín, "or I'll throw you into the sea." Tintín's screams reached a feverish pitch, inciting a new round of crying among the boys left with me. I could see that the task of caring for the carriers would never be totally out of my hands.

"Now, now, boys," I hushed them. "See, Tintín is fine. Let's all wave to him." From the deck of the *Pita*, Don Basilio grabbed the terrified child's hand and forced a wave back, eliciting more screams, almost destroying the calm I had wrought.

*Pascual Aniceto!* The next child was called. I had selected each boy for Don Francisco's examination and approval, but our director had made the final pick, writing down each name—or as much of each name as was known—that the herald was now proclaiming in a booming voice.

*Cándido! Clemente! José Jorge Nicolás de los Dolores! Vicente Ferrer!*

As more names were called, the boys grew bolder in their ascent up the gangway to the *María Pita.*

*Francisco Antonio! Juan Francisco! Francisco Florencio! Juan Antonio!*

I buttoned up Juan Antonio's jacket, which had come undone, and wiped his runny nose. Perhaps, our sickly Juan Antonio had been a bad choice. But we were running out of boys whose pasts I could fully account for. And Juan Antonio had come to us from the hospital next door with his mother's blood still caked on his scalp. I would have to watch over him carefully so he would not catch a bad cold and imperil his vaccination.

*Jacinto! José!*

José was the worst of my bed-wetters. Back at La Casa, we had forbidden him any drink after supper, but even so the boy inevitably wet his bed. "What is it with you," Nati would scold him as she collected his bedding many a morning. "Do you dream every night that you're pissing in a pot?" I would have to be sure to wake him; indeed, it would be best to wake all the boys mid-night to relieve themselves. No wonder Don Francisco had asked for additional chamber pots. He thinks of everything, I marveled once again.

*Gerónimo María! José Manuel María! Manuel María!*

The three brothers went up together. Indeed, they did all things as a trinity. It was going to be difficult vaccinating only two of them at a time.

*Tomás Melitón!*

Tomás was a swarthy little fellow; his father or mother must have been a Moor. The other boys teased him relentlessly. Doña Teresa thought he'd be snatched up by a noble family, as the fashion had become—with the Duchess of Alba's adoption of María de la Luz—to have negritos as part of one's retinue, along with little dogs and monkeys. But the ways of the court did not always take in Galicia.

*Andrés Naya! Domingo Naya!*

Too late, I noted the wet spot on the back of Andrés's breeches. Unlike the ones who had cried loudly as we were departing from the orphanage,

Andrés had clung to the leg of a table, mute with terror. Somehow that silence had been more disturbing than the din of crying surrounding him.

*Benito Vélez!*

Our director had been coming down from the deck to carry the toddlers aboard as they were called. Benito, of course, refused to go with him. The boy clung to me, burying his face in my neck, curling himself up and digging into my side like Adam's lost rib. "Best I bring him up, Don Francisco." Our director nodded and stretched out his hand to the last boy as his name was called.

*Antonio Veredia!*

Antonio was our little scholar. He had picked up reading easily and had started in on a Bible he had discovered in the chapel. But Father Ignacio had taken it away. The boy was only seven. "He is too young to be navigating these complex waters by himself," the priest ruled. Now Antonio would be navigating real waters. Lord keep him and all the others.

*Isabel López Gandalla!*

Had I misheard? Our director had recorded the wrong name! He had so many important things to attend to, I excused him to myself. Still, it pained me to think that I was of no consequence to him: one more member of his expedition to discard from his acquaintance once it was over.

The wind was blowing strong. I heard the clang of a bell and the clinking sound of chains. The gangway swayed. How would I keep my footing, a child in my arms, my heart in my throat, my mind tangled with guilt? High in the rigging, sailors were cocking their heads, trying to make out the one woman who would be on board. It was bad luck to allow a woman on a ship. In fact, Captain Pedro del Barco had out-and-out refused to admit me at first, so Don Francisco had reported to me. The captain had finally come around, I knew not by what means, sending me his personal welcome and a little bag of smelling salts that would prevent any seasickness in myself or the boys. Quite the turnabout! Had Don Francisco been any other kind of man, I might have suspected him of having exaggerated his first report in order to incur my gratitude over his efforts.

"Doña Isabel!" the boys were calling out my name. If nothing else, my boys now needed me more than ever. Some good might still come of what I had done for my own reasons. I kissed my little Benito's head and whispered, "Here we go!" No matter that Don Francisco had recorded the wrong name in the official documents. I had wanted a whole new life, so why not have a new name to go with it? Up the swaying gangway I climbed, toward the sloping deck where my boys and Don Francisco were waiting for me.

# 3

Alma turns into their driveway after seeing Richard off at the airport, and the sight of their house gives her a hollowed-out feeling in the gut. On the radio, the guys on *Car Talk* are having a grand old time. Do they ever get depressed? she wonders. Does one brother ever turn to the other and say, Jesus, I can't go on and talk about carburetors, not today, I can't!

Their house looms before her, a lot of wood, a lot of glass, very Vermont. They bought it from a couple who were divorcing after doing the usual crazy thing: Having marital troubles? Have a baby. Build a house. Alma remembers, now that she is about to go into it alone, that she didn't want to buy it. That she thought it was bad luck to buy a house from a couple that hadn't made it, that Richard had talked her into it, as he often did, by being reasonable. The house was cheap, considering the state's increasingly expensive real-estate market. "The chic-ifying of Vermont," Tera calls it. For weeks after they moved in, Alma did cleansings while Richard was at the office. Cleansings don't have a lifetime guarantee, she is thinking. Maybe she should begin by cleansing the house again before she tries to write a novel in it?

A horn toot-toots. Claudine's SUV going by. She recognizes Alma's car. Probably wondering why Alma is sitting halfway down her driveway looking at her own house.

If only you knew, Claudine, Alma thinks. Her down-the-road neighbor, Claudine, is one of the people Alma could never become, which

makes her sad or used to anyhow. Competent, the mother of two dar-
ling little girls who are as good-looking as she is, Claudine stayed
home with them when they were little, loved it; now works part time
as a real-estate agent, loves it; has read all of Alma's books, loves them.
If things get bad, Alma can call up Claudine and become friends.
Maybe it will rub off on her, Claudine's talent for happiness.

This is nothing new, Alma reminds herself, this terror whenever
Richard leaves for any trip that'll take him away overnight, though it's
never really made sense. Unlike the monkey experiment Alma once
read about, she wasn't torn from her mother's side as a baby and
placed in a cage with a mechanical lookalike that delivered shocks
whenever Alma climbed into its arms. But clinging to her capricious
Mamasita had created its own kind of trouble: never knowing when
she'd be given the tit, when the dart. Though Alma had figured it out
soon enough.

That was a half century ago, Alma tells herself now, recognizing
Richard's tone of voice in her head. Richard has no patience with
adults who go on and on about what their parents did to them. "Everyone's going to make mistakes!" he always says after some confessional
moment by a troubled friend almost derails a lively and fun supper
party. The saga of a wicked-witch mother. An alcoholic father revisited. They will be brushing their teeth after the guests have left, and
almost always Alma will be the one championing such courage. "We
all so seldom talk to each other about what really matters," she'll say
to Richard, spewing toothpaste suds on her side of the mirror.

"*That's* what really matters?" he'll reply after he's done brushing,
rinsing, and patting his mouth dry. Even in this, Alma thinks, Richard
has the cleaner windshield.

And now her cleaner windshield is gone. She drives the rest of the
way down to the house and gets out of the car. Upstairs, a boatload
of orphans and their hopeful rectoress are waiting to cross the Atlantic
with a crazed visionary.

Alma decides not to go inside just yet. Instead, she heads across the
back field to Helen's house.

"HELEN, IT'S ME!" Alma hollers, after knocking at the back
door and turning the knob. She doesn't want to scare the half-blind
old woman who's not expecting her at this hour of the morning. Usually, Alma tries to come once or twice a week in the late afternoon for
an hour and read to Helen. Lately, Alma has fallen off, letting weeks
go by, which she feels bad about, but tells herself it doesn't really matter. Claudine and another woman on their road alternate days checking on Helen and reading her the necessaries: her mail, the local
gossipy paper she likes, and anything else she might ask them for.
Alma is supposed to do the frills, as Helen calls them. Some good
book. Sometimes Helen asks Alma to read something she has written,
which is sweet of her, and Alma has obliged a few times but stopped
because Helen always falls asleep. But then Helen also naps for Toni
Morrison and Robert Frost, so Alma doesn't feel so bad.

"Is that you, Alma?" Helen calls out. Her voice sounds wobbly,
croaky, as if maybe she's coming down with a cold.

"Yeah, it's me, Helen," Alma says, trying to figure out where Helen
is since she isn't in the kitchen in back where she usually hangs out all
day. Helen is sitting at her telephone-table seat that reminds Alma of
being a kid. Amazing to think that forty-some years ago that item was
shipped down to a little backwater dictatorship. Some stuff, like bubble gum, found its way everywhere, even back then.

"Hi, dear," Helen says, her voice brightening. She's looking in
Alma's general direction. Helen's hazelish eyes have that cloudy look
of the planet Earth seen from outer space. And though Alma knows
Helen's vision's almost gone because of glaucoma, Alma always feels
as if Helen does see her. "I do, dear," Helen has told her when Alma
has mentioned this feeling in the past, "with the eyes of my heart."

"What a nice surprise!" she says now, like she means it, but there's
something in her voice that doesn't sound like the Helen Alma is
used to.

"Everything okay?" Alma asks, wondering if Helen will tell her. Her
old friend is not a complainer and avoids ever mentioning any problems in her life—even when Alma has pressed her. Helen doesn't

want to dwell on the negative, Alma can accept that, but sometimes she has the feeling that Helen is afraid people won't come back if she doesn't make them feel better.

"I'm fine, especially now that you're here. Let's go on back to the kitchen and get us some tea. If you're not in a hurry?"

"No, no," Alma assures her, holding back on trying to help as Helen pulls her walker over and leans into it, struggling to her feet. There's an extra heaviness in her movements. Maybe she has gotten an upsetting phone call and that's why she was at her phone seat. The AIDS caller from a few weeks back pops into Alma's head—but that woman has since been taken into custody and committed somewhere, Tera caught her up. Better not bring up something upsetting and make Helen feel unsafe and even more fragile.

"I'm surprised to see you so early, dear. What time is it anyway?" The radio usually keeps her posted. But the radio is off. Another odd detail. Helen, not being predictable.

"I'm giving myself a day off," Alma tells her. Helen knows all about Alma's writing schedule—how Alma makes herself sit at her desk, come muse or not. Helen, however, also knows the truth—the only person Alma has told. She has given up on her novel. Instead she is reading and brooding about some orphan kids crossing the Atlantic. She has told Helen the whole expedition story.

"A good thing to give yourself a day off," Helen is saying now, tentatively, as if she doubts that's what Alma is up to and is giving her a chance to refute it. Helen is standing in the little corral of her walker, catching her breath from the exertion of getting up. It makes Alma feel tender to see the old woman in there.

"What about you, Helen. What are you up to? I always find you in your kitchen."

"You'd be surprised," Helen says, chuckling. "If you'd come any earlier, you might've found me in the bedroom in my nightie."

"All alone or with a honey?" Alma plays along. Helen has alluded to her past, a long-ago rocky marriage and a son, who periodically drops off the face of the earth and then reappears. Alma has gotten the story mostly from Claudine, whose husband's a "local boy" and so knows all about the old-timers in town. For almost fifty years, Helen worked at the high school in the lunchroom and saw several generations in this town go through their adolescence; she retired when she started going blind. Everyone loved her so much, they gave her a little parade on her last day of work. Small towns. You gotta love them.

"A honey at my age, ha!" Helen is laughing, as she clumps around the kitchen, making tea. Alma loves to watch how Helen finds things, her hands tentative, but somehow landing true, like a puzzle piece that snaps in place. "How's *your* honey doing, by the way?"

"He's gone away on an assignment." Alma tries to keep her voice even. She doesn't want Helen to think the real reason she came over on a Saturday morning was to get away from her own loneliness. "It's one of those projects his company has in different countries." Alma goes on to tell Helen about the green center, as they sip from their chipped mugs. Probably because Helen is blind and bumps into things, a lot of her cups and plates have chips in them, but at least she doesn't have to see them. In their house, Richard is always holding up his favorite bowl or martini glass and saying, "So what happened to this?" "Why is it always me?" Alma has countered. For the next five months, she is going to have to be careful. If something breaks, she will not be able to convince Richard that he might have done it.

"So he's going to be gone for a while, is he?" Helen wonders.

"Uh-hum." Alma takes a sip of her tea, swallowing down that weepy feeling.

"Any time you feeling lonesome you come over here, you hear?"

"Thanks, Helen, I will." Helen can tell. Of course, Helen can tell. Just like Alma can tell that Helen has got something on her mind. "Helen, you'd tell me if something was wrong?"

For a moment, Helen looks unsure as if she has been caught keeping something to herself, but then she smiles, bemused, the old Helen. "I'll try," she says, almost shyly. "You, too," she adds, turning the conversation back to Alma. "A woman can get blue without her man."

"And *with* him, too," Alma reminds her. Helen has heard about

Alma's dark moods of the last few months. "Don't you worry," she has told Alma. "God has a plan for you. You just have to keep your eyes and ears open so you don't miss it."

Unlike other religious people who can drive her nuts, when Helen mentions God, Alma just does an instantaneous translation in her head—God as a metaphor for the stunning, baffling, painful, beautiful spirit of the universe—bypassing the whole thorny question of whether God even exists, and instead dealing directly with the little quandaries that really are the places people get stuck in for life.

"He wanted me to go with him, and maybe I should've, Helen, but . . . I don't know." If indecisiveness hits her now, Alma is a goner. She'll be on a plane tomorrow.

"Maybe you needed him out of your hair so you could hear yourself think," Helen offers. For a moment, Alma wonders if Helen is talking about her own solitary life—her difficult husband, who disappeared ages ago; her on-again, off-again son who reappears whenever he wants. "Sometimes you need to be alone so you can hear that quiet, little voice of God inside." Helen's voice is hushed, as if she's hearing it now.

"Hmm," Alma puzzles. Did she really stay to hear the baffling, painful spirit of the universe inside her? "It's just that I lied to him, Helen. I told him I was staying to finish my novel."

Helen smiles, bemused again. "He'll understand," she says. "Goodness gracious, saving the world isn't for everybody. You've got your own work to do."

Has she misrepresented Richard, Alma wonders. He isn't saving the world. Just greening one tiny bit of it. The bit of it that has her country's name on it. She should have gone with him if only for that reason. As for saving the world? Alma used to tell herself that writing was a way to do that, but deep down she has to agree with Helen that "you can't use a tractor to weed the garden." Literature does one thing; activism and good works do another. But Alma doesn't want to keep plaguing Helen with her self-doubts right now, especially when her old friend doesn't seem herself. If nothing else, Alma wants to give

Helen the pleasure of thinking that right here, right now, all's well with the two of them anyhow.

They sit together, quietly sipping tea, the muted sun coming in through the curtains and giving the paneled room a reassuringly old-fashioned sepia look. All is well. "It's good to be here, Helen." Alma reaches for the spotted hand, which startles at first at her touch, but then holds Alma's hand back.

As ALMA IS GETTING ready to go, perhaps because she broached wanting to help, Helen asks if Alma might be stopping in town anytime soon.

"Sure," Alma tells her. That was going to be her next stop after leaving Helen's. So as not to have to go home to a place where everything reminds her of Richard. "You need some groceries?"

"Claudine got me all supplied yesterday. It's a prescription. Over at the drugstore." There are actually two drugstores in town, some chain just out of town and Peters' Drugs downtown, which Alma knows is the one Helen means. Mr. Peters is another local "boy," only a little younger than Helen. "It's been called in," Helen explains, as if the doctor did her a special favor by doing this. Helen reaches for her purse hanging from the back of her chair, burrowing in it for her wallet.

"Pay me later when I bring it," Alma tells her.

"You sure?"

"You stiff me, Helen, and I'll make you sit through *Paradise Lost* again!" Alma had had some misguided idea that since Milton was blind, Helen would somehow feel connected to his work. Plus, Helen is Christian, there was that. But Milton and Helen were not a match. Alma actually only read the first two books, skipping whenever she'd hear Helen sigh. Finally, Helen had her stop. "Is it too depressing?" Alma had asked. "No, it's not that. It sounds like those Congress hearings on C-Span," Helen had laughed. All those devils double-talking must've been what turned Helen off.

She's laughing now at Alma's threat, and Alma is laughing, too, feeling her mood lifting. Five months, five years, they're going to make it,

Helen and Alma. They're going to stare that old loneliness in the face until it backs down and turns into productive and soulful solitude.

But when Alma picks up Helen's prescription, she is not so sure. Helen on Paxil? So, it's not as easy as it looks. Of course, Alma has no business reading the label on Helen's little bottle, but she was surprised when Mr. Peters rang it up and she had to hand over a bunch of twenties. She finds herself wishing Helen had told her before dishing out top dollar for antidepressants. If nothing else, Alma could have offered her stash, which have, no doubt, disintegrated into the soil by now. One more bit of human trash littering up HI's green world.

AFTER DROPPING OFF HELEN'S prescription, Alma spends the day running all the errands she hasn't gotten to in months. By the time Richard returns, the torn shower curtain will be replaced, the overgrown houseplants repotted in new pots, the portrait of Ben by his artist girlfriend (actually, Lauren's already an ex) matted, framed, and hung.

It's not until late afternoon that Alma finally enters her house, bracing herself for its eerie tranquillity. Beeps on the answering machine, messages! And there's a sizable packet of mail she just picked up from their box on the road. Groceries to put away. Busy work—today she welcomes it.

The message machine is full of hang-ups, weird open-line sounds. Just what Alma needs now that Richard is gone: the AIDS caller back at it or some thief checking to see if anyone's home. Alma now wishes she'd left Richard's curt male voice on the machine. Maybe she can borrow Claudine's Dwayne to come over and tape a new message.

Between the hang-ups the other messages are reassuringly normal: a reminder of a dentist appointment, a book Alma requested is in at the library, some lady getting back to Richard about bags of raked leaves from the hospital grounds he had called about. He must have forgotten about them. Alma will surprise him with her resourcefulness, pick them up, lay them on the garden. There's also one from Lavinia, just calling to say hi, which probably means Veevee just called her about the saga of the saga; and one from Tera, about their plan to get together next weekend, an overnight, which Tera better not cancel, as Alma has nailed down a great big stake of solace on her friend's being around for a couple of days. The final one is from Claudine, cheery but uncharacteristically vague, could Alma call her back please, it's about . . . well, Helen. So Alma's hunch was right! Something *is* wrong with Helen. Why didn't Helen tell her directly? Alma feels a pang of jealousy at Claudine's being the preferred one. True, Claudine is also the dependable one, there every other day. Still, Helen knows Alma loves her and cares about her problems.

Alma dials Claudine's number, venting on the numbers, punch-punch-punch, punch-punch, punch-punch, but when Claudine's message machine clicks on, Alma hangs up, then keeps hitting the redial, over and over, while putting the groceries away. Finally, she stops when she realizes she's behaving like Mamasita! "The apple does not fall far from the tree," Helen always says whenever some local kid gets in trouble, a saying that Claudine uses a lot, too, whenever she reports on the antics of her two clone daughters.

Claudine, Helen, it's struck Alma before: how alike they are. Determined optimists. Somehow, though, Helen being older, struggling to keep that kind of attitude through almost eight decades instead of just three and a half makes Alma gravitate toward the old woman more than toward Claudine. Besides, Helen is poor, not poor poor—she does own her one acre, "more or less," with its ramshackle farmhouse—but like Tera, Helen is on a tight budget. Alma has always preferred poor people to rich ones, probably a guilt holdover from coming from a place where you're not offered that gray area—the middle class—a buffer zone where you can live a decent life and not feel like it's coming off the hide of someone whose yearly food money equals last night's tab at a fancy restaurant.

This is where Richard is right now—her homeland, where buffer zones are in short supply. Alma starts punching in the airline's 800-number to hear that automated voice of comfort tell her the plane has landed, having successfully evaded the Scylla of mechanical failure and the Charybdis of terrorists. Dear Richard, her love, her only one, is going to help create a whole new space for her countrymen, a green center, where they can enjoy clean air and viable rivers and forests full of songbirds that summer in the United States. But Alma knows her countrymen. They're going to want cell phones and sneakers for their kids with heels that light up when they take a step and houses with satellite dishes and cable TV. How will they react when they learn that's not at all what Richard has come to deliver in the name of HI?

Alma feels a pang. A loved one moving through a world of people who do not love him, who would smash his skull for the cash in his money clip or blow up his plane for a God he doesn't believe in. Even with her stepsons, Alma can't bear to see them depart, thus the many good-byes, the walk to the door, the walk to their cars, with shopping bags of snack food they don't really want. Alma wonders how Helen feels having her son drop off the face of the earth, Claudine's description. Like watching the *María Pita* sail off that windy November day, past the Tower of Hercules, heading south and west, the crew working the ropes to get the sails angled just so, the ship becoming smaller and smaller, until it cleared the horizon, and was gone! What a gloomy evening that must have been, back at La Casa de Expósitos, Nati and the remaining boys trying not to notice the many empty spaces at the long table. In her own darkening house several blocks away, Doña Teresa might have wondered if she'd done the right thing, letting her boys go on this questionable expedition.

It's enough to draw Alma upstairs to her study, wondering about all of them. But as she is going past the landing, she glances out, and her breath catches. A jolt of fear rivets her to the spot. The stranger is back, headed up the field this time, not stopping at the boulder to scope the lay of the land but coming straight toward the house! Somehow, Alma wrenches herself away, races downstairs just to be sure the doors are locked, first to the back door as that's the direction he's coming from—already locked! Then dashing to the side door—also locked! Finally, the front door—locked, thank God! Snatching up the portable, Alma races upstairs to her study, locks that door, her heart pounding like mad. She dials Tera, and the phone rings and rings. Damn! Why can't Tera have a machine where in case of emergency, Alma can leave her best friend her last words? Next, she tries Claudine, and gets her machine, but Alma can't leave Claudine her last words, because what if they're not her last words, she'll feel totally embarrassed next time she sees Claudine. So, Alma dials Helen, which is crazy, what's Helen going to do—clomp up the field in her walker to rescue Alma? But Alma is not thinking straight, and the moment Helen answers, Alma blurts out, "Helen, I'm sorry. I don't want to worry you, but there's this weird guy coming up the back field to my house, he doesn't look armed but—" Alma stops to catch her breath.

"Oh, dear, I'm so sorry. That's Mickey," Helen says, that croaky voice again. "My son. I sent him up there to check on you."

"Your son?" Alma gasps. Why didn't Helen tell her this morning her son was around?

"I couldn't reach you all afternoon"—of course not: Alma has been driving around the county, avoiding her own house—"and seeing as you're alone, I just wanted to be sure you were all right."

Alma hears Mickey pounding on the door downstairs, a sound she mistakes at first for the pounding of her own heart. She hangs up. If she is not careful, she is going to end up with a heart attack in a locked-up house that the rescue squad has to break into.

"Hallo!" Mickey says when Alma opens the door, trying to look composed. What's the use? The minute he gets home, Helen's going to tell him their neighbor mistook him for a murderer. "I'm to look and see you're okay."

"I know," Alma says. Might as well fess up. "I just called your mom. I got spooked when I saw a stranger on our property."

He looks over his shoulder as if Alma is talking about someone else, then gets it, crosses his arms in front of him, amused. He has his mother's eyes, hazel but without the cloud cover, which makes Alma feel as if she should trust him even though she has never met him before.

"My imagination, I can get carried away." Alma laughs at herself, inviting him to laugh at her, too. But he doesn't, just that bemused look, as if he's watching a little chicken peck herself out of a half shell he could easily reach over and remove.

"You're an artist," he finally says. Artist–imagination–getting carried away: Alma can sort of see how his mind works, but she has to connect all his dots. He actually looks like an artist himself, blond gray shaggy hair, not long enough for a ponytail but getting there. "Helen said you were an artist."

Helen? Wonder why he doesn't call his mother Mother? "Well, I don't know about that."

After a moment, he says, "Nice being an artist." A man of few words. But from the few he's said, Alma has noticed an occasional odd intonation, not quite an accent, a trace of an English from somewhere else. Maybe New Zealand or one of the English-speaking islands near where she comes from. *Off the face of the earth,* the phrase comes to mind.

"Anyhow, I'm fine."

He nods, one deep nod. "I can see that." His hands are at his hips as if he's going to stick around a while and watch. He's still wearing only a shirt, a worn plaid, and old jeans—a street-person look anywhere else, but here in rural Vermont it's the outfit de rigueur of the wardrobe righteous—while Alma is shivering in her turtleneck and sweater, standing on the warm side of an open door.

"Thanks for stopping by. That was nice of your mom to worry about me. I worry about her sometimes, too. We call and check on each other from time to time." Alma pauses. Come on, she thinks, put some money in the meter, say something to conclude. Maybe this man is a Buddhist. Alma heard from Tera how she invited a new adjunct in her department to dinner, a Buddhist, and he hardly said a word. So how does he lecture in class? Alma had wondered later. Alma keeps forgetting to ask Tera every time they talk. "So. . . anyhow, thanks." Alma starts shutting the door, but the man's still standing there on her front step, as if he's not going anywhere. She can't just be rude to Helen's son and shut the door in his face. "Bye," Alma says in warning; then, exasperated, she says straight out, "I'm going to shut the door now."

He must think that's funny because suddenly he's grinning widely, his hazel eyes full of recognizable response. "I can see why Helen would worry about a woman like you all alone." For some reason, Alma finds herself wishing Helen hadn't told her son that she is alone. His comment makes her feel uneasy, as if men are out there on the prowl and she is going to need protection from their savage lustiness for the next five months Richard is away.

She catches herself. For heaven's sake, she is fifty years old! Besides, didn't this attitude go out with their generation? This guy has a weathered and leathery look, hard to guess his age, but he looks to be in his late forties. Maybe he's harmless and nonverbal, and this is his clumsy way of delivering a compliment? "Helen sure has some attractive neighbors," he goes on, shaking his head, downright talkative now. "There's another one, hair a little lighter than yours." Claudine. If he wants to be the gallant, he should know a compliment to a woman is best left in the singular. Though in this instance, let Claudine be the beauty. Claudine, who is about fifteen years younger and whose big, husky local husband should be getting home just about now.

"Don't mean to keep you." A Helen phrase. "But anything you need, you just let Helen know."

Alma nods, the quiet one now.

"I'll be staying on with Helen for a bit. I'll come by, now and then, to check on you."

"You don't need to do that," Alma tells him. Better stop this right at the start.

"I know," he says, finally letting his arms drop to his side, a motion that might mean he's leaving, might not.

Alma closes the door while he's still standing there—hopefully, he'll leave—then leans back on it and closes her eyes. Poor Helen. Alma sighs. No wonder she's on Paxil.

• • •

ALMA FINALLY REACHES CLAUDINE later that night. She and
Dwayne and the girls were at a neighborhood potluck. Alma feels a
pang, as if she were back in high school, a *neighborhood* potluck and
no one invited her. Who wants a sad, tofu-bearing woman with a near-
empty dinner plate, announcing she's vegetarian?

"I didn't mean to sound so mysterious," Claudine explains. She intended to talk to Alma this morning when she saw Alma's car in the
driveway, but she had to go home first and put her groceries away, ice
cream, the girls go through a gallon in two days, both have a bad sweet
tooth, she should talk, the apple doesn't fall far from the tree, but
when she came back, there was no one in the house. Just wanting to
fill Alma in. In case Alma has noticed how Helen hasn't been herself
for the last month.

Another pang. A whole month of Helen's not being okay, and Alma
just noticed this morning! But then, Alma hasn't seen much of Helen
these last few weeks before Richard's departure. "Yes?" Alma says,
bracing herself for that old weather report: The winds of time are
about to blow hard. Batten down the hatches.

"Helen . . . well, she's not doing so well." Claudine is hesitating her
way through words that might blow up in both their faces.

"I picked up some medication for her today," Alma confesses. "I
couldn't help noticing it was Paxil." Maybe Claudine doesn't know
what Paxil is. "An antidepressant," Alma adds.

"That should help. But it's . . . Alma, Helen's got cancer, really bad,
it's in her liver, in her lungs, it's everywhere." Claudine's voice goes
shaky. "She didn't want me to tell anyone, but I'd be upset if someone
didn't tell me."

"I'm glad you told me," Alma manages, her head spinning. Cancer
everywhere. Why didn't Helen tell her? Suddenly, it makes sense that
Helen's son is here. "I met her son. Is that why he came home?"

"Yes and no. Dwayne's mom got a hold of Mickey through his wife's
family who were trying to get a hold of him, too." It flashes through
Alma's head that the guy has no business being a gallant with a wife
in the wings, not to mention his mother, whom he doesn't even call

Mother, dying of cancer. "Mickey was told to come home if he wanted to see his mother alive. He's been around for the last month. His wife's not doing well either, you know."

"No, I didn't know," Alma says, feeling ashamed at how hastily and harshly she judged the guy a moment ago. He can't be all that bad: he's taking care of a sick wife and a dying mother. "How long does Helen have?" Does she really want to know? Wouldn't it be better to just leave it like the old parental estimate for that childhood question, Are we almost there? Almost. An almost that can last a long time?

"They can never be sure," Claudine sighs. "But the doctor said two, three months, at the most six."

One down. At best, five more to go. Richard might not even get to see Helen again. But then Helen doesn't mean as much to Richard. To him, she's just a kindly old woman who reminds him of his mother. "Oh, Claudine," Alma says, feeling suddenly bereft, as if they're two kids stuck in a dark forest together, waiting for someone to lead them safely home. "Is there anything we can do? I mean, I'm not even supposed to know, right?"

"Well, Helen's mad at me already for telling Dwayne's mom to call Mickey, so she might as well be mad at me that I told you." Claudine laughs, a sad laugh. "But like I told her: people don't just belong to themselves, Helen, they belong to the people who love them."

Alma loves this woman! Why hasn't she noticed before how wise and good Claudine is? *We belong to the people who love us.* That's the best advice going on getting a lost soul out of the dark wood, back to the human fold.

"Sorry to be the bearer of bad news," Claudine is saying.

"No, it's a wake-up call," Alma says, and is surprised to hear Claudine agree, "I know what you mean."

"You take care," Claudine concludes. Alma has noticed before how Claudine always personalizes the throwaway phrase, as if to let you know she really means it in your case. Today, Alma believes her. "Take care," she says back.

Alma lays the receiver down carefully in its cradle as if everything in this world is suddenly too fragile; any abrupt move, and she's likely to snag a thread or step on a bit of pulsing matter. Was it Richard who told her about some Far Eastern monks in a remote place, totally removed from what'd been happening in the world for the last century, who in addition to being strict vegetarians, could not harm any living thing, no matter how small or insignificant, so they had to watch where they stepped, check before they sat down, and so on. Can you imagine, Richard had said, if these monks found out about microscopic life? They'd be unable to move or breathe or *be*. What was Richard's point? Something about the collateral damage of just being alive, how you can't live with that kind of knowledge, how you just do the best you can.

So Alma fortifies herself now with arguments: Helen is an old woman, she has lived a long, good life, not without its bumps. Lots of people don't even get to live this long. She'll have decent medical care. Neighbors and friends and a son, who are going to be by her side. Alma feels like one of those devils in *Paradise Lost*, full of logical reasons why it's okay that somebody else is going to die.

BY THE TIME ALMA talks to Richard that night, she has been on the phone with Helen with the excuse that she wanted to thank Helen for sending her son over, but no need to worry, Alma is fine, she'll be by tomorrow, hope that's okay. Helen is full of apologies all over again for scaring Alma, and as Alma listens to her old friend, she is hearing a new background sound, ticktock, ticktock. Next, Alma calls Tera back, and sure enough, Tera tries to talk Alma into spending part of their weekend together at a rally for wind power at the Sheraton where some energy summit is going on. Alma explains about Helen. Can't they just have a quiet weekend together? Surprisingly, Tera agrees, though almost immediately she starts peppering Alma with questions: Is Helen in touch with Home Health? Does she know about its excellent hospice program? There's this wonderful advocacy group fighting for death with dignity rights—Tera'll dig up some info. Alma can hear Helen's dying of cancer becoming Tera's next cause.

Oh, Tera. Alma should know by now. There's no stopping people from being who they are.

And the nagging question through all these conversations is, Why hasn't Richard called? Alma knows from the automated airline number that his flight landed about a half hour late, in the early afternoon, and it's already eight at night. Several scenarios run through her artist mind, none of them nice.

When the phone rings, Alma promises Helen's God—since she knows that the baffling, painful spirit of the Universe doesn't make deals—that if it's Richard, she will not let the first, second, or even third thing out of her mouth be *Why haven't you called?* And, in fact, when she hears his dear voice, everything falls away, and she is flooded with pure and simple joy that he's back in real time on the other end of the line.

"¡Hola! ¡Querida!" He's already talking with exclamation marks. "¿Cómo estás?" For the last few weeks Richard has been dutifully listening to some State Department tapes from HI's library. Alma hasn't had the heart to remind him that no one in her homeland is going to talk Spanish that fancy.

"Honey!" Alma laughs. "It's so good to hear your voice!" She almost asks—before she remembers her part of the deal—why he has waited to call her until eight o'clock at night.

"I've been trying you on and off since I landed," he says, leaving Alma to wonder if she did ask her question out loud. "We kept stopping at every roadside phone. My calling card wouldn't work, and the meanest operators, they wouldn't let me leave a message. Where have you been?"

"Oh," she says airily, as if she has been having an exciting life here in the backwoods of Vermont since he left. But who is she kidding? "I've been missing you too much," she admits. "I didn't want to come home and find you gone. I don't know if I'm going to be able to stand it."

"I know," he agrees. But a certain airiness in his voice, plus the fun-sounding background noise—music, laughter, is he at a bar?—tells

Alma separation is not going to be as hard on him. The debit is on her side again. She is the one whose love is alloyed with need; his is the genuine article. "I'm calling you from this neat little hotel on the road—adobe-style, you'd love it. The owner's so nice, there's a fiesta going on."

They haven't been parted a full day yet, and already there are so many stories to exchange! Bienvenido, that's the Dominican intern he'll be working with, picked him up at the airport. "And I swear we stopped at every pay phone." So that's what the hang-ups on the answering machine were all about!

Rather than drive up the mountain in the dark, he and Bienvenido have decided to stop overnight on the road. "It's good because it's giving Bienvenido a chance to catch me up on some of what's been going on." The project has been off to a rocky start. "Remember the clinic I mentioned? Well, all these patients have been brought in from coastal towns near resort areas to be treated with experimental drugs. I guess there's a lot of HIV in the country because of sexual tourism—and the locals aren't too happy about this."

AIDS? "But you must have known this AIDS clinic was there, Richard." Richard, not honey. He knows what that means.

"Well, don't go getting angry at me, or I'm not going to be able to tell you things!"

A threat. Tears fill Alma's eyes. "I feel like you only told me part of the story. I would've come with you if I'd known there was going to be trouble."

"No, you wouldn't have. You're finishing your novel, remember?"

That silences her. He is not the only one telling little lies.

"And there's no trouble, that's what I was going to tell you: everything's been smoothed out. The clinic sponsors have donated money to the locals, and they've also hired a communications-liaison person to explain to the community that they're not going to get AIDS just because the clinic is there. Bienvenido says there's been a complete turnaround. Trust me," he adds.

Why did he trouble her with the story then? He has probably had a drink, two drinks, and he's a little sloshed, his guard down. Alma should be grateful he's being straight with her, even if it's taken one-hundred-proof Dominican rum to do it.

"Truly, querida, I'm not going to run any risk. I promise."

"You'll tell me if anything's wrong?" Alma pleads.

"Of course, I will," he assures her, a little too broadly—the rum, no doubt. But he won't tell her, Alma can bet on it. He knows that if he intimates that there's any trouble, Alma will drop everything and go rescue him. Something she should have learned by now: husbands do not appreciate their wives in shining armor. But Alma can go down without armor, just hang out, nothing is holding her here, except . . . except Helen. Helen is dying!

"I don't want you to come down," Richard is saying, and then realizing how that sounds, he backtracks. "Not right now anyhow. I want to think I can handle this myself."

It can't be easy for Richard to be in her country when she is along: a native wife correcting his pronunciation, rescuing him from being overcharged at the market, and then feeling uneasy herself, like some bargain-hunting Malinche, betraying her own people by telling Cortés that a dollar a mango is okay in Vermont, but here, well, it's a rip-off. It will be good for Richard to establish his very own relationship with her homeland, make it his. "But please promise you won't take any risks?"

"What do you take me for, a fool?"

Alma reminds herself now is not the time for honesty. If they have a bad phone call, she can't just walk into the next room in a few minutes and explain what she really meant by not agreeing he wasn't a fool. So she changes the subject, tells him about Helen, what a shock it's been, how she is going to try to go over there every day. "Poor Helen." Richard sighs. He knows Alma is attached to their neighbor. "Are you going to be okay? You promise you'll take care of yourself?"

"I will," Alma promises. "But you have to promise you'll do the same for me, right?" *Our lives belong not just to us but to the people who love us.* How long before it's a bumper sticker?

"I'm sorry," Richard says, and Alma knows he's back to Helen.

"It sure puts everything into perspective, let me tell you," Alma says.

There's a momentary silence. This is usually Richard's line. Alma probably took it out of his mouth. "That's for sure," he finally says.

Before they say good-bye, he promises he'll call soon. "Tomorrow?" Alma tries to pin him down. But he can't commit because then she'll worry. Bienvenido has told him that cell phones don't receive signals on the mountain. He's going to check into other options. Meanwhile, the clinic has its own hookup, and Alma can call him at that number if she needs to reach him. "Do you have a pen and paper handy?"

"You already gave it to me," Alma reminds him. She recites it back, just to be sure.

"There's also a fax number, which is easier as we don't have to coordinate times."

Faxing her beloved? *How do I love thee? Let me fax the ways.* No! Alma wants to talk to Richard; she wants him to come home at the end of the day, tired, brimming with stories, and as they get dinner ready or sit and have a glass of wine, a martini, one or the other will begin: *So, how did your day go?*

Miserable, Alma thinks, as she hangs up. Helen is dying. Richard is headed into what sounds like a momentarily becalmed hornet's nest. She is fifty years old and she doesn't know who she is or where she is going anymore and to top it off she has abandonment attacks when her husband leaves home. How did people in the past maintain that single-mindedness of purpose that history at least makes it sound like they had? Balmis, for instance. Did he ever waver? And Isabel, once those kids started getting seasick and feverish from their vaccinations? How did she keep believing—or did she?— that what she'd done was the right thing?

Alma looks out the kitchen window and far off, she can make out the twinkle of Helen's lights among the trees now that the leaves are gone.

# III

---

31 diciembre 1803

Mi querida Nati,

I hope that this finds you in good health along with all our boys. I write you from the island of Tenerife where, as I understand it, most ships stop before they make the ocean crossing. How I have missed you and that most pleasurable hour at La Casa, after our little ones were abed, when you and I would sit and exchange stories of what had happened that day!

To be the lone woman in a world of men and little boys makes one yearn for the company of another daughter of Eve. That yearning has been granted these three weeks of our stay here at Santa Cruz de Tenerife. My boys and I have been housed at the convent of the Dominican Sisters, who have plied us with many attentions.

I trust you passed a good Noche Buena and that Doña Teresa brought her usual candies and clothes for the boys. And now on to a new year to-morrow! I wish you and all our boys joy and peace in this coming eighteen hundredth and fourth year of our Lord!

I had not thought to write until we reached Puerto Rico, but then the op-portunity presented itself with the *Espíritu Santo,* departing in several days to Cádiz, where, hopefully, this letter will be put on a packet to La Coruña. We, too, are readying for departure, awaiting only the final provisioning of the ship and a prevailing northeast wind to make our crossing. I confess I have been dreading the renewal of our journey, after the terrible seasickness

I endured en route here. I have prayed to the Blessed Virgin, kissed the cross at the plaza, and packed all our things. Only to unpack them the next morning.

Outside, I could hear the crowds beginning to gather. Vaccinations would not start until three, and the church bell had not yet tolled two. Downstairs in the refectory, the tables had been pushed aside, the mats laid down, and the boys were sleeping their siesta. I hoped the bell would not wake them.

My own room was upstairs, a tiny cell, narrow and plain with a cot and a prie-dieu I was using blasphemously as my writing desk. A small casement window looked down onto the square. After the cramped quarters of the *María Pita,* it seemed a royal chamber.

I put my quill aside and stood to stretch my limbs. I was wearying of this letter. Of ever being able to capture on paper the sights and sounds of the last few weeks. Why even make the attempt? And yet, I knew how happy Nati would be to hear from me that the boys and I were well.

The boys are all thriving, and except for having picked up some foul curses from the crew, they have recovered from all sea ailments. These three weeks of rest have worked wonders on their little constitutions. Indeed, I think His Majesty should consider sending all our orphans to be raised in Tenerife, for the climate here is temperate and lovely, an eternal spring, and we feast on the fruits of the earth and air and sea! Even our sickly Juan Antonio has recovered from the nasty cold he caught waiting on the wharf while the royal proclamation was read out loud to us. Our scholar, Antonio, has all the boys convinced that we have landed in Paradise. Perhaps we have, though my confinement in this small convent makes a golden cage of my heaven. My tasks keep me busy and mostly indoors.

There was the bell, two loud strokes. The convent stood beside the church and so time was palpable here, the walls hummed with the vibration, the floors as well. The crucifix opposite my cot sometimes fell at the stroke of midnight, twelve reverberating bongs. I waited now, anticipating footsteps up the stairs, a small hand at the door, a boy wanting my attention. But thankfully the convent was still. The nuns were resting as well.

I should have been resting, too. These last three weeks on land I had had sole care of the boys. The Sisters were kind, but they were not used to having children about. They deferred to me in all matters. Often they would ask me, rather than the boy in question, Is he hungry? Is he sleepy? Is he hurt? Why is he crying?

As their guests, I was at pains trying to keep my flock of little boys from being a bother to them. Curses issued from the mouths of my toddlers, making the little nuns blanch. Nights, I often fell to sleep, too tired to say my prayers or even wash my hands and feet.

None of our expedition could be spared to help me. Daily, but for Sundays, crowds thronged the plaza for their vaccinations, long lines of men and women and children eager to be saved from the smallpox. Upon our arrival in Santa Cruz, the bishop had extolled our blessed mission. "Our Holy Father has offered an indulgence to all who undergo this holy procedure," the bishop proclaimed, stopping just short of calling it the Sacrament of Vaccination.

From the vesicles of our two carriers, a dozen had been vaccinated that first day. I was amazed how much vaccine one vesicle could yield. Just a drop was needed on the arm. From that dozen came vaccine enough for dozens more. By now, several hundred had been saved. Indeed, many of the believers who came to the plaza were convinced they were receiving a drop of the blood of Christ on their skin that would guard them from all evil and keep them from sin.

By the time this expedition is over, dear Nati, I wager I will be vaccinating on my own! Don Francisco especially loves to be teaching. In fact, many of the members of our expedition have been his students. Some do seem rather young. Why the second in command, Dr. Salvany, has only just turned twenty-six! A pale young man, in love with poetry, he will not say something in ten words that can be embellished into twice that number. I wonder how such a tender-hearted young man will fare on this rigorous journey. Our director has also brought along a pair of nephews, Don Antonio and Don

Francisco Pastor, very able young men. All in all, we are ten, assisting Don Francisco.

I include myself, yes! for our director himself has taught me the procedure. It really is quite simple, the vaccinating part. I dare say, deworming the boys is a far more unpleasant task. First: the skin is pierced with a lancet. The difficulty here is keeping the boys distracted. How they howl as if they were being murdered! Then the cowpox fluid is harvested from the vesicles of the last carrier and laid upon the pierced skin. In three days, the skin begins to show signs of inflammation. Remember Tintín's and Bello's "boils"? These continue to grow and fill with fluid until the whole area becomes quite painful. To varying degrees our carriers have suffered soreness and indisposition, which Don Francisco says are quite within the norm.

How I had fretted when Tintín began thrashing with fever and vomits on board the ship! "No ill effects," Don Francisco had assured me back in La Coruña. When I confronted him, our director smiled a sheepish smile. "Perhaps I overstated," he admitted. "I meant only to persuade you of a truth you might have doubted had it been qualified. I hope you forgive my enthusiasm, Doña Isabel." It was a tender moment between us. Of course, I forgave him.

The most difficult part is keeping the vesicles intact—no small matter, Nati, when you consider how restless our little boys get confined to a small area on a small ship. Inside each vesicle is the precious limpid fluid that must reach full potency before it can be harvested to the next set of carriers. What I still cannot decipher is how long that maturation takes.

"Excellent question, Doña Isabel!" Don Francisco had praised me when I had asked. How I loved to hear him say so! The vesicle had to be fully engorged, the grain at the center beginning to sink—as few as seven, as many as ten, days. "In science, theory must be ruled by observation, and, of course, necessity." As in life, I thought, but I did not offer my opinion.

I am happy to report that so far all of the boys we so carefully selected have reacted to the vaccine. From Tintín's and Bello's vesicles, we have gone on to vaccinate Pascual and Florencio at sea. On land, the two oldest boys. I do hope that none of our little carriers will fail us . . .

Nati, of course, knew about Benito, but I dared not allude to him in writing. What if my letter should fall into the wrong hands? Several times I had come close to confessing to our director. I had forgiven him his enthusiasm. Would he forgive me mine?

You are no doubt wondering how I have fared on a ship surrounded by so many men (thirty-seven in total, not counting our boys). In truth, I barely noticed them those first days out of La Coruña. Oh, Nati, I thought I would die of seasickness. Nothing helped settle my stomach or quiet my pounding head. Not the smelling salts the captain had given me before setting off, not the wine of ipecac that Don Francisco urged upon me. Of course, it did not help that my berth was with the boys down in the lower deck ("orlop," the sailors call it). Captain del Barco, a former Armada officer, more used to a ship full of mariners than of passengers, would not allow a *woman* in his officers' quarters where the cabins are located. He pronounces the word as if it had a bad taste. How to describe him? Think of our porter, another of those burly-type little fellows whose muscles resemble nothing other than sausages packed with far too much meat.

But I suppose our captain owed Don Francisco a favor. Remember the substitute boy who was to replace our little Carlito? (I hope he has fully recovered?) He is none other than the captain's young cabin boy, a sweet, cherub-faced child, Orlando, no older than our own Francisco. There is some rumor that he is the captain's son and a darker rumor that I will not repeat. A ship is not unlike our own city of La Coruña, full of gossip and hearsay.

The captain finally conceded to Don Francisco's petitions. But the true kindness came from the first mate who offered his own cabin for the lady's use. I was moved "aft," as the back part of the ship is known—a whole new language is spoken on board. At the time, I was too sick to properly thank the kind lieutenant. But a few days into our sail when I had grown more accustomed to the rocking ship, I made a point of finding him out. The tall, taciturn man stiffened and stammered so painfully, I had to cut my gratitude short. I can see why the captain might not want a woman in the midst of his officers if such is the effect of a pocked female of ripe age upon his right-hand man.

From my upstairs window, I could see the bay to the east, the ships posed as if in a painting, their sails slack, such a pretty picture! Of course, I now knew how unwelcome this very sight was to the captains of each of those outbound vessels, cursing the stillness that kept them from plying their trade. And though, I, like them, was eager to reach our destination, I was reluctant to board a rolling ship and be seasick once again.

"Virgen María," I prayed, not knowing what to ask for.

Below, in the square, the line already stretched past the marble cross and down the narrow streets. Knowing that our expedition would soon be leaving, larger crowds had been showing up. The captain-general had published an announcement that a local board was being set up, staffed by physicians trained by Don Francisco and his assistants, who would continue vaccinating after we were gone. But, still, many came from inland towns and other islands, wanting to be vaccinated by one of "the king's men."

This Saturday afternoon would be the last vaccination session until Monday morning, if we had not left by then. Tomorrow, Sunday, this same square would fill with traders from many nations come to sell and buy African slaves. I had watched the scene from my window and seen it up close as we returned from mass, a veritable Tower of Babel loosed in Santa Cruz: Dutch and French, Danish and British, Portuguese and American traders, and of course, our own Spaniards; and then the slaves, barely clothed, men and women and children, fetters at their feet or around their necks, their eyes wide with terror. I did not want to look at them and yet I could not help but look at them in wonderment, as the traders inspected them, prodding them to turn and show what they were made of.

"I no longer go near the plaza on Sundays!" the captain-general's wife had admitted at the Noche Buena celebration she threw for the boys at the palace. "The bishop kindly comes to say Mass in our chapel." She was a marchesa, the first marchesa I had ever spoken to, richly dressed for the occasion in a silk gown with pearls stitched in the bodice and sleeves; the Spanish rage of dressing like peasant majas had not caught here. "But I am sorry for you, dear, and for the poor Sisters, having to witness such sights, week after week. The slave market should be moved to the docks. I have been importuning the marquis. But he argues that this is where our good fortune comes from. 'Let the Sisters shut their windows!'"

Not that all new sights are pleasurable to behold. We have witnessed several horrid hangings of pirates captured by the *Venganza*. One in particular, a young man, who swore so foully, a rag was stuffed in his mouth to protect delicate ears in the crowd from hearing such uncivil utterings, as if the dangling of a man at the end of the rope were not uncivil and indelicate itself. I took the opportunity to instill fear in my little ones should they persist in their bad habit of swearing. Later, I felt ashamed to have used the suffering of another as the text for their improvement.

On Sundays in the plaza, in front of our lodgings, a slave market takes place. The savages are lined up on a block and bid upon. On the way back from Mass, I saw one African, a woman, naked but for a cloth tied about the waist to hide her sex; she was in fetters, sores where the chains had cut her skin. I could smell her fear, and the look in her eyes when she saw me gazing at her was one of such desolation it took my breath away.

The boys being boys have begun teasing our poor little Moor, threatening to sell him at the market. Needless to say, Tomás Melitón is now in a state of terror. Where does this unkindness in these children come from, Nati? Most of them have been with us from the very day they first drew breath or shortly thereafter, and though we have punished them when deserved, we have never taken relish in their sufferings. Another sagrado misterio to lay before our wise confessor, Father Ignacio. How is he? No doubt glad to be rid of the rectoress with her troublesome questions.

When I asked Don Ángel Crespo (the kindliest of the nurses; his name well suits him!) if these savages were to be vaccinated, he said they should be, for of those who do not die on the middle passage many are lost to the smallpox once they've crossed the water. But the traders, being fearful lest the vaccination make their merchandise sickly, and so bring in a lower price, prefer to forego this precaution and let the loss accrue to the buyer's account.

Why was I telling Nati such disturbing things? Why darken her day with a letter meant to bring her glad tidings? Why not tell of the sweetness and light abounding all about me? I could hear laughter now, as two men exchanged greetings and good wishes for the upcoming new year. The vaccination sessions often turned into festive gatherings, with street vendors selling all manner of fruits and sweets and boys piping tunes while a capuchin monkey danced a jig.

Ay, Nati, I should not complain of confinement, for in our three weeks here, I have had more outings than in a year in La Coruña. As I mentioned, I have curtsied before a marchesa and received many visitors and well-wishers at the convent. I have also kissed the ring of a bishop, each time a different one, I noted. You must wonder, no doubt, that I, who always sought the shadows and feared the scrutiny of the public eye, should now yearn to be out and about. But my curiosity once kindled cannot easily be snuffed out. And as I am only "the woman who takes care of the children," I am of no consequence to the eyes that gaze in my direction. Not once have I had to wield the pin with which you armed me for my protection!

In fact, the pin was stowed among my personal effects in the chest that was ready and packed at the foot of my cot. For days at a time at sea and here on land, I forgot my scarred face, my wounded vanity, my old losses. Only in *his* presence, or sometimes when a stranger's head turned to stare too boldly, was I thrust back into the cramped cell of my own story, and a fury would rise up, a desire to do damage such as the smallpox had done to me. Perhaps I should not be so astonished at slavers trading in human misery or crowds hurling abuse at some poor wretch at a hanging!

We went on an outing to the small town of Oratava, where there are many gardens. Our steward had to go to secure provisions and invited us along, no doubt trying to make amends for the loss of some of our cargo. I will not bother you with the details, only to say that some cases with Doña Teresa's treats have vanished into thin air! The steward, whom everyone calls Steward, a red-faced, shifty-eyed fellow, who doubles as our purser, is the one responsible for the ship's provisions. He blamed the loss on rats, but when pressed by the mate he charged the cook, who accused the seamen who returned the blame to the rats! They behave like our boys, do they not?

The outing was a welcomed treat for the boys, who will soon enough be closeted in a small wooden vessel. Ahead of us rose the enormous, snow-covered peak that, if reports are to be believed, spews out fire and pours out a burning river from time to time. The boys' eyes were big with wonder, hearing the stories. They sat in the square in Oratava, waiting and growing impatient. "When is the damned thing going to throw out bloody fire?" (Forgive me for transcribing their very words. Judge for yourself what foulness falls from the mouths of our innocents!)

I'm afraid the outing was a disappointment to them, but I enjoyed seeing such different sights. Palm trees and banana trees, fields of corn, and vegetables such as I had never known before, thriving now in the winter season! The houses are many of them painted a white color and the red tiled roofs become them very well. The people are dusky, as if from proximity to Africa, their skin had darkened. But they put great store on their purity and would rather, I wager, have my scarred white face than a Moor's unblemished dark skin.

I must mention a troubling incident, for my head still spins at the thought, and I have no one in this world but you, Nati, to whom I can confess it. We had to spend the night in Oratava, for though the distance from Santa Cruz is not great, what passes for a road is in very bad condition. As I bid our hosts good night—the local authority, something like our alcalde, and his kindly wife—the steward followed me to the door of my bedchamber and made a most improper proposition—

There was a tapping at my door now. One of the boys had no doubt awakened, and there was an end to my solitude. "Yes?" I called out wearily.

Sor Catalina pushed open the door gently. "Some members of your expedition." She spoke so softly, I could hardly hear her. The little nuns were not used to tending to children, and they walked on tiptoes and spoke in whispers whenever the boys were asleep.

I was surprised. If there was a message to be delivered, one of our expedition was sufficient for the task. Why several members? Perhaps we were sailing this very day and a number of helpers had come to assist me with rounding up the boys. So much for my letter to Nati. "Is Don Francisco with them?"

Sor Catalina was not sure. The convent had been beset with officials and well-wishers, who came to pay their respects to twenty-one little sons of the king. (Orlando was staying with our captain at the captain-general's palace.) Sor Catalina had met so many people in the last few weeks, she could not be sure who was who. The captain-general had decorated the expedition members with a red satin honor band to wear over their uniforms, which identified them. These men, she explained, were wearing those bands.

In the front receiving room, I found Don Francisco and Dr. Salvany as well as Dr. Gutiérrez, Don Francisco's personal assistant in Madrid whom he had enticed to join our expedition. My own little Francisco was with them.

Of course! Francisco's vaccination must be ripe for harvesting—today was already the tenth day. On shore, Don Francisco had been vaccinating only one of our boys at a time in order to conserve carriers in case of any mishap in our crossing. He might have dispensed with vaccinating any of our own boys altogether, as there were plenty of reserves here. But so careful was he of any possible corruption, he wanted to maintain a pure line of continuance from our original number.

"Gentlemen," I said, giving them each my hand in greeting. "My child," I added, bending to kiss Francisco's forehead. He was of the age that such womanly affection embarrassed him. He lifted his hand, as if to prevent me, but Dr. Gutiérrez caught him by the wrist. I do not think his intention was to prevent the boy's discourtesy, as much as to protect the big, blooming vesicle on the boy's left arm.

"The boys are napping," I explained. "Whom shall I fetch next?"

"I would ask you to choose among the sturdiest," Don Francisco replied. In fact, all the boys were fat and well. We had all been gorging ourselves on the fruits of the land, sweet milk and oozing cheeses, bananas and figs and grapes, every kind of verdura mixed with spiced rice, all of the treasures of this island of eternal spring, plied upon us by our little nuns and visitors.

"How about the little Neptune who clings to you like a barnacle," Dr. Salvany suggested, smiling at his own cleverness. After ten days at sea, his descriptions had become decidedly nautical.

I nodded agreement, trying to hide my immense relief. It would be no great tragedy if Benito's vaccination did not take here. There were dozens of carriers whose vesicles could be harvested and the vaccine not lost. At sea was another matter.

"We are departing any day," Don Francisco reminded me. "We must go back to a pair of carriers again."

My heart sunk. The voyage I had been fearing. The return of my seasickness. And now, the added uncertainty about Benito. What if the vaccine did not take on him? The second in the pair of carriers must not fail.

"You need only bring the boy, as Orlando will serve as our second carrier," Don Francisco went on. I had been at the point of suggesting José, a sure second, as I had wiped the boy's birth caul from his face and could vouch for every illness and ailment he had suffered. But the captain had already asked that his cabin boy be vaccinated during our land stay, so that Orlando might be free to perform his duties once we set sail. But the boy had come down with something and our director had thought it ill advised to vaccinate him until he was well. "He seems to have made a full recovery."

Orlando and Benito, two unknown carriers! I turned to go, full of foreboding.

"Stay a moment, Doña Isabel." Don Francisco's voice stopped me. I was almost at the door, Sor Catalina at my heels. Quaintly, the nuns did not permit me to receive male visitors alone. Whom did they think had been chaperoning me on board the *María Pita*? Who would protect me from the lusty steward when we resumed our journey?

I turned back. Had our director found me out? He looked weary, they all did, but Don Francisco especially, his face lined and leaner, though he had good color from the browning of the sun. Only the younger Francisco looked healthy and strong. The boy had not even raised a fever with his vaccination. In fact, we were all convinced that the boy had lied, that he was, in fact, immune. But the vesicle had finally formed on his arm on the sixth day and grown apace.

"You have heard, no doubt, of our success here?" Don Francisco questioned me.

I nodded. "We see the crowds daily from these very windows." I pointed to the half-open casements behind him. "And of course, we have followed your reports closely." Daily an expedition member would come to the convent to inquire after us, to send Don Francisco's regards, to explain what had occurred that day.

"The five hundred copies of the *Tratado* will not be enough to carry us through. I am having to send to Madrid for two thousand more copies to be printed and forwarded by packet directly to Havana. How many have we vaccinated by now?" He turned to Dr. Gutiérrez.

"Several hundred," his assistant guessed.

"Several hundred?" Dr. Salvany objected. "Your ocular apparatus fails you, Dr. Gutiérrez. I might sooner number the waves on shore than the multitudes we have saved from the ravages of smallpox. I wager a thousand!"

"There are records," Dr. Gutiérrez muttered. He was a practical man. No doubt Dr. Salvany's flights of fancy wearied him. But he did not insist on his count, loath, no doubt, to be the one to reduce the expedition's glory with a mere actual number.

"We have vanquished smallpox in Tenerife," Don Francisco pronounced, ending all argument.

I was glad that our mission had met with this first great success. But it was a bittersweet victory. On shore, I had lost our director to his work. Sequestered in this convent with my boys, I ached for the world beyond my doorstep, though sometimes I wondered if it was not him I ached for. "I wish I could be of more help to you!"

"Oh, but you are of immeasurable help, Doña Isabel. Taking care of all our boys is no small task." Of course, he was right. Many invisible hands were needed to lay the stones of a great cathedral. And I did not mind laboring without recognition. I needed only him to notice.

"We sail as soon as our good wind blows. The captain informs me it should be within the week. His steward has been busily provisioning the *María Pita.*" He was telling me nothing I didn't already know. I wondered why he was choosing to go over such details with me. I glanced at Dr. Salvany, who smiled uneasily and looked away. Dr. Gutiérrez stood behind the young Francisco, his hands on the boy's shoulders as if to fix him there.

"With God's help and Aeolus's wafting, it shall be a swift crossing," Dr. Salvany ventured.

"May God grant it," Dr. Gutiérrez echoed more plainly.

"We have been sorely crowded on the *María Pita*," Don Francisco continued. "As my colleagues will surely tell you"—here he indicated Dr. Salvany and Dr. Gutiérrez with a nod—"we had planned on the *Sylph*, a much larger ship at four hundred tons. But the repairs would have delayed us another month or two. We would still be in La Coruña to this day."

A long road was being paved, leading, no doubt, somewhere I did not want to go. I waited in silence as our director belabored the subject of our ship's small size, our crowded accommodations. Perhaps he was preparing to move me back to the orlop deck with my boys. The first mate, Lieutenant Pozo—I had since learned his name—had kindly hung a hammock with the crew in order to release his cabin to me. Ceding it for ten days was one thing, for the forty days or so of our crossing another.

"As you know the merchant ship, the *Espíritu Santo*, sails soon for Cádiz, and from that port many vessels depart for La Coruña."

"Indeed, I am writing our friends in La Coruña," I mentioned. "We were informed of the ship's departure."

"Many of our Sisters have family . . ." Sor Catalina began, but halfway through her sentence, she stopped. Three pairs of male eyes had turned in her direction. Her small voice trailed off before such immodest attention.

Don Francisco waited politely for the young nun to continue. But Sor Catalina could not summon the courage to go on. She was among the shyest of the nuns. I wondered why she was ever put on door duty.

"The *Espíritu Santo* is a fine ship," Don Francisco explained. A slaver, it was returning to Spain for repairs after years transporting human cargo from Africa to America. "We are thinking of sending back the boys who have already been vaccinated. It would only amount to six—"

"No!" little Francisco cried out, wresting himself from Dr. Gutiérrez's grasp. To have come so far and behaved so well, only to be denied the adventure he had dreamed about. "I will not go back," he defied the three men before him, looking from one to the other for a champion, his eyes bright with tears.

I was glad for his outburst, for it mirrored my own sentiments. Had Don Francisco forgotten the agreement he had made through me with Doña Teresa? The boys were to remain *together* under my care.

"I don't have to go back, do I, Doña Isabel?" the boy appealed to me.

I reached for him, but he pulled back, perhaps fearing any caress would turn into restraint. He looked around wildly like a trapped animal, searching for an escape. The men stood by, baffled by his reaction. It was Sor Catalina who stepped forward to try her hand with this little creature shouting at his elders. "There, there," she soothed him, gingerly touching his hair. Oddly enough, the boy accepted her comfort. "You can stay here with us," she added, nodding to confirm her special offer.

That was not what Francisco wanted to hear. He pulled away from Sor Catalina and wept a child's tears.

"A man does not cry," Dr. Gutiérrez reminded him, and though, I, too, had used this argument often, I now found myself rejecting it. Break a man's heart and he would weep as surely as he would bleed if you cut off a limb. Had I not heard the African men on Sundays wailing horribly when they were parted from their wives and children?

And now my own heart was crying in silence at our director's deception. But had I myself not deceived him about Benito and misled Doña Teresa about my participation? How could I think to save the world and not begin with my own salvation?

I looked from Dr. Gutiérrez to Dr. Salvany, then turned to Don Francisco, the most difficult to defy. "That was not our agreement." I tried to sound firm, but my voice was quivering. "We are a family. I cannot allow the boys to be separated."

"But they have served their use," Dr. Salvany spoke plainly. The truth was so obvious, it did not merit a metaphor to embellish it.

"And what shall be done when they have served their use midocean? Perhaps we will toss them overboard like the peel of so much fruit—"

"How could you think so, Doña Isabel!" Dr. Salvany's hand was at his heart, as if wounded by my sharp remark. Indeed, I had seen our director wince at my accusation. "Why those boys are our *divino tesoro,*" Dr. Salvany protested. "It is only that, as our director has mentioned, we are so crowded on the *María Pita,* and we have a long distance still to go."

"No harm will come to them," Dr. Gutiérrez added, his voice sharp, his look impatient. No doubt he thought my opposition out of order, not deserving of the consideration they were giving it. "The captain of the *Espíritu Santo* will be sure to put the boys on a ship bound for La Coruña."

The very same captain who was trading in human misery. What might he do with six hapless boys, whom no one would hold him to account for?

"We shall all be on that ship together then." I might have been agreeing with them for the soft tone of my voice, but there was iron in my will.

"You would be defying Don Francisco," Dr. Gutiérrez reminded me. "Defying our king!" he added, no doubt ready to manacle me right then and lead me to the gallows.

"The contract would have been breached already and so we could not be held to it," I countered.

"That is not so," Dr. Gutiérrez persisted. Had he not read the proclamation? Certainly he had heard it read at our departure ceremony at La Coruña. No doubt, his was a blind loyalty to his director and teacher. A woman could be bullied; a woman could be pushed aside. "Our director was named director to lead us. If he sees the wisdom of a certain action, we must comply."

Indeed, I had set out with every intention of complying. After all, I had come in awe of this same man. I had helped him convince Doña Teresa and risked my boys in the bargain. But in spite of my desire to please him, I was diverging from the path he was directing me to take. What had been only a pretext for my coming had become my purpose. I could not abandon my boys. I could not allow them to be abused. "I shall comply in all things with our director." I addressed myself to Dr. Gutiérrez, as if Don Francisco were not there. "Always and when my boys are not put in any danger."

Dr. Gutiérrez could think of no further argument. He looked to our director for help. "She must obey," he stated blankly. But his voice was less sure than before.

I could feel the color rising in my face, my legs turning to butter in the heat of the day. My courage would have failed me had I not looked up at that moment and caught Don Francisco's eye. The cold sternness I had expected was not there; in its stead, I discerned a kind of respect; I would almost say, a touch of admiration, which encouraged me to plead my case to him. "As you said, Don Francisco, there are only six boys in question: four of them are scarce able to feed and dress themselves, no less to travel alone, and the other two are old enough to be of help to me on our expedition."

My little Francisco nodded readily. "I have been helping, haven't I, Doña Isabel?"

"You have been indispensable!" I drew out the word as if it were a proclamation.

I doubt the boy knew exactly what the word meant, but he could tell he was being praised. His tearful face broke into a wide grin.

"Six will scarcely take up two berths. Little Benito can sleep with me. And sir," I added, addressing Don Francisco. I took a deep breath and confessed the secret I had held in my heart for months.

No one said a word. In the silence we could hear the crowd milling in the square. The hearty greetings, the laughter seemed so at odds with what was now to be decided in this room: my fate.

"So you cannot vouch for the boy?" Don Francisco finally spoke up. "He is not your son?"

I had only presented Benito as my own so that if he were not selected as one of the carriers, he might still go with me. There had not been enough time for me to adopt him in La Coruña. Upon my return, or in New Spain, I would institute the proceedings. "He is not my child, but he is my son," I explained, "as they are all my sons."

Our director and his assistants had come quite determined to carry out their plan. They had not anticipated the opposition they had encountered from the quiet, accommodating rectoress.

"We have been quite crowded on board, as you say," I went on. "And I know our mate has been most inconvenienced by ceding his cabin to me."

Don Francisco held up his hand in contradiction. "That is not it, Doña Isabel."

"My place is with the children," I persisted. "Had I not been so ill, I would not have abandoned them." I was determined not to accept any further favors. But the thought of the lewd steward only a thin partition away from where I would be sleeping qualified my determination. "Perhaps some other spot can be found for me on the ship."

I had a spot in mind. Soon after our arrival, and before the outing to Oratava, I had returned to the *María Pita* in hopes of retrieving Doña Teresa's treats. Those cases, which I had marked with my own hand, had not been delivered, along with our chests, to the convent. I had brought several of the older boys along to help me carry them back. Our captain was ashore—for which I was secretly glad—but his first mate, Lieutenant Pozo, had been left in charge. Correct and stern while sailing, the mate seemed to be rendered powerless by being becalmed in a quiet bay. And by the presence of a woman inquiring after some missing items. The steward was summoned and it was soon clear that some thievery had been going on. Candied almonds, dried fruits, sugar balls?

"Rats, sir," the steward replied to each item.

"See that those rats are discharged from the crew," Lieutenant Pozo ordered.

The steward put on a face of baffled innocence. "I do not understand, sir."

"See that you do!" Lieutenant Pozo shot back.

The surly man muttered that it was not his fault the cat, Sirena, had fled our ship, what with two dozen damned boys pulling at her bloody tail, but finally he withdrew.

"I will report this to our captain upon his return," Lieutenant Pozo promised me.

"No need for that, Lieutenant," I put in quickly. I did not want to give our captain another instance of the rectoress being a bother.

The lieutenant stiffened as if I'd been encouraging him to mutiny. "It is the rule," he informed me.

"Oh, but you are more than equal to this task, Lieutenant."

He wavered. I could see, as if through the tiniest of cracks, a ray of pride enter the forthright face. "I suppose . . . I could handle it myself."

"I would be most grateful, Lieutenant Pozo. Our captain has plenty to

do. I am sure he depends on you to resolve minor problems with the crew."
Had I always been so adept at handling men's natures? Why should it surprise me? For a dozen years, I had been handling younger specimens in
similar situations. I, too, worked by calculation. Why then judge Don
Francisco so harshly for his shrewdness? Why else? Because he was using
it against me.

Our lieutenant seemed to expand with the increased responsibility I had
conferred on him, offering me and the boys a refreshment before our return.
He had a drink on hand, an experiment, he explained, which Don Francisco
would be conducting during our crossing. A daily infusion meant to combat the dreaded scurvy. It consisted of a lemon drink sweetened with molasses. I complimented it, and Lieutenant Pozo agreed it was very tasty and
refreshing. "Whether it is a medicine against the scurvy, I cannot say." He
himself was a believer in "a daily dosing of vinegar."

"But this will do the men no harm," he added, holding up his glass and
quaffing it in one swallow. "And as long as Dr. Balmis does not experiment
with denying the men's daily ration of rum, we should be all right." I almost
detected a smile on the stern but not unkind face.

At the boys' request, Lieutenant Pozo obliged us with a tour of the ship.
Often I was on the point of reminding him to beware a beam—the man's
height ill befits the low ceilings between decks! But it seems the first mate
has lived much of his life at sea, as have many in his family—two cousins
are among the crew—so he knows as if by instinct when to stoop and
where to watch his step.

I had never fully understood how our wooden house was put together,
as the various compartments seemed to roll around on the heavy seas.
How wonderful to peer into all its little spaces! At the entrance to the
wardroom and officers' quarters we passed a compartment where Don
Francisco's five hundred copies of the *Tratado* had been stowed along with
some of his instruments. That space was now vacant. Perhaps room could
be made for me to sleep there?

The church bell startled us with its sonorous tolling. Once, twice, three
times. In the ensuing silence, we could hear the crowd in the plaza. The
afternoon vaccinations would soon begin. I needed to fetch our next

carrier: the sure José in place of Benito. Still, I lingered. I had yet to receive his assurance that we would all continue together.

As children often do, sensing the unasked question among their elders, the boy spoke up. "Am I to go on with you?" he asked Don Francisco directly.

Our director nodded toward me. "We must ask your rectoress." The color flew to my face. Was he jesting in anger or was he in earnest? "What do you say, Doña Isabel? Do we continue? "

He knew my answer. Why was he forcing my hand? Perhaps it was the largesse of someone with power, flattering an underling with the control of an empty purse's strings. Surely, he could overrule whatever I chose. "We continue all together," I answered him, my trembling voice betraying me.

"We continue all together." Don Francisco held up his hands as if he had no power against such a ruling. But there was a leniency to his tone and a smile on his face that belied such surrender. He was being gracious, to be sure. I swallowed, my face burning, my hands in fists lest he be mocking me. But the boy took him at his word. He leapt up, wild with relief and joy, so much so, that Dr. Gutiérrez stepped forward, alarmed less his jostling break the vesicle before we could make use of its precious fluid.

As I turned to go, my eyes met Don Francisco's. I could not be sure, for I was indeed flustered with my triumph and still angry with him, but the look he cast my way seemed to say, *I see that I have brought along a formidable foe as well as a noble friend to our mission. It will not be an easy journey.*

I dared not reply, *You are right, Don Francisco.*

6 enero 1804

Nati, dearest, how many times haven't I meant to continue and now must resign myself to make a hurried finish. The wind is in our sails and we are off before the day is over. The last of the water casks are being rowed on board as well as those provisions that would have spoiled if stowed earlier. All our chests are readied, and the cart should be here any minute now to carry them away. I will entrust this letter to the Sisters to send along with their own letters to the *Espíritu Santo* when the wind turns in its favor.

We will again parade down to the docks just as we did in La Coruña. The preparations outside are in progress, as I write. A large crowd is gathering, which will accompany us, led by the marquis and the marchesa and the bishop, singing a Te Deum, in gratitude for our work. The cannons at Castillo San Juan will fire and no doubt terrify the boys. The Sisters are presently helping them dress in their red and gold uniforms, finally at ease (just as we depart!) with these little men who are, they have discovered, not much different from little women.

And so farewell, Nati. Who knows when I shall be able to send you a letter again? But please do not worry on our account. I give thanks to be granted this opportunity to serve, for I am convinced that this is God's work, especially when I review the great labor that has been accomplished here in Santa Cruz. Hundreds of souls vaccinated! How apt that we leave on Epiphany. Like the three wise men of long ago we bear a precious gift to all—or most of our brothers and sisters. May God bless our journey.

Please give each and every one of our boys a sweet kiss from Doña Isabel and my greetings and gratitude to Doña Teresa for her thoughtfulness toward us. (I trust you will not tell her about the missing cases as her righteous rage would surely make her ill!)

As for me, I am not much changed: good only because I am not often given the opportunity to behave otherwise! I assure you I have not had to use your pin once. And though the sun has improved my complexion and the salt air invigorated me, I am afraid I will go to my grave as *immaculate* as the Blessed Virgin.

I miss you, my dear friend, and hope you are all, every one of you, well. Trust that we are in God's hands and safe in His care.

I finished just as Sor Octavia came to my door to announce that the cart was here. Could the men come up to carry my chest downstairs?

"I will be ready shortly," I assured her. "They can start with the boys' chests in the front room."

She hurried away with my instructions.

I folded up the letter. There was no time to seal it properly as my wax and seal were packed away. Hopefully, the Sisters would not read my missive and pale at my blasphemous comparison, though by then I would be far away.

And yet . . . God's eyes were all-seeing. He might well send down a heavy rain and a stormy sea to punish me!

And so it was that with so little time for such frivolity, I took up my quill again and blotted out the sacrilegious sentence. Quickly, my eyes ran down the page and caught at the mention of the steward's lewd offer. Why worry Nati with news that could only trouble her? That passage, too, I blotted out, and refolded the letter.

Enough! I had better hurry. I cast a quick glance around the room to make sure all my possessions were packed away. Only what I could carry in my small purse would go with me on the parade down to the dock. I knelt at my chest to lock it, and as I did, I heard the heavy tread of the men downstairs moving the trunks, the shouts and excitement of the boys among them, the steward ordering the little devils out of his goddamn, bloody way.

The steward . . . His image rose before me: his wet breath in my ear; his flushed, drunken face; his hands fumbling in the dark for me.

Quickly, I pulled open my chest and rummaged about until I found the small box with needles and thread. I withdrew Nati's gift and pinned it to the inside bodice of my dress. May the Virgin protect me, I prayed, and keep me from having to use my only weapon as I crossed the unchaperoned sea.

# 4

November 12, late Friday afternoon

TO: Mi amor                      FAX: 802-388-4344

FROM: Ricardo                 FAX: 809-682-0800

¡Hola, querida! I'm so sorry you've been having problems reaching me. Hard to believe it's already been almost a week and I haven't heard your sweet voice. The clinic phone/fax machine was down, as you probably guessed, but a tech guy from the capital got it up and running, and your faxes all came through, so I know you've been trying. Turns out nothing was wrong with the machine. The cable outside had been cut. Some campesino with his machete hacking away at the yerba. Getting pretty good with the old español, eh?

I didn't make it down the mountain all week: been doing a survey of the area—what the needs are, what's viable. Locals have been a little pulled back, which is natural, given earlier trouble with clinic, but you know how hard it is to resist that old Midwestern charm. By the way, you mentioned that Emerson left a message? Weird. He knows I'm here. Maybe he's been trying to reach me, too, and thought you might have had better luck?

I'm staying with Bienvenido in a casita next to the clinic. Well, he doesn't spend all his nights here. Every Saturday he goes to see his wife and kid in the capital. Turns out women here—once they get a little up on the class scale—develop a downright phobia of el campo! I guess the age of women following their beloveds to the ends of the earth is over. (Sigh.) Just joking!

I'll write more later, just wanted to send this off before the clinic closes, so you don't worry. I'll also try calling, but I think you said Tera was coming this weekend, so you're probably out on a picket line. How's Helen? Give her my love. You can give Tera my love, too. And as for you, querida, I love you with a love too big to put into words, Ricardo.

Richard's fax is waiting when Alma gets back from having to pick up Tera, as Paul needs their one car for the weekend. Alma is so relieved, she reads it through greedily—no gunshot wounds, no scorpion bites—Tera at her side. Just in time, Alma spots her friend's name in the last paragraph and pulls the sheet to her bosom, suddenly a demure heroine from the nineteenth century.

"Excuse me! This *is* a love letter!" Alma gives Tera a coy look.

"A love fax," Tera corrects. "What's this about trouble and a clinic?"

Alma hasn't told Tera about the clinic, knowing her friend will probably plug it into some high-voltage story she has read about and blow Alma right off the worry charts. All week she hasn't heard from Richard. Actually, there was a call from Bienvenido's wife, Charmin, who'd heard from Bienvenido, who'd asked her to call Alma with a message from Richard that he was fine, that the phone/fax wasn't working, that he hadn't been down the mountain as he'd been involved in a survey, everything he later explained in his fax. But all Alma was thinking was how come Bienvenido could find a way to call his wife and Richard couldn't do the same for her.

Tera's glancing around—she hasn't been down to visit in a while. Probably looking at all the extras Alma doesn't need. "I thought you told me Richard was setting up some green center?"

"He is. This is just some clinic that's nearby." Alma shrugs it off, but then her own Achilles' heels, yes two of them, double strength, trip her up: her need to tell the dear ones in her life the intriguing little stories that happen left and right. "It's actually an AIDS treatment center of some kind, which is really strange, because remember that call I got a few weeks back? I mean, back to back, like that."

"AIDS is an epidemic." Tera states matter-of-factly as if, of course, Alma already knows this and shares all the feelings appertaining, which is something refreshing about Tera. She's not righteous with her outrage. It's a bright light shining in her own as well as everyone else's eyes. "So what's the clinic about, an offshore drug-testing site of some kind?"

It doesn't sound good, and Tera does keep up on everything horrible. "No, it's a center for treating AIDS patients who can't afford treatment." Alma can't keep the righteousness out of her own voice, which is ridiculous as she is improvising on what this clinic is all about.

"Hmm."

"Hmm what?" But before Tera can elaborate on her hmm of suspicion, Alma blurts out, "I'm going to ask you a big favor, Tera. I don't want to worry about Richard, okay? I know it's politically regressive of me to say this, but let's have a moratorium on south-of-the-border horrors this weekend, okay?" Alma is surprised at her own angry words, even more so, when she glances over and sees the hurt look on Tera's face. Is she really the bully who just stomped on the fat girl's sand castle and then smashed her pail in the bargain? And because Alma knows that she is partly that mean kid, she backs down. "Ay, Tera, I'm sorry, I didn't mean it—"

"Of course, you meant it," Tera says intelligently. "I know what a pain in the ass I can be. Cassandra syndrome. You start talking truth to power and you can't stop."

She said it better than Alma could. She looks away so Tera can't see in her eyes that Alma agrees with her. "It was still a mean way to say it," Alma admits, then goes on to tell Tera about the week of worrying, about how Helen is going downhill, how she might not even make it to Christmas, before Alma leaves for Florida, where the plan is to meet up with Richard at her parents', who aren't doing so well themselves. And all these things are true. But there's still just the sheer rush that comes from letting her mean streak have a go at it. Honestly, and she talks about her capricious Mamasita!

"If it weren't for you, I'd have such a petite soul, I mean it, Tera. You keep us all on our toes." Alma goes on defending Tera, as if ganging up on herself will make up for wanting to hurt her friend, turning the meanness on herself, more of the same.

Tera has started unpacking her overnight bag, which looks like a big flowered carpetbag. Everything in it seems to be pamphlets. She stops for a moment, a stack of info in her hand, and scowls. "Who wants to be on their toes all the time?"

Alma can't help herself. "You do!"

Tera narrows her eyes at Alma in mock anger, then hurls the stack in her hands, pelting Alma with pale blue hospice care pamphlets.

<br>

|                  | November 13, Saturday noon |
|------------------|----------------------------|
| TO: Mi amor      | FAX: 802-388-4344          |
| FROM: Ricardo    | FAX: 809-682-0800          |

Mi amor, yesterday, after faxing you and calling you (Did you get my message? So sorry to have missed you!), I ran into the new liaison person for the clinic, Starr Bell—yep, that's her name. Texas, what can I say. She said it's crazy for me not to have access to the phone and fax, and so now I have my own key to the main office, so I don't have to be on their schedule to fax or call you.

Don't know what to make of her, Starr, that is. She's youngish (midthirties?), attractive, a take-charge person. Everyone seems to like her. She's done a lot to calm things down. Perfect Spanish, thanks to a Mexican nanny, she told me. Drives a pickup and comes loaded up with food from the capital. Ms. Santa Claus with a cowboy hat. She totally supports our green center. Says we can create a model community here, count on Swan's support. Swan's the drug company she does PR for. Starr actually knew Emerson from an on-site internship she did with HI back when she was in college (our Haitian outhouse initiative) and so when Swan was looking to sponsor a community project of some kind, she suggested us. I guess Swan always does some sort of goodwill project when they go into an area. I mean, even Tera can't find fault with that.

Speaking of whom, how's the weekend going?

This place is beautiful, I mean absolutely hands-down gorgeous. Shangri-la, if it weren't for the poverty. Really bad. So, our Centro Verde del Caribe is a godsend, as I think it will create jobs and also encourage locals to stay on the land and make a living at farming.

Our little casita was one of several built by Swan for their staff, but they're fine about letting Bienvenido and me stay in it. So, mi amor, I'm living in the lap of luxury: electricity from their generator, on-and-off hot water, and get this: a lighted toilet seat, works with some sort of solar battery, though how and why it got here, nobody knows. But just so you don't get too jealous, remember, you wouldn't get much writing done here—solitude is in short supply. Only time I'm alone is nights Bienvenido is gone or when I wake up early, sip coffee (toasted and ground by our neighbor), watch the sunrise, and miss you.

Anyhow, please don't worry. Tell me about Helen, how everything is going. Thanks for getting those leaves. Wow, my wife is turning into quite the gardener! Please call the boys and tell them I'm fine. I'll call once I've got a better phone setup. Take care of yourself. Remember, te adoro, mi amor querida, Ricardo.

ON SATURDAY, TERA, of course, wants to go over to see Helen and hand-deliver the pamphlets she brought. They have met several times before, and one meeting with Tera and you're in her clan, especially if you're female and have had a hard life. Alma was going to drop by anyhow with a flan she made for Helen, but she exacts a promise from Tera that the pamphlets are to stay in her bag and not come out until they can talk to Mickey privately.

"Who's Mickey?" And then, before Alma can tell her, Tera breaks out with the Mickey Mouse song. "M-i-c K-e-y M-o-u-s-e. So does Mickey wear his ears?"

Alma loves it when Tera acts goofy. "His real name's Michael, Michael McMullen. Helen's son, a character."

"Michael McMullen . . ." Tera puzzles over the name. "It sounds so familiar. Maybe from meeting Helen before?"

Alma shakes her head. "Helen's last name's Marshall. According to

Claudine, the McMullen comes from Mickey's wife. He changed his name to hers." It is strange when simple salt-of-the-earth folk end up having lives as complex and troubled as those of Alma and her friends. Were Helen not sick, Alma would pelt her with questions about why her son changed his name, why he doesn't call her Mother, why he periodically falls off the face of the earth.

They drive over to Helen's, releasing their trail of hydrocarbons in the air, when they could just walk across the back field. But Alma vetoes that suggestion. There is a north wind blowing, and flans are tropical critters.

Mickey's out in the front yard, unloading wood from a rusted blue pickup. He stops when they pull in, doesn't come forward to greet them, doesn't go on with his work, just stands there, watching. The here's-looking-at-you routine. "Is that Mickey?" Tera wants to know.

"Uh-huh," Alma says under her breath, her heart quickening again, some Pavlovian reaction triggered by this guy, who has unnerved her both times she has seen him before. It's not attraction, at least she doesn't think so. It's the same feeling she gets with people who stand too close when they talk to her. Some psychic trespassing going on. Mickey's still wearing that plaid shirt, except now he's donned a down vest, in deference to the north wind, she supposes. It is wicked cold, even Tera says so.

"I'll bring in the flan," Tera says, "Can you grab the pamphlets?"

"Let's leave them here for now," Alma suggests. Watching Mickey watching them, Alma just knows pamphlets are not his thing. "Hi!" she calls out as she gets out of the car, as if he's some strange dog she wants to be sure won't bite before she leaves the safety of her vehicle behind. "Brought Helen a flan and my friend to visit."

Again a time delay in which he stands and watches, having received her words, an envelope he's not going to open yet. "Just keep walking into the house," Alma tells Tera under her breath, which in this cold shows up as a plume of white breath like a cartoon character's balloon, so it's dumb trying to be discreet. Besides, it's too late. Tera is making a beeline over to Mickey. Alma swears her best friend looks for trouble. And what can she do but follow.

"Ta da!" Tera imitates a drumroll and lifts the cake lid from the flan. "Flan!" And by God, the man laughs. Tera can be so cool sometimes.

Tera introduces herself.

"Tera?" Mickey asks, like there might be something wrong with her name.

Tera gives him a firm nod. "From Teresa. And you?"

"Mickey." Mickey grins, daring her to make something of it.

Of course, Tera does. "Mickey? Like in Mickey Mouse?" She grins back, a little taunting game going on between these two.

"Is Helen inside?" Alma steps in, worried that Tera might start in on her Mickey Mouse routine.

Time lapse. Message received. Time lapse. Mickey nods.

"Thanks," Alma says, nudging Tera, who—Alma can tell— is intrigued by this odd guy. But Tera takes Alma's cue and starts down the path. Alma falls in beside her, both women looking straight ahead, holding in their laughter, that unspoken female communication going on between them—*Just keep walking, don't turn around, we're being watched*—both feeling that old chagrin at how men always seem to have the last word, their eyes sizing up your butt as you walk away.

INSIDE, HELEN IS SITTING in a big chair by the fireplace, a fire going. This is the first time in ages that Alma has come in the front door, because in the past, even when she drove, she'd go around to the back door into the kitchen, where Helen almost always was sitting.

Alma can feel it in the air, like a season turning. The kitchen era is over. Soon the time of the living room shall pass. How long before Helen is confined to her bed, where she has let it be known she wants to die? How long before she's part of Snake Mountain where she wants her ashes scattered? "In the summertime, when it's convenient," she told Alma a few days ago. "Oh, Helen," Alma had scolded, "let yourself make a few demands!" But Helen explained that the top of a Vermont mountain in winter with gale-force winds blowing wasn't her idea of a pleasant funeral. Besides, she wants to stay on Snake Mountain, not be blown clear down to New York City.

"Hey! Look at you, all cozy!" Alma says, bluffing it. Helen looks terrible. It's as if now that people know about it, her disease can have a go at her, no holds barred. Her skin is deathly pale and seems to hang on her, a size too big. Her bones poke out, and for a split second Alma's heart stops because what she is seeing is the skeleton Helen will soon become. But then the skeleton smiles, and Helen is back again!

"Mickey made me a nice little fire. It's been so long since I had a good fire." She's feeling around for her walker, so she must sense there is company, as she never stands up to greet Alma anymore when it's just the two of them.

"Don't get up, Helen! I brought my friend, Tera. She's here for the weekend. You remember Tera, don't you?"

"What do you mean, don't get up?" Helen fusses. "Of course, I remember Tera!" And then, as if to prove it, she reels off a brief bio of Tera, full of glowing highlights Alma has told her, with all the complaints Alma has ever made about her best friend left out. Alma tells Helen everything, or used to, until this new knowledge turned her friend into this new person: a person who is going to die on her.

Alma was always bringing up Helen in her sessions with Dr. Payne. Why did this old woman mean so much to her? Usually, Dr. Payne tossed the question back: why did Alma think Helen was so important to her? But one time, he told her straight out what he thought. Helen is the mother Alma never had in childhood.

"You're paying this guy a hundred bucks an hour to tell you stuff like that?" Richard had said, a look of total incredulity on his face. "How about she's your friend. You like her. Period." It was Alma's own fault for telling Richard, but then she was always running Dr. Payne's observations by him. She supposed she shared Richard's deep mistrust of people who charged money to heal your spirit.

Whatever the reason, it did seem that with Helen, all Alma's usual safeguards were out the window, and she loved the old woman without a whole lot of second guessing, no periodic flaring up of mistrust or dislike. Oh, now and then Alma felt a little bored, because there was none of the exciting, edgy stuff that was usually going on with other people. But it had taken her by surprise that she could love someone without the usual big-brand bonds: not Lover or Husband, not Son or Daughter, not Familia or Boss or some other powerful person. A 100 percent unimportant, generic person. Helen was living proof. It was a revelation.

"Alma made you this flan," Tera is saying, maybe as a way of letting Helen know why she, Tera, is not giving her a full frontal hug. One of Tera's hands is occupied. Still, a half hug from Tera is a mighty thing. Helen's fragile little figure totters — she never did find her walker, tucked behind the box of kindling — and Alma catches her just in time to help her back down into her chair.

"This fire is yummy, Helen," Alma says, feeling its warmth radiate right down into her cold bones. "I wish I'd known you loved them so." She wonders if this will be one of her regrets months from now, how she never came over and made Helen a nice fire. "You feel like having a little flan now, Helen?"

"How did you know?" She's pretending again. Helen hasn't had much of an appetite all week. Every day, Alma has dropped by with a dish, and after seven days, her repertoire of recipes is close to used up. Helen always takes a few nibbles in Alma's presence, but Alma can tell Helen can't keep stuff down. Some pain medication she's on, no doubt. Alma has asked Mickey about it, but each time he just looks back at her, that watchful look that makes Alma want to withdraw the question. "She's okay," he always says.

Alma takes the flan from Tera to serve up in the kitchen, since she knows where everything is. The place is surprisingly tidy: the dishes are done; the floor looks mopped. Mickey is running a tight ship, good for him. Alma opens the cabinets and finds the small plates with their dainty, chipped flowers, so old-fashioned, so Helen; the brass utensils with rosewood handles that Mickey got for his mother somewhere during his world postings, with the marines — so Alma learned a few days back; the tray with the peeling decal that once said HOME SWEET HOME but now reads like a phrase written in a foreign tongue, HOM EET OME. Alma is taking it all in: everything, everything making one sound, ticktock, ticktock. She turns on the water and lets it get hot and holds her hands under it, until it's scalding, until she can't stand it. So much for conservation, this trick she has for making something else hurt when her heart's about to crack.

Finally, she has got everything on a tray, ready to go, and the back door opens. It's Mickey, clapping his hands together, like he, too, feels the cold!

"I don't see how you do it without a coat." Alma shakes her head, startled into this confession by seeing him responding like a regular person, not a man she can't understand and is half afraid of.

Instead of explaining himself, he looks down at her tray. "You got one for me?"

"Of course," Alma says, pleased to pass herself off as a good cook, which she supposes she is, a big frog as long as she sticks to her little pond of six, seven recipes. She sets the tray down, and when she goes to pull open the fridge to get the flan, there on the door, stuck on with a magnet, staring back at her is a picture of a boy, Mickey, unmistakable, the eyes, the grin. He's holding up some certificate that he's obviously proud of, too young for it to be a high school degree. Maybe some scout thing, who knows? It's a picture Alma has seen hundreds of times before, Helen has had it here for a while, from before she went totally blind, Alma assumes, because why else stick a photo on your fridge if you can't see it. How odd to be in the presence of the man who was once this boy, the kind of perspective she seldom has with people.

"I won that calf."

Alma smiles. "How'd you do that?"

"A 4-H contest. Had to write five hundred words on the four Hs: head, hands, heart . . ."

He can't remember the fourth *H*. Alma tries to help him out. What other major body part starts with an *H*? She gives up.

She bends to look more closely at the photo, and sure enough she can make out the long, makeshift buildings, the grandstand, the stalls for animals, the usual fairgrounds paraphernalia. A Ferris wheel is vaguely visible in the background. Strange that for years Alma didn't see it back there, didn't see the boy's smile of pride, the flank of the prize calf, the rope in his hand, a luminous moment that will be there whenever she looks at the grown man from now on.

"Helen took that picture. Just before my father left us. Last good day in a long time."

Alma has brought the flan over to the table, and she starts assembling another dish and spoon, keeping busy, feeling surprised and a little flattered that he's confiding in her but also uncomfortable lest he make it a habit.

"Is your father around? I mean, maybe he should be notified? Maybe he's someone Helen might want to see?"

"He's not welcome here," Mickey says, the quickest reply Alma has ever gotten back from him.

She waits a moment, not knowing if Mickey wants to say more. Finally, she murmurs, "I'm sorry," sensing that she has bumped up against a wound that still hurts to be touched.

After a moment, Mickey nods. End of conversation. Back to being Paul Bunyan. But now he's also a boy who won a calf and lost a father.

A man who is losing his mother, Alma thinks, as she dishes him up an extra big serving.

THEY SIT IN THE parlor, Mickey, Tera, Helen, and Alma, eating flan and running the topic of the cold weather to the ground. Alma and Helen and Tera would have no problem coming up with any number of things to talk about. But Mickey seems to tense up the room, the way he sits back, watching their chitchat as if conversation were a spectator sport.

Tera breaks the rather thin ice with a pick. "Helen, I hear you've elected not to undergo treatments?"

Alma has confided this to Tera, not knowing if she is supposed to. She glares at her friend, hoping to stop Tera from continuing.

But Helen seems unfazed by the comment. "That's right, dear. It's pretty near spread into everything, like dandelions. There's not much the doctors can do. It's my time to go." She says this so matter-of-factly, like the oven beeper just went off and the flan is done.

"Doctors'd just nuke her to death," Mickey interjects clunkily.

"You said it," Tera says, and Alma can almost feel the easing of tension in the room. Two potential foes have found a common enemy: the medical profession.

"As long as it's what you want, Helen," Alma puts in. Is she the only one here who isn't 100 percent sure? If she is, she should keep her mouth shut. "I know how you are about not wanting to be a bother," Alma reminds her.

"It'd be a big bother to *me* to be in the hospital, hooked up to a lot of machines." Helen shakes her head at this bleak vision of her last days. As frail and blind as Helen is, it is surprising how seldom she visits doctors, so unlike Papote and Mamasita and most old people Alma knows. No doubt this is why Helen's cancer spread all over without some earlier diagnosis. "It's what I want," Helen says, quietly, firmly, and Alma knows she can trust the sureness in Helen's voice.

"Sometimes they do a lot of procedures where they know it's no use just so they can collect the insurance," Mickey elaborates.

"I read about that case." Tera is nodding eagerly. "The guy in Florida with total metastasis, liver, lung, everything involved, and they did this whole stem-cell treatment, hundreds upon hundreds of dollars."

"Thousands," Mickey corrects. "They cooked that poor guy."

Excuse me, Alma feels like snapping at them. You *are* talking in front of a terminally ill person! She tries to catch Tera's eye, but her friend is too busy stockpiling evidence with Mickey to notice Alma beaming a big red stop sign.

"Don't get me started on the health system," she says, shaking her head.

"Good idea," Alma says pointedly, which stops Tera momentarily. But Mickey goes on undaunted. "I've seen those fellows up close. They're operators all right. Know what the MD stands for? Money dealers."

Soon he's launched into the ills of the health system in this country, and Tera is launched right alongside him. A half-dozen *I hear yous* and *you said its* later, and the two have hit their stride, comrades. Only when Mickey stands up and says he's going out to bring in some wood and Tera stands up and says she has something she has to get in the car does Alma realize that Tera hasn't just been mouthing off, she has been preparing the ground to hand over her pamphlets.

Alma is relieved to see them go. And glad that Helen is the first to laugh. "Those two, my word." Helen is shaking her head.

"Makes me mad. Honestly, they're so clueless. I'm sorry, Helen." Mickey is not her fault, but Alma did bring Tera over.

"What for? No, no, no," Helen adds, refusing to let Alma feel bad about the conversation. "I'm sure I agree with what they say. But all that angry talk. It's just like that book you read me."

She must mean *Paradise Lost,* all those devils arguing, but it's funny how for Helen, all books seem to melt into one book, which is sometimes *Paradise Lost* and sometimes *The Bluest Eye* and sometimes the *Selected Poems of Emily Dickinson.*

Alma takes Helen's hand. "So you're okay with your decision?" All week, one way or another, Alma has been asking Helen this question.

"Yes," Helen says, almost shyly, like she didn't know she'd elected an option that would get her this much attention. "When I heard what all they had to do just to buy me a few more months, it just wasn't worth it."

"I can understand that," Alma tells her, knowing she probably would have chosen the opposite, believing as she does in plots she can revise, endings she can rewrite. Unless, of course, the story is over, the expedition completed, Balmis's mission accomplished, Isabel's name misremembered, and the child carriers all but forgotten, their names briefly noted in some dusty tome in the library. "Anything you need, you let me know," Alma squeezes Helen's hand. She's thinking about Helen's Paxil. The way Mickey talks, he probably won't buy his mother anything that makes money for the drug companies.

"I will," Helen squeezes back.

"Anyone you want me to call . . ." Alma hints. She doesn't want to bring up any sad memories. And Helen will know what Alma is offering. She has always read between Alma's lines. Why it's always been hard for Alma to believe that Helen is really blind.

"I think Claudine's got the phone calling all covered." Helen laughs again.

"Nothing you're worried about?" Why does she keep insisting? Alma should shut up. But she has known Helen long enough to read between her lines, and Alma thinks she has spotted some fine print.

Helen hesitates. "Only thing I suppose I worry about is . . . well, Mickey. He's just had some hard times. I hope he's going to be all right." She sounds not sure, as if she needs a second opinion.

"Is he in trouble?" Alma asks.

"Yes and no," Helen confides. "His wife's been ill, you know. Mental disease. And sometimes she's brought him down with her."

"I'm sorry to hear that. Maybe he can get some help?"

Helen sighs and shakes her head. "You just heard what he thinks of doctors. And he's not mental, I'm not saying that. Just gets some strange ideas. When I try to talk sense into him, he goes off. Always comes back, though, always with a present in his hands." She smiles, remembering those homecomings. The brass and rosewood flatware, the little Dutch clogs, the fan with the painted butterflies.

"It hurt him, losing his father," she goes on. "Up and left us just like that. Mickey took it hard. And I wasn't much help. Had to put Mickey in foster care while I got myself together. But like the song says, amazing grace. I don't know where I'd have ended up without it. But Mickey never did forgive me. Said I wasn't a mother to him. At school, I can't say he got in with the wrong crowd, as he was the troublemaker. Dropped out."

Alma stares at her old friend point-blank. Incredible to think that her strong-as-a-rock Helen was once a bad single mom. But then sweet Jesus came and put her back together again. No such luck for her son.

"Next I knew, Mickey'd joined up. I thought the marines would be good for him, give him the discipline he needed. But I guess there, too, he went places and saw things that hurt him some more, never was the same again."

Helen seems suddenly bereft, as if she just got the really bad news, a cancer that can destroy her peace of mind: her son will not fare well in the world she is leaving behind.

"I'm sorry you've had this worry, Helen." Alma wishes her old friend had confided in her before. What would Alma have done? Introduced Mickey to Tera, she supposes. Maybe Mickey would have learned from Tera how to marshal personal hurt into purposeful action.

"I hope I'm not fooling myself," Helen pauses to catch her breath. All this sad talk must be tiring. "But I think he's okay now." It's really a question. She wants Alma's reassurance. Alma doesn't want to lie to Helen, but she wants her friend to be at peace in the time left her.

"I don't know Mickey well enough to say," Alma hedges. Helen waits. Her face is a mask of worry she wants Alma to take off. Alma hesitates. "He seems fine to me, Helen, he really does."

"You think so?" Helen's face tilts up, even though they are sitting side by side, holding hands. It is the face of a child gazing up at an adult with a look of total trust.

Alma takes a deep breath. "Yes, I do." And then, lest Helen's keen vision see through Alma's bluff, she adds, "He told me about winning that calf."

Helen laughs. "Oh yes. My oh my, was that boy ever proud."

"He said he won it with something he wrote about the four *H*s. Heart, head, hands, but he couldn't remember the fourth *H*."

"Health," Helen says right off. "Head, heart, hands, and health."

That's not an organ or a part of the body, Alma is thinking. But it's not surprising that it's the one *H* that Mickey would forget, given the kind of life he has led and the difficult days that lie ahead.

ON THEIR WAY OUT, Tera needs to use the bathroom. Alma is waiting in the entryway when Mickey approaches from the kitchen, flan plate in hand.

"Guess I didn't like it," Mickey says, nodding at the empty plate.

There was over half a flan left after Alma spooned out his serving! "You ate the whole thing?"

He grins, watching her. He seems to get a kick out of shocking her. "I put what was left over on one of Helen's plates," he admits finally. Alma has noticed how prompt Mickey is about returning her plates and platters, as if he's trying to prove his honesty, the showy scrupulosity of the shoplifter, paying for the gum after stuffing his pockets with candy bars. "That was some good—what'd you call it?"

"Flan, a kind of custard." Alma braces herself for his usual question. Last few times, he has asked if the recipe is from her native land.

It's odd how he never mentions Alma's country by name, as if he's not real sure where she comes from, some foreign place where the marines have landed, no doubt, though probably not during his watch or surely he'd remember the name. But since quite a few of Helen's gifts have come from places like Thailand, Indonesia, Korea, Alma imagines Mickey did most of his invading in the Far East, probably served in Vietnam, he's that vintage.

Each time he asked, Alma was glad to prove him wrong. The polenta was Italian. "Actually, it's sort of like cornmeal mush." The potato salad, pure Indiana. "From my husband's family." She wanted him to know there was a man with a clan in her life. Alma hoped Mickey would imagine a big, beefy Midwestern guy such as he knew in the marines, instead of her pale, lanky Richard who's half blind without his glasses. She doesn't know why Mickey's question should make her feel defensive, when the guy's probably just being curious about her background. She supposes it's resentment that Mickey doesn't even know the name of her country, wariness that she is about to be trapped by a label that leaves out a big part of who she is.

The last time before the flan, the polenta time, Mickey hadn't even registered what Alma had said about the dish. He'd gone off on one of his non sequiturs, same vein as his co-rant with Tera this afternoon. "I bet lots of people in your country don't get much to eat. They get sick, they die. Life is cheap." Alma had bristled at the implication that she was some corrupt, exiled native because here she was, not only eating well but doling it out to neighbors, while "her people" were dying off like flies. But as he went on talking, Alma realized that Mickey was trying to voice some deep unease. He and his wife—his first mention, Alma noted—had been working to wake people up, to face the facts. "Until she got sick." In fact, Mickey was apologizing for inequities—misguidedly to her. He wasn't some gung-ho former marine; he was a maverick in his politics as he was in his personality, a man who'd been transformed by what he'd seen. Had he been a more coherent fellow, Alma would have pursued the topic. But instead she'd just nodded and taken back her dish.

But this time, he hasn't asked if the flan is a native recipe, and he's still holding on to her dish, as if Alma has to come up with the magic word to get it back.

And maybe that's why she thinks of it. "Health," she tells him smartly. There is something about this man that makes her want to get him back. She doesn't even want to imagine what his fellow marines might have done with his personality type.

Mickey laughs. He gets it, without Alma explaining, as if the same ability that he requires of listeners to connect his loose dots, he has for their random thoughts. "Hot damn, you're right. Head, heart, hands, and health. What do you want for your calf?"

Her *calf?* Mickey grins. Slowly, the boy is surfacing, the boy who won a prize calf for his essay on the four *H*s. It takes Alma a minute to work out his meaning: what does she want as a prize for coming up with the fourth *H*?

"I want my dish back," she tells him, holding out her hands.

"Ta da!" he says, setting it down with a flourish on her uplifted palms.

TERA AND ALMA DECIDE to go out to dinner, Alma's treat, she tells her friend. She wants to be out and about among people. All week, she has been housebound, except for visiting Helen and running errands, not knowing how to introduce herself into social situations without Richard.

The fax phone rings as they're setting out.
Alma runs back in, just in case the fax is from Richard.

November 13, 2004

TO: Alma Rodríguez                    FAX: 802-388-4344
FROM: Lavinia Lecourt Literary Agency      FAX: 212-777-6565

Dear Alma, Just got back late last night from the regional book-
sellers' conference, so I'm in the office trying to catch up on the pile
on my desk. I called you before I left, as I knew I'd be seeing Veevee at
the conference and she'd ask. Since you didn't return my call, I assume
you are avoiding me.

Rather than trying to chase you down by phone or put you on the
spot, I'm faxing you the enclosed contract. Veevee sent it over—prior
to the conference—after her assistant noted that the due date (already
extended twice) was the last day of the past year, and still no manuscript.
I can't keep making excuses, Alma. Veevee very kindly (took some arm
twisting, believe me) agreed to one last extension, but that's it.

You've got to level with me. Do you want my agency to sign this new
contract? Will you be able to deliver by the end of next year? My cred-
ibility and yours are on the line. I would love to continue representing
you, but I've got to know where I stand.

Please think about it and let's talk at the beginning of the week.

Reading Lavinia's fax, Alma feels that old anxiety perking in the pit
of her stomach. Her writing career's about to go up in smoke, and now
it's not history taking a wrong turn, it's her, adrift in purposelessness,
self-doubt, second-guessing, all the ills attendant to petite souls in
crisis.

And it's not just Alma, who will pay, but the people who love her,
who will feel the deeper gloom. Life ain't easy; some people can't even
take it, as Richard would say, so why make it harder on everybody?
What were those lines from Dante that Papote used to quote, back
when he could remember things? Some story about a father in a dun-

geon with his kids, all of them being starved to death, but the kids being kids are clueless. They don't know that tonight there will be no supper, tomorrow there will be no lunch. But the father knows, and when his kids ask him why he looks so scared the father decides not to alarm them. "For them I held my tears back, saying nothing; I calmed myself to make them less unhappy."

So what do I tell Lavinia? Alma wonders.

That she's sorry. That she has lied. That she lost heart. That she got distracted. That she started listening to the songs of the losers. The still sad music of humanity that'll drown out any story. The terror reports from Tera. HI's feasibility studies, flow charts and graphs, a whole industry of help to stem the tide of human misery. The AIDS caller. Isabel and the orphans, the helpless, the powerless, on whose backs civilization carries itself forward, for the greater good.

So what does she tell Lavinia?

The truth is going to bring the card house down on her head, turn the wheel toward the edge, and her guardrail is gone, her clean windshield is far away, Helen is dying, and she'll owe Veevee & company a hell of a lot of money.

"You want to talk about it?" Tera has come down to the basement room where Richard keeps his little office. The fax machine is still rolling out page after page of the contract, all that fine print full of promises Alma is not going to be able to keep.

"Not really," Alma says.

"Not from Richard, right?"

Alma shakes her head. "From my agent."

"Oh." Tera, Alma knows, does not believe in agents. Literature should be free, along with medical care. There's enough money to go around to be charging people for listening to the song of the species. Alma is inclined to agree with her, especially now when she is in a free fall toward Veevee's bottom line, fifty grand in the red, and her only song a stupid refrain going through her head, *What do I tell Lavinia?*

• • •

THE HARD DAY'S NIGHT Cafe sits right next to the creek, a small purple house with star cutouts in the shutters. It's a soulful place owned by former hippies, who feature a lot of vegetarian dishes. Soft lights, hanging plants, loose and laid-back, Alma half expects to find reefer on the menu. Commune morphed into funky cafe. Alma loves to come here with Tera. It reminds her of her pre-Richard days when she fancied herself a woman on the verge of a great breakthrough.

Tonight she feels distracted. But she rallies. Otherwise she is going to get all the help she doesn't need from Tera. They order a bottle of wine instead of their usual individual glasses. Why not? "It's been a hard day's night for days," Alma jokes with the young waitress, who smiles wanly. "Have you noticed," she asks Tera when the girl departs, "how the young people don't get our jokes anymore?"

"I know," Tera agrees. "I'll tell a joke in class and I'm the only one laughing."

Alma remembers to ask about the Buddhist in Tera's department. "How'd he do as a lecturer?"

"Evaluations were glowing," Tera tells her. "Kids loved him."

"I assume he talked to them? I mean you said he was almost moribund in his silence."

"No complaints. Everybody did really well in the class. All A's."

They look at each other, the same thought going through their heads, the same giggles bursting out. Soon they're laughing too loud. Alma looks around. Better keep it down. She still has to live in this town after Tera is gone.

The restaurant is almost empty. A cold night mid-November. The two women have the waitstaff mostly to themselves. They're making Alma nervous, constantly alighting by their table, asking if everything is okay.

"Don't ask her that!" Alma says, pointing to Tera. The young woman who seems to be their assigned waitress looks from one tipsy broad to the other, smiling awkwardly. "She might just tell you," Alma tries to explain.

Tera swats Alma with her napkin. Alma grabs her wineglass just in time. It strikes her that they're back in yesterday's arena, that charged moment when Alma was mean and Tera was Tera. But now they're laughing at themselves, which is probably how they've managed to stay good friends now going on a third decade.

In the same light vein, Alma tells Tera about Mickey's imitation of Tera's drumroll as he put the platter back in Alma's hands. "By the way, did you get a chance to give him your pamphlets?"

"He wouldn't take them." Tera sighs. Alma can just imagine the scene. "I tried to tell him that these were resources he could tap if he needed to. He said he could take care of Helen himself just fine."

Oh yeah? "He doesn't have a great track record." Alma wishes she hadn't brought up the subject. They're both quickly sobering.

Tera pours herself another glass of wine; Alma shakes her head, no, she doesn't want any more. Somebody's got to drive them home. "I guess it's like you said yesterday, most people want to stick their heads in the sand."

That's what Alma said? Her pronouncements always sound ridiculous in somebody else's mouth, especially Tera's.

"I told him I'd just leave them in case he wanted to look them over, and it was like I was going to dump contaminated waste in his backyard. He said he didn't want them around."

"Oh, Tera," Alma says, touching her friend's arm. Alma can tell Tera is—hurt is too strong a word—baffled. It's rare that her friend meets someone who's more enraged than she is. Secretly, Alma is thinking, this might be good for Tera. "Don't take it personally. Mickey's a hard nut to crack. I guess he hasn't had an easy life." Alma discloses her conversation with Helen. How Helen wanted to be reassured that Mickey would be all right.

As Alma is talking, Tera's gaze strays: something has caught her mind's eye. "I have this feeling, I don't know, that Mickey is up to something."

"What?" Suddenly, Alma's alarm feelers are out. A prodigal son, a dying mother, a difficult past, a score to settle. A plot so easy to assemble, you'd think, nah, nobody would try that. But an odd person might. Mickey might. "You mean, he'd try to hurt Helen?"

"No, actually, I think it's more that Helen has asked him, I don't know. You know Mickey used to be a nurse in the marines?"

How do people find out these surprising things about strangers they've just met whom Alma has known for years? Okay, she hasn't known Mickey, but she has known his mother, and Alma only just found out this last week that Mickey was an ex-marine, which seems like something a mother would let a friend know about her son. But then Helen has never talked much about Mickey, and Alma has always respected Helen's silence, willing enough to fill it up with her own complaints and quandaries. "So what does Mickey's being a marine nurse have to do with Helen?" Alma has already worked out the plot herself, but she wants a different ending.

"Just that she might have asked him to help her die." Tera shrugs. Like it wouldn't be the end of the world. But it would, for Helen.

"I'm not sure how I feel about that," Alma admits, surprised in part that her feelings aren't as cut-and-dry as she would have them. Helping someone to die is murder: murder is bad. But Alma also feels a gleam of relief. It can be quick, painless, and not just for Helen but for those left behind.

One of their waitresses suddenly descends on their table again. Tera and Alma both jump, startled from their grim thoughts. "Will there be anything else I can get you?"

The two women look at each other, then back at the waitress, and shake their heads.

"Just the bill," Alma tells her.

AFTER TERA GOES UP to bed, Alma heads downstairs to compose an answer to Lavinia, a brief fax in the telegram style. *No saga. Stop. Tell Veevee I messed up. Stop. I'm sorry. Stop. I will pay back the fifty grand.*

That stops her.

She and Richard don't have a spare fifty thousand dollars lying around in the bank. But they do own their house; they can refinance it. If worst comes to worst, Alma could ask Mamasita for a loan, though she couldn't tell Mamasita the truth, what it's for: book money being no better than blood money, helping finance this way Alma has of disgracing the family. But, actually, this time Alma could tell Mamasita the truth. This is money to pay back an advance for a saga novel Alma is not writing. Mamasita will be delighted. She might even make the loan a gift if Alma agrees never to write it.

It has crossed Alma's mind that she could offer Veevee the Balmis story as a substitute for the saga novel. But she keeps backing off from even thinking about this option. She knows what would happen. Lavinia and Veevee and her assistant and their marketing department would soon be climbing aboard the *María Pita*, wanting more orphan scenes, wondering if Isabel shouldn't have sex with Balmis. It would ruin everything. And Alma needs this story too much right now to risk it. Besides Veevee wants a saga. She doesn't want orphans and a woman scarred by smallpox. She wants the dying generations, with a Latin accent.

When Alma comes into Richard's study, she finds another of his faxes waiting for her.

November 13, Saturday night

TO: Mi amor                                    FAX: 802-388-4344
FROM: Ricardo                              FAX: 809-682-0800

I just this moment tried calling, but the machine came on, so I hung up. I didn't want to leave a message, afraid that you'd hear the loneliness in my voice and think something's wrong, especially since I just faxed you this afternoon. Missing you so much tonight! Bienvenido went off to the capital and invited me to go along, but I figure the guy needs time with just his wife and kid. Maybe, if he offers again next weekend, I'll say yes.

I cooked myself up a supper of local yuca with fried cheese and a hunk of longaniza. (Sorry, my vegetarian honey.) Dessert was some of the chocolates you stashed away here and there in my luggage—made me miss you all the more. So I wandered into the poblado, an after-dinner, chase-away-the-blues stroll. Everybody came out to greet me, pulled up chairs, invited me to sit down, but I didn't want to intrude, as I could tell most were in the middle of their supper, if you can call it that, a bowl of boiled roots, yuca, rábano and maybe a plátano, with some rock salt, for a family of eight. Made me ashamed, remembering my own feast. Can't afford to be a sentimentalist about this. As Emerson says, bleeding hearts are ineffective, end up needing emotional triage, so get a grip. Has he called again?

On the way back, heard music and laughter in the residential dormitorios of the clinic compound: one for men, one for women patients. They must have a boom box in there. Sounded like a party. Think I saw some locals going in and out. Hope everyone's being careful. Last thing we need is a case of AIDS among the locals in the community.

I had the key to the clinic office in my pocket, so I came here to call you. No luck. So, instead, here's this second fax of the day—my good night kiss to my querida honey, whom I wish were here with me, from your Ricardo.

Richard must have sent the fax while Alma and Tera were out at the restaurant. Alma tries calling the clinic number on the off chance that Richard might still be around and will pick up. It's awful how good she felt reading that Richard is sad, that he is missing her so much. It means he won't forget her, won't run off with Starr Bell in her pickup to spend the rest of their lives saving the world together. Of course, Alma wants Richard to be happy, just as long as she's the one drawing the smile on his smiley face. Another small thought to tuck away in that back room full of things Alma doesn't want to admit about herself.

Alma lets the phone ring and ring, though by now Richard would have picked up if he were within hearing distance. But even if she can't talk to him, Alma wants to hear the phone ringing, to be able to at least cause a sound in the world in which Richard is probably brushing his teeth this very moment, maybe peeing in the dark with a glowing ring to help him hit the bull's-eye of the bowl. And so she lets it ring and ring, thinking oh my God, this is just like Mamasita, and the more it rings, the more it does sound like a baby bawling, wanting someone, anyone to pick up the other end and ask, Is everything all right?

Isn't that why Richard tried to call? He'd taken a stroll into the dark and dirty village, and heard it loud and clear, the song of the losers, that plaintive cry that sent him to the phone, hoping to hear Alma tell him, *Everything is going to be all right.* Isn't that what Helen wanted to hear from Alma, that Mickey was going to be all right. That they are all, every one of them, going to be all right?

Alma hangs up, takes a deep breath, and tries to compose a fax to Lavinia. Before she knows it, she has written a half-dozen drafts of a one-page fax. No wonder she can't get through a whole saga novel.

She gives up and heads upstairs, past Sam and Ben's old bedroom where Tera is fast asleep already. For someone with her dark vision, Tera is amazingly light on her psychic feet, sleeps well, eats and drinks well, and knows how to have a hearty good time even in the midst of the many horrors she does not fail to see.

And seeing those horrors, one might be driven to do something noble for the world, Alma thinks, pulled yet again by Isabel and Balmis into her study, just as the *María Pita* departs the waters off Santa Cruz de Tenerife. The sailors are aloft, letting out sail as orders are shouted through a trumpet between the booms of the far-off cannons.

That first night out at sea, Isabel is too excited to sleep. After putting the boys to bed, she comes back on deck, staying close to the mate and the pilot manning the wheel, wary of encountering the steward or the rougher type of man who forms the crew—the mate has warned her. The seas are calm, the wind is light from the northeast, the pilot calls out these observations in a chanting voice that Isabel finds comforting.

Alma stays up late, as if to keep company with this lone woman, sitting on a stoop the mate has dried off for her, wondering what the next forty days at sea will hold, whether her seasickness will return—already her stomach feels a bit queasy, whether the boys will fare well. Don Francisco has forgiven her over the Benito matter; the boy will be saved as a carrier until they reach Puerto Rico. Isabel can feel something changing between her and the director. A new closeness she must be careful not to overstep. She has no secrets now from him, or rather only one secret. The secret she must never tell.

She has learned that the director has a wife. Not that Don Francisco has mentioned her; the director seldom speaks of his own private life. But his nephew and namesake, Don Francisco Pastor, is open and talkative and has alluded to his uncle's wife, Doña Josefa Mataseco, who has stayed behind in their house in Madrid. How can a woman let a man she loves go on a journey that will last for years? Had Isabel such a love, she would grapple him to her with hoops of steel! She would follow him, as she is doing now, for much less recompense. For love of a dream he has shared with her. Nothing more.

*Josefa Mataseco.* The ship now seems to rock to those three syllables: *Josefa, Josefa, Josefa.* The name will become a constant irritation, a grain of sand inside the oyster of her mind. What pearl will she make of her disappointment?

They are still close enough to shore that Isabel can see the far-off lights of Tenerife, nothing so sad as a retreating view, as Lot's wife well knew. Above, the stars arrange themselves in shapes the mate points out: the Great Bear, the Chained Lady, the Twins. Perhaps because it is late, her eyes begin playing tricks on her, undoing their shapes and connecting them into her own creation, an ark, plowing through the dark sky full of little boys made of stars. Finally, eyes drooping, she tires of her game, bids the pilot and mate good night and descends to her own quarters.

But Alma goes on, filling in the blue black of the night sky with its zillion stars like those Indian molas, a panel of black fabric with cutouts showing the bright yellow beneath, the soft brown of Isabel's serge dress, which matches the boys' onboard tunics, the pink of her whimsy, the dark red of her passionate soul, Don Francisco's deepening, pale lavender conscience.

Alma writes and writes, and then she prints out her handful of pages and goes downstairs to the fax machine, and first she faxes

Lavinia a handwritten note, full of sorrys, and then she faxes Richard the pages she has printed out with a cover sheet that only later she realizes Starr Bell might read.

то: Richard Huebner            FAX: 809-682-0800
FROM: Alma                     FAX: 802-388-4344

My love, I've trashed the saga novel. This is what I'm really working on. Trying to save the world on paper, I guess. Starr Bell with a pickup full of words, instead of goodies from the capital. Please forgive me for not being there with you to hold your hand and swat away the blues. I'll come if you tell me to.

Alma is too worked up to go to sleep, so she prowls the house in the dark. It's after midnight and lights are still on over at Helen's house. Alma wonders if Mickey is an insomniac, or maybe it's poor Helen, who can't sleep, alone with her mortal thoughts. If Mickey weren't there, Alma would call and offer to come over, make Helen a nice fire, stay up, eating the rest of the flan together. But Alma doesn't call. Instead she continues her wanderings, liking the feel of rooms at rest without the hype of activity, forlorn spaces with their trinkets and hopefulness. Finally, what she has been wanting to do but hasn't because she worries that she'll wake Tera and have to explain herself, she pushes open the door to Tera's room and finds her way to the bed and crawls in.

"You having a bad dream or something?" Tera mumbles, making room.

"Yeah," Alma tells her.

# IV

*I, ISABEL SENDALES Y GÓMEZ, mean to keep this record of our crossing. Perhaps in a future I cannot yet imagine for myself, I will have it to look back upon and recollect these nightmare days at sea in the sunny light of memory.*

*Sunday, January 8, stormy day, on board the* María Pita

We have been two days at sea, and stormy as it has been we have kept mostly below. And so again, bouts of seasickness have afflicted me, but in a milder form, thanks to the mate's prescription of a half cup of salt water each morning upon waking and then again at night before retiring.

I dare not breathe that I am being treated by a lieutenant when there are so many skilled physicians on board. But in science, as we know, we must be ruled by observation, and the bite of salt in my stomach seems to have abated the mal de mar a lot better than Don Francisco's wine of ipecac and deck exercise, albeit the latter has been difficult owing to the heavy seas we are encountering.

It seems a common opinion among the crew that this is one of the stormiest Januarys they have seen in the north Atlantic, and the month just over a week old! Our cook, an irascible old salt with one good arm and a hook for a left hand — which intrigues our boys to no end — claims that we're in for a bad crossing as we left Tenerife on a Friday. "The day of Our Lord's crucifixion bodes ill for setting out on a journey."

"But it *was* Epiphany," Orlando, the cabin boy who is not much older than our oldest carriers, spoke up. "And the three kings were traveling."

The cook glared at him. No doubt the young apprentice would soon learn not to contradict the shipmate in charge of feeding him. "You just wait and see," Cook warned, jabbing his hooked arm in the boy's direction, nearly cuffing the steward in the jaw as the ship heaved to one side. Cook should know better than to wield that thing about so freely on a heavy sea. "If you live to see it, that is," the cook growled as he stirred the greasy stew, which was to be the crew's supper.

The poor boy blinked, fighting back tears. As he lifted his bowl for his ladleful, the buttons on his sleeve caught the gleam of the galley fire. The mate had told me these buttons were purposely sewn on the sleeves of young apprentices to prevent them from wiping their noses when they sniffle with homesickness. I doubt that a few mere buttons would prevent my own boys from wailing at will when they want.

And they have been whiny and bored with being confined below. I join them in the galley for meals to help with feeding the youngest. Afterward, depending on the cook's mood, we stay sitting at the tables, playing games and telling stories rather than withdrawing to their darker, smellier quarters below.

If anything will get us across this ocean, it will be the telling of stories. I have devised a game the boys seem to enjoy, a variation of the one I used to play in my head to relieve the tedium and hopelessness of my days back at La Coruña. I take each one in turn and imagine a lovely future ahead for him, describing in great detail the house he will live in, the color and character of the horse he will ride, the important post he will fill, the gatherings he will attend, the foods he will eat. I set before them trays filled with exquisite cakes and little candies in colors that tease the eye. And for an hour at a time, the boys are mesmerized, having forgotten the rocking ship, their confinement below, their queasy stomachs, their homesickness, seasickness, weariness of travel. "Are we almost there?" they keep asking.

"Soon," I reply—with a month or more to go!

Yesterday, I waxed on about the future of our little Francisco: "You will be a respected merchant in a satin waistcoat with buttons of gold and ride in a carriage to the viceroy's palace pulled by two black stallions with bells at their bridles that ring wherever you go." I looked up and saw I had a larger audience than just the cook and the steward, sitting nearby, picking his teeth, drinking his noon ration of rum. Don Francisco had come forward to see after us, and he stood by, listening. When I stopped in embarrassment, he urged me to go on.

Later, when I went back to my quarters in the aft part of the ship, he complimented me on my skill in invention. "Or can you actually foretell the future?" He cocked one brow. I knew better than to tell a man of science that I believe in fortune-telling.

"They are just stories I tell the boys," I explained. "To give them something to hope for."

He seemed almost disappointed with my answer. As if he would have preferred I claim special powers that I might tell him what lay ahead for our risky expedition.

And who knows, perhaps my stories do have special powers? Little filaments of hope thrown out into the unknown, which might carry a boy somewhere he would not otherwise go. For my own part, I cannot imagine any future for myself beyond this watery waste that seems to have no end. Perhaps the common lore of seamen is correct and our women constitutions are not made for the sea. Were it solely up to me, I would not choose to travel by ship again.

Yet how can I complain? My accommodations are among the best. The mate would not hear of letting me move out of his quarters. I have a small but pleasant cabin all to myself, with two hooks for a hammock, a tiny desk that pulls down, and a small hatch from whence blows in a lovely, revitalizing breeze — though in these heavy seas, I have mostly kept it closed.

Slowly, I am learning everyone's name. Thank goodness many are called by what they do: Cook, Steward, Boatswain ("Bosun," I've been instructed to say). We are all told sixty souls on this ship. Besides the twenty-two boys, there are eleven members of our expedition (including myself) and twenty-seven in the crew. According to the mate, this is a small number, purposely so, to accommodate the rest of us. I see now why our director thought of sending six boys back and why Captain del Barco felt compelled to have his own cabin boy double as a carrier. It is amazing to think we are all to live in a space only slightly bigger than our orphanage for the next month or so!

Don Francisco brought along six blank books. He is writing in one, keeping a second in reserve. He has given one to Dr. Salvany, another to Dr. Gutiérrez, and a fifth to Don Ángel, who is to be secretary of the expedition. Don Francisco asked if I would like one, which I was pleased to accept. (The second book he has given me! This one, a blank, which I have already begun to fill.)

It seems everyone is writing a book: Dr. Gutiérrez writes in his blank book, as does Dr. Salvany, who has also brought along a small book with gold leaf on the cover, which he is filling with poetry he sometimes reads to the wardroom at night; Don Ángel writes what he is told; and Don Francisco keeps a record of his vaccinations as well as other experiments he is conducting. Then the captain and pilot write a daily log of our weather, which they read out at supper to the officers: "rainy with heavy seas; cloudy with fresh gales and squally; the same uncomfortable weather with a long westerly swell." They are also constantly taking measurements with all manner of complex instruments among which I recognize only the compass, kept in a binnacle, which measurements they then use to chart our way across the ocean. These they keep secret, because, as the mate, Lieutenant Pozo, who has warmed to the point of being quite chatty with me, confesses, it is a danger to let the crew of a ship know exactly where they are; it encourages mutiny. It makes my heart sink to hear such talk. As if I didn't have enough fears already to worry my mind about!

Evenings in the aft part of the ship, with these many men writing, one would think one was in a schoolroom rather than in the wardroom of a ship crossing an ocean.

Until the floor tilts and the ink spills and the quill slips!

I, myself, cannot join these scribblers. For after I have put the boys to bed, I visit with our carriers in the sick bay: little José and the captain's cabin boy, Orlando, whose vaccine has not yet taken. Thank goodness, José's vesicle proceeds apace.

From the sick bay, I then rock back to these quarters—I cannot call the stumbling perambulation that takes place upon this rolling ship "walking." I barely have the energy to eat my own supper, do whatever mending and care the boys' clothing requires, arrange for the next day's meals, confer with Don Francisco about the condition of our carriers and the health and spirits of all the other boys, but I am ready to retire. I open the door of this small cabin, tumble upon my bed, taking care to drink my half cup of salt water courtesy of Lieutenant Pozo's cask, and I do not sleep, no, not immediately. Instead, I lie, resting, listening to the voices in the wardroom. Perhaps it will get easier as I become accustomed to performing all these duties myself, without the expert help of another woman's hands, in this floating world in which we are all truly orphans of the land.

Only on Sundays am I to have this brief respite of the morning to myself. We have no priest on board, so we shall not have Mass, only a reading from the gospels by the captain in the evening. We are all Catholics, though the mate claims we have a Lutheran or two among the crew, but that said, the name of God and the Virgin are taken so many times in vain they might as well all be heathens. I worry that despite all my efforts, the boys will have forgotten how to say the Our Father or make the sign of the cross by the time we make landfall.

Today, especially, I am glad for this morning of rest, having just begun my menstrual flow yesterday, so that between my menses and mild seasickness, I am feeling quite indisposed. And, of course, now a new problem presents itself: What to do with my sullied napkins? Whom to ask? Where is there privacy to wash them or sun to dry them out in this rainy weather? My hope is that in a month's time when I shall need them again, we will be safely landed in San Juan, my bloody bundle discreetly smuggled ashore to whatever convent we will be housed at. Or will it be a convent this next time? Perhaps I am imagining a future for myself after all, not dazzling with promise, but provident with clean napkins and terra firma under my feet. Indeed, such a future seems much to be desired at present, and the mere act of setting it down on paper seems to draw it closer. All the more reason to continue navigating my way through my blank book on my Sunday mornings.

Blank no more! How odd just now to look back on pages I have filled with my own hand. So this is the way our poets and philosophers write their great works!

*Sunday, January 15, lashing rain, frightful wind*

We have been nine days at sea and it is still squally, everything wet from the quantity of rain which keeps falling. At the very least, we will not have to worry about water, as the barrels are overflowing. There has been such an excess that I was able to soak my rags, now a damp bundle stowed in the far corner of my sleeping closet. Nothing dries aboard. Soon, we shall all have webbed fingers and toes.

I also attempted to wash the boys' hair, or rather heads, for the boatswain, who doubles as barber, shaved them so closely they look like newborns with their bald pates. Better a shorn head than one full of the lice which had begun afflicting some of the smaller boys. I am tempted to cut off my own hair, for I can see it will be difficult to wash it on board. Where is there privacy (my baths are cat washes in my cabin) and when is there time? I have been applying pomade and keeping it combed under my lace cap, but it is beginning to feel as stiff as a cap itself. And yet I waver. How I miss having Nati to consult!

Yesterday, before dinner I finally steeled myself and approached the boatswain-barber, but the gruff man refused to do the honors. He stammered that my long hair was too pretty. Later, I heard from Don Ángel that a bidding war was in progress in the galley. The boatswain had been offered as much as six pesos—by the steward!— for a bracelet made of the lady's braid.

That settles it. I will keep my mane for now. Better dirty on my head than binding the wrist of that lusty, pesky man. Nati's pin is close at hand should the man dare approach me again. A bidding war indeed! And yet, I confess, hearing such compliments, I take even more pains, busy as I am, to keep my hair nicely braided, the coils looping around my ears, the ends gathered under my cap. Ah, the vanity of those who have nothing else to be vain about but a shank of lustrous hair or a nice turn of the foot or a handsome set of shoulders! (I wonder if these are the sorts of things one writes down in a book?)

We had our new round of vaccinations on Tuesday—little José passing the cowpox on to Tomás Melitón and Manuel María, two of our three-year-olds. (Orlando's vaccine never took, though the boy and captain swore he had never been exposed to the smallpox.) What a heartbreaking task it has been to separate one out of the trinity of María brothers. The little one wails all night in the sick bay like a lone puppy, and his two brothers call out from the front of the ship when they hear him. But we cannot risk vaccinating two brothers at a time, as our most vital concern is sustaining the chain of vaccinations across this ocean. Indeed, no one sleeps well the days after a transfer, all of us waiting anxiously for the first sign of a vesicle forming on the arms of the new carriers.

Yesterday evening, to raise our spirits, Dr. Salvany read us a poem he had written about twenty-two miniscule volcanoes erupting with mankind's good fortune. I had to drink a full glass of salt water to regain a settled stomach. (Are these the sorts of verses poets write down in their books, I wonder.)

I am happy to report that now on the fifth day, Manuel María's vesicles are defined and growing. But our little Moor shows no sign of forming a vesicle. Don

Francisco has questioned me repeatedly, and I can only repeat that Tomás came to us as a mere infant, deposited in the hospital drawer next door, and he was never ill with the smallpox at the orphanage. Our director has finally sent him back to the other boys, though I asked the nurses not to mention why. I dread to think of the mistreatment Tomás would endure if the word got out that he failed to make a *vehicle*, as the boys mistakenly call it.

Orlando, too, never developed a reaction, and we did not lose the vaccine, I keep reminding Don Francisco. But our director does not easily accept events not going according to his plan. Presently, he checks the boys so continually that they are more worked up than they should be. I dread to think what would happen to our director if for any reason the expedition should fail. What an intense man! He aims everything at the stars and keeps nothing to light his own lamp. But is this not why I, and others, are drawn to him?

His special worry is that Manuel María will scratch his vesicles and the precious fluid be lost from our only carrier. To guarantee the safety of these vesicles, I myself have kept vigil over the boy these last few nights. Over and over, I promise the bereft child that if he is very good and does not disturb his vaccine, he will be reunited with his brothers. But this consolation only works for a short while.

I will be very relieved when this round is over.

Orlando. The boy is not well, his skin has a deathly pallor, and there is a general feverish cast to his whole appearance. Our captain has made insinuations that the boy's illness is a result of the vaccination. Don Francisco keeps reminding him that the boy was ill in Tenerife before he was ever vaccinated. Our captain is keeping the boy on a bland diet of biscuit and broth. How foolish of the captain to persist in a regimen that is not working. Don Francisco has asked permission to dose the boy with his special concoction against scurvy, which he is giving to all our carriers, but the captain refuses. God grant that Orlando be back in good health soon, for our captain seems quite attached to him.

"I do wish the captain would allow Don Francisco complete charge of the boy," I confess to Lieutenant Pozo, as he pours out my first dose of salt water this morning. I am on my way back from the sick bay, weary from lack of sleep, glad to have this morning to myself.

The lieutenant seems uncomfortable with my implied criticism of his superior. "The boy is a bit better today. You need not worry, Doña Isabel."

"One worries so much when any child is ill."

The mate bows his head as if he has had direct experience of the truth of my remark. He is still holding on to my cup, so I cannot leave him alone with his memories.

The wardroom is empty but for some members of our expedition engrossed in a card game at one end of the long table. Most of the officers not on duty are catching a few hours of sleep before their watch begins. Everything on board is timed by watches, four hours the length of any responsibility, barring a call for all hands on deck in an emergency.

Finally, the mate stirs himself from whatever recollection had drawn him away. "Where will all the boys go once the journey is over?" Before I can begin to explain His Majesty's arrangement, he stammers on. "I ask because . . . perhaps I could, as you have done with your little Benito, take some boys to raise." I am touched by his sweetness, though I wonder how a man who is always at sea can raise boys? Some wife on shore will no doubt be saddled with the work. Shouldn't he confer with her first? "Do you have a family, a wife with whom to leave the boys?" I ask.

The lieutenant sighs and shakes his head. He seems ready to say more, but just that moment Don Francisco comes down the companionway. He looks oddly from one to the other. "Doña Isabel, just who I wanted to speak to," he says, as if wanting a word with me privately.

My heart lifts—as if the matter our director wishes to discuss were something other than the condition of our carriers, their appetites, the state of their vesicles, the movements of their bowels. After my disappointment with him in Tenerife when he sought to amend our agreement and send the boys who had already served their purpose back to Spain, alone and unprotected, I confess I have been wary with him. But his intense passion for his mission and his thoughtfulness toward me have won back my good opinion. For a moment he faltered. How many times don't we all do so in the course of some enterprise far less noble?

I notice too late that the mate has let go of the cup before I have hold of it. It tumbles to the floor, spilling its contents upon Don Francisco's and my own clothes. Quickly, the mate bends to retrieve it, all apology as if my clumsiness were his doing.

"The ship could use some spirits," Don Francisco jokes, believing the contents of the cup to be rum. The men get a pint a day in two servings, the crew's watered down but the officers' undiluted. Often Don Francisco foregoes his own portion in favor of doling it out to this or that expedition or crew member who has done him some small favor.

"It's not rum, sir. Just some salt water." The mate is honest to a fault. "Good for seasickness," he goes on to explain. I am tempted to poke the man in the ribs to quiet him. But I do not have that kind of intimacy with anyone on board except my little boys. I look down at the wet floor and wait for trouble to unfold.

"Seasickness? I hope you are not giving this out as a *remedy*?" Don Francisco scowls at the empty cup in the mate's hand. "I especially caution you not to give such an unwholesome drink to Orlando, for it could very well be aggravating his condition." Don Francisco's tone is that of an adult chastising a child.

I glance up, wondering if the mate has taken offense. His face is flushed, as if he is indeed perturbed to be given this interdiction by a mere *passenger*.

"The captain has always dosed with salt water," the mate speaks up, reminding Don Francisco who is the ship's, and therefore his, commander.

"The captain is not a doctor," Don Francisco reminds the mate in turn. "I am not trying to sail this ship. The captain should not attempt to heal the sick."

The mate stiffens, at a loss for words, holding my cup like a mendicant awaiting alms. If he is anything at all like me, he will wake in the middle of the night or some other inconvenient time with a whole volley of words to shoot back at his adversary.

"I say this only for the child's good," Don Francisco goes on more kindly. Then bidding the lieutenant farewell, he leads me away by the elbow. At my door, he bids me good day as well. Has he forgotten his greeting: he needed to speak with me?

"Wasn't there something you wanted to tell me, Don Francisco?"

Our director looks at me a long moment, then makes a curious remark. "Doña Isabel, you might put some distance between yourself and Lieutenant Pozo. Any impropriety, do not hesitate to inform me."

Surely, our director does not suspect the kindly lieutenant of any indiscretion! What would he do if he knew about our steward? Have him flogged? Punishment is harsh on board. That much I know. Men grow bestial at sea, the mate himself has warned me, separated for long periods from the beneficent influence of female company. Perhaps that is why our director grows more and more protective of me.

I doubt any of the men have much in mind at the present but the storm we are expecting. A moment ago, I heard the mate announce to the wardroom that a swirling tempest is bearing down upon us. I will soon have to put book and quill away for the agitation of the ship is making it near impossible for me to proceed. And yet I cling to my quill as a sailor might to a floating beam from a sinking ship.

Cries and the sounds of running above, the bell clangs frantically, all hands on deck. The wind is howling about us like a crazed evil spirit, lifting the ship like a plaything and dashing it against the water. I hear the horrible sounds of cracking timbers, glass shattering. I can only imagine how terrified all my small boys are. My poor little Benito! I should not have left him behind with the others, but at the time it seemed unfair to single out one boy, even if he is my son. I must somehow make my way to their quarters and offer what comfort I can. Though I doubt any story I tell the boys now will calm their terror, or mine.

*Sunday, January 22, who knows where on this watery waste*

We have been sixteen days at sea; the bad weather continues, though the worst storm so far was last Sunday. Two men washed overboard while they were bringing down sail. We had a time trying to rescue them! One was a mere boy, eighteen, who had only been to sea once before. The other was our mate's cousin, an experienced seaman who should have known better than to let go both hands even for a moment to tie up sail! The lieutenant himself was lowered with a rope round him to rescue them. Back on board, the cousin claimed that his salvation was due not to his cousin's efforts but to the precaution he took in Tenerife of having a rooster and a pig tattooed on either foot, which is suppose to protect a man from drowning.

"I don't care what you have marked on you, one hand for the ship, one for yourself," the mate said sternly. He certainly runs a tight ship and makes a point of not favoring his relations.

I had such a time trying to find the boys' quarters during the storm. Somehow, I managed to grope my way toward where I could hear the children wailing, even as the ship slammed and tossed on the waves. I am still full of black-and-blues from the banging I took trying to reunite with my poor little ones.

The storm has abated but we have still to see a clear sky or a ray of sunshine. On deck, repairs are under way: the top of the mizzen mast was snapped off like a matchstick and the main topsail carried away as if made of gauze. Now I see why a ship must carry a carpenter and sailmaker—its own repair crew—on board!

The captain is weary with lack of sleep and the travails of this stormy crossing. Meanwhile, Orlando does not improve. This despite the attentions of expert physicians on board. But what good is a diagnosis, as Don Francisco explains, if nothing is done to carry out the prescribed cure? Our director is convinced that the boy is suffering from scurvy, and he is ready to overpower the captain and force his lemon drink down the boy's throat. But the last thing we need in these stormy seas is a captainless ship! Say what you will about our prickly commander, he is a skilled seaman. The crew swears that were it not for the captain, we would all be food for fish by now.

And so I have convinced our director to allow me to find a way to dose Orlando. "Only a spoonful at a time," Don Francisco explains, "and he will improve." The boy seems soothed by my presence, especially by my stories. Indeed, the captain now seeks me out to attend to the boy when his duties force him on deck for long watches at a time. Quite the change from those first days, when my very presence seemed to offend him. You can catch more flies with honey than you can with bile, as Nati was wont to say. Dear Nati! If only she knew what a dreadful passage we have been having.

But even the humpback gets used to carrying his hump around, as she herself would say. I seem to have grown accustomed to this rocking house, for I am no longer seasick, even though I am no longer dosing myself with the mate's salt water, or smelling the captain's smelling salts, or walking upon the deck—Lord forbid!—to look up at the great swells of water.

This past Friday we vaccinated two new carriers, José Jorge and Juan Antonio, from Manuel María's vesicle. We had already sent Tomás back to the other boys before the storm, but right afterward I noted that he had indeed grown a vesicle *under* his arm where he must have scratched himself. It was small and unremarkable but a vesicle no less, recently broken, the fluid still dampening his arm. I did not give it a second thought, until that night when it occurred to me that the way those boys tumble and roughhouse with each other, and especially the way many take it upon themselves to pounce upon our little Moor, it was likely that the fluid from Tomás vesicle had been smeared on future carriers.

I did not sleep a wink, worrying that all our boys had been infected and we had at the very least a fortnight still to go. The very next morning, I sought out Don Ángel, who inspected Tomás's arm and corroborated my findings.

Of course, we should have reported the incident to Don Francisco. But why not spare our director this mortification and ourselves his ire? We had probably caught the contagion in time. As a further precaution, we separated Tomás from the other carriers just in case he was still capable of infecting them. Meanwhile, Don Ángel advised washing down all the boys with vinegar and water, with just a drop of vitriolic acid in the solution.

I had eighteen boys stripped in a heartbeat, their clothes piled in a great heap. It might have been deworming day in La Coruña. I doled out new sets of clothes from opened chests, sponging down the smallest boys from the bucket we kept for hand washing, then changing them into clean shirts and trousers. "Why are we putting on clean clothes?" some of the oldest wanted to know.

"Mine are all damp," another complained. Indeed, the sea had leaked in through the hull and several chests had been soaked in water. The crew had been busily pumping out the hold for days. Once we made landfall, if we ever made landfall, the ship would need to be caulked and made more watertight.

Tomás, meanwhile, was sent aft to my quarters to wait for me. I would have to think up some excuse why I had to have the boy by my side. Perhaps the very fears I had voiced to Don Francisco that the other boys would beat up on the little Moor for not being a "good carrier."

Once the soiled clothes were piled upon a sheet, I tied the ends together into a great bundle. With Don Ángel's help, I dragged the bulky load to the opening that led down to the hold and let it tumble onto a raised platform where barrels of salt pork and casks of rum were stowed. I was perspiring heavily by now and ready for a change of clothes myself.

At dinner this noon, Don Francisco noted how nice the boys all looked, clean in fresh clothes. Don Ángel glanced over at me and we exchanged a look of heartsick collusion.

*Friday, January 27, late night and smooth sailing on the* Pita

I am not wont to write midweek, but late as it is I cannot sleep, reflecting over this evening's conversation.

I have learned a little more about our director and his wife, Doña Josefa.

Her name did not come from his own lips. In fact, Don Francisco is not one to converse about himself. I would not know his age, had his fiftieth birthday not occurred on board. Or that he has a sister, had his nephew not told us so. (There are actually two nephews; the older one, Don Antonio Pastor, seems to be a nephew-in-law.) Don Francisco Pastor—he insists we call him plain Pastor— is a fun-loving young fellow, as garrulous as his uncle is reserved.

"Ever since he was a boy, my uncle has been driven to help mankind," the young man gabbed. We were sitting in the galley, having just put the boys to bed below. Evenings, the nurses and nephews liked to visit with the crew in the galley, where they found livelier company than the officers and surgeons, writing away in the wardroom. Often Lieutenant Pozo dropped by to check on his cousins. But he was on watch this evening, which made for a merrier gathering. He does have a rather stern presence, but excepting the steward, the entire crew heartily respects him.

"Of course, medicine runs in my mother's family," Pastor went on. "Our grandfather was a surgeon as was his father. My mother says it is a wonder the men in our family marry, for the only way a lady can attract the regard of a Balmis male is by being ill. I myself seem to have been spared that family trait!"

The young nephew grinned proudly. He was eager to arrive in America, where, he had heard, the women were very taken with pure Spaniards. He wore his hair long and had refused the boatswain's scissors. "Saving your curls for the girls on shore, eh?" the boatswain had joked. Everyone seemed to enjoy teasing him.

"We were all very surprised when Uncle brought a bride home from America a decade ago," the young nephew went on. "We thought it might settle him down for good. But this trip should take . . . What do you say, Bosun? Two years?"

"To circumnavigate the globe?" The boatswain took a long draft of his rum as if to stimulate his navigational calculations. "Two to three years at least."

"At least," the cook agreed.

Two to three years! And then Don Francisco will return to Madrid, to his duties as royal surgeon to the court, to Doña Josefa. Meanwhile, the boys will have settled down with their new families. And where will Benito and I be? That is one story that fails me.

"Uncle wanted Doña Josefa to stay with our family in Alicante. But my aunt protested that if he was to be away that long, she wanted to stay in Madrid. She detests the provinces. You would think her family came from Paris, not Mexico City."

I felt emboldened, detecting a criticism of his aunt. "Do they have any children to keep her busy?" I asked.

The young man shook his head, but before he could elaborate, his cousin, Don Antonio Pastor, put in, "How could they when he is never home!"

"Now, now, cousin," the nephew chided him. "You yourself are never at home and yet you have a half dozen. But I suppose your wife does not need your help to conceive them."

Don Antonio Pastor reached for his cousin's curls, but Pastor ducked just in time, laughing.

Wives and mistresses and cuckold husbands — the topics were never far off. It was time for me to go.

"We are driving Doña Isabel away," Don Ángel rebuked the cousins. "Do stay," he urged me. "Tell us one of your stories."

I shook my head. I was not bold enough to speak up in this company. But I did sit back down, not wanting to end the evening for Don Ángel, who would insist on escorting me back to my cabin, as Lieutenant Pozo was not present to accompany me.

My curiosity remains unassuaged. Why doesn't Don Francisco ever mention his wife? Why has he taken her so far from her home to then wander off, saving the world, leaving her all alone? How can we possibly understand another's life when our very own lives elude us, swift and secret currents, carrying us hither and yon while we turn a toy wheel, thinking ourselves in charge.

As I close, I cannot help noting that today would have been my dear mother's birthday. To think she was thirty-six, my own age exactly, when she perished. Even now twenty years after her death, I grieve for those happy days. How full of promise they seemed! Papá's quill business was thriving; Mamá was busily preparing for my sister's betrothal; and I, at sixteen, spent my days absently going from one activity to another, careless of time, a deep chest full of golden hours I could squander at will.

Even the horrid news that an infection of smallpox had broken out among pilgrims in nearby Santiago de Compostela could not tarnish my happiness. But then, overnight it seemed, the infection arrived in La Coruña. Panic ensued. Great houses were suddenly deserted. Carriages left for the mountains, and households embarked by sea for noninfected cities: Lisbon, Naples, Cádiz. Papá made preparations to send us away to my uncle at the goose farm where our quill feathers came from.

His precautions came too late. We all succumbed to the fever. I alone survived, but with a heart so crushed and a face so scarred, I wanted to die. I tremble now thinking how close I came to taking my own life, relenting only because I would lose the one happiness I could still envision: joining my beloved mother and father and sister in heaven.

No suffering lasts a century, nor a body that can withstand it, as the saying goes. Soon a path opened. Those of us who had survived the smallpox were in much demand as nurses, for we were able to tend to the infected without danger. I was offered employment at the new charity hospital, and when the orphanage opened I took the reins there, leading a life of duty and obligation which might win for me future redemption . . . until the day Don Francisco showed up at our door.

How can I ever regret his visitation?

After years of resignation, I am alive again with passion and intention! His heart, I know, belongs to Doña Josefa, but there is still a place for me in this expedition, this child of his — and now my own imagination.

*Sunday, January 29, bored on board the* Pita!

I don't even want to think how many days we have been at sea! The boys grow restless, behave badly, curse like heathens. They climb in the rigging like little monkeys, ring the bell off hours, play hide-and-seek in every nook and cranny, and generally get underfoot so that the steward threatens to throw them into the sea which tells no tales. I am hoarse with chastising them. But who can blame them, cooped up in this floating gaol with no deliverance in sight. Even a prisoner can look through the bars of his cell and see the world he yearns for out there.

My own eyes are hungry for the sight of land, and my mouth for the taste of fresh fruits of the land. What I wouldn't give for a slice of fresh bread with a dollop of butter, a fried egg, a good fat fowl. I know this shows ingratitude when I consider that our table in the officers' quarters is much better provisioned than the boys' or the crew's. Even so. Ambition does not stop when we acquire what we first desire. If it were so, we should all still be happy as babies with a mere rattle.

We have had several glorious days of blue skies, full sun, a good wind, and calm seas, all that I have been fervently praying for. But I grow ambitious for more: sea-weed in that sea, a bird in that sky—both of which would betoken land nearby.

"How long before we arrive, do you suppose?" I've asked the poor mate this question more than a few times, echoing my boys. All bad habits are catching, an-other favorite saying of Nati.

"Another week or so."

Another week! It seems an eternity.

Excitement is growing on board—I can feel it. Everywhere there are prepara-tions being made for our arrival. Most of the damage done by the storm has been repaired, but now the brass is being polished, the figurehead touched with paint, the cook's kettles brought up and scoured as if they were to be used as mirrors in a lady's chamber. The crew have been on their knees all week, scrubbing the deck with holystones. "The most religion you'll get out of me," one old salt exclaimed. Everything must be shipshape for our entry into the port of San Juan.

And a glorious welcome it will be, our first landfall in the new world! Don Francisco has been rehearsing the boys. Letters preceded us from Tenerife to Puerto Rico, alerting Governor Castro to be ready "any time after the first of Feb-ruary, with a landing party, and all the honors due a royal expedition." The very day we land we are to start vaccinating, for the sooner the vaccine begins to spread, the better. Even before we left Tenerife, reports reached us of new outbreaks of smallpox throughout the territories of America. Thousands have been perishing, bodies piled as high as houses, the smoke from burning pyres darkening the skies for days, just as Don Francisco described to me at our first meeting four months ago—it seems a lifetime!—in La Coruña.

There is an added reason for our director's desperation. As we feared, several boys were infected by Tomás's vaccine—at least three: Cándido, Clemente, and Jacinto, though there may be more, and the fear is that we may run short on car-riers. "How could this have happened?" Don Francisco questioned the nurses. But his eye fell on me, as if he guessed where he might discover the solution to the mystery.

I searched for my tongue but could not find it.

"You have all been following the correct procedures, I trust?" he went on, his voice tense with barely contained anger. Don Basilio affirmed that we had indeed kept the carriers separated from the rest of the boys, sending them back only after their vesicles had healed, the scabs fallen off.

Don Ángel looked down, nodding vaguely.

"Tomás," I spoke up. My voice sounded foreign to my ears. As if I had finally found, not my own, but some stranger's tongue. "We sent him back before his time." I went on to explain my discovery, omitting Don Ángel's participation in the cover-up. I dared not lift my eyes as I spoke, but I could feel the heat of our director's eyes branding my forehead with blame. "I didn't want to worry you, especially as there was nothing to do but wait."

"And instead you took it upon yourself—" He stopped short of condemning me. But it did not matter. I knew his faith in me was shattered.

How many conversations haven't I had in my head, exculpating myself to him? But I know whatever grace I win will only increase his recriminations upon himself. It was he, after all, who sent Tomás below to join the others. And so I suffer in silence, trusting that these stormy clouds will soon dispel, and all shall be well. And indeed, as the days pass and only the three boys seem to have been infected, our director breathes a little easier, and so do I. Tomorrow, we shall vaccinate Domingo Naya and José María, the two youngest who have shown no sign of contamination.

This dark cloud has diminished but not totally destroyed the joy of the good weather we have been enjoying at last: days full of sun and fair winds. We have carried all our bedding on deck to air, as well as the footlockers and chests that were damp from the leaks sprung in the hull with the bashing of the stormy waves. Every sodden, soggy, moldy object has been brought up to dry out and feel the blessed rays of sunshine. And though seawater renders clothes stiff and rough, many in the crew have washed some of their things, and with the boys' help, I myself have scrubbed two dozen or more kerchiefs, shirts, and trousers, the latter reeking of urine, particularly those belonging to the younger boys. In addition, I lathered up and rinsed my napkins, which I then stuffed in a pillowcase and hung up to dry. What a sight we are, flying our wash from rigging and masts: boys' and men's trousers, shirts, sheets, and a pillowcase of napkins! The captain admits he will be mortified if we meet another ship, as he will never live down the embarrassment of having commanded a corvette of floating laundry.

The captain is a different person. He smiles and jokes and speaks quite pleasantly to the crew. I don't think it is only the fair weather and good wind which has made him so, but the improvement of his cabin boy, which he ascribes to my care and ministrations. Little does he know how right he is. Ministrations indeed! "And your wonderful stories," he added, "have lifted all our spirits!"

*All* our spirits? I did not know my tales at Orlando's bedside were being listened to by a wardroom of eavesdroppers.

The captain lifted a glass to me at supper. And grim and preoccupied as Don Francisco has been, he joined the toast and smiled at me.

Later, on deck, he offered me a lovely apology by way of a story. "Once upon a time," he began, "there was a kind lady and a willful, ungrateful doctor . . ."

Not so willful, not so ungrateful, I thought, before I stopped myself. I wanted to hear his story, where it would take us. But he stopped too soon, in my opinion. The doctor apologized, the lady accepted.

*Sunday, February 5, ever so eager to reach Puerto Rico*

I have lost count of how many days we have been at sea. "Another week," the mate said a week ago. The prize is now up to five pesos to the first man who sights Puerto Rico.

I admit that I no longer feel the thrill of our looming arrival. Our work will be over: the vaccine safely carried across the Atlantic by my boys. Don Francisco has explained that we are to stay all together, stopping first in Puerto Rico, then Caracas, on to Cuba, and finally Veracruz. There, the boys and I can choose to return to Spain or remain in Mexico. He and the other members of the expedition will pick up a new group of young carriers and continue across the Pacific to the Philippines and China.

Suddenly, I want desperately both to make landfall and never to reach it.

It is unusually quiet for a Sabbath morning. The boys have been sent below to their smelly quarters in the orlop deck—harsh punishment on this sunny day. But then, they did almost kill the steward. Here's what happened.

The boatswain, a surly type with a barking-mastiff personality meant to deceive us into thinking he is tough, indulges the boys to no end. He got it in his head to carve them a bow and arrow during the idle time that these mild days afford. What a plaything to bestow on a rowdy band of restless boys! The little troop

promised to aim only at the target the fellow had set up, a tarp with a drawn circle. But I needed no fortune-telling skills to predict how long that would last. They
soon tired of this easy target and commenced aiming at the seabirds that have begun alighting here and there on the ship. The cook had set up a trap on top of a
cask baited with salted cod, and the steward, happening by, got the arrow intended
for our supper in his right shoulder. God forgive me for my first thought upon hearing that he had been struck: I can put away my pin for now.

"He will be fine," Don Francisco reported after treating the groaning steward
in the sick bay. As for the bow and arrow, the mate snapped them in two and
threw them over the side. "You are lucky you did not kill a man," he lectured the
boys, pretending to more outrage than he felt. The steward is not a popular fellow.
"This is a peaceful expedition," the mate reminded them. Indeed, though we have
several cannons on deck and four crew members who know how to work them,
we do have safe conduct from France and England. Hopefully, our guns will only
be fired for the ceremonies of arrival and departure, unless we should be attacked
by corsairs.

"Corsairs?" I could hardly believe my ears when the mate told me.

"Oh yes, they are everywhere these days." The mate puffed his chest out
bravely as if inviting the corsairs to attack us, so he could prove his bravery.

Perhaps Don Francisco is right and the mate has taken a fancy to me!

I now study the man a little more closely. He is no youngster, a few years
younger than myself, I would guess. He is not in actual fact a lieutenant, he informed me today. The captain has dubbed him that title as a mark of distinction
and the name has stuck. The poor soul is dreadfully honest and felt he should
come clean with this fact. We all have our secrets, I suppose. He is handsome,
in a partial way. His body is strong and stalwart, but his head seems an after-
thought: a little too small for the rest of him, as if all the energy of growth had
gone into the mighty trunk and only a meager amount had been left to turn out
the foliage.

So we are on a sharp lookout, not just for land, but for corsairs, who favor the
warm, tropical waters of the Caribbean we have entered. The captain has called
several drills, but after the stumbling, inept performance of the crew he vows that
it will be a better defense to fly a black pennant and pretend to have smallpox on
board. Strange how we get past one danger only to worry about another. I suppose

that is no different at sea than on land. If it were not so, we would all become sailors.

The captain puts out as much sail as possible, racing to reach landfall. It is not just attacks from corsairs that compels us but the danger of losing the chain of vaccinations we have so far maintained across the ocean. Two more boys have been infected, which means only *three* carriers are left, and two of them will be vaccinated in the next week. That leaves only Benito, whom I cannot account for. Our director suspects foul play, for how else could these contaminations be happening? They can no longer be the result of Tomás's vaccination. Someone must be infecting the boys on purpose, sabotaging our expedition.

"But why would anyone do such a thing?" I ask him.

We are on deck enjoying the coolness of the night after the sweltering heat of the day. The boys were allowed one quick constitutional this evening to mark the end of their punishment. Now they are asleep in their quarters, guarded by Don Basilio and Don Ángel, though usually only one nurse attends them at night. But Don Francisco is taking no chances.

"Someone who wishes us ill. Who wants our expedition to fail."

I run my mind over the crew. True, any number of men are capable of meanness, starting with our steward, angry at having been wounded. But the mystery can be more simply solved. Not foul play, but plain and simple play gone awry. The boys are crazed with confinement. Little moles, they burrow in every dark cavity of the ship. There is no policing them. I keep my eye on a dozen and three sneak away. I round up those three and two more run off! Last Friday, I discovered Gerónimo and Clemente in the sick bay, crouched behind the medicine chest during one of their hide-and-seek games. On another occasion, Jacinto hid himself inside a recently emptied barrel of rum and, growing hot, commenced licking the damp insides and came out reeling drunk.

"It could be as simple as that," I suggest to Don Francisco.

"Let us hope so," he murmurs. But I can tell he is not convinced. Some heavy cloud hangs over him. Odd that now that victory is in sight, his faith should be flagging.

A strong breeze is blowing; the splashing rhythm of the water as we move forward is lulling. We are quiet for a while, listening to the pilot, singing an old sea chantey as he turns the wheel.

"Tell me a story, Doña Isabel," Don Francisco says. "Something hopeful, like the stories you tell the boys." He laughs, no doubt embarrassed by his whimsical request.

I would excuse myself, but I can tell he is in earnest. Man of science or not, he needs a distraction from his grim worries. And so I begin, describing our arrival, the crowds waiting at the port of San Juan, the hundreds who will be vaccinated before we depart. I mention all the places he has told me the expedition will visit, taking myself boldly along with it.

I stop when I hear him sigh, worried that I might be wearying him.

"Go on," he urges me.

But I have run out of inspiration. Or perhaps I am afraid that if I continue, I will betray myself. "History will remember you," I close. "And your own time will celebrate you."

"I won't pretend I am immune to recognition," he admits. I smile at his apt choice of words. "But immortality, true immortality comes by not granting history the last word."

For a moment I wonder that Don Francisco is expressing Christian sentiments. Up until this moment, he has not seemed particularly religious.

"We must not live entirely, or even mainly, for our own time. The soul exceeds its circumstances."

*The soul exceeds its circumstances.* I am not sure I understand his full meaning, but hearing those words, my heart soars up to those very stars the mate taught me to connect into the shapes of gods and goddesses: Orion, the hunter; Andromeda; Perseus. Romance, reputation, glory, our director has attained them all already. Wedded love. Surgeon of the royal court. But still he strives for more than the world can give him.

"You will exceed your circumstances," I portend.

"We shall see," he says, as if he fears a different ending, and that is precisely why he asked me to tell him a hopeful story.

*Thursday, February 9, port of San Juan*

We are in the bay and going ashore soon. The boys are in their uniforms and I in mine. We sighted land yesterday late and none too soon. Today, Antonio Veredia and Andrés Naya are to be vaccinated, which will leave us only Benito. But now there will be plenty of carriers in Puerto Rico.

"Faith!" I keep telling Don Francisco.

He smiles a weary smile when I say so. "Yes, indeed, faith, that great virtue without which neither hope nor charity can live."

A cannon is firing from shore, and our ship shakes with a booming reply of our own. And yet, despite this welcome, the mate looked through his spyglass a moment ago and reported the dock is deserted. Perhaps this epidemic we heard of has been even more devastating than we imagined. All the more glorious our timely arrival, bearing the cure on the arms of two little boys, and the nineteen who had preceded them.

A lone boat makes its way toward us, two Africans rowing, an official in uniform facing us. Certainly not the grand welcome I described to Don Francisco.

"Faith," I tell myself, and write it down to make it more real. But the word looks strange, captured in ink, like a stuffed bird, so unlike the thing with beating wings.

# 5

Helen decides she wants to have a party, and since Thanksgiving is coming round, why not have it then. "It'd save everybody a lot of trouble," Helen observes.

"You know, Helen, I might just kill you before your time," Alma growls, a mock anger that she has settled on as the best pose before her dying friend. It's either that or nonstop sobbing every time she looks at the old woman, visibly diminishing before her. They now weigh about the same one hundred pounds, "more or less," which on the big-boned Helen is a lot less weight than on the birdlike Alma.

"It's just all that cooking on Thanksgiving." Helen waves a hand vaguely in the air, a form of ellipses she is using a lot these days, meaning, "You know what I mean."

"I'm surprised she'd throw herself a party," Claudine confides in Alma one day when their visits overlap—Claudine is leaving as Alma is dropping by. "I bet it's that hospice social worker. I bet she talked Helen into having a party, a way to say good-bye to folks."

"Knowing Helen, she's having the party to make her social worker happy." Alma laughs ruefully, a sob in her throat. But the longer she knows them, the more she doubts any of the hospice women would be conned even by the likes of sweet Helen.

They have been wonderful, the hospice "team," as they call themselves, a nurse, a social worker, an aide, a nurse practitioner: Cheryl and Shawn and Sherry and Becky, a constant cycling through Helen's house of the same kind of woman, short-haired, with strong, capable arms and the most soulful eyes, a very tribal feel to them.

Occasionally, they confer with the new minister at Helen's church because Helen asks them to. "So as not to hurt his feelings," she admits. Reverend Don is young and far too enthusiastic about the afterlife, in Alma's opinion. But the hospice team has been great, not just with Helen but with Helen's friends, Alma among them, gently leading her through this whole new world, old as can be, of the dying. What's truly amazing is how they've managed to negotiate their way around Mickey. By the end of their first week of visits, the glaring former nurse marine is eating right out of their hands.

Alma supposes it has to do with how these women don't fool around with gripes and grievances. They've got work to do and they won't take no for an answer. And what is Mickey supposed to do when Cheryl, the nurse, hollers from the bedroom, "Hey, Mickey, give us a hand won't you," as she lifts his mother up so as to put a clean sheet under her?

Claudine, meanwhile, has slipped Alma some of the self-help books she has borrowed from the social worker. Manuals about dying, among them the classic Kübler-Ross, which Alma devours overnight. What baffles her is that Helen doesn't seem to have gone through all the stages the dying are supposed to go through. No denial, anger, bargaining, or depression; it's acceptance right from the start.

"We don't know that," the social worker, Becky, explains to both women during one of their impromptu conferences out in the cold in the driveway of Helen's house. Always what breaks up these "meetings" is Mickey coming out to get some wood from the woodpile or check on something in his pickup. "You gals still out here? Why don't you come in and talk by the fire where it's warm?"

Laughter and thanks and excuses. Everyone's got somewhere to go. Besides, who wants to talk about all this stuff in Helen's house, with her smells, increasingly unpleasant ones, in the air; her walker abandoned in the corner, an artifact from a time when the situation was grim but manageable.

"She probably has been going through all the stages for a while. And, besides, as you know better than I do," Becky adds, "Helen's always put a bright face on whatever is happening. So she's going to do that now. People die the way they live, in character."

It sounds like in a novel, Alma thinks. And Helen's will have a happy ending, complete with roast turkey and three kinds of pie, and for the vegetarians, a lasagna with spinach. Helen is having part of the food catered by the Hard Day's Night Cafe and the other part by a woman who used to work with her in the school lunchroom but now does Christmas office parties, weddings, anniversaries, and the occasional funeral.

MAYBE BECAUSE OF WHAT everyone is now calling Helen's "courage," Alma decides to face up to what she has been avoiding in her own life. Following up on her fax, she calls Lavinia, breathing a sigh of relief when the answering machine kicks in. But as soon as she identifies herself, Lavinia picks up.

"I don't get it," Lavinia says after a pause in which she is swallowing or smoking something. "You told me you were done. You were about to send it in."

She goes on to detail the numerous instances, three years running, in which Alma has misled her. "I know," Alma keeps saying in a small, sorry voice. This is her punishment, watching reruns of her shabby past that she thought was over.

Lavinia turns to what they can do now. Why not cobble together some of the saga chapters and call it a novel in stories? Stories seem to be making a comeback. When Alma refuses, Lavinia tries a part pep talk, part scolding approach. Alma is too hard on herself, too much of a perfectionist. Finally, Lavinia gives up. "Okay, okay. I'm not going to keep trying to talk you into it. You should call Veevee yourself. I mean, as a courtesy, if nothing else."

Lavinia sounds genuinely sad. As does Veevee after Alma jogs the young woman's memory—Veevee is at least a decade and a half younger than Alma. What is her excuse? Maybe people in cities age like dogs, one year of a New Yorker's life equals seven of a Vermonter's?

"Alma Rodríguez, you know, Fulana de Tal with the Latino saga novel?" Except she isn't Fulana de Tal and there is no saga novel.

"Of course!" Veevee laughs. Alma imagines her, blonde and beautiful, fully sprung from an F. Scott Fitzgerald novel. It makes her sad, thinking of all the heartaches this young woman is going to have to live through, until one day she ends up on the other side of a phone call, not unlike this one, apologizing for messing up.

"You want another year? I could give you two years. How about if we just tear up the contract and you hand it in when you want?"

Alma feels like crying. These women don't want her to mess up. So much good-hearted energy should be harnessed and shipped somewhere, like to her own native country. This is what HI is supposed to do, Alma reminds herself, and nine times out of ten, to hear Richard talk, it doesn't work.

But then, that one time out of ten, it does happen. And hope and history rhyme, a line in a poem she read Helen the other day. Helen is back to wanting things read to her. Alma suspects that it has less to do with Helen needing entertainment and more to do with keeping all the visitors that are coming by these days busy. Helen has so little energy. Getting herself in and out of bed, feeding herself, chewing food—just the minimal maintenance stuff exhausts her. And visiting is hard work. Especially the way Helen does it, paying attention, making the other person feel good.

"Sometimes when there's no pressure, things really start to flow," Veevee tries to persuade Alma. But as with Lavinia, Alma holds firm to her resolve. "Veevee, it's not that." Does she tell the young woman that she has lost heart? That she doesn't want to work on a product that Lavinia can peddle, Veevee sell, and some poor soul pay to read? That'll just make Veevee feel foolish, like some corrupt little cog in a wheel that is turning, turning, and going nowhere.

And it's not that either. Veevee and Lavinia, and Sherry and Cheryl and Shawn and Becky, Claudine—they keep the world running. Somebody's got to do it. Just like someone has to go to the edge and look and come back and tell about it. That was always her part, Alma thought. But what if what she has seen is not something she wants to broadcast? What if there's nothing but the still, sad music of humanity over that edge? What does she come back and tell? *We're floating on faith. We're floating on love. We, the lucky ones.*

And the rest of the poor souls? The nine failed times out of ten? The ones caught between those opposing wheels of history and hope?

"Alma?" Veevee's voice is concerned. "Are you with me? I mean, what I'm trying to say is that we'll work with you on this. Why don't you just let it rest for a few weeks, and then let's talk?"

"Sure," Alma says. Maybe if she hangs in there long enough, her publisher will be bought up by an even bigger publisher, for whom fifty grand is nothing, a small debt that can be forgiven, especially if Alma can't be traced. Fulana de Tal. Last seen on the island of Tenerife, headed west, to save the world with a certain Don Francisco.

ALMA AND EMERSON HAVE been playing phone tag for days, so next time Alma drives out by the barnlike building where the offices of HI are housed, she pulls into the parking lot. Strange to be entering Richard's stomping grounds and Richard so far away. A kind of nostalgia washes over her for those old times when she'd be joining Richard at an office party or coming to pick him up because one of their vehicles was in the shop. That first glimpse after an absence of someone you love, his face lighting up.

Now it's Emerson's face lighting up. So glad to see her. "You'd think we lived on opposite sides of the state! You're looking terrific. Did I tell you my daughter's reading your book in one of her classes?" Emerson says all the right things. He is the same age as Richard, born within days—they worked it out at a supper party—and both have the same basic, straightforward disposition: they are men of action, though a bigger engine drives Emerson, which is probably why Emerson is the head of the company while Richard is a mere site supervisor. But Richard has just taken a big step up, on-site directing, though Alma has sensed from the messages Emerson has left on her machine that he is a little worried that Richard might not be able to handle this assignment.

"I told Richard you were trying to reach him," Alma says as she sits down on the other side of Emerson's immense desk, a desktop computer to one side, a diminutive, humming portable beside it, stacks of files, a phone center with lots of options. Missing are the usual photos of wife and kids, rather *wives* and kids in Emerson's case. Emerson has led a complicated life. Just the desk makes Alma feel that the power equation is off. She needs a reason to be here. To report a phone call. To bring him news of Richard. "He said he would try to call you."

"We connected." Emerson beams her his broad, appealing smile. Everything's going to be just fine, the smile tells her. After all, the world is his apple, which he means to share with everyone. You've got to love this guy, Alma thinks. He is banking on it.

"I've been wanting to touch base with you," Emerson begins, but almost immediately he is distracted by a letter that has been brought in for him to sign. There's always a flurry of secretarial activity around him, a memo to initial, someone on the line, the file he requested being placed on one of the many piles on his desk. But Emerson is unperturbed. Alma doesn't ever remember seeing him flustered or overwhelmed. He seems to thrive on a lot of things needing his attention.

"Why don't we have lunch," he suggests just as his telephone buzzer sounds. Someone getting back to him on line 1. "So we can talk," he adds. "Give me a second."

"Sure," Alma says, though the conversation goes on and on. Somebody is very unhappy in the West Bank, and Emerson is trying to figure out how to remedy the situation. Alma gets up and strolls around the large office, looking at Emerson's collection of art objects from around the world. Everything has a story, she is sure of it, the masks, the silken veil with bangles, the mortar and pestle big enough to grind human bones.

"Sorry about that," Emerson says, sighing as he hangs up.

"Trouble?"

"No, not really." Emerson smiles his handsome smile. It would take a lot to make Emerson admit there is trouble, Alma surmises. She recalls her own beloved Richard. Trouble is a state of mind and only the weak of will live there. Even the time they went over the side of the mountain in an ice storm, the car smashing through the guardrail, floating over the edge, and then miraculously— it was a miracle!— coming to rest by a tree stump, Richard kept assuring her, "It's okay. A little ice, that's all."

"Just the usual. Personnel problems," Emerson elaborates as he grabs his leather bomber jacket and calls good-bye to the flank of secretaries up front. Nothing he wants to talk about. He wants lunch. "The steakhouse be okay?" he asks as he leads her out. It's either that or Hard Day's Night Cafe, which would seem logical. They have known each other now for the decade she has been married to Richard, and Emerson still can't get it through his head that Alma is vegetarian. "Steakhouse sounds fine," she lies. Why make a fuss? There's always salad, a big, tall glass of Bloody Mary mix. This is the trick to avoiding trouble, she thinks as she gets into Emerson's sports car. No personnel problems at all if you just go along with the boss.

BUT BY THE TIME her salad comes, Alma isn't getting along with Richard's boss. "Richard never said you were counting on my going."

Emerson's look is apologetic. "I assumed you would go. He seemed to think so, too."

"Emerson, I've got a life, you know!" Though it doesn't amount to much right now, Alma thinks. Still, it annoys her that Emerson should assume that she would go along. "Did you tell him that you were counting on my going, too?"

"Of course not. I didn't want him to feel I didn't have full confidence in him—"

"But you don't, do you?" she interrupts.

There is a hesitation, a moment in which he is assessing her as he might a proposal by someone on his staff. "I have full confidence in Richard, or I wouldn't have let him go. I just thought it would be easier with you along. You're native. You're fluent. That counts for a lot, you know."

"If that's the way you feel, you should have offered me the job."

The smile is back. "You want one?"

He's got her there. Of course, she doesn't want a job smooth-talking the locals. "Richard says there's this person who just got hired. It sounds like she's smoothing out the rough spots. Starr Bell."

"Starr's terrific." Emerson's eyes take on the soft glow of a happy memory. An intern he mentored. Did it go beyond that? Alma wonders. Emerson has been through several wives. He seems to have any number of children and stepchildren—all of whom he keeps up with, joking about tuitions, orthodontist bills, holiday schedules. A complicated family, broken, melded, amended, which Emerson seems to manage with minimal ill will all around, not unlike his style at HI.

"So, let me get this straight," Alma says, wondering if Emerson will level with her. He is not one to display his hand even in the best of times. And he's now got an anxious wife, worried about her man. "Richard's gone down to set up a green center that this drug company, Swan, that's doing clinical trials with an AIDS vaccine, is financing for what?"

"A green center is a good thing," Emerson says, as if surprised Alma should doubt this. But he knows what she means. "It's a many-pronged approach. Medical care, education, sustainability. I personally think it's the way to go: you provide a model."

"It sounds to me like sugar-coating. And I'm surprised you would go along with it, Emerson." Alma stares at her Bloody Mary mix in its short, fat glass she can't get her hand around. The drink is sweaty, making a ring on the coaster. There is a little tropical-looking umbrella posed on the brim. She feels disheartened by the picture she is putting together. Surely, Richard would be smart enough to see through some travesty green project, a front for some clinical-testing sweatshop? But no, she thinks, Richard with his goals and his projects wouldn't be deterred once his heart is set on something.

Emerson is staring down at his steak, which he has not touched. She has ruined his lunch and she doesn't care. When he glances up, he looks weary and misunderstood, a man who is trying to do good in a troubled world where the solutions are not simple. "Listen to me, Alma. And I'll back this up with statistics, studies, reports, so you don't have to take my word for it. Swan is hands-down *the* most ethical of drug companies—and I've worked with several, believe me. Not only do they have informed consent forms that every single participant has to sign, but they commit to continued treatment of all volunteers *after* the study is over. You can't just use somebody's body because they're poor and oppressed."

Alma finds herself ruing her quick temper. Emerson is a good guy. He has been a crusader for social justice in the business world from the get-go. In fact, every year a certain percentage of HI's profits goes into a fund that bails out the likes of Doctors without Borders, Save the Children, Project Hope. But even Emerson has to admit, this two-pronged project is, at best, odd: a green center helping local farmers *and* a clinic testing an AIDS vaccine? A tractor to weed the garden? "So, why aren't they testing this vaccine in the States—"

"Oh, but they are. It's just that, let's face it, AIDS is much more prevalent in other parts of the world, a lot more sick people in need of drugs, which they can get for free by entering the trials and continue to get until virological failure, and ultimately"—Emerson cocks his head as if to earmark what he's about to say—"these are the people who stand to gain the most from some breakthrough—"

"And the people who will least be able to afford those medications once they're approved!" It's her turn to interrupt.

"There you go!" He beams at her, as if this were the exact conclusion he wanted her to reach, a conclusion that proves him wrong. "Alma, don't you see? That's why these other models are important. You have to create sustainability, not just health. These countries have to get organized. Connect to global markets with green products that can bring them top dollar. Then they're players. They don't have to prostitute themselves; they don't have to be the pleasure palaces for the rich of the world."

The man is either a saint or a master of spin. And since her husband works for him, Alma has got to believe that Emerson is trying to save the world a lot of grief and given what he's got to work with, he's doing the best he can. In fact, this strange bedfellow approach is nothing new. It's everywhere these days: athletes sporting milk mustaches, beer companies promoting literacy, sports equipment chains giving free flu shots to senior citizens. There's even a lunch-meat company that once featured one of her books on their Web site. A contest aimed at attracting the sizable population of Latino customers. Win a signed book by Fulana de Tal and a year's supply of bologna. No matter that the author is vegetarian. Why make a fuss? These spin-offs sell books. Everybody stands to win. No wonder Mario González-Echavarriga went for her literary-integrity jugular.

"Oh, Emerson, I believe you. I know HI's got an amazing track record. I just want to know Richard's going to be okay." Her eyes fill in spite of herself. So much for righteous indignation. She is the weepy, tagalong wife, after all. "It just seemed like if this project is so good, why were the locals so upset with it?"

Emerson has taken a bite of his steak and it is not the way he likes it, she can tell. "Sweetheart," he'll tell the waitress later, "you know I like it rare." He nudges the plate away to show his disapproval and folds his hands before him, as if he means to pray. "That's my question, too, and believe me, I grilled Starr about this. Why were they so upset? You know what it amounts to? Rumors. Half-digested facts. They hear things and they just knee-jerk react. They don't know any better." He could be describing Alma's own reaction, politely, under the cover of the poor and the ignorant of the third world. "And you know what? I don't blame them. They've been conned before."

He stares down gloomily at his steak, and his mouth pulls to one side as if to say, And so have I, well done for rare.

AFTER LUNCH, EMERSON ASKS Alma to come up to his office a minute so he can print out some reports for her.

She would rather take off, hide her head in the sand. But she is feeling penitent on so many fronts, and this is one of them. Here she virtually accused her husband's boss of wrongdoing! Has she ruined something for Richard? she wonders. Maybe she can make it up to Emerson by becoming one of the women he mentors, an older version of Starr Bell, inspired by his soulful genius to go forth and be a force for good in the world.

She enters his office meekly. Everything seems to accuse her, including the screen saver on his big computer, the earth spinning in outer space, *Help International* unwrapping itself from it like a bandage coming off. He clicks it away, calls up file after file. He is a man intent on her conversion.

The statistics are mind-boggling and heart-stopping. Of the annual global expenditure on health care, 87 percent is spent on 16 percent of the population who represent only 7 percent of the world's sick. No wonder the drug companies want to focus on that 7 percent, refusing to manufacture drugs that could eradicate third-world epidemics but that people there can't pay for. Millions of dollars worth of antidepressants (Alma's heart sinks, thinking of her own wasteful stash); meanwhile, the pill for sleeping sickness that could eliminate the disease in sub-Saharan Africa can't be found. But AIDS, ah, AIDS has cut across those first- and third-world borders. These plagues, the great levelers, might end up inadvertently tying the world together.

"Drug companies are willing to invest in finding a solution," Emerson explains. "Okay, so maybe they're thinking about their profit margins in the wealthy countries, but you know what? Everyone stands to benefit."

It's this conclusion Alma doesn't quite get to with Emerson. How poor countries are going to benefit from a silver bullet that's so expensive.

"What?" Emerson has suddenly realized Alma is not with him. "You don't believe me?"

"Dinero," Alma says simply. Emerson has a working knowledge of a half-dozen languages, and surely the word for money is one he is familiar with in all of them. "Who is going to make sure—once the third-world trials are over—that the poor folks who can't afford it get the vaccine?"

"People like you and me," Emerson says, pointing to her, then himself. It's so refreshingly naive, she almost laughs in joyful glee. But under the joy, she feels uneasy. How can this guy be running a top-notch international aid company and think like this? Robin Hood in a pinstriped suit. Except it's Vermont. He's wearing fancy dress jeans and a bomber jacket. Her beloved is now in the hands of this possible messiah or madman, she can't be sure. But one thing she does know (this much history she has absorbed): in any salvation scenario there are bound to be casualties.

"Think about it, Alma, seriously. In this world where we're all so interconnected—travel, migrations, e-mail—you're going to tell me that we in the first world will have a vaccine for AIDS, and we're going to keep it to ourselves. Nope. The world won't stand for it. You and I won't stand for it."

He's damn right. She finds herself nodding agreement.

"But we've got to go at it step by step. Paul Farmer calls it the long defeat, fighting the long defeat, making common cause with the losers. But you know what? We're going to win. But first we've got to help the Pharmas find the solution."

"Yeah," she says, overcome by his passionate intensity. "We have to." This guy could be Balmis, she thinks. Then who is Richard? Who is she?

"And meanwhile, while the testing is going on, the DR ends up with a green center. Folks participating in the study get free treatment. This is just the beginning, Alma."

She's looking over his shoulder as he's calling up Web site after Web site on his big computer, studies he keeps printing out for her. Already her hands are full. She's not going to read all this stuff. In fact, she's going to put it in her recycle box and use it for grocery lists, to fill the fax machine for printouts of Richard's faxes. To make hard copies of her own musings about Isabel, the orphans, Balmis.

"Emerson, really, this is enough." She tries to stop him, but he has already pressed the button, and his printer is jetting out a copy of yet another article.

"Last one, promise!" He laughs, as he collects the printout and staples it together for her. Should she tell him not to staple it, that it's going straight into the recycle box, that she has already decided what he has probably been hoping for all along, she is going to join Richard?

"Just one last question," Alma says, as the phone buzzer goes off. "Does Swan know what you're up to?" They can't know this guy's not just working for them. He's trying to save the world!

Emerson lifts his eyebrows. The smile is vague. Alma doesn't live in his world, and her ideas about it are formed by biased, left-hearted compatriots, Tera and friends, the *Nation*, Richard after hours. She doesn't know how to read between the lines of the powerful.

"Mr. Armstrong, Mozambique is on line 2."

"How about Starr," Alma persists. "Does she know?"

"Starr is terrific." Emerson beams his disarming smile. He lifts a hand in farewell and turns his attention to the receiver at his ear. "Emerson here. What's up?"

Alma feels shaky as she walks out of the offices of Help International, loaded down with the statistics of sadness. Hope and history have to rhyme. Emerson is working toward it; Tera is working toward it, Richard. Alma should be, too! But she has gotten in her own way—no one else to blame. She recalls how when Richard's dad was dying, a man she dearly loved, she hovered over him in the hospital, reluctant even when visiting time was up to leave him alone. In his final hours, he became agitated, hallucinating that he was driving a runaway car. He kept gripping the wheel, struggling to get control of this imaginary vehicle, headed for death. "Oh, Dad!" Alma wept. "How can I help?"

And the answer came back to her, his last words on earth, which stung with their appropriateness, "Just get out of the way!"

ON THE WAY HOME, Alma decides to drop in on Helen. She's debating whether to tell Helen of her plan to join Richard. One thing for sure, Alma will stick around until after Thanksgiving. No way she is going to miss Helen's good-bye party. But afterward, well, Helen will understand. She has plenty of people around—maybe too many—and as the team has explained, toward the end people are just plain tired. All their systems are shutting down. Family members and friends should not feel hurt if a loved one only wants one or two people by her side. All the more reason to tell Helen now, so she knows that Alma might not be around for the final good-bye.

One person she is sure she can't tell ahead of time is Richard. It has to be a surprise. Otherwise, he will surely say no. Especially if he senses her decision has anything to do with even the tiniest doubt about his competence. His safety. Her jealousy. Yes, she might as well admit it to herself, she doesn't like the idea of this terrific Starr hanging out with her beloved, who goes on lonely after-dinner strolls through the village. She has given him his own key to the Swan office. What next? If her husband runs into trouble with her countrymen, Alma wants to be the one to save him. She feels ashamed of her small-minded intention. So much for altruism as her sole motivation.

Alma knocks on Helen's door. Another change, knocking, instead of what used to be her knock: opening the door and calling out, Helen! And it's not only because Mickey and other people are around. Alma feels a new formality around Helen. A respect due to the dying, which is what Helen has become, instead of her old friend whose house she can walk into, whose fridge she can open and help herself to its contents.

When no one answers or calls out for her to come in, Alma nudges the door open. Angry voices are coming from the back of the house, Mickey's and, now and then, Helen's. A fight is going on.

"Please, Mickey, please," Helen is pleading. "I can't let you do this."

"You can, but you won't help me," Mickey accuses. What a time to be asking Helen for help! Doesn't Mickey know his mother is at death's door? The doctor has amended his hopeful prognosis of six months. Helen might not last the year. The guy is unbalanced, Helen as much as said so. With a queasy feeling in her gut, Alma remembers Tera's remark about Mickey's being up to something.

She considers calling out. Surely, that would break up the argument. But then, after Alma leaves, Helen will be left in whatever untenable situation she is in. And knowing Helen, she won't complain about it. Alma should find out what Mickey is up to and report him to the team. They'll know what to do with the former nurse marine. They're trained to handle difficult situations at these dire junctions when, so they've explained, unfinished family business is likely to get stirred up again.

"I always want to help you. I do." Helen sounds so frail. What is she doing up? Has she returned to using her walker? "But this thing is crazy, Mickey. You can't let Hannah talk you into this!"

Hannah . . . Hannah. The name sounds familiar, but Alma is too caught up trying to figure out what crazy thing Mickey is talking about to unravel who this Hannah person might be.

"Forget it, okay? Just forget it! I knew you wouldn't do it. You can be everybody else's mother! But you won't help your own son!"

Helen is sobbing now. Alma cannot bear to hear her old friend cry this way. She feels pulled to the rescue as a mother might by the sound of her infant wailing in another room. "Hello!" Alma calls out. "Helen! It's me! Hello!"

A deathly silence follows her call. Alma walks down the front hall, craning her neck to look into the empty living room. She is pretty sure the voices were coming from the kitchen.

In a matter of seconds that seem endless, she hears the clomping of Helen's walker on the linoleum. Then the bang of the back door. In a moment Helen will turn that corner into the hall, her face distraught; her eyes red; her thin, white hair falling out of its plaintive ponytail; and there's a fifty-fifty chance that when Alma asks her, "Helen, are you all right?" the old woman will say, "I'm fine, dear."

And it's as she is waiting for this moment that Alma's memory finally makes the connection. The AIDS caller was named Hannah, so Tera said. Hannah McSomething. There can't be two of them. Hannah McMullen, Mickey's sick wife!

When Helen comes into view, Alma doesn't even ask. "I heard the fighting, Helen," she confesses. "You shouldn't have to put up with this."

The old woman bows her head, sobbing inside her walker.

ALMA IS STILL AIMING on leaving after Thanksgiving to join Richard, but she keeps delaying calling the airlines. She wants to be sure Helen will be all right. Surprisingly, Helen has been on the upswing since the Mickey incident. Maybe Helen will stick around for a lot longer than the doctor predicted. Maybe fighting with her son gives her a reason to go on living— she can't die until she makes peace with him.

Alma has not been able to pin Helen down on what the fight was about. Helen has been vague. Mickey was upset because he wants to take care of his mother himself, wants this whole team of busybody women to back off.

"Families shouldn't treat families." Alma reminds Helen. Is this really what the fight was about? It sounds fishy. Alma is sure she heard Mickey asking for Helen's help, not asking to take care of her. "Besides, Mickey hasn't even been practicing as a nurse, has he?"

Helen isn't sure. She hasn't kept up with the particulars of her son's life. He still has some friends in the medical field. They get him jobs from time to time. One of these friends is a medical missionary. Another heads a lab where Mickey last worked. Helen is straying from the issue at hand. What does Mickey want? "He wants . . ." Helen waves her hand vaguely, gets weepy again. She won't say. No doubt she will protect Mickey till the bitter end. He is her son, the boy who won the 4-H contest and who now needs her help. "Has anybody heard from him?" Helen asks. The plaintive upward tilt of the old woman's face reminds Alma of being young, in love with someone who was going to break her heart.

No one has seen or heard from Mickey. He hasn't come back to the house since the day of the incident. Claudine with her local connections makes a bunch of phone calls and finds out from Mickey's wife's family that Hannah has left the treatment center. No law's been broken as she was released into the custody of her husband. She had been doing very well, but the worry is that she might stop her medications and have another full-blown psychotic breakdown. And, yes, this Hannah is the very same woman who was making disturbing phone calls, claiming she had AIDS. She was tested at the center, and the results were negative. But she insists that she has an invisible strain of the disease, which won't show up on any test. She has brought it to Vermont, to infect everyone she calls, an AIDS of conscience that will wake up this country as to how the rest of the world is dying for lack of a little of the too much we have here. Except for strategy, Alma thinks, this woman sounds like Tera. Except for the rage, Alma finds herself agreeing with what both women have to say.

"Things are really crazy around here," she tells Richard when he reaches her late one night. She feels gratified that he is calling her, missing her at bedtime. It's her and only her he wants, why should she doubt this? She fills him in on the Mickey fight and the follow-up. Her AIDS caller was Mickey's wife! "The very same woman, can you believe it?"

"I don't know," Richard says. "I used to think Vermont was a safe place. Maybe you should come down here?"

Is he serious? Has he read her mind? "Don't think I haven't been thinking about it."

"But it sounds like you've started on something new?"

"Not really." Alma has learned her lesson about stringing people along with the promise of a novel she hasn't written. She has already told Richard about the call with Lavinia, with Veevee. Richard is all for waiting and offering Veevee whatever Alma ends up writing. Fifty grand is a lot of money.

"How about that smallpox story you faxed me?"

"It's just an idea." Who is she kidding? The story is already inside her, string in the labyrinth, as she makes her blind way out into that big-hearted life she wants to be living with him.

"Well, any time you want to come down."

"I just want to be sure Helen's going to be okay." She had been doing so well after the Mickey incident. But she has taken a downturn again. The doctor says Helen should consider having hospice in the hospital. "Claudine and I were over there last night talking to her. I know she really doesn't want to go, but she is saying yes, she doesn't want to be a bother to all of us."

"My wife, Florence Nightingale." Richard laughs, but Alma can tell he is only half joking.

Florence Nightingale with the dark soul, full of self-doubt and mixed motives. But there are worse things to be in the world, Alma decides. Look at Mickey, making a dying woman's last days miserable. The spark is gone from Helen's eye. The party is called off. She is going to die as she has lived for the last few decades. Without her son.

ALMA OFFERS TO SPEND Thanksgiving with Helen. Tera's off to DC on a march with Paul and Richard is a world away. "We're the two turkey orphans," Alma teases Helen, who smiles weakly after the lapse of a second. That lapse reminds Alma of Mickey's slow absorption of conversation, but in Helen's case it is the slowing down of her brain. What was it the team called it? All systems are shutting down. The body is saving its energy for the things that must absolutely be working for life to go on. Soon those, too, will stop, and like the astronauts in their fragile capsule, Helen will go behind the moon. But she won't be coming round again.

As for her trip, Alma has gone back to the original plan. She'll fly down for Christmas at her parents' condo in Miami, where she'll meet up with Richard. There she'll present him with his Christmas gift: she will be joining him for the next three, four months. Surprise! She hopes it will be a surprise he wants. Every phone call, he mentions that he's missing her lots, that she sure would be welcome if she decides to come, that he doesn't want to pressure her. And these last few days, he has sounded downright forlorn. Holiday blues kicking in, no doubt. Since his divorce, the boys have always spent Thanksgiving with their father, Christmas with their mother. Even now that they are grown men, the "tradition" has continued, the two older boys driving up from the city with their current girlfriends, the tumbleweed Sam flying in from wherever he is currently living. But this year Richard will be eating his yucca and plantains and fried cheese all alone on a Dominican mountainside. Bienvenido is in the capital attending a workshop. Starr is back in Texas for a family wedding, staying on for Thanksgiving.

Alma's new plan makes a lot more sense all around. Richard will have had almost two months to get settled in, making the project his. And Alma will have three more weeks to be with Helen. It seems the mantle has fallen on her, maybe by default: Alma is the one Helen seems to want around as her energy is diminishing. "Read to me," Helen will say. "Anything you want," she answers when Alma asks what kind of book Helen would like. So Alma reads her what she is writing, the story of Balmis and Isabel and the orphan carriers and the wide Atlantic they have just finished crossing. Helen mostly dozes. But, like a child, if Alma stops for more than a few moments, Helen's eyes open. "Is it already over?" she asks.

EARLY THANKSGIVING AFTERNOON, on the way to Helen's, Alma stops at Jerry's Market for the jellied cranberry sauce Helen likes. Alma thought of making the sauce from scratch—can't be that hard—but Helen insisted she really likes the canned brand. The truth is, Helen is unlikely to eat more than a tiny spoonful. She just is not hungry anymore and eating in general makes her feel sick. Stomach and intestines signing off. Roger. Next to go will be the synapses in her head, then the muscles of her heart. Alma finds herself torn, wanting Helen to hang on and then wanting Helen to die before the old woman suffers any more than she has to, before Alma leaves for four months, heartsick that she isn't waiting until Helen is done with her dying before going on with her life.

As Alma turns into the aisle where the woman at the cashier said she'd find the jellied cranberry sauce—there it is, only one brand, this is a mom-and-pop store, after all—she sees Mickey, coming up from the back of the store, swinging the red plastic grocery basket as if he's on a picnic. By his side, an arm through his, is a tall, thin blonde woman who looks almost ethereal in the very paleness of her coloring. For a moment, Alma considers turning on her heels, pretending she

hasn't seen them. What can she say to Mickey? You've made your mom
miserable? What good will that do? What if the prodigal son repents
and decides to return to the fold? Can that be good for Helen?

Mickey spots her and his face lights up. He murmurs something to
the woman at his side, who turns to look at Alma. There is nothing for
Alma to do but wait as they approach her.

"Hey!" Mickey stops that one step closer than Alma likes for people
to stand talking to her. Hannah comes up beside him, smiling, a kind
of free-floating smile, maybe medicated, maybe shy.

"Hello, Mickey," Alma says briskly. Should she tell him she's on her
way to have Thanksgiving with his dying mother? Don't be mean,
Alma cautions herself. This is Helen's son. The boy on the refrigerator. But Alma is still too upset with Mickey to care if he was once that
boy. All she knows is that he is now the man making Helen's last days
miserable.

"Sorry about the other day," Mickey says. He must have recognized
her voice from the front hall. His penitence, if indeed it is penitence,
surprises her. He has always seemed implacable in his oddness. Well,
if he is sorry, it's not Alma he should be apologizing to, but his
mother.

"Your mother is very sick," she says. "She doesn't have much longer
to live."

"Poor Helen," the woman says. Her voice is surprisingly normal-
sounding, not the ugly voice that called down curses on the other end
of the line. But this must be Hannah. Who else could she be? Alma
waits for Mickey to introduce his wife, but those civilities are beyond
him. And, at this moment, beyond her.

Mickey is watching Alma with that look that pulls her in, so that she
feels trapped in his mind, a mind she doesn't understand, so she can't
pick the lock, let herself out. She looks away, her eye caught by the
two frozen turkey dinners in his basket. Jesus. The boy is back, the
4-H kid who will grow up to live a pitiful life.

"Your mom's very sad," Alma says in a kindlier tone. "She needs to
make peace with you so she can die in peace." The team is going to kill

her! How dare Alma take it upon herself to engineer a reconciliation between a dying woman too weak to get through a whole meal and her angry son? Dry tinder to his lit fuse! But Helen would never forgive Alma if she knew that Alma had a chance to bring her boy home and Alma didn't do it.

Mickey is still watching her, but his eyes, Helen's eyes, glisten with tears. If Alma has been hard on him, it was only in telling him the truth he needs to hear.

"We just called Helen." Hannah nods to the front of the store, where an old rotary phone, not unlike Tera's, is mounted on the wall, a little sign above it advising customers to limit themselves to short calls, please, no long distance. Homey touches abound throughout the store. There is a bulletin board with Polaroids of the latest newborns. Raffle tickets for sale to sponsor the local ball team. The place has a following. Today it is empty. But now and then someone hurries in. A convenience to our customers, Alma has heard the woman say about the store being open on Thanksgiving Day. "But there was no answer."

No answer? Alma's heart quickens. "I just spoke to Helen about an hour ago." Could something have happened since then? Helen had said that she was feeling better. It could be she is napping or didn't get to the phone on time. That happens a lot. There is no jack in the bedroom, and though Claudine has loaned Helen a portable, Helen often knocks it over as she flails around trying to reach it. More than once, Alma has had to get down on all fours to retrieve it from under the bed or the chest of drawers by the door.

"Well, I'm going over there right now," Alma says, cranberry sauce can in hand. She'd better hurry, just in case. But, as she turns to go, it occurs to her that if Helen is dying this might be the last chance to see her son. She turns back. "You want to come?"

She can tell from Hannah's brightened look that this is precisely what she had in mind. It's Mickey who seems unsure, scanning the shelves as if avoiding Alma's gaze, for once. From what she's seen, Alma would say that Hannah is a lot more with it than Mickey. But then Hannah's probably still on her meds. And Helen is Mickey's mother. So much easier to access equanimity toward someone else's painful childhood.

Mickey turns his eyes back on her. What he says surprises her. "I don't have anything for her."

Of course, Alma thinks. That was always the pattern. Mickey came back with a gift, his peace offering. It could be he is speaking metaphorically, he has nothing left in his heart to give his mother, but Alma takes him at his word, his literal word. "Here," she says, handing him the can of cranberry sauce. It's not flatware from Thailand or a painted fan from Taiwan or a silver spoon from Ireland. "She said this was all she wanted for Thanksgiving. That and seeing you." Since when did Alma earn the right to make a story out of other people's lives?

Mickey stares at the can in his hand for a long moment, then sets it in the basket. This must mean he is coming.

"My name is Hannah," the woman says, oddly introducing herself just as they are parting. She holds out a wan hand for Alma. "Mickey's told me all about you."

For some reason, Alma doesn't like the sound of this. What all is there for Mickey to tell about? A few driveway and hallway conversations. She could come back to Hannah with her own rejoinder. I'm one of the people you infected with your psychic AIDS. Don't be mean, Alma reminds herself. This is Helen's daughter-in-law. And they are all about to have Thanksgiving together. Thanks to Alma.

LATER, THE SEQUENCE OF events will seem like a historic film clip of a moment gone awry, to be played over and over by the networks, the gunshot incredibly hitting the president in his motorcade, the airplanes impossibly flying into the towers.

Alma will replay these Thanksgiving moments over and over, trying to register that indeed unfortunate things do happen on a balmy November day with the sky slightly overcast, too warm for children to be skating on the pond at the edge of the woods. She is wearing only a sweater, and as she drives by on her way to Helen's she notices the opened windows in the houses along the road. It must be downright hot inside with all the baking going on.

The pickup pulls in beside her car, but Alma is already at the door knocking, not expecting Helen to answer, wondering if to go in first and alert her. She waves to Mickey and Hannah, then enters the house, calling out in the old way, "Helen, it's me!" No answer. She hurries toward the bedroom, trying to stay calm, an apprehensive sense growing in her gut, because already Alma knows what she will see, although she will want to rewind to the very moment and look at it in disbelief, Helen unconscious on the floor, maybe en route to the phone, who knows, but still alive, still breathing, which is why Alma cries out, "Helen! Helen!" as if she can bring Helen back if only she calls out loud enough.

Mickey is suddenly beside her, no lapsing synapses now, springing into action—the nurse marine under fire—taking a pulse, checking Helen's vital signs, calling to Hannah to bring him something from his pickup, in the glove compartment, a first-aid kit, his nurse bag, Alma can't be sure, because meanwhile she is crawling around, searching for the portable, which she finds right where it should be, by Helen's bedside. She steps out in the hall to call 911 for an ambulance, suspecting Mickey might not approve and not caring to ask him either.

And here is another moment to rewind and look at, this moment with the hysterical sound of the sirens coming closer, stopping at their very driveway, and Mickey looking up startled from the bed where he has carried his mother, "Did you call an ambulance?" as if there were something so very wrong in calling for help when someone has collapsed!

Then the huge bangs at the door, and Alma transfixed, all of her focused on that syringe in Mickey's hand, wondering, What the hell is Mickey about to inject Helen with? And maybe it's because both Hannah, standing on the other side, and Mickey, sitting on this side of the bed, are glaring at the offending portable in her hand that Alma gets the idea, which is too trigger-quick a response to be a full-blown idea, of hurling the phone at Mickey and knocking the syringe out of his hand, and then as he cries out, racing down the hall, flinging the door open, grabbing the paramedics by the arms, screaming, "Please, please, help, he's trying to kill her!"

The two men look around, alarmed. "Who? What?"

But Alma doesn't answer because already she is running back down the hall, the two men behind her, into the bedroom, where they find Mickey on his knees picking up the broken pieces of whatever the phone knocked out of his hands, dabbing at the floor with the towel he had used to wipe Helen's face.

"What is wrong with you?" Mickey stumbles to his feet and comes toward her, as the two paramedics, animal instinct kicking in, lunge toward the other male in the room. They each grab Mickey by an arm. Meanwhile, a third man, the driver, has hurried in and is calling the police on his cell phone, as Alma sobs out that Mickey was about to give his mother an injection when he isn't her doctor. And everyone sort of calming down when she says so and looking at her, as if to say, Is that all?

"He's not her doctor," she repeats, sobbing. "They've been estranged. He shouldn't be treating her." Each accusation less vehement than the one before, because Alma is already asking herself if she hasn't overreacted after all.

What exonerates her: the commotion that ensues when the paramedics try to approach the bed and Mickey plants himself before them, refusing to let them get near his mother. One of the paramedics—the one who keeps advising everyone to stay calm—tries to go around him, but Mickey swings, and so the guy backs off, and Hannah starts to scream, and the paramedic guy holds up both hands and says, "Hey, buddy, we're just trying to help out. Let's take it easy, okay?"

Then there are more sirens as the sheriff, who lives only a mile away—his cruiser always parked front end out in his driveway giving Alma a scare when she is speeding home the back way—pulls in, followed by his deputy, and the men all start trying to talk to Mickey, who takes a few more swings and manages only to hit the sheriff, who brings Mickey down with him, the deputy diving on top, securing

Mickey, handcuffing him, leading him out the door to the cruiser, the sheriff following, massaging his bruised jaw.

And Alma will rewind to this crazed and wild moment because otherwise she might miss Hannah, slinking into the shadows, terrified, mute, after what seemed an interminable bout of screaming, and slipping out of the bedroom just as the thought crosses Alma's mind that Hannah has been released into the custody of her husband who is now in the sheriff's custody, and will she be all right?

The paramedics spring into swift action, checking on Helen, hooking her up to oxygen, lifting her onto a stretcher that materializes from who knows where, and rolling her out, Alma hurrying alongside, trying to get a hold of Helen's hand, thinking, Oh Helen, forgive me, what a miserable last Thanksgiving I've brought to your house.

AT THE HOSPITAL, THE sheriff drops by to get Alma's testimony of what she witnessed at the Marshall residence. Alma doesn't know what to say. She doesn't want to get Mickey into any more trouble than he's already in. The sheriff's jaw is swollen. "Is it broken?" Alma asks. "It's fine," he says curtly. He doesn't want to talk about it. He wants to talk about what Alma saw over at Helen's house, and he is getting increasingly impatient with her vague answers, with her not being sure.

"I want to call someone from Helen's hospice team," Alma tells him. He looks too young to be a sheriff, with his big hands and pink skin showing under his severe crew cut. A half century ago he would have been milking cows on his father's farm. Now he has a cruiser and at his hip a holster with what looks like a toy gun.

Claudine drives over, followed by Becky and Shawn, little pieces of pie crumbs still in the laps of their skirts and pants, vague scent of food on their breath. A little later Cheryl joins them. Sherry is out of town. No one thinks to call Reverend Don. Who wants a twenty-something-year-old trying to cheer them all up in the waiting room with talk of paradise?

"I made a mistake," Alma admits to the assembled team. "I never should have invited Mickey over." And then she tells them the whole story, how she can't swear that Mickey was going to harm his mother, just that he was about to inject Helen with some medication that could have been harmless. "I mean he is a nurse. Maybe I just panicked." The deputy and another officer have been back to the house, and no one has come up with what they are calling hard evidence, the syringe, its contents. As for Hannah, she has vanished in the pickup, and there is a call out to the state police to stop her if they find her.

The doctor on call comes out to announce to the hodgepodge collection of people in the waiting room that Helen is stable. She has had a ministroke, but she is going to be okay.

Okay? Alma wonders if the doctor even knows Helen has cancer. Maybe he doesn't realize how bad things are. Helen has told Alma that she has a living will. Should Alma bring that up now?

"Nothing more to do tonight," the doctor advises the team. He seems weary, bags under his eyes, his hair looks unwashed. What a life, bringing people news of their mortality. "Why don't we all touch base tomorrow?"

Soon after the doctor leaves, the group disperses as if taking his advice. Claudine better get back to her girls and Dwayne and both their assembled families. "You all take care." Shawn follows. "You going to be all right?" Becky asks Alma, before taking off herself. Now that it's dark outside, the large picture window in the waiting room reflects all these leave-takings. The clouds have dispersed. The night is turning cold. The stars are sharp-edged, numerous, bold.

Before Alma leaves, she asks the on-duty nurse if she can just go in a minute to say good-bye to Helen.

The woman glances up from her island where she has been checking paperwork. She is tired, overworked. The cheerful demeanor of a few hours ago is gone. All of this commotion she has heard about is nothing that can be helpful to her patient. "It's better if she rests," she tells Alma, but then, maybe because it's Thanksgiving—a cutout turkey hangs from an orange streamer above her head—she relents. "She was asking for Mickey." Maybe the nurse thinks Alma is Mickey? Alma holds her tongue.

The room is dark except for the lighted-up dials of machines, the indirect light falling in from the hall. Helen is getting oxygen, her arm's hooked up to an IV. Tubes crisscross the bed, connecting Helen to sundry ticking machines. As Alma looks for a patch of un-occupied skin to stroke, Helen's eyes open, and her scared and sorry look is the saddest thing in the world.

"You just had a little setback," Alma whispers. "The doctor said you'll be home in no time."

Helen's eyes close, but from the edges of them tears roll out. This isn't what Helen wants, Alma thinks. Whatever Mickey was going to give her in that injection was probably a lot better than this. Alma wonders if Helen knows what is going on. Could she have heard the whole commotion in her house even if she'd had a stroke?

The nurse is at the door. Time to go. Alma squeezes Helen's hand. "I'm sorry, Helen," she says, brushing her lips against Helen's forehead. It feels damp, smells cold-creamy, Helen's smell the hospital odors haven't completely obscured. "Everything's going to be okay," she adds, lamely.

Pulling into the driveway of her dark house, Alma wants Richard to be home so much, she could weep. She wants to tell him the story of this crazy day, so he can tell her that she did the right thing, that she had no way of knowing what Mickey was up to. It is a little after mid-night. Maybe she'll try calling him. Maybe luck is on her side and Richard'll just happen to be in the Swan office, reading by the office's generator light, who knows. Or maybe she'll dispense with long dis-tance altogether and instead call the airlines, buy a ticket, get on a plane tomorrow, be gone by the time the sheriff comes by to get her sworn testimony, before Mickey is released on bail.

She walks into the house, feeling unsure, shaken, suddenly fright-ened: of Mickey, of Hannah, of this bad blood in the air. The answer-ing machine is emitting its reassuring beep that means a message is waiting for her. Four to be exact. She plays them in the dark, the voices seeming strangely present. Happy Thanksgiving from her par-ents! Happy Thanksgiving from David and Ben, together in New York!

How sweet of them to remember her. Sam out in San Francisco will probably not call, as his father's not around. The third message makes her breath catch. Emerson. His voice too calm, controlled. Could Alma please call him no matter what time she gets in. He gives her his cell phone number, which Alma scrambles to write down, then several alternative numbers in case she doesn't get through on his cell.

His cell phone number goes right into voice mail. He's probably talking to someone else. "Emerson, I'm home. Please call me." The other numbers are busy. But Alma feels so desperate she keeps trying one number after another, reminding herself of how Emerson closed his message. "Richard is okay. I don't want you to worry about that. But do call me no matter what time you get in."

Finally, the call goes through. The phone is ringing at his end.

"Emerson here," Emerson answers. And then he tells her, how Richard is okay, but there's been some trouble at the center. The locals have taken it over, and Richard, her Richard, is a hostage.

"What do you mean, a hostage?" Alma manages to get out stupidly. She knows what a hostage is. "What do they want?" Whoever these angry people are, they can have anything they want—this house, the car, the pickup, all of her royalties for the rest of her writing life, anything, anything, in exchange for Richard.

"They want the testing to stop. The clinic turned into a clinic for locals. The chance to tell the world their story." Emerson sighs as if he's heard all this before. "I'm leaving tomorrow," he adds. "The head of International Research from Swan is joining me. Starr'll meet us there."

"I'm going with you."

"I thought you might want to," Emerson says. Maybe he is thinking what she is thinking. This would not be happening if Alma had gone along with Richard in the first place. "I booked you a seat, too." Emerson'll meet her at the airport in a few hours, early-bird flight to Newark, connecting to the island.

After the call, Alma races upstairs, stuffing clothes wildly in a bag. What to pack? Underwear-pants-tops, a nice dress in case—in case what?—hiking shoes–socks–nightgown–toothbrush, her jewelry bag.

Maybe she can trade Richard for her old charm bracelet, the gold hoops he surprised her with on their last anniversary, the pearl necklace Mamasita and Papote gave her when she graduated from college. Closer to dawn, she calls Claudine but gets her machine, probably the family is sleeping in. Alma leaves the clinic number because what other place can she tell Claudine to call in case anything happens to Helen? How to reach Tera? Tera on the protest circuit with no answering machine at home! Alma scribbles her best friend a note. Maybe by the time Tera gets it, Alma will be home with Richard. As for her stepsons? Alma decides not to alarm them, to wait until they need to know.

It's in her wild zigzags through the house that Alma remembers to listen to the fourth message she had ignored. A woman's garbled voice, a truck roaring by, a roadside phone. "Please don't let them hurt Mickey. He was just trying to do what's right."

Hannah! Alma feels a surge of anger. *Are you happy now that your curse is working? Is this what you wanted?* But what good will it do to rage at this distraught and scared woman, as scared and distraught as Alma is herself? They are all now hurtling over the edge, floating on faith, floating on love. Nothing for Alma to do but make a deal with Helen's God. Mickey for Richard, both men back in the arms of the women who love them, unharmed.

# V

WHEN THE SMALL BOAT was within earshot, our captain called down the name of our ship.

"We are the Royal Philanthropic Expedition of the Vaccine!" Don Francisco added. "We've come in peace!" Surely, the letter he had written from Tenerife and sent ahead by packet ship to Puerto Rico had arrived. Where was our welcome?

We were lined up in our uniforms, the boys and I, looking toward the calm bay, the city of San Juan, the green hills beyond. Land, land, land! How beautiful and unreal it seemed after a month at sea. For the moment this was welcome enough, at least for me.

Don Francisco's face was flushed. He seemed tired and feverish. Again it struck me that with the prize almost within reach, his faith was faltering.

"They are probably being cautious," Captain del Barco assured him. "False flags have been flown before." He went on to explain that a few years ago, San Juan had been attacked by the English. In fact, the present governor had distinguished himself in that battle. And though San Juan had been victorious, even victors remain wary.

Our director was shaking his head, unconvinced. Perhaps he already had an inkling of what awaited us. So much time and money and passion had gone into this enterprise. Anything short of a magnificent welcome would have disappointed him.

I had been worrying about other things. After this last round, only Benito would be left to vaccinate. Our task was almost finished. Would we return with the *María Pita* to Spain after its final stop in Veracruz—the mate had stammered a question about my plans, as if his own depended on mine—or continue with Don Francisco as far as Mexico City and part ways there? No matter where, the inevitable was bound to come.

And yet, when I saw him so downcast, I worried not only for him but for the future of our expedition. This worry grew in the ensuing weeks as our director's conduct began to threaten the very spirit of our mission. That is why I did not continue writing in my book. I did not want there to be a record of our fiasco in Puerto Rico.

I, too, had an inkling of what was to come. What was to be my mission from now on.

THE HOUSE WAS ELEGANT and large, no spare convent or plain-spoken public building; we were to be housed in our very own mansion. The cook came out, a Creole woman, along with a handful of servants to welcome us. Several uniformed militiamen were posted at the door, I suppose to protect our royal persons!

The boys' eyes were round with wonder. All the stories I had told them on board the ship were coming true. Even I was half convinced that perhaps I had foreseen the future.

A wonderful smell was wafting from the kitchen, onions frying, meat roasting. My mouth watered at the prospect of a meal of savory, fresh food. Soon I would indulge in a bath, soaking the salty stickiness out of my skin and hair. How luscious that would feel! We had not drowned at sea, terra firma was under our feet. I was a happy woman.

Our director had gone ahead in the first carriage, so that as we came in the entryway, he was descending the stairs. His face had not lost its flushed, weary cast. I hoped he was not falling ill. He was not, after all, a young man.

"There are no sheets on our beds," I heard him tell the emissary who had rowed out to the ship.

"No sheets on the bed?" Señor Mexía was perplexed. Someone else had been in charge of that detail. Of course, he would attend to it. But first things first. Governor Castro and Bishop Arizmendi and Dr. Oller would soon be here to greet our party personally.

Dr. Francisco shrugged, unappeased. No grand reception had awaited us at the docks. No processional to the cathedral for a Te Deum, as he had specified in his letter. We looked silly in our fancy attire, people dressed up for a grand occasion that had not transpired. "Did the governor not receive the Tenerife mail?"

Señor Mexía could not say except to say how glad the governor was that we were here. Poor man, I thought, trying to pacify a wounded dignitary.

"Where are we to conduct the vaccinations?" Don Francisco wanted to know. "I sent instructions not to hold the sessions in the hospital. People will not come. Hospitals are for the ill. We want the vaccine to be thought of as an agent of health."

Señor Mexía nodded every assurance he could.

But our director ranted on. It was a rant. The large swath of sunlight through the windows brought him no joy. The inside of the house opened into an inner courtyard from which a lovely breeze was blowing. Water splashed from a fountain beside a tree with red blossoms like flames whose like I had never seen before.

"We need to start vaccinating immediately. Have the boys I requested been selected?"

Señor Mexía faltered and looked unsure of what to say. "The governor will explain everything," he assured our director with a nervous smile.

Now I was intrigued. What was going on? Our reception had been nothing short of courteous but, upon reflection, in no way remarkable. As if what we had risked our lives to bring was a kind but unnecessary trifle. As if we had come to paradise, offering salvation.

From managing La Casa for many years, I had learned where one could go for whatever one needed to know. At the first opportunity, I slipped away, following my nose toward the smell of our wonderful dinner cooking. Most of the servants had withdrawn to the back of the house and were sitting about the kitchen. They scrambled to their feet at attention when I came in.

I gestured for them to take their seats. "It has been so long since I smelled such delicious smells!" I exclaimed. "It is a meal just to smell them!"

Everyone watched me, mouths agape. I was a strange creature. A

Spaniard who spoke a Spanish only vaguely recognizable to their Creole ears. A woman who had come with a medicine for the smallpox but who had obviously not had the benefit of the cure herself. For the first time in months, I felt conscious of my scarred face. But I would never go back to covering myself. Somewhere, midsea, I had lost that much of my vanity.

At my heels, Benito came running in. "Mamá!" he called. He had something to show me, a flower dropped from the flame tree. It was then I realized I had not seen a flower for weeks. It seemed a heartbreakingly beautiful thing.

When I glanced up again, the guarded looks had vanished. Strange woman or not, we shared a stronger bond, motherhood. As they indulged me with a taste of the roast pork and a slice of pineapple for the boy, I began to ask questions.

THE SOUND OF BLOWING trumpets drew me back to the front room. Governor Castro was entering the front parlor, a lovely little girl in either hand, his two young daughters, each bearing a posy for Don Francisco. His wife, Doña María Teresa, sent her greetings. She would receive Don Francisco and the members of his expedition this evening for a banquet.

The governor motioned for a man about our director's age to step forward. "Dr. Oller," he introduced himself, giving our director a curt, correct bow as if he did not want to be too enthusiastic and be deemed a provincial. "We are honored by your visit."

A bishop in a scarlet robe that matched the blossoms on the flame tree spread his arms in a blessing. When he was done, he embraced our director warmly. Bishop Arizmendi had been born on the island and did not have the reserve of his Spanish cohorts.

I saw the worry and ill temper fall away from our director's face. At last, we were being properly welcomed. Though he still looked weary, he seemed to breathe easier. Indeed everyone around him did. In a minute he would begin asking what preparations had been made for vaccinations to begin immediately.

I was the only one in our party who knew that this moment was the great calm before the storms, such as we had experienced at sea. But the governor breathed not a word to Don Francisco, and the pageant of welcome went on without a hitch.

It was only later in the day that a letter arrived from the governor's palace, enjoining Don Francisco to have a relaxed if brief stay in the lovely city of San Juan. *For there will not be much for you to do here,* the letter went on. Our director requested I read it after he had done so, but I had already heard the news from the cook and servants in the kitchen. A smallpox epidemic had threatened in December, and learning that the vaccine had been safely transported by the British, encrusted on threads, to St. Thomas, Dr. Oller had arranged for it to be brought over on the arm of a slave girl. Hundreds of people had already been vaccinated. The epidemic had been averted.

"On threads?" I was perplexed. Don Francisco had mentioned an alternative way of preserving the vaccine, impregnating threads with the cowpox fluid. But he had said the method would not work for long transports.

No wonder crowds had not thronged us at the port. The vaccine had preceded us. For the moment, it must have seemed to Don Francisco that he had crossed the oceans for nothing.

"What a show they put on this morning!" Don Francisco shook his head bitterly. "What do they take me for, a fool?"

"And to acquire the vaccine from an enemy! I thought the British attacked this city. Oh, uncle," his nephew commiserated.

Soon, I thought, our director would get past his disappointment and recognize the stronger pull: an epidemic had been threatening the island. To wait for a ship that could take weeks upon weeks to arrive with a vaccine that might have expired midocean when the cure was a boat's ride away, why surely everyone could see the reason on the far side of our grievance.

Some members of our expedition did. Dr. Salvany, for one. During the morning welcome, he and Dr. Oller had discovered they had attended the same college of medicine in Barcelona, albeit more than twenty-five years apart. Dr. Oller had invited Dr. Salvany as well as our director to stay at his house in San Juan during our visit. Dr. Salvany had obliged. But our director—even before he knew the truth—did not want to be diverted from his mission. "Since we are to vaccinate here and in the house across the way, it's best for me to be right on these premises. I thank you for your kind offer, Dr. Oller."

Our director did not see the color drain from the doctor's face. Of course, by then I knew it would be difficult to find anyone to vaccinate in San Juan.

The truth from the start would have been most honorable. Certainly, it would have cleared Dr. Oller and the governor from any blame over what ensued.

When the carriages arrived that evening to take our party to the banquet prepared for us, Don Francisco sent his excuses. The expedition was divided over whether to attend out of courtesy to the governor or stay back in support of Don Francisco.

It was not a contest for me. As I said, I now had a new mission. Don Francisco's faith was faltering. It was up to me to keep alive his belief in a dream that from the very beginning had been too deeply rooted in his self-esteem.

I stayed back, and perhaps that was the night I felt the closest to him.


DON ÁNGEL WAS AT my door. "The director is ill," he said. I had no idea what hour it was. Without a large sky above and the pilot's voice calling out the hour of the watch, I had lost the ability to tell time. "He wants to speak with you."

I threw my shawl over my shoulders and hurried my loose hair back into its cap. Down the long gallery I followed to the room where Don Francisco sat collapsed in a chair. His face was pale, beaded with perspiration. "Doña Isabel, I have a favor to ask," he began, trying to rouse himself but sinking back, unable to summon the strength he thought he had at his command.

"He won't let me call for help," Don Ángel said. In the flickering candlelight the nurse's face was portentous with shadows.

"We have sent for my things," Don Francisco corrected. His nephew and Dr. Gutiérrez were this very moment rowing out to the ship to fetch Don Francisco's bloodletting equipment and apothecary. Don Pedro

Ortega and Don Antonio Pastor were sleeping with the boys in the large dormitory room downstairs, tired out after their first day on land chasing after the little boys, wild with their release from the confines of a ship. Meanwhile, Dr. Salvany, Dr. Grajales, and the practicante Lozano and nurse Bolaños had gone off to the palace for the banquet and comedy performance afterward.

"Perhaps we should send for Dr. Oller?" I inquired of Don Ángel. The name had come to mind, as all I knew of Puerto Rico was the governor, the bishop, two little girls, and a half-dozen servants who knew gossip but could not bloodlet. And of course, the doctor who had beaten Don Francisco to the prize and brought the vaccine to the island.

The name Oller did what a lancet might not have done. Don Francisco struggled forward in his chair. He was fine. No one was to call anyone. He had probably caught some dysentery from the change in diet.

Reluctantly, Don Ángel agreed not to seek further help from our hosts. Instead, he was sent below for a tisana. "Ask the cook. She will know what leaves to brew," Don Francisco smiled wanly. The country people knew more than our science gave them credit for. I remembered what his nephew had told me, the begonia and agave cure for the great pox Don Francisco had learned from a medicine man in Mexico.

"Meanwhile, Doña Isabel. I want you to write down some instructions for me." I wondered why he did not have his very own secretary transcribe his words. I understood once Don Ángel had disappeared. Our director had a personal letter to dictate, in case anything should happen to him. I suppose he was not so sure he would recover from whatever fever was afflicting him. *My dear Josefa,* it began. Though by the following day after several infusions of Juana's tisana and bloodletting by Dr. Gutiérrez, Don Francisco felt considerably improved, and by the second day "cured," and by then, too, the letter he had entrusted me to deliver was back in his hands, its contents were etched forever in my memory:

My dear Josefa, I do not know whether I shall succeed in the great enterprise for which I forsook you and all that I hold dear. After a most trying crossing, with what might possibly have been sabotaging by members of our

expedition either from jealousy of my appointment or as a means of returning us to Spain owing to cowardice, we arrived in Puerto Rico only to find
that various inept ingrates, as a means of garnering honor to themselves and
perhaps causing His Highness to call off our glorious mission, have introduced a so-called vaccine, using that dubious method of threads, which will
prove injurious, I have no doubt. Now I find myself ill and perhaps foresee-
ing an abrupt end to all my efforts, I want to assure you that it was not for
lack of love that I left your side. Although I now begin to doubt my own in-
tentions, I trust that what first sent me off on this risky journey was the very
love I feel for you extended to every living being. Perhaps it was an error to
think that I could carry such a large soul in my narrow character and mortal body. But if we do not make the attempt, we shall not enlarge our humanity even by the smallest whit. In the dark days ahead, no matter what
evil tongues might say of me, remember that what I bore to the far reaches
of the world was not only the vaccine but the love, which you, Josefa,
planted deep inside me.

By the time he had finished, tears were coursing down my face. Indeed,
I worried that I would blur the very words I was writing down.

I don't know if our director heard me sniffling or saw that I was crying.
He had closed his eyes as he had been dictating, his head resting back in
his chair, as if imagining his beloved Josefa. "What is it, Doña Isabel?" he
asked in a kind voice.

I shook my head. What was I to tell him? That I wept because no man
would ever write me such a letter?

I collected myself and did not breathe a word, but Don Francisco knew.
"Some day someone will write you such a letter, Doña Isabel. And you will
think of me, perhaps."

"I will think of you always, Don Francisco," I confessed. "You have carried that love already into many hearts. We will not let it go out. And *you*
must not let it go out either," I dared. "No matter the storms that blow," I
added more faintly.

He let his head fall back on his chair. His eyes were closed again, but he was smiling. "Doña Isabel, I would be a better man if you were by my side every step of this journey."

My heart leapt. If only he knew how much I hoped to be! "If you could use my help," I managed. "But what would be my duties?"

"To remind me," he replied, opening his eyes, smiling.

IN THE DAYS AHEAD, I tried to remind him.

But along with his good health, his stubbornness returned. The very next evening, he was already afoot, issuing announcements, preparing instructions for local doctors, not listening to reason. Even Juana, the cook, had said that the infusions worked best with rest. No, no. Our director knew better than all of us put together. He had already waited a day more than he should to vaccinate Andrés Naya and Antonio Veredia and to hold our first public session. Vaccinations must commence immediately!

The problem was that everyone who needed a vaccination in San Juan had gotten one. So common had the procedure become that children were vaccinating each other as a game in the schoolyard.

"How can this be?" Don Francisco questioned Señor Mexía, who bowed his head as if beseeching the very tiles on the floor for help. As a city councilor and general factotum, he no doubt knew the right answer could be the wrong answer depending on who was questioning him. I could not help thinking of Doña Teresa's rages, how it was always best at those moments to refrain from crossing her. "Does the governor and the so-called doctor Oller know that by doing so they might have imperiled His Majesty's expedition? Where are we to acquire the next set of carriers? Do they not know that one must not vaccinate wholesale but in succession in order to perpetuate the vaccine over time for the next generation?" Our director paced back and forth, wringing his hands.

I admit I, too, worried about the fate of our mission. Only one carrier would soon be left, Benito, whom I could not vouch for. Of course, I had inspected the boy thoroughly, and there was not a mark on him. But he might still prove immune. A second, sure carrier had to be found to receive the fluid from Antonio's and Andrés's vesicles in another week or so. Woe to our expedition should this last vaccination fail us. And woe to me: the fault would lie directly at my feet.

I hurried downstairs with two urgent requests for Juana: one was for a tea to calm the director's nerves, the second for a baby who had not received Dr. Oller's vaccine. In exchange, I offered her my necklace of rosary beads and a few trifles of jewelry I had inherited from my mother and sister (an ivory bracelet, a silver mourning pin). Juana had told me that many servants had been hiding their babies from Dr. Oller, disbelieving that "you could have smallpox not having it." But Juana trusted me. After all, I was putting my own little Benito forward as a carrier of "the safe vaccine from the king."

I went back upstairs with good news for our director. First, I offered him a cup of guanabana tea. I had already sipped a cup downstairs and felt much relieved, though my relief might have come from the good news I now delivered to him. Juana had a niece who had given birth a month ago. That healthy baby boy had not yet been vaccinated!

"That is wonderful news, Doña Isabel," Don Francisco agreed absently. He nodded for me to set the cup down wherever I might find a clear surface. He would drink it presently. He was in the midst of dictating a letter to Don Ángel, addressed to Governor Castro. Dr. Oller's vaccine was false and must be publicly discredited on pain of treason to His Majesty!

Don Ángel shot me a grim glance. As I stood by, while they finished the letter, I was sure we would all be hanged once the governor read it.

ALONG WITH THE LETTER, Don Francisco sent the governor a copy of his translation of Moreau's treatise on the vaccine. Hopefully, His Grace would study it, *as high as your penetration might go, lacking as Your Lordship is in these lights.*

I don't know what angel was looking down on us, but instead of militiamen with a rope and manacles, the governor came in person to respond to Don Francisco's missive. Perhaps after fighting off the English invaders, he was determined not to let a mere doctor shake his equanimity.

His greetings were cordial as if our director's incendiary letter had been written to some other person. He brought along toys for the children, tops and little carved soldiers, as well as sugarcane candies stuffed in a painted basket made of straw, which we were to hang from a high branch and which the blindfolded boys were to strike at with sticks. Oh dear, what a wild time they had in the courtyard! I tried to keep down the uproar but to no avail. A few of the boys were clobbered over the head, but at least no one was shot through with an arrow. From the ship had come the news that the steward was going to wring the neck of every last one of the boys should he see them again.

The shouts and screams of my little piñata warriors probably accounted for why I did not hear the strong words that were exchanged between the governor and our director. It seems Don Francisco took a long time in coming out to greet His Grace, and then with a dark look and a curt bow. Don Ángel told me that the governor produced a list of all those whom Dr. Oller and his assistants had vaccinated. Every prominent name was on it, including Bishop Arizmendi, Dr. Oller's own sons, the governor's two daughters.

"All of these people are in grave danger," Don Francisco declared. "Your Grace must send out a proclamation stating that Oller's vaccine is in error. Revaccinations must begin immediately!"

In a more reasonable tone, the governor advised that instead of trying to summon hundreds of people, why not test a handful? He had perused the Moreau book that Don Francisco had so graciously sent him—Don Ángel said the knife flashing in the word *graciously* was sharp enough to cut a hangman's rope. The good doctor Moreau himself had written in his prologue that even an average talent who knew no medicine could form a correct idea of vaccination. (Indeed, *I* had learned to vaccinate!) By revaccinating a handful, Dr. Balmis would be able to verify whether the earlier vaccinations were false or not. If there was no reaction to the new vaccine, Dr. Oller's vaccine would be proven to be effective after all and the island of Puerto Rico be spared an enormous and undue cost.

How could the director argue with that? But he did, according to Don Ángel. He had not come across an ocean, enduring tribulations, risking the lives of so many innocents, in order to do the cleanup work of some local charlatan. Either all 1,557 vaccinations were redone, or Don Francisco would not repeat a one. And with a nod and a "Good day," he left the room, and the governor was left still holding the list. It is a wonder, Don Ángel claimed, that the paper did not burst into flames, so fiery red was the govenor's face.

DR. SALVANY WAS ILL with the same fevers and faint feeling that had afflicted Don Francisco. From on board the ship, news came that Orlando and several of the crew were suffering the same indisposition. Could it be a mild dysentery or malaria or the dreaded ship's fever? Don Francisco planned a trip to the *María Pita* to examine his shipmates. As for Dr. Salvany, who was still a guest in Dr. Oller's home, Don Francisco ordered him back to our house to be treated by a legitimate physician.

Perhaps to clear his good name or to argue the inadvisability of moving Dr. Salvany at the moment, Dr. Oller appeared at the house that same afternoon during the siesta hour. I was having my coffee cup read by Juana in the back of the house. *A long journey*. ("Come, come, Juana," I chided. "There needs no soothsayer to divine that!") *No children, many sons*. (I sighed impatiently.) *A broken heart, a happy life*. I sat up. How could that be? Wasn't love necessary for happiness? Juana shrugged. She only read the future, she didn't invent it.

Don Ángel and Don Antonio Pastor were resting in hammocks strung from post to post of the open gallery as the boys played in the courtyard. Periodically, when their games became rough, one or the other nurse would threaten to send them all to their mats in enforced siesta if they didn't behave. When I heard that Dr. Oller had come to have a little talk with our director, I headed for the front room. I didn't need coffee stains to predict what would happen if spark and gunpowder should come together.

Dr. Oller looked nervous as he waited to be received by our director. They were about the same height and age, though Dr. Oller seemed shorter and older with the stout paunch of a successful professional. He was blind in one eye, which stayed blank and unmoving while the other gazed back at you, giving him an unfortunate sly look. "Doña Isabel," he bowed when I entered. He had remembered my name! "I come with news of your colleague and to explain . . . this unfortunate matter."

Like all frightened people he had begun his explanations to the first ready listener. "I trust Dr. Salvany is better?" I put in, hoping to set him at his ease by talking about a mutual concern of ours. I was also hoping to convince Dr. Oller that I would carry whatever news to our director who was upstairs resting. In his present agitated state, Don Francisco would not, I was almost sure, be open to Dr. Oller's explanations.

Dr. Oller finished his report on his guest, which I promised to deliver to our director. I was steering him toward the door when we heard Don Francisco's voice behind us. "Stay, Dr. Oller. I want you to repeat your lies to my face." The doctor continued out the door, which only incensed our director further. His next command was a shout, heard, no doubt, all the way down the street. Later, I learned that Dr. Oller was deaf in one ear, and what the director had taken as an affront and a sign of the local doctor's guilt was the mere faultiness of his hearing.

This time, the doctor heard the shout. He turned, and stood, shaking visibly, his face pale with anger. Both eyes seemed now to be looking boldly back at his accuser. "You will be proven the liar," he returned, throwing fire into the fire.

HOW HAD THINGS GONE so horribly wrong! All of San Juan was now transfixed, waiting to know the outcome: Was the vaccine which most everyone in the city had received a good vaccine or a bad vaccine? Should one trust the British or the Spanish cowpox, as they were becoming known? Meanwhile, the outlying towns were left to battle the epidemic with no vaccinations at all.

Finally, Bishop Arizmendi interceded. He convinced the governor to recall the earlier vaccination and have everyone revaccinated "so that the public will be served as the king wills." The bishop came to deliver the news to our director. He himself would be revaccinated as an example so that others would be persuaded.

By now, Don Francisco's fevers and faints had returned. But there was no tea Juana knew of that could change a person's character. Meanwhile, Dr. Salvany returned to our side, much recuperated and growing stronger every day, while our director became paler and weaker. I wondered if he would survive Puerto Rico.

THE DAY OF REVACCINATIONS was set for February 28, a Tuesday. Given the large numbers expected from outlying provinces, all members of our expedition were to be in attendance, including the nurses and myself. I had become quite adept at assisting the doctors, handing them instruments, and, most especially, calming the children to be pierced with the lancet.

How did I do it? I told them stories, how this wonderful spirit of love was about to enter them, how it would work magic, how it would keep them in good health. How a little prick or sting was the footprint of the spirit coming in.

It worked. I did not know if it was the story or the way I held their attention with my eyes. *I am here with you,* my look said. *You are not alone.* By the end of an hour, I felt black and blue all over my arms as if I, too, had been pricked a dozen times.

The servants took charge of the boys that day, so that all the nurses and I could assist with the large crowds that might keep us vaccinating until late into the night. Only little Benito and the infant boy Juana had found for me and whom I had nicknamed Salvador were kept apart. Both had been vaccinated on the nineteenth with the fluid from Andrés Naya's and Antonio Veredia's vesicles and both vaccines had taken! I kissed my little Benito so mightily, he wondered what he had done to earn such joy. We had succeeded: an unbroken chain of vaccinations we could trace all the way back to La Coruña!

Juana had also convinced several servants to allow their babies to be vaccinated. There was now enough cowpox fluid to go around. That being the case, Don Francisco decided to wait a day to harvest Benito's vesicle. Our director had demanded and was granted four boys to carry the vaccine to Caracas. They were to be delivered without fail tomorrow. Juana told me that the city was being combed for four children whose families were willing to release them to accompany us to Venezuela.

"Perhaps you know of some other children?" I suggested to Juana.

"No, señora." The cook shook her head adamantly. One thing was letting your babies be vaccinated—and more and more of the poor were coming forward to have their sons and daughters saved from smallpox. It was another thing altogether giving over your child to a dangerous sea voyage so far from home. "What do we poor have but our children?" Juana explained to me. She was wearing my necklace of beads. Her niece had taken the bracelet and mourning pin.

"Any child on the voyage would be under my special care," I assured her.

"Not even under the Virgin's care," Juana replied. What blasphemy! But I understood her point. It had been difficult for me to part with my Benito. In fact, I had imperiled our mission to keep him by my side. I hoped there would never come a time when I would be asked to leave him behind.

MIDMORNING OF THAT eventful day, the bishop arrived with several eminent colleagues. This first group was followed by Dr. Oller, solemn-faced and seemingly tongue-tied, saying not a word. He brought along his sons as well as several prominent citizens and their families. The receiving room downstairs was bustling with talk and anticipation. A few servants were positioned near the windows with large fans made of palm fronds to blow in fresh breezes.

Finally, the governor arrived with his two daughters, who were to be revaccinated along with everyone else. The trumpets blew, and in a booming voice the standard-bearer announced that the vaccinations could now officially begin.

But where was Dr. Balmis?

A look passed between the governor and Dr. Oller, a sneer of a smile that did not become them.

I had come down to greet our illustrious guests. The unenviable duty now fell to me to inform them that Don Francisco had already begun vaccinating in the large hall upstairs.

"But the governor is the one to give the command," Governor Castro said, as if the governor were a separate person from himself. "The illustrious señor bishop and other esteemed guests are waiting for the doctor downstairs." He gestured with that exquisite calm of the truly furious.

"There is much better light upstairs," I excused our director. Of course, I knew it was highly improper of Don Francisco to begin without observing the formalities due high-ranking officials and families. It was an affront, one that I was trying with every grace learned under the tutelage of Doña Teresa's character to soften and present as professional enthusiasm.

But I could tell that my explanations had done nothing to soothe the indignation of the governor. Later, I heard him say that he would rather fight off the British any day than deal with this director.

A child's screams from upstairs reminded me of my own duties. I excused myself and arrived just in time to see Don Basilio holding a boy by the neck, a hand clapped over his mouth. Suddenly, the nurse gave out a cry and jerked his hand away. "Bloody cannibal!" he cuffed the boy's ear. He showed the director the marks where the child had bitten his fingers.

"A little more self-control, Don Basilio," Don Francisco reminded him. I could not help but think of the irony—how wise our director could be with someone else's imbecility.

SEÑOR MEXÍA CAME UPSTAIRS several times to inform the good doctor that his guests were waiting downstairs.

"I am not here to be an actor performing in a play for them," Don Francisco tossed over his shoulder. "Lift your sleeve a little higher, thank you," he advised the young woman who was already wincing at the sight of the lancet.

*Look here*, my eyes told her, and she looked. I could see the fear draining out of her.

"But, sir," Señor Mexía persisted, wiping his brow. Poor weary ambassador! I knew just how he was feeling. "His Eminence, the governor, and the bishop—"

"Do you not understand plain Spanish?" Our director turned, lancet in hand, and glared at the frightened councilor. "I am at work. If the illustrious eminences want to see me, let them come here."

Incredibly, a while later we heard a dozen or so illustrious eminences climbing up the stairs.

WHY DIDN'T OUR HOSTS indulge a tired and ill man in his need to deliver the vaccine he had brought for them?

Why didn't our director remember that the world is a big place, that there would be other spots where his efforts would bear fruit? Why didn't he listen to Dr. Salvany's explanations, which he had heard from several sources, regarding the straitened circumstances of the public coffers?

It seems that the island had not been receiving its subsidy for the past five years. There were no funds to run the government. The militiamen at our door, Señor Mexía, and God knows all the servants in the house had been at half pay since June of last year. The governor and ayuntamiento could ill afford to host an expedition whose services they no longer needed. And yet, out of courtesy to the expedition members, the council had unanimously voted to cover our expenses in Puerto Rico, while at the same time, urge us not to linger. No wonder our governor had looked askance at the horrid prospect and expense of revaccination after having undergone the cost of the first vaccination already.

I suppose only an almighty God can see all of our differing stories. Only He can love each narrow, aggrieved, and petty self and applaud each time one of us, inflamed by love or enlarged by loss, manages to see briefly beyond the confines of our own self-interest into another's being. *I see you. You are not alone. We are here together.*

The governor entered the upstairs room, putting on the best face he could on a bad situation. Near the window, Don Francisco was vaccinating a screaming child. All around the room at their different posts, Dr. Salvany and Dr. Grajales and Dr. Gutiérrez stopped their own vaccinations to greet the governor and bishop and other eminences. The nurses quickly ushered the patients who had already been vaccinated out the door. I could hear Don Basilio in the hall explaining the schedule, how the vaccinated area should be treated, the growing vesicle safeguarded. A peso was to be awarded for each good vesicle harvested. (How would the governor and ayuntamiento meet this new financial obligation that our expedition was imposing on them?)

"Don Francisco!" the governor greeted him in a genial voice that did not convince anyone. Our director waved. He would be with his guests in a minute, he was vaccinating.

"Oh, but I can perhaps spare you all this work," Dr. Oller taunted, directing his two sons and the governor's daughters to come forward. "I re-vaccinated these children myself with *your* vaccine, and look, not one has taken."

Don Francisco turned now, his jaw set, his face livid. He was too furious to inquire how Dr. Oller had obtained *our* vaccine, but I saw Dr. Salvany's face grow deathly pale. Our director advanced past the glaring proof of the children's arms bared at him, ignoring them, as if they were not there. He stopped directly in front of Bishop Arizmendi, who smiled uneasily.

"Your Most Illustrious Grace," Don Francisco addressed the bishop. "Can you believe that I have not seen one good vaccine in Puerto Rico? Or— excepting yourself—one honest man either."

"Remember you talk in my presence, the highest authority on this isle," the governor said in a voice of steel. "I will report you to the king."

"I, too, speak to the same king, and I will do so in person," Dr. Balmis countered.

By now, the children in the room were wailing, for in addition to their fear of vaccination, there was now the added fearful prospect of grown men shouting at each other. An overzealous militiaman fired a shot at the ceiling in warning. A woman screamed.

"You are disrupting my work," Don Francisco informed the governor. "I must ask you to leave immediately."

Who knew what would happen next, the two men were staring each other down in the center of the room. The militiamen were called to attention. Were we to have a bloodbath over such trifles? I came toward them. "Gentlemen, please, for the love of all that is good." I held now one, now another with my eyes, until I could see that their animal fury had abated, that they had become human once again.

THE VERY NEXT DAY, we began preparations to leave. A message arrived from the governor's palace in the person of Señor Mexía. No apology, no allusion to the events of the day before. Just a message that the four boys promised for our trip to Caracas would be on our doorstep by evening. A good thing as Benito's vesicle was now fully engorged and ready to be harvested, the fluid transmitted to a new set of carriers.

By the same poor, weary vehicle, a response was returned to the governor. No apology, no allusion to the events of the day before. The Royal Expedition of the Vaccine would vacate the premises as soon as the four boys were received.

As he waited for the promised boys, Don Francisco brooded on Dr. Oller's trickery. How had the bogus doctor gotten hold of our vaccine? Perhaps there was a traitor in our midst? Don Ángel, ever the kind soul, reminded our director that Dr. Oller might have obtained fluid from any number of provincials we ourselves had vaccinated. Thank goodness that sufficed for an explanation or our own number would have been riven with contention.

Hours went by and no boys appeared; Don Francisco began to doubt the governor's word. Without carriers, the vaccine might be lost after all. I had a suggestion I dared not make to our director. Since hearing that the vaccine had successfully traveled from England to St. Thomas on silk threads, I had begun wondering, Why not use this method from now on? Why expose more children as carriers when this simple procedure might be just as effective?

I sought out Dr. Salvany, who corrected my misapprehension. Threads were not reliable; rarely was the vaccine active upon arrival. "In this I have to give the reason to our . . . director." He hesitated before the word *director* as if there were some doubt in his mind about its applicability to Don Francisco.

"I am glad to hear it." I felt relieved.

"Rest your mind on that regard, Doña Isabel," Dr. Salvany smiled wanly. He himself did not seem relieved. Since the scene yesterday, the young doctor had gone about the house with a numb, unhappy look. He had made friends with Dr. Oller, dined with the governor, recited his poetry to the local literati. The skilled painter, Campeche, had invited him to sit for a portrait. He was caught between loyalties, but it was more than that. His romantic illusions of the expedition were quickly falling away. His poetry was of no help at all in the present crisis. He had embarked on a journey with a madman! A person so driven by his mission, he was turning into a kind of monster. What would happen as they crossed the Americas and sailed the Pacific and on to the Philippines and China?

"Our director has not been himself," I tried assuring the young doctor, though the same worries were running through my mind. I told him about the fevers Don Francisco had suffered that first night, which upon questioning I learned had returned on and off since then. "I am sure he will recover and all will be well."

"It is I. I'm not sure I will recover," Dr. Salvany said vaguely.

I asked him if he was feeling a renewal of his fevers as well.

"It's not that," he said, sighing. "I was wrong in accepting this commission. I do not have the temper for these continual battles and intrigues."

"Don't lose faith, Dr. Salvany," I urged him. I tried to hold him with my eyes, but his gaze could not be held. His own eyes were thousands of leagues away in a drawing room in Spain. Later, after dinner, I collected his coffee cup and took it back to the kitchen for Juana to read. She looked down into the empty cup and shook her head. I did not ask her what she saw. Instead, I watched as she filled the cup again with coffee and a shake of sugar and drank it in one draft.

THE FOUR PROMISED BOYS arrived later that day, escorted by Bishop Arizmendi, who had heard that the expedition was leaving Puerto Rico. Wouldn't Don Francisco reconsider and stay at least long enough to set up a junta that would perpetuate and administer future vaccinations?

"Your governor and his doctor have taken matters out of my hands, Señor Bishop. Let them vaccinate as they will."

Bishop Arizmendi conceded that the situation had been poorly handled. But he reminded Dr. Balmis that there were many more inhabitants on the island who would benefit from the royal doctor's vaccinations.

But Don Francisco was implacable. Our trunks were packed, the carriages had been ordered, and a letter sent ahead to the audiencia of Venezuela to be ready to receive us.

"It grieves us to have you leave in this way." The bishop stretched out his arms as if speaking for everyone in Puerto Rico. Then turning to the four carriers he had brought for us, he reminded them to behave themselves. They were to obey whatever instructions Don Francisco and Doña Isabel gave them. The poor little boys began wailing that they did not want to leave Puerto Rico.

This was too much for our director, for whom that name had become as poison in his ears. Off he went to complete his own preparations for leaving. Dr. Salvany accompanied the bishop to the door while I sought to soothe the boys: Juan Ortiz, Manuel Antonio Rodríguez, Cándido de los Santos, and José Fragoso, four more sons to add to my growing list of children.

THE PROBLEM WITH A grand exit is that sometimes nature will not cooperate. We sat in a becalmed bay for ten days unable to sail away. The small boat was sent ashore daily, refilling our water casks, procuring added supplies. The heat on board was terrible. For the first time I understood what it meant to be in the tropics. The boys slept on deck because no one could bear the sweltering heat below. Fevers raged on board. And every day that passed Don Francisco fretted. We had four carriers left, two had been vaccinated on the twenty-ninth. Their vesicles matured in ten days and we were still sitting in the bay, with only two carriers to go.

That should have been no problem as our next stop, the port of La Guayra, in Venezuela, was at most eight days away. Or so, the port official assured our captain, who had never sailed those waters before. Perhaps we should take a local pilot with us? But our director refused to do further business with anyone at all on the island, and so the *María Pita* waited in the harbor to make its aggrieved departure out of Puerto Rico.

Finally, oh finally, our respite came. A breeze began to blow that night and the very next morning we sailed off. Perhaps it was an error to sail with so many in the crew still weak with fever in waters unknown to our captain and crew, but by now error was piled so high on error that all one could do was pray that hope had sturdy sails and that good sense would prevail.

# 6

Alma's faith is in short supply as she wings her way down to the island to try to bargain for her hostage husband. Everywhere she looks, she feels implicated by the dozens upon dozens of little perks and privileges her life is built upon.

It's ridiculous where this guilt first seizes her, in the airport bathroom in Vermont. She enters the bright, cleanser-smelling room with its bank of mirrors, its stalls with backup rolls that drop into place to offer more paper when the bottom one is used up, the extra hand towels held together by a brown band and stacked atop the too-full dispenser. She tries to imagine *them*, the kidnappers, the way they would see this room; there is so much here, and more where that came from, and this is a public place. Not a rich man's home, not a dictator's palace, not a swanky suite for state functions but a small airport in a rural state with its own pockets of poverty.

She hates looking at her life this way, through grievance. How can this pettiness be good for anyone? Counting the petals wasted on a rose as if the distribution were suddenly her fault. But that is precisely the way she is imagining these kidnappers seeing her world. It's as if they're an infection inside her, and she can't get rid of them.

In the waiting area, Emerson has set up a workstation, his little computer connected to his cell phone plugged into an outlet—how can the man be so enterprising? Alma sits numbly by, her carry-on suitcase with its leather tag and wheels propped beside her, more evidence against her. She recalls the first time she went home with one of these wheeled suitcases, which had not yet made their appearance on the island. The airport porters rushed forward, grabbing at her bag, each one wanting the job of carrying it. She didn't need their help anymore, she pointed out: she could now pull it along by the handle herself. She demonstrated, as if they should be intrigued by the ingenious device; instead, they walked off, disgusted. All but one man who snatched the handle out of her hand and insisted on rolling the bag for her out of Customs. This man's son probably grew up to become one of the kidnappers, whom Alma now imagines taking one look at her bag and saying, *So you are one of the ones who drove my father out of business.*

Why is she torturing herself this way? No one really knows who these kidnappers are or why they are aggrieved. Alma is already putting words in their mouths, writing out their manifestos in her head, viewing the video they will make in which an unshaved, pale, petrified Richard pleads for his life to some head of state.

On the short flight down to Newark, Emerson tries to engage Alma in conversation. But he forgets about her when they meet up with Jim Larsen, the soft-spoken Swan representative, for their connecting flight down to Santo Domingo in first class. What kind of an aid operation is he running, spending all this money to travel in luxury to help the impoverished of the world? Such violent either-or distinctions! Alma better watch out or she'll soon find her own left hand chopped off by her right.

Emerson changes seats so he and Jim can confer and brainstorm and order up what seems like a lot of martinis for what is not yet lunch. Just as well. Alma can't seem to concentrate on anything, not her Coetzee novel, her Dante paperback, her journal, or the Balmis material she stuck in her satchel before leaving. To distract herself, she picks up the newspaper Emerson has left behind in his seat pocket. In the Vermont section, her eye is caught by a short piece titled "Trouble on Turkey Day." Unbelievable that the wheels of this sleepy, little state can turn so quickly, but then it was Thanksgiving and the paper was probably strapped for news. Alma is mentioned only as "a neighbor" who claims to have seen Michael McMullen about to inject his mother, Helen Marshall, with an unknown substance. Meanwhile, Michael McMullen maintains that he was only trying to give his mother her diabetes medication; he was not trying to do her in by infecting her with a deadly virus. He lost his head and struck the sheriff by mistake.

How do you strike somebody by mistake? Alma wonders. Probably, Mickey was aiming to strike her, and the sheriff got in the way. But more to the point, what strikes Alma now sitting on this plane, flying away from the scene of one possible crime to the scene of another probable one, is, Who said anything about a *deadly virus?* Why would Mickey defend himself against an accusation she never made? Hasn't he inadvertently implicated himself? Where in the world would Mickey get hold of a deadly virus? Is that what was in the syringe that Alma knocked out of his hand and that the sheriff's men later couldn't find? Maybe Hannah picked it up after they all left and before she fled? Has she been found? Even the life Alma might go back to if she manages to save Richard seems suddenly unmoored, rickety.

A deadly virus. Like this one infecting her head. Everywhere she looks she sees signs of dread. She takes a deep breath. She'll call the sheriff's office as soon as she lands. Meanwhile, she makes herself think of Isabel and Balmis, wandering the waters not far from the island where Alma's plane has just landed.

THE AIRSTRIP SEEMS DESERTED, the sunshine blinding. The few planes out on the tarmac look unsafe in their odd colors, a huge pink airbus with a flag that could be a T-shirt logo for a reggae band, a lavender plane with propellers.

Only their own and another American carrier seem trustworthy with their silver wings and bully flag and blond, noli me tangere pilots, who come inside the terminal briefly to buy cheap rum at the duty-free shops and use the airline's premium-club-members-only facilities.

As she descends the rolling stairwell—the jetway is not working—as she follows the other passengers down a long outdoor corridor, Alma is hoping against all hope that Richard will be just around the corner, tapping on the glass partition, craning his neck to get a glimpse of her.

But no, he is not here, he is not there. Instead, pictures of him flash in her head: Richard driving the pickup over snowdrifts, Richard and the boys laughing on the deck, Richard falling asleep, his body curled around hers as she reads in bed. How will she ever sleep in that bed again if Richard is killed?

Her heart starts that jumpy rhythm that makes her feel as if she's going to faint, her head pounding with stupidities that convince her she is going to go mad unless she takes a deep breath.

Suddenly, a picture, not of Richard, hangs before her. That famous Munch painting of a terrified face, hands over her ears, mouth ripped open in a mute cry. Now Alma knows what that poor waif was screaming about: the loss of her beloved.

JUST INSIDE IMMIGRATION, Starr Bell is waiting for them. "I flew into Miami last night," she explains. "Got here about an hour ago." She doesn't look a bit tarnished by the long journey, blonde and tanned and a head taller than the contingent of about a dozen men who stand by while the señorita greets her friends. Half of the men in the group are dressed in street clothes, undercover guys must be, with their dark glasses and slick look of professionals. The other half are military men with gold braid and heroic glitter on their chests. They give the group a semiofficial air as if they are receiving representatives from somewhere not important enough to merit more fanfare.

One man doesn't seem to fit either bill, a pudgy, Baby Huey–looking guy with soft brown skin. Before Starr even introduces him, Alma guesses this is Bienvenido. What's he doing here? Why wasn't he taken hostage? Probably the same reason that Bienvenido got to call his wife while Richard couldn't come down the mountain to call her. Maybe the guy is in league with the kidnappers?

"I am so sorry about what is occurring to your husband," he assures Alma, taking her hand in both of his. He has a lazy eye, which keeps wandering off. It gives him a sly look, as if he doesn't trust his own sincerity. "As you know," he adds, "this type of situation is a very rare occurrence in our country."

Alma's eyes fill. *Our* country. Not hers, not anymore, not if they hurt Richard. As for rare occurrence. This type of situation is going to start happening more and more everywhere. The perks and privileges are going to go up in flames like so much paper fortifications.

Their passports and papers are collected by one of the plainclothesmen who goes off to get them stamped by Immigration. Meanwhile, Emerson and his group are escorted into a VIP room to be briefed about what has been happening on this the second day of the seizure of the Swan center.

"We are very unaccustomed to this type of occurrence," one of the men in uniform says, echoing Bienvenido. "In our country, we are not radicals, we are not revolutionaries. There is no tradition of such movements on this soil." With his overdecorated, puffed-out chest and declamatory lift of the hand with each sentence, he reminds Alma of an opera singer with a minor but nevertheless critical part.

"These people, they have no electricity, no schools, no medicines," the military spokesman continues. "But they come down to the barras with the cable TV, and in the news they see all over the world these terrorists. They get ideas." His colleagues, plainclothes and in uniform, are nodding agreement, as if the speaker has set a whole shelf of little figures with springs in their necks bobbing.

So the kidnappers got the idea from cable TV. "But what do they want?" Alma feels impatient at the bureaucratic wheels she sees turning in rhetorical revolution. "Have they issued a statement?"

"Señora." The military man shakes his head sadly at her. He is doing all the talking, so he must be in charge. Probably some big general, Alma guesses; at any rate, best to call him that. She remembers one of her cousins telling her that years back. Always address an official with a higher title than the one you think he has. It makes for smooth handling of the situation. A tip also helps. "You mean a bribe," Alma had corrected him. Her cousins stopped giving her pointers when they realized she was always coming down with ideas on how to improve things. "These are boy terrorists, local kids, they do not know how to read or write. How can they issue a statement?"

"But they must have said something about why they've taken over the center?" Alma looks over at Emerson for help. "Didn't you say the kidnappers were asking for their own clinic for the community? No more AIDS vaccine testing?" Emerson looks over at Starr and Bienvenido, who nod in agreement. Emerson nods back. What is this? Alma thinks angrily—a convention of nodding people?

"Ah . . . You are referring to *those* matters." The general seems to be drawing out his answers as if to remind Alma that she must speak with more calm and consideration herself. "Yesterday they say they want a termination to testing. They say they want a clinic for the community. That was yesterday. Then they saw the cable TV. They heard the radio. All the publicity. Today they add more things."

"Like what?" Alma gasps. She feels like the dog in that Goya painting, its head poking out of a sloping mass of—is it quicksand?—that will shortly swallow him up. *Dog Drowning,* it was called. Alma feels like she is drowning, like she can't get enough air in her lungs.

"Señora, it is not clear to me what these individuals want." The general says with showy regret. He doesn't want to talk to her, Alma can tell. She is being a nuisance. *Get out of the way.* Dad's last words keep running through her head. "We will review this matter with the troops on-site."

Troops. That doesn't sound good.

"But you must understand," he continues, addressing his remarks now to Emerson. "Our government's policy is like yours, we do not negotiate with terrorists. We are trying to reason with them. What will they gain if the center is bombarded?"

Alma's mouth drops. She looks over at Starr and Emerson, shocked when they don't immediately protest. They both understand Spanish, so it can't be that. And Jim has been sent down as Swan's rep, so one would hope he knows the language. Don't they realize what this guy is suggesting? "What do you mean bombard the place?" Alma challenges when no one else does. "My husband is in that center."

"Señora," the general reminds her, "there are forty-six patients and personnel in there, along with your husband, and three women who clean and cook and their children who help them. All these lives are very valuable to us."

Alma feels rebuked. Of course, all these lives are valuable. But she doesn't like hearing *him* say so. This is the kind of platitude that will allow him to give the signal to bomb the center because none of those fifty or so lives are the one life he cannot bear to destroy, his own beloved child, his beautiful mistress, his old mother whose hand he kisses when he visits her for Sunday dinner.

The room is frigid—the air conditioner must be cranked up to top dollar—and unnerving with its heavy drapes and fluorescent lighting, a place where a shady deal is being brokered. She can't stand to listen to this guy talk. Any moment she is going to lose control, reach over and yank off his medals, call him corporal, tell him he can't go bombing innocent people.

Take a deep breath, she coaches herself. Make believe you're Isabel. (This is slowly becoming her mantra.) You've brought the vaccine across an ocean without a single casualty. You saved the day in Puerto Rico. Surprisingly, she does feel calmer.

"Emerson, can I talk to you a second," Alma says, standing. The group falls silent. Emerson follows her to the far side of the room, where there is a bar with stools. A waiter in a tuxedo is preparing a tray of cafecitos. He looks up; Alma shakes her head. No, there is nothing he can get for her. Behind her, the men continue their discussion.

"Emerson, do you realize they're talking about *bombing* the place," Alma explains, just in case he didn't understand. "You're not going to let them do that!" It's not a question. She hopes he knows it's not a question.

"Nothing like that is going to happen," he assures her. But he doesn't flash her his customary smile that seals his words with confidence.

"These guys have to talk a hard line. They're not going to do something stupid."

Alma is not so sure. Everything is taking too much time! "So when are we going up there?"

Emerson gives her one of his long, assessing looks. No doubt he can see right to the heart of her terror. "I'm going up now with Jim. And Starr knows these people, the ones in the village, and maybe even some of the guys involved. But Alma, it might be best for you to stay until we assess the situation. Don't you have relatives in the capital?"

"I'm going!" she cries out angrily. The room again falls silent. The men sitting in their circle of chairs and couches look over at her. She doesn't care what they think of her. They're not going to usher her away to her old aunts with a sedative and a pat on the head, while they go wreak their havoc. She is going up there! If need be, she is going to stand guard in front of the clinic and let cable TV catch the footage of how her country treats the lives of innocent people! "Why do you think I came all this way? Richard is up there."

Emerson puts a calming hand on her shoulder. "I know this is difficult, Alma. We're not going to leave you out of anything. I promise. Okay?" He gives her a kindly *Ah, come on now, give us a little smile* look. She hates herself for letting go of her anger, for nodding meekly yes. But she better run with the pack. Who else is there to trust? Everybody seems suspect, including herself. This is what it means to live in a fallen world, she thinks. If only she'd been paying closer attention when she read to Helen from *Paradise Lost*.

That, too, seems laughable here. The idea that literature would have made her live her life any differently than she has. And besides, she doesn't have the luxury right now of being an individual. Setting herself apart. The same broad brush is painting over everyone. She feels the invisible bristles moving over her skin. She shivers as if to shake it off.

"Can you believe how cold it is in here?" Starr has left the group of men just as Emerson is returning to them. Was there an invisible nod between them, Alma wonders. *Your turn to try some female mollifica-*

*tion.* Starr is holding on to her bare arms, which are covered with goose bumps. Alma has to bite her tongue to keep from saying something mean. Why take it out on these people just because they've been spared instead of Richard?

"You smoke?" Starr asks, digging around in her purse, a little leather knapsack with nifty brass fittings. "You mind?" She lights up, when Alma shakes her head. "One thing I love about this country," she begins, and then, as if recalling the situation, she gives Alma an *Oops, sorry about that* smile, before adding, "You can smoke anywhere you want here."

"So do you know what else these terrorists are now asking for?" Alma returns to the point everybody seems to be avoiding. All this verbal red tape is making her even more afraid.

"*Terrorists?* Oh please, Alma. Like he said, they're kids. They're probably starting to have second thoughts and want to be sure they get amnesty when it's all over." Starr twists her head to exhale her smoke away from Alma. "I know all those guys, Moncho and Rubio and Tomás and Salvador. They want attention. And just remember, the last thing anyone wants is a . . . tragedy."

Alma can tell Starr considered and discarded a word or two before landing on the literary and elegant-sounding *tragedy.* She probably knows Alma is a writer with a big imagination. Better not use a word that calls up blasted bodies, severed limbs, bloodied faces, the casualties that come when you bomb a place. "You *know* the guys who are doing this?"

Starr needs a drag before answering. She pulls on her cigarette; smoke pours from her nostrils, her mouth. It is an ugly habit, Alma thinks. And Starr is not just pretty, but beautiful. The classic features, the good cheekbones. Plus she is tall and big eyed and pouty-mouthed. Maybe the kidnappers all want to sleep with her. Alma remembers a Southern woman at a party recounting how Savannah was saved from burning during the Civil War. The place was surrounded by Union troops, and the city fathers, trying to ward off the impending tragedy, sent out twenty volunteer beauties to give the soldiers whatever they wanted in exchange for sparing Savannah. It worked. It's even been done in the Bible. Negotiate for salvation with a beautiful woman. Alma would offer herself if she could. But she's fifty years old. And face it, even when she was Starr's age, she didn't have the goods.

"I'm not sure who all is in on this," Starr explains. "But I can take a good guess." She leans in closer for a confidence, holding the hand with the cigarette as far as possible from Alma and waving the smoke away with her other hand. "One thing I can tell you is these guys are not the ones in charge." She indicates the men behind her, who are, unbelievably, laughing at something. "They're like the welcome wagon."

Alma feels like a lucky ten-year-old befriended by a cool teenager. She listens, impressed, and vaguely hopeful. Starr will get Richard out. She'll drive up with her pickup full of goodies and a negligee in her purse. "So who *is* in charge?"

"Of the guys inside, probably Salvador. And outside, I'd say the United States of America." She laughs at Alma's surprised look. "Seriously, nobody here's going to do something unless Jim tells them to."

"Isn't Jim with Swan?"

"Yes and no," Starr says, but before Alma can get an explanation, the plainclothesman comes in with their stamped papers and passports. The vans are waiting outside. Alma tries to stick close to Starr and Emerson and, God knows, Jim, but at the last minute, the divvying up lands her in a black sedan. Inside, she finds a woman journalist, who has gotten permission to cover this news item discreetly, so as not to encourage the situation; a plainclothesman who drives; and two of the military guys, including the one Alma thought of as the general in charge, who is calling his wife on his cell phone to say he won't be home for his daughter's quinceañera rehearsal. So much for Alma's native ability to read her culture.

One good thing about her car: nobody seems to be a smoker. They ride into the interior in sealed, air-conditioned comfort. The general lectures for a while on the continuing theme, his two cohorts chiming in: This situation is a rare occurrence. It all comes of this cable television. Alma says nothing. Globalization be blamed. Everybody wants to wash their hands clean of what is wrong in their corner of the world. But they might be right, like those viral infections that Emerson mentioned, that start somewhere else but spread everywhere and end up bringing the suffering world together.

Alma tries without success to pump the occupants of her car for information. Who is this Jim Larsen fellow? Is anyone—okay, not *negotiating*, but talking to these boy terrorists? What are the new demands they are making? She feels weepy with unanswered questions.

"Señora," the quieter military man finally speaks up. "We do not know any more than you do." And she believes him. They were all pulled out of their lives abruptly to attend to this rare occurrence. They, too, were on their way somewhere else, not wanting this to happen. Only the journalist whose job it is to be prepared for the unexpected was ready. She holds up her little overnight case. "It goes with me everywhere."

By the time they take the turnoff into the mountains, the general has turned genial. It seems he knows several of Alma's relatives. Has done business with her cousin. Once dated another cousin. Hard to believe this chesty, antique character is Alma's age, actually six years younger. He has a wife, a fifteen-year-old daughter, a son with leukemia. His eyes fill. He can't afford to take the boy to the United States, where surely the best doctors could save him.

No, Alma thinks, this guy is not a general.

It's NOT UNTIL THEY'VE started up the mountain that Alma thinks about calling the sheriff back in Vermont. A lot of good it will do now, late in the day. Still, maybe Alma can avoid a tragedy there. Was Mickey's deadly virus idea what Helen was refusing to go along with that day Alma walked in on their argument? Hard to believe Helen would keep this disturbing secret to herself. Maybe she knew Mickey and Hannah were just fantasizing. And no matter what, Mickey is her son, the boy on her refrigerator holding up his 4-H prize: head, hands, health, heart.

Poor Helen. Her hands weak, her heart ailing, her head muddled, her health gone. Her boy in jail. Does she know about the scuffle in her bedroom, how Mickey hit the sheriff by mistake? Yesterday afternoon seems so long ago.

Alma asks the occupants of her car if they know where she can make a phone call. She has seen them all using cell phones, so she's hoping they'll oblige. But no one's cell phone seems to be working right now; the most promising, belonging to the attractive journalist, gets a signal but does not have an international plan. "Perhaps your American friends," the general who is surely not a general suggests. He must think his neighbors to the north are godlike: they can cure leukemia; they can produce cell phones with interplanetary capacities.

The ride is endless. The caravan stops here and there so that the men can take a pit stop, right on the shoulder, their backs to the road. What need for modesty? The road is deserted at this late afternoon hour. Anybody who has to get up or down the mountain has done so. Starr and Alma and the journalist trek out a little farther afield, airing the usual female grievance about the ease with which men can urinate publicly. "The only penis envy I've ever had is when I need to take a leak," Starr laughs. "So there, Mister Freud." Her drawl makes a lot of what she says sound funnier than it is.

As for Alma's wanting to make a phone call, Starr's cell won't get a signal until they're on the mountaintop. Of course, her cell works up here, she replies when Alma voices surprise. Bienvenido doesn't know what he's talking about if he told Richard cell phones don't work at the Centro. And the general is right. Starr can call the United States on her plan. Her daddy would die if he didn't hear from her every day. *So there, Mister Freud*, Alma thinks.

After forty or so minutes on the slow-going, winding mountain road, the caravan comes to a halt. Alma cranes her neck trying to see who all has stopped them. A roadblock ahead. Troops in camouflage stream by either side of their car. A soldier peers in the driver's window, saluting when he sees the uniformed men inside. Alma half expects him to ask, Any of you bringing a cable TV into the area?

By the time they reach the mountaintop village, it is dusk. The huts cast ominous shadows; electric lines haven't made it up to this remote spot. The caravan rides down the narrow, dirt street, windows down, greetings called out to the people who come to their doorways to watch. Troops are visible everywhere. This is probably the most excitement these poor people will see in a lifetime. Except for hurricanes, the journalist reminds them, which rip through the island, leaving behind their trail of destruction, uprooting forests, houses, crops, people. To this day, you fly over the island, the journalist explains, and you see the new green coming up. "Avenidas de esperanza," she calls them. Avenues of hope. And then because the thought inspires the kind of religiosity that comes easy to those not on the spot, she touches Alma's hand. "Your husband is going to be fine. God is taking care of him and the others. Don't worry." Alma feels a surge of cheap hope. She always regresses when she comes back home. Actually, she reminds herself, she was regressing long before she got here, back in Vermont, trying to strike a deal with Helen's God.

Suddenly, Alma catches herself. *Her man for Hannah's, both free, unharmed.* But if Alma calls the sheriff to warn him about Mickey's craziness, isn't she going back on her part of the deal? It's late. The sheriff is home by now, his car facing out on the road giving some other motorist speeding home a scare. And the sheriff might be young, but he's smart with a sore jaw. He's not going to let Mickey out of jail just like that. Whatever harm might have been done was averted by Alma's throwing the phone. As for "deadly virus," it's probably another imaginary strain of Hannah's AIDS of conscience. Tomorrow will be soon enough to call the sheriff if Alma decides to do so.

And maybe, oh please God, maybe by tomorrow, Richard will be free. Getting Mickey into a good therapy program might be the only way for Hannah to really have him back. "He was just trying to do what's right," Hannah had said. So were we all, Alma thinks, remembering Emerson's grassroots revolution, hope and history rhyming. So why have things gone so terribly wrong? Who can she call on?

She remembers an article she once read about how in moments of

terror or pain or grief, most people, no matter their age, cry out for
their mothers. Not their wives or mistresses, sons or daughters, but
their mothers! Maybe as an infant this was true for Alma, but not
since her early teens has she thought of Mamasita as a soothing presence. A few months back, Alma probably would have cried out
*Richard* or *Helen,* but neither of these names is a helpful invocation
right this moment. Who to call?

*Isabel!* The name comes unbidden, the one person who might understand the tangled web of head, hands, heart, and health Alma finds
herself caught in right now.

Why not Isabel? Who cares if her story took place a long time ago,
if it is half made up, if history wants control of the facts? History can
keep the facts. But Alma mustn't lose faith. Isabel's story is keeping
the knowledge of something alive in Alma, belief in a saving grace.

THEIR CAR STOPS AND pulls over behind the cars and vans
ahead. Everybody is getting out and walking down the main street
toward what looks to be the only lit-up house around. Beyond the
village, the street dead-ends at a cluster of concrete houses surrounded by a chain-link fence. On this side of the fence there are
sandbags and crouching figures. Just inside, Alma can make out a
sign, but it's too dark to read what it says. It has to be! The Centro
with its clinic, cloaked in darkness. Did the troops shoot out the gen-
erators? Maybe the boys who laid siege to the place—she has got to
stop calling them terrorists—are saving fuel, just in case they're in
for the long haul.

A *long* haul! How long is that? Another week? A month? Before the
generals who are in charge lose all patience and begin to bomb the
place. Alma's panic kicks in again. *Richard!* she feels like screaming.
*Are you there?*

"Hey." Starr is waiting for her in front of the concrete house. "We've
just been getting an update. They released the local women who do
the cleaning and cooking and their kids about an hour ago, and the
women gave a complete list of all the names. The guys are just the

ones I thought!" Starr is elated, as if she just guessed the right question in a quiz show.

Alma is glad for the women and children. But it's amazing how shallow her gladness is except for how it may connect to her deeper concern. "What about Richard?"

"Come on in, you can talk to them yourself." Starr hurries ahead.

Alma follows, her body breaking out in a cold sweat. Why can't Starr give her a simple answer: Yes, Richard's okay? Maybe something horrible has happened to him? Or maybe he is inside, a big surprise Starr doesn't want to ruin?

Inside, the room is packed with men who are not Richard, soldiers, plainclothesmen, barefoot men in rags who stand in the shadows, obviously the locals. The room is small but looks even smaller with everyone standing. A coil in the ceiling gives out a vague, milky light, probably solar panel lights, the batteries run down. The men all turn to greet the three ladies, the journalist coming in behind them. Everybody, of course, knows Starr. And the journalist turns out to be a minor celebrity who has a weekly column in which she interviews people who are making news. Alma is introduced as the wife of the americano. "Is my husband all right?" she blurts out.

"Your husband is fine," the soldier in camouflage who had been speaking when the women walked in assures her. "Camacho," he introduces himself. He is a tall man, heart-stoppingly handsome, a rich mahogany color, with long-fingered hands, which when he turns them up in answer to questions he can't answer are endearingly pink. His teeth flash white. Were she not so terrified, Alma could watch this beautiful man for a long time.

"I know they released the local women and children. Did they say when they might release—" She catches herself in time. "The rest of the hostages." Of course, she cares about the-rest-of-the-hostages. But first and foremost, there is Richard.

"Señora—"

"Call me Alma, please." Alma doesn't know why she hasn't said this before to all the officials calling her señora, her usual home-country mode, no titles por favor. Most likely, she has just been too panicked to be shrewd. But now she senses that she is finally meeting the person who, if not in charge, then has one of those big, beautiful hands on the pulse of what is going on. She wants him on her side.

"We expect this situation will be resolved very soon. The women have given us the names of the individuals involved." He holds up a piece of paper with what looks like a lot of names.

Alma asks to see the list as if she is going to know anybody on it. Some of the names are the ones Starr mentioned. Moncho. Rubio. Salvador. Tomás. There are three Josés and a couple of Franciscos. Then numbers without names. Young men the women didn't recognize, strangers from somewhere else.

The crowd toward the back of the room parts: two young men walk in, dressed in windbreakers, Walter and Frank from the U.S. embassy in the capital. Big handshakes for Jim and Emerson and a hug for Starr. They seem confident if a little weary. They have been here for two days, talking to the villagers, talking to the kidnappers, just talked to the released women. They could resolve this mess in no time. But it's not their country. These people have to learn to do it for themselves. They remind Alma of parents, vowing to stay out of their children's arguments.

"But there's an American citizen in there," Alma puts in. "My husband's in there. And these guys have been talking about bombing the place." She feels like a tattletale, spilling the beans on naughty classmates.

Walter—or maybe it's Frank— rolls his eyes privately at her. "No one is going to bomb anything," he tells her flatly. They're here precisely to protect an American life and American property. The Centro and clinic and surrounding lands belong to Swan. Normally, Alma wouldn't approve of the USA meddling in another country's business, but this is one time she can't help feeling glad. Cooler heads will prevail.

"So what's up?" Jim asks the embassy fellows, who nod for Camacho to join them. He strides over, smiling hugely, one pink palm clapped on a revolver, another patting his belt of ammo. They all make room for him in their now segregated American huddle. Alma suddenly realizes where the strong smell of cologne has been coming from.

Jim repeats his question, this time in impressively good Spanish. He wants to know the latest news, what the local women have reported, where the water line is, all the entrances into the compound. As he asks his questions, Alma feels she is watching a champion analyze pieces on a board in a game whose rules she does not understand.

Camacho summarizes. His Spanish is so slow and well enunciated, it sounds like a foreign language, even to Alma. The local women were released in exchange for some concessions. "The men want food brought in. They want a journalist to interview them. They want cigarettes."

"We can let them have that." Jim nods. "What else?"

It turns out Starr is right. The kidnappers want amnesty. But in an untenable form. They all want tickets to the United States of America and guaranteed visas so they can stay there and get jobs.

"Fat chance," one of the embassy men says under his breath.

Alma looks over at him, Frank or Walter. He gives her a collusive look, as if what she just heard was in total confidence. "So what'll you do to make them give up the hostages if you're not going to negotiate?" Alma asks stupidly, as if these embassy guys are going to spell out the battle plan. "I know you're not going to bomb or anything, but some-body might do something rash and someone might get . . ." She can't let herself think no less say the terrible word.

The two embassy men defer to Jim as the spokesperson. Alma re-calls what Starr said. Nobody's going to do something unless Jim tells them to. "We're going to work something out," he assures her, but his eyes are somewhere else. "You'll be back home with your husband in time to eat leftover turkey." This is supposed to comfort her. Little does he know that she's vegetarian. He smiles—at least he's cheered by the thought—and then, casting a look that includes Emerson, the em-bassy boys, and Camacho, he adds, "Maybe we can find a place to talk?"

The mayor, whose house it turns out this is, comes up to their group. He would like to invite them to sit down on the crude chairs several boys have carried in. He is a short, slight man, with missing teeth, who is way over his head with so much fancy company. A journalist! Americanos! Not since the gente from Swan came to negotiate for the clinic and Centro has there been such distinguished company in his humble house, which is at their orders. Alma feels sorry for the poor guy, knocking himself out to be their welcome mat. To think this is the grand moment of his life. "Those boys, they are just sinvergüenzas," he starts to declaim in a loud voice. He has asked to be allowed to go inside the compound and talk with them. They're not going to shoot him. He wiped this one's snot from his face. He baptized this other one. His wife was like a mother to a third one who was orphaned young. He goes through a rather long list of favors he has done for each one. Again Alma wonders, How many kidnappers are there anyhow?

"Thank you, Don Jacobo," Camacho says, courteously and definitively shutting up the old man. "We will go in here to talk." He invites himself and the American men into an adjoining room. Then, turning to Alma and the crowd of compatriots left behind, he adds, "Perhaps you could offer our tired visitors a refresco."

"It would be an honor," Mayor Jacobo says, again in that loud voice, which he must think is the way to talk to important people, a voice of declamation. The old man backs out of his own back door. A moment later, Alma will hear him in the outside kitchen, ordering his wife and daughters to get together some refrescos. All the glasses in the town will have to be collected in order to serve these many visitors.

It's as he's bowing his way out that Alma looks down, and her heart catches. The mayor is wearing big, floppy shoes, obviously too big for his feet, like a clown's shoes. God bless us, one and all, she thinks.

DOES SHE SLEEP THAT night at all? She and Starr and the journalist, whose name Alma finally catches, Mariana from *El noticiero*, are given the mayor's daughters' room. It seems there are two other sleeping rooms: a big house for the area. The americanos, Emerson and Jim, and the U.S. embassy guys from the capital get the bigger bedroom where the mayor sleeps with his wife when he isn't out mujeriando through town. There is another room, which Alma guesses is the boys' bedroom, and that's where she assumes a few of the plain-clothesmen and generals are staying; the majority, though, hunker down in their cars and vans lining the one and only street of the little village. Who knows where the mayor, his deferential wife, his shy, giggling daughters, his four seemingly mute sons, and a grandchild some other daughter has left behind with her parents end up sleeping. But by dawn, when Alma comes out to the open-aired kitchen, hoping for a cup of coffee, the whole family is there, awake, and at her service.

"How did you sleep?" the mayor wants to know.

"Thank you," she says, so as not to go into details.

She did sleep some. In her carry-on, along with a half-dozen items she looked at last night uncomprehendingly—why did she bring so many books? why her jewelry? a pair of heels?—she also packed the sleeping pills Richard always talked her out of taking nights when she couldn't sleep worrying over some important performance the next day that she had to be at her best for; worrying about Mamasita and Papote, what would become of one when the other died; worrying about Helen's glaucoma and diabetes, not knowing there was an even bigger danger already replicating itself endlessly in the old woman's body; worrying about her saga novel that she wasn't writing. You'd think all those worries would vanish, surpassed by this bigger worry, but last night, in a feeding frenzy, all those little worries came into her head, as if to snatch at the crumbs that might fall from the big worry's feasting on her peace of mind.

As a last resort, after hours of tossing and turning, Alma tried invoking Isabel again, the twenty-two boys, who sometimes turned into the kidnappers and sometimes into the bashful sons of Mayor Jacobo carrying in chairs. What had become of Isabel's boys once they had served their use as carriers? Alma tried inventing futures for them. One would become a lawyer, another a teacher, a third a general with no teeth in his mouth and big boots he couldn't take off. Finally, she fell asleep with the help of Ambien and Isabel reminding her in Helen's voice that God was taking care of all of them.

"And you? You slept well?" Alma asks the mayor as he offers her a cup of what turns out to be wonderfully strong but too sweet coffee she can hardly get down.

He slept very well, thank you.

She does not go on to ask him where he slept, because she wants to drink her coffee quietly, look around, shake off this foggy feeling and pounding headache and growing sense of dread of a world without Richard. She walks beyond the kitchen, with its sweet smell of wood smoke, a zinc roof protecting the cooking fire from rain, and looks around. Not more than fifty feet away, she sees the chain-link fence, the sign she couldn't read last night: CENTRO VERDE DEL CARIBE, and below, in smaller letters: CLÍNICA DE INVESTIGACIONES SWAN. The sun is just beginning to rise in the east. She wonders if Richard is watching it. If he is scared, hungry. If he slept at all. If he is getting any coffee.

*Richard, are you there?* Alma is again tempted to cry out. But what if her voice is enough to snap some terrorist's frayed nerves, to jerk a trigger finger, to spill the life she loves more than anything on the ground forever? *Oh, Jesus God, no! Isabel!*

As she guessed last night, the compound is surrounded by sandbags, crouching soldiers in camouflage, leaning against the bags, some of them catching a snooze before Camacho comes by to inspect and kick ass. A few of the soldiers who are awake look over at her. They are boys—no more than seventeen, eighteen years old—boys who stayed up all night, boys who are hungry and staring at the coffee cup in her hand.

She waves without thinking, and without thinking they wave back, giving away their position to the enemy, who are not the enemy, but— if the mayor is to be believed, a bunch of young boys he has known since they were this high.

Just inside the fence, there is a picnic table with an umbrella. She wishes she could go in through the little pedestrian gate, drink her coffee. Her journal is in her jacket pocket, a pen. She wants to write

Richard a love note, give it to the little boys to deliver when they take in those big pots of boiled roots the mayor's wife and daughters are cooking. Or is this breakfast for the young soldiers behind sandbags? Or for the patients locked up in their dormitorios, who periodically call out? They are hungry. They are hot. They are sick, innocent people. *Have a conscience for the love of God!*

"We were offered such an oportunidad, señora." The mayor has come up beside her to gaze upon what he hoped would be the bright future of his little village. In the morning light, Alma sees Don Jacobo is not so old, at most in his late thirties, just worn out with a life of hard work, a hundred lean pounds, more or less. He has donned a baseball cap with the logo of an American feed company, one of the many articles Richard picked up at recycling to take down in a duffel bag. "Señora, it grieves my heart to see this hen killed because we could not eat her golden eggs."

He has got the story garbled, but no matter. The grief is real. So much hope gone to waste, the packed duffel bags, the pickup full of goodies. But maybe that hope was misplaced. A clinic testing an experimental AIDS vaccine laying the gold egg of a green center? Boys infected with a virus to save the world from smallpox? Every good threaded through with, at best, dubious goods. Hope and history rhyming, but only by violence or sheer accident.

"And now no hen, no eggs."

Alma is not going to be able to get rid of Don Jacobo. In fact, it is a courtesy to her to keep her company. "El problema is these jóvenes, they can't get jobs, but they can get sick, that is what they worry about. La señorita Starr explained to them they can't get AIDS just because the clinic is here. That is not how it works. I am a bruto who never learned letters, but I believe her. And they believe her, too. She told them they are going to get jobs with the programa your husband is starting, but la señorita Starr leaves, the money she gives them to help their families until the work starts, they spend it all, and they start drinking, fooling with drogas, talking to other elements. Well, you can imagine, one thing leads to another."

So much for the cable TV theory, Alma thinks. "Are they armed, do you know, Don Jacobo?"

"Desgraciadamente, there are some bad elements in the group. They are not from this village," Mayor Jacobo is quick to add.

"But are they armed?" Why won't people give her straight answers? Are they trying to protect her from a truth she is going to have to face anyway?

The mayor takes off his cap, as if in deference to the truth he is about to pronounce. "Desgraciadamente, I do not know but that these other elements are armed."

Alma feels herself breaking out again in a cold sweat. This is not going to turn out as the journalist led her to hope. Last night, after she and Starr and Mariana said their good nights, she could hear Emerson and Jim and the embassy guys, talking in their room with Camacho. What were they plotting? She strained to hear, but she could not make out their words, just that serious murmuring of men at the wheel. She feels desperate. She has got to save Richard before these guys mount some stupid operation. "Don Jacobo, please," she pleads. "Tell me in your estimation. Do you think they would hurt my husband?"

"Absolutamente, no." Don Jacobo shakes his head with his whole body. "Not my boys. They are malcriado and hardheaded but they are not criminal types. But desgraciadamente, the elements, not from this village, are not to be trusted."

Alma sighs. What a roller coaster, talking to this guy.

"La señorita Starr talked to them. Your husband talked to them. Those elements have been making trouble for everyone."

Alma watches the sun reflecting off the roofs and solar panels of the Swan compound while the mayor talks on at her side. Soon, the others will begin stirring, car and van doors banging, and he will leave her alone to attend to them. For now, though, he needs to pour out his heart to someone who will listen, how the building of the clinic brought everyone jobs, how all the houses—he points and she turns to the skyline of the little village behind her—every one of those houses was going to get a solar panel, a good latrine, running water;

his was the first. And then, when the patients came, the local women got jobs cooking and cleaning, and then the señorita Starr came and explained and helped everyone out with a regalía, and then Don Ricardo came, and the local men were starting to get jobs working for the green center.

Alma can see the main building, where the clinic is housed, flanked on either side by little adobe houses. The slopes behind look newly planted. This has been Richard's world for the last month and a half. Alma feels a nostalgia that makes her afraid, as if she has come back years from now to see the place that cost him his life. She shivers. Isabel and Balmis and most of the little boys survived, she reminds herself. *Isabel!*

"That little house is where your husband and Bienvenido stay. All that land around is planted already with many, many hectares of coffee. It will bring in good money. That is what I tell the boys. But now ¿quién sabe?"

That's right. This green pipe dream has gone down the tubes at least for now. But maybe Swan and HI can let the locals pick and sell the coffee? Maybe something can be salvaged?

"I want to write my husband a note," Alma explains. She wants to tell Richard she is here. She loves him. Everything is going to be okay. Hold tight. Hold tight for what? The vision takes her breath away. "Are the boys going to take food in to them?"

Mayor Jacobo looks down at the empty inside of his cap as if the future were pictured there. "This I cannot confirm. There is a clinic kitchen, but the women last night said the food is running out."

A phone has started ringing, such an odd sound in this isolated spot. On and on, it rings. It could be any number of cell phones, now getting signals, belonging to the visitors. Wives and daughters and mistresses and mothers calling up, worried about their men who did not come home last night. Finally somebody picks it up. But it's as if this ringing phone were the wakeup signal. The village comes awake behind them. Car doors bang, voices call out, a rooster crows lustily, a donkey brays, a baby wails.

And as the world comes awake in all its beautiful, baffling detail, Alma can't help but think of other mornings with Richard. The sounds and smells wafting up from the kitchen, the silverware drawer opening, the coffee perking, Richard letting in the cats, the furnace kicking in. She needs to be with him. If anything is going to happen to Richard, she must not survive him.

Mayor Jacobo excuses himself, and as he heads back to his house, Alma walks toward where the young men recline on their sandbags. *Duck down!* one of them gestures desperately. Alma obliges, running forward, and as she thrusts herself beside them they turn to face the compound, suddenly remembering their mission, now that she has joined them.

"You must go back, señora," one of the tougher, older-looking boys tells her.

"It's okay. I have permission," she lies, avoiding his eyes, because surely he'll be able to tell. She remembers what Tera has told her about civil disobedience. Stay calm. Act like you know what you are doing. We have the right. The world is ours. We need to take it back. There are forty-some patients locked in those dormitories; Richard and the staff are in the clinic, guarded by dozens of local boys and their friends, the elements not from here. So many expendable lives. Alma is another American life, another reason not to bombard or storm the place and cause a tragedy. Hope and history might rhyme, especially if Alma doesn't let her fear and indecision keep her from what might work out just this one time.

"I have permission," Alma repeats. And suddenly, she is standing up, scrambling quickly over the mound of sandbags as several soldiers lunge, trying to grab her back. But she is too quick for them, too scared, too lucky-unlucky, and the pedestrian gate is so close by, unlocked, so that she has slipped inside and is heading up the cobbled path with her hands in the air before the soldiers begin yelling for her to halt.

Soon other voices are joining in, Emerson and Starr calling her back, Camacho shouting orders to hold fire! The commotion, of course, has not gone unnoticed on this side of the chain-link fence. Just ahead of Alma, two figures emerge onto the front porch; the one in front, the shield, is Richard! Standing behind him is a young man with a kerchief over half his face and what looks like a real-life gun he is holding up to Richard's head.

"Get away!" Richard calls out. The guy holding him by the collar gives him a jerk to shut up.

"It's okay," Alma calls back. "I'm not armed!" she calls out to the man with the kerchief. It is the longest walk she has ever had to take, those twenty steps toward a man holding a gun to the head of the man she loves. And all that way, she feels as if another woman inside her is leading her forward, the woman she once saw out of the corner of her eye, whom she has identified as Isabel because sometimes a story can take over your life. If you are desperate enough to let it happen. Which Alma is. Which is why she tells Richard again, "I'm okay. This is where I want to be." And to the man now screaming in a voice muffled by his kerchief "Stop!" she repeats, "I'm not armed."

Behind her, she feels the sudden deafening silence of the troops and Starr and Emerson and Jim and the embassy folks and Camacho, watching her. Thinking she is crazy, which she probably is, stepping out like this from where they were all headed and might still be headed if she doesn't succeed.

# VI

---

L ATER, THE MANY PORTS of call, the welcome or unwelcome we received, the thousands we vaccinated, the bared arms, the ripe vesicles, the many officials proclaiming us saviors or setting up impediments to our smallpox salvation—all of it seemed to blur together into one great tapestry of the expedition.

One would think that I hung that whole tapestry in my memory. Curious indeed how the mind works! For what I remembered was a particular scene, a seemingly insignificant incident, a certain face such as an artist might draw.

During our crossing, on those long evenings aboard the *Pita*, Dr. Salvany often perused a book of prints he had purchased in Madrid by the artist Francisco de Goya. *Los Caprichos*, it was called. Once, when I asked if I might view it, Dr. Salvany's face turned quite pink. They were not for the eyes of a lady, he claimed.

It was not until our departure from Puerto Rico, as we were hurriedly assembling our equipage that the book came into my hands. A servant had found it fallen behind the night table of Dr. Salvany's chamber and turned it over to me.

I confess that before I returned it, I could not help but peek. I had imagined something far naughtier than I found. They were etchings of moments in our human lives, some dark, some light. Each one bore a caption that bespoke what the etching was about. A dozing figure was beset by horrid blackbirds and owls. *The sleep of human reason produces monsters*, read the note. Another showed a donkey mounted on a poor laborer, jabbing at him with a golden spur. I knew the saying that served as its caption: *The poor carry the rich on their backs.* Those who do thus, the artist seemed to suggest, were indeed asses. I suppose the book was naughty enough.

I was only able to view a few of the prints before I was summoned to some task or other. But even that quick glimpse left quite the impression on me. As the expedition unfolded, I would catch myself making a mental drawing of this or that moment, inscribing it with a message, storing it in my memory. Later, reviewing those moments, each place would come alive again in my mind's eye, complete with its own caption: Caracas, Havana, Veracruz, Mexico City, Puebla de los Ángeles . . .

*GOLFO TRISTE—EN ROUTE FROM PUERTO RICO TO VENEZUELA: Afloat on gray waters, a small ship wanders. In the background, veiled in mist, officials are assembling at a port.*

*But such foreknowledge is denied to those on board. We see faces distorted with anger, suspicion. The captain, his eyes dark pools of despair, holds a dead child in his arms, his mouth ripped open with a cry we cannot hear.*

Days upon days, we were lost at sea. Yellow fever raged on board. Our director himself was stricken with fever and worry, for it seemed we would not find landfall by the time our last carrier's vesicle reached its tenth day.

That morning when I heard the wailing of a man, I thought my own heart had found a voice. It was our captain, crying over the body of his cabin boy. For days afterward, he locked himself up in his cabin, refusing to let us bury the boy at sea, neglecting his duties. Lieutenant Pozo and the pilot did the best they could, but a ship without a captain is a body without a soul.

Puerto Rico had been a disaster. It had brought out the worst in our director, in all the men. They were at odds with each other. There was talk of returning to Spain; there was talk of the crew taking a knife to our throats, talk of the expedition arming themselves against this attempt.

And, of course, there was the murderous look in the steward's eye each time he spotted one of our boys. He claimed they had tried to kill him with bow and arrow and should all be hung from the starboard foreyard, then thrown in the sea. I kept a close eye on my charges. No longer did we linger in the forward part of the ship, sitting in the galley with the crew. Besides, most of my boys were ill with the fever and the cook was no friend to a vomiter around his steaming pots of stew—as if his fare were not already beyond spoiling!

The aft part of the ship was no less peaceable.

Dr. Salvany no longer trusted our director. Dr. Grajales and Don Basilio Bolaños and Don Rafael Lozano fell in with him. The rest of the expedition members defended Don Francisco, who no longer trusted anyone. Only one person seemed to be agreeable to all members on that ship. I had turned into what I had hoped Don Francisco would be. Someone to remind us all of how grandly we could dream.

We were indeed lost at sea, which in an odd way seemed the correct state for our embattled expedition to be.

VENEZUELA—*LAST NIGHT IN* CARACAS: *A much lighter scene. The great hall is filled with guests, ladies and gentlemen lined up for a quadrille. So many bright, happy faces. And yet at the edges of the party one lady has a face covered with—are they scars or letters? How dreadful that she should be so disfigured. We yearn for the artist to provide us with an explanation.*

*But wait, look closely at the other faces and they are all similarly marked. Here is the guest of honor with the letters of shame written across his features. A young man holds a book whose words are crawling up his arms toward his proud face. Ah, the carnival of human desires!*

*In the background, faces, hundreds of them. They have been saved by those who are now enjoying this grand celebration in their honor.*

We became whole again in Caracas.

After being lost at sea, we finally sighted land just in time. The vesicle was ripe on our last boy. Don Francisco was distraught with the impending loss of the fluid and the debacle of his expedition. The last thing I wanted I forced myself to do.

We were lowered into the sea on the small boat, Don Ángel accompanying us—oh, paint wings on that dear, angelic man! Lieutenant Pozo guided two crew members to row toward an indistinct shape that might be a storm cloud, a pirate ship, the Leviathan, or the coast of Venezuela. My heart was in my throat as we moved through that thick fog.

When we landed, it seemed a miracle. The local comandante was waiting for us with the leading families of the town, who had brought with them twenty-eight carriers!

I looked at each fresh, young face and reminded myself: no, not *carriers*, but children, dear, worthy human beings.

From the port, we traveled inland, arriving in Caracas during Holy Week. The whole city turned out to celebrate us with fireworks and tributes. This was the welcome that Don Francisco had so sorely missed in Puerto Rico. Honorary regidor, concerts, masses, our director turned back into the noble man who had inspired me to be the woman I was struggling to become.

By the first of May, we had vaccinated twenty thousand and set up the Junta Central de la Vacuna so that there would always be vaccine available for the future generations. The last night before we were to leave, Captain-General Guevara threw a lavish banquet for us at his palace. The tables were covered with fruits and fine pastries. The boys claimed they counted forty-four plates of food at each service of which there were three. I had to keep a close eye on them to prevent them from overeating or stuffing food in their pockets. Poor dears. Once you have known need, its phantom hangs over any luxury.

After the tables were cleared, the entertainment began. A poet was introduced, a young man with the knowing eyes of an old man, who read a rather long ode—over two hundred verses! My boys grew restless. I was getting ready to round them up, but Don Francisco stopped me. There were servants enough to take care of the boys for this one night.

I was touched that he wanted me to stay to enjoy the evening with the rest of the expedition.

"You have kept us together," Don Francisco acknowledged as he led me onto the dance floor. I had protested that I did not know how to dance, and he had smiled. "Neither do I, so we are well matched."

But amazingly, my feet retained the memory of the steps I had danced as a girl. "As with other matters, you underestimate yourself, Doña Isabel," Don Francisco complimented me. Was it time to ask him to call me Isabel?

His color was back, though he had not put on the weight he had lost. Still, the hospitality of our hosts, the good food and rest had restored him to his health. We should stay here forever, I thought, for as long as it lasts.

The music had ended, and a new spirited fandango was starting up. Dr. Salvany asked for this next dance, and though I pleaded that I was tired, he persisted and I indulged. "I am happy to see that all is mended between you and Don Francisco," I mentioned during one of our spins around the room.

He lifted his eyebrows as if questioning the accuracy of my observation, but he was in good humor. Poetry brought out the best in him. "Wasn't he marvelous?" I was still thinking of our director and so must have looked puzzled, because Dr. Salvany added, "The poet, Andrés Bello."

I loved a poem, especially one set to music on a romantic theme. But a long ode to the vaccine . . .

"Do you think it would be too bold of me to show him my own productions?" Don Salvany was flushed with the exertion of the dance. He, too, had recovered, but there was still a fragile look to him.

"I should think he would be honored," I offered.

Just then, the dance ended and we found ourselves standing near the poet. Dr. Salvany gave him a deep bow.

The poet bowed back. "Andrés Bello, a sus órdenes."

That was all the invitation Dr. Salvany needed. "May I commend you on a true masterpiece of the pen and of the spirit."

The color heightened on the young man's cheeks. He had that glow of success, touched perhaps by shame of that success. How we feel when we are much feted and wonder if there is room for our darker nature in this bright acclamation.

"I hear that you have also written a theatrical work about us?" Dr. Salvany was all eagerness. "*Venezuela salvada.*"

"*Consolada,*" the poet corrected. "*Venezuela consolada.*"

I wondered if indeed a work with that title could be *about* us. Perhaps from now on, we would be a consolation to others. Perhaps it was good of this poet to write such a work. We might be forced to live up to the grand and noble passions his words would hold us to.

As Don Andrés Bello outlined the action of his theatrical piece to Dr. Salvany, I glanced toward our director, now seated at his place at the table, the bishop on one side, the captain-general on the other, his face radiant. I could not help thinking how I had seen him in all his many phases, noble and base, humble and vain, like a moon that wanes and disappears but returns again with its soft, insistent light.

When he glanced in my direction, he dropped his gaze as if embarrassed at being seen so nakedly.

I had not been the only one hiding my true face from the world.

The poet was introducing me to several prominent members of the city council. Dr. Salvany had gone off to retrieve his book of poems to show his newfound friend. "This is the guardian angel of the little carriers of the vaccine," Don Andrés Bello was saying with a bow, "Doña Isabel López Gandarillas."

Another name for me! By the time the expedition was over, I would have been so many Isabels.

Don Francisco was at my side, ready to escort me back to my seat. "You looked lost in that sea of Creoles," he noted in a low voice. "I thought I had better come rescue you."

I took his arm, indulging him in his role as my savior.

*E*N *ROUTE TO* C*UBA: A large canvas with several scenes.*

*First, a busy port, a parting of ways: one group rows out to a ship, the other stays ashore.*

*Another scene shows the deck of that ship. A lone female passenger interrogates a lineup of children. Her face is a study of worry, dread, grief.*

*Last comes a panel depicting a lady conversing with the captain of the ship. The man weeps; the woman looks downcast into the deep. The stars are silvery and sweet, and yet the scene seems to be another one in this triptych of grief.*

Upon leaving Venezuela, our expedition parted in two.

Our director had originally intended that the vaccinations in the territories of New Granada, Peru, and Río de la Plata would be conducted by his colleague from Spain, Dr. Verges, who had gone ahead to Bogotá several months before our expedition had set out. One of our members was to take the fresh vaccine we had brought across the ocean to Dr. Verges when we landed in Venezuela.

But the news reached us in Caracas that Dr. Verges had died of a mysterious fever. We were sobered in the midst of our celebrations. How many of us would be lost to our expedition? It was a question that loomed in my mind as we boarded the small boats that would conduct us out to the *María Pita*, waiting for us in the waters beyond the shallow bay. The ship would take us on to Cuba and Veracruz before returning to Spain.

On shore, we were leaving behind Dr. Salvany and three of our number: Dr. Grajales, Don Rafael Lozano, Don Basilio Bolaños. It crossed my mind that Don Francisco had separated out those members who had always shown partiality for his younger colleague. (How glad I was that Don Ángel, that pacifying angel of our expedition, had been retained in our group!)

Dr. Salvany was pale and looked almost frightened by his new commission. "Do you think he will succeed?" I found myself asking our director as the men on shore became smaller and smaller, toys, figments of our imagination.

Don Francisco sighed. "All he needs to do is continue south down the length of the Americas." Our director raised a hand, parting the air easily in two.

But as we moved away, I saw in my mind's eye the high peaks of the Andes and footpaths through dark jungles, the rapids and rivers and rocky falls. I wondered how easy the task would be for our young colleague in love with poetry.

Perhaps I sensed I would never see him alive again.

As for our own group, Dr. Balmis was taking no chances: he had petitioned for and been granted six boys to carry the vaccine from Venezuela to Cuba.

They were older boys, which made them both easier and more difficult for me to manage. The oldest was thirteen; the youngest, seven. They stayed together, avoiding our own children at first, for the Galician accent was foreign to their ears. But they all soon found plenty of naughtiness in common.

Among their mischief was tormenting our timid little Moor, Tomás Melitón. Even more than our own boys, these young Creoles teased the boy relentlessly, calling him negrito, and threatening to put him in a cask of lye to see if his color would come off and prove him the Spaniard he claimed he was.

Our third morning out at sea, I could not find the boy. I searched every-where on the ship. But the child seemed to have vanished into thin air.

I lined up the boys and interrogated them, threatening to punish all of them, no supper, no coming on deck to see the stars, no stories. There were guilty looks, but the most they would confess to was that they had been chasing Tomás, threatening to throw him in that cask. "But all it has in it is seawater, we swear—"

"No swearing!" I scolded. It was a battle I was losing, keeping the boys from cursing on a ship full of foul-mouthed sailors.

"Tomás!" we all shouted, sometimes individually, sometimes in chorus. My own voice tinged with increasing panic and despair.

Seven days out we found him by his smell. In his effort to evade his tor-mentors, he must have fallen down the steep ladder into the hold and drowned in the bilge water. Already the rats had made a meal of his soft flesh. I wept for the poor unfortunate, who had passed through this life without anyone cherishing him enough. Even my own love was composed largely of obligation.

Captain del Barco, who had become quiet and removed in his grief, found me on the quarterdeck that evening. He stood by me, saying noth-ing. We gazed out at the endless watery world, which now held two of our children.

"You seem to be the soul of this expedition, Doña Isabel. Tell me—" Our captain turned to face me. Though it was dusk, I wished I had my veil, so I could hide the uncertainty I always felt when a superior interrogated me. "Is it worth it?"

I wanted to tell him that it was a calculation we must never make: weighing lives against any cause. Orlando and Tomás had lost the only lives they had. There was nothing to balance against that loss. No platitude, no poetry.

"We must believe we are doing more good than ill," I managed. I meant that it should always be a struggle to believe this. Otherwise, we would push ahead with certainty like our director or founder in doubts like Dr. Salvany. But my words sounded hollow even to my own ears.

*CUBA—ARRIVAL IN HAVANA: In the distant bay, a ship drops anchor, while in the foreground, a welcome party assembles on the wharf. Yet another port scene.*

*A short, nervous man, his shirt misbuttoned, his hat in his hands. By his side a large, ballooning woman, children coming out from under her petticoats, points to a waiting carriage.*

*Behind them stretches the city of Havana with its irregular houses, their fronts painted red and pale blue. The parade of carriages leads to a commodious residence, which fills with dozens of boys. A pet monkey shrieks. Cages full of songbirds twitter. A frisky puppy barks and barks out of sheer exuberance. The cheer on all the faces tells that in this vale of tears pockets of paradise exist.*

Our destination again eluded us, owing to a stormy sea. The eight-day journey took us eighteen days. But in spite of the fact that we were not expected, we were warmly greeted at the port of Havana by the governor, the Marquis of Someruelos, and a hastily assembled group of officials.

Right up front, without any subterfuge, the marquis informed us that the vaccine had preceded us to the island. It turned out that a Cuban lady had been visiting relatives in Puerto Rico and while there had taken the opportunity to have Dr. Oller vaccinate her young son and two servant girls.

*Oller.* Just the name made my heart stop. I dared not look over at our director. I braced myself for a repeat of our first landfall.

As if he knew no reason not to continue, the marquis went on with his explanations. Upon their return to Havana, the vesicles were ripe on all three children. Dr. Romay, their family doctor, took the opportunity to harvest the fluid and vaccinate the entire city. The dreaded epidemic that was spreading across the island had been averted.

A short man stepped forward, his cravat twisted, his buttons askew, a stain on his sleeve. He looked as if he himself had just been assembled hurriedly. "Dr. Romay," he introduced himself. "Our esteemed governor gives me too much credit. I have done the best I could with little training in this field or supervision. So I am most grateful that your illustrious person and colleagues have arrived on our shores to review my work and improve upon my errors." Then, with a smile that could win the devil back to goodness, he insisted that our director and expedition be lodged at his own house.

Five sons, from youngster to young man, came forward to second their father's invitation, offering to take the smaller boys in hand, relieving me of the carpetbag I was carrying. A fat, open-faced woman directed them. She turned out to be the good doctor's wife, Señora Romay. Her largeness was amplified by the voluminous skirts spread out around her. It seemed five more boys might issue from beneath them if she should sneeze or laugh too heartily.

Our director's face was softening, won over, as who wouldn't be, by such good-heartedness. "We are too many to burden any one household."

Señora Romay declared that even twice our number would not be too many. "You will break my heart if you do not do me this honor, Don Francisco!"

There was no arguing with this kind clan. Already the Romay boys were loading the smaller boys into the waiting carriages. Señora Romay hooked her arm through mine. "You poor dear," she commiserated. "I, too, live my life surrounded by men!" She smiled broadly, gap-toothed and proud of her brood.

Yes, I thought, but you have command over yours.

The very next day we began reviewing vaccinations and setting up a junta as we had done in Caracas. Thank goodness the outlying towns provided us with new carriers to spread the vaccine to the other parts of the island.

Benito loved Havana. He had found five older brothers in the Romay boys. I must say, my son was no longer the frightened, clinging waif of days gone by. In the small world of our expedition, he had become the special one with a mother along, a position I struggled to downplay. You are all my sons, I told them. But anyone could see—and children are especially adept at this—that I had a special weakness for my little Benito. "Let's stay here, Mamá," he pleaded.

"We have a mission to accomplish," I explained, recalling a similar moment in Caracas, when I had wished to stay forever. "But perhaps we can come back later when it is over."

But to a child the word *later* might as well be *never*. He pleaded and cried and finally our hostess's words came out of his mouth, "My heart will break, Mamá."

"Then we will put it back together again," I said, trying hard not to smile, to take his small sorrows seriously.

And so, in spite of the fact that as in Puerto Rico, the vaccine had also preceded us here in Cuba, the warm welcome of our hosts, their honesty from the start, their deference to Don Francisco's direction—all of this made a world of difference. Any request, the marquis was at our service. And Dr. Romay and his family continued in their many kindnesses.

In only one regard our hosts were unable to indulge us. We had been promised four boys to carry the vaccine from Havana to Veracruz. But days passed and no one would volunteer a child; unfortunately, the orphans at the local hospicio had all been vaccinated. It seemed that my Benito's wish might come true after all, and here we would stay.

Frustrated, as only he could get, Don Francisco finally resorted to the only means he could think of. "I've bought them," he told me when I asked about the three African girls, the oldest no more than twelve, who had been delivered at Dr. Romay's back door in a cart one morning. "They will carry the vaccine to Veracruz. There I will sell them and recuperate my expense."

"Bought them?" Why was I so surprised? I had seen the slave market in Tenerife. At our many hosts' houses in San Juan, Caracas, here in Havana, any number of servant slaves had attended to our needs. Yet a new wind was blowing in the Americas. I could feel it all about me. On the way to Cuba, we had passed by Saint Domingue, avoiding the shore, for a revolt had taken place there and the slaves had freed themselves. I had felt a surge of fear—no doubt if seized, our white throats would be cut!—but I had also felt a secret surge of hope, this was as it should be, every one of us born free.

Out in the courtyard, the girls were moaning, begging to be returned to their families.

"We came to save all our brothers and sisters who have cried to us in need." I was repeating the very words our director had spoken to me months ago at the orphanage.

"This is necessity, Doña Isabel. I have no other recourse." Don Francisco would not meet my eye. I could see him withdrawing, shutting the doors of his heart against my influence.

And so three Negresses joined our expedition, and at the last minute, the boy drummer of a local regiment was thrown in for good measure by the marquis. Perhaps I was wrong to question our director's choice. He had merely brought out in the open what my moral delicacy had sought to hide. How free had my own boys been to choose their destiny? Whether they were *slave* girls or *orphan* boys, our mission's success depended on those who had ever carried the burden of sacrifice—the poor, the powerless, the helpless, among them the children I myself had compromised in order to join the expedition.

Until late that night, I could hear the girls wailing, Mercy! Mercy! I went down several times thinking to comfort them with treats or a song or a story. But they pushed away the sweets I offered. They cried when I sang and wailed when I spoke. They wanted nothing from me but what I had failed to secure for them, enough freedom to remain with their enslaved families.

NEW SPAIN—PARTING IN VERACRUZ: *A man and a woman in private interview. The man is tall, well formed, no youngster. Only his head seems not to have been drawn to scale, too small, too delicate for such a stalwart figure. He is awkward before the woman who regards him with a kind smile.*

*And she, a mature lady—these are not young lovers, stormy with desperation—has a handsome figure as well. Her face is freckled . . . or pocked? Perhaps the painter has not yet made up his mind whether she will be handsome or homely, old or young.*

*In the miniature over her shoulder, we see her riding a mule train into the mountains, a trail of boys, two to a mount behind her. As for the man, we see him board a miniature ship blown by Aeolus with his puffy cheeks across the ocean to Spain, which is just now bursting into flames.*

We were greeted in the port of Veracruz with what should now have been accustomed news. The vaccine had preceded us to New Spain.

But in this instance, there was a sinister twist. No epidemic had threatened. No visitor with a ripe vesicle happened to have landed. Viceroy Iturrigaray, jealous of the honor that would accrue to our expedition, had taken it upon himself to introduce the vaccine in his domain. He had sent for it to Puerto Rico while we detoured to Venezuela and Cuba. The vaccine had arrived on the arms of five musicians, the viceroy making a grand show, bearing his own small son, dressed in regal robes, to the hospital to receive the first vaccination. This had been precisely our own director's strategy, creating a spectacle in order to convince the masses to be vaccinated.

"But he knew we were coming!" Don Francisco was furious.

"There will still be plenty for us to do," Don Ángel tried to soothe our director. It was only the capital and these thriving port cities that had received the vaccine. Many remote areas were desperately awaiting our arrival.

But Don Francisco would not be comforted. Upon reflection, I could see why. New Spain was his former home. He had been director of the very hospital where the viceroy had taken his son to be vaccinated. Don Francisco had wanted this grand moment for himself. To return to a place he loved, a place where he himself had fallen in love—Doña Josefa's family was from New Spain, I recalled—in triumph with salvation from the smallpox.

In a rage, Don Francisco sought out the returning musicians with a whip in hand. By evening, he was ill again with a bloody dysentery. The rumor spread that our director was on his deathbed. It did not seem such a far-fetched possibility. Dr. Verges had died, Orlando, Tomás; our sickly Juan Antonio sank into a stupor and by morning was dead of fever. Three boys already sacrificed to our mission! Perhaps we should all return to Spain with the *María Pita*.

I was confused as to what to do. I knew our work—the boys' and mine—was done. I had not thought past the conclusion of our mission, or if I did, it was to imagine myself continuing with Don Francisco, Benito at my side. Yet something had happened since Cuba and the buying of those slave girls. I had lost heart. I felt weary of the envy of officials who impeded our work; weary of the self-importance of our director, who confused the vaccine with his self-esteem; weary of policing the deeds of our expedition; weary of the boys—their cursing, their neediness, their bad behavior. I wanted to hide my thin, scarred face again behind my black veil.

Had I come so far to a new world only to find my old sad self?

Perhaps it was my illness. I, too, had caught the dysentery. I felt feverish. My stomach could not hold food. I worried what would become of my boys—most especially my little Benito—if something should happen to me.

"What are your plans, Doña Isabel?" Lieutenant Pozo stood before me, tall and stammering, hat in hand. It was as if my own mind were interrogating me.

"Plans?" It seemed too grand a word for the jumble of possibilities and questions in my head. I let out a sigh and smiled at him. I haven't any idea what the future holds. I was not unaware that the smile could be taken as encouragement. And in fact, I was open to the possibility of a connection. Years of caring for orphan boys, many of whom I had no reason or inclination to love, had taught me that the heart is a trainable creature. Passion might arise unbidden, but love is a discipline. "And your own plans?" I wondered if he was still considering what he had once mentioned, possibly adopting one or more of the boys.

"My plans?" He looked as baffled as I had been a moment before. But he, in fact, had much more of a settled plan than I did. His contract with the ship, which as a man of honor he would fulfill, required him to return to La Coruña with its captain. Once there, he could apply for his release. From what he stuttered and blurted out, I pieced together his story. He had been briefly married but had lost his wife and young son to the plague, another epidemic. Nothing was holding him in Spain unless I would be returning. "If you could see your way . . ." He was turning and turning his hat in his hands as if it were the gears of his courage. He dared not set that hat down.

I both wanted to rescue him from his own mortal embarrassment and to be given proof that he could be gallant and eloquent, a lover from a romance. But I let the former win the day. By now in our journey, I prized kindness above all. "I will be happy to entertain your company."

"Where will you be?" the mate spoke almost instantly. If he waited, he might find himself ambushed by shyness and incapacity.

I don't know why it was that suddenly I knew what I would do. I was infected with America. There was an open, unfinished feel to these territories that invigorated me. The air seemed to have more air, the sky more sky. Every place we visited, there was talk of new ideas, the rights of human beings. The poor, the powerless, the enslaved were rising up and demanding their rights—in the back rooms and kitchen of our house in Puerto Rico, in the parlor chatter after the dances in Caracas, in Havana, and now in this port city. My boys stood a better chance here, peninsulares, with every advantage. Why, Spain was full of destitute souls seeking a new life on these very shores. "We will accompany Don Francisco to Mexico City. The viceroy will take charge of the boys there, as I understand it."

"And you, where will you be?" the mate asked again, his voice surer now.

"Wherever you hear the boys might be." In that general vicinity, he'd be likely to find me.

For days following, I thought, surely, I had imagined his proposal. After all, I had a penchant for constructing scenes to console myself and my young charges. Could it be possible that I was being courted, a none-too-young woman of thirty-six, scarred by smallpox, and thinned by the exigencies of our journey? So many years wasted in thinking I did not deserve such love! I remembered the prayer for orphans we had read daily at chapel in La Coruña: *We are saved not because we are worthy; we are saved because we are loved.*

We parted company before the ship had left port, for our director was in a great hurry to reach Mexico City. The lieutenant—the name now stuck—accompanied us several days out of town before returning to honor his contract. Our last moments, we were surrounded by boys, by mule drivers, by Don Francisco and my colleagues. But for once, the modest man lifted his gaze and I held him with my eyes. *We will soon be together.*

*New Spain—triumphant entry into Mexico City? Do not expect a grand encounter between the fair-skinned Conquistador Cortés and the gold-clad Aztec emperor Montezuma.*

*A viceroy in his nightshirt shakes his fists in a temper; his wife descends the stairs in a robe of rich satin, her hair undressed, her face a struggle between politeness and suspicion, as nineteen little youngsters wail their claims upon her husband. A woman quiets them. The palace guards look worriedly upon the scene.*

We entered the city at night, having waited in the outskirts all day for the viceroy to receive us. When it seemed our welcome would not come, Don Francisco led us down the wide avenues. There were forty of us, all told, including ten soldiers from the regiment who had carried the vaccine from Veracruz.

I could not help but admire the many grand houses we passed, their windows lit up, displaying that enviable warmth of a home seen from the outside at night. This was as large a city as La Coruña, grander, richer. At the palace gate, we were stopped by guards, who were advised to inform the viceroy that His Royal Highness's expedition had arrived.

It was ten at night. The guards looked unsure.

But our director was not to be deterred. We were to be announced immediately. Somehow—perhaps it was the six soldiers accompanying us that gave our group an official air—our director convinced the head guard not only to summon the viceroy but to let us wait for his audience *inside* the palace.

Viceroy Iturrigaray descended from upstairs having been informed that the king's sons were at his door and would not leave. "How there, sir?" he confronted our director. This was most unprecedented, that he should be importuned at this time of night in his private residence.

"And this is very unprecedented," our director returned the indignation, "that a *royal* expedition should not be met with due ceremony. I sent word this morning," Don Francisco added. "We have brought the precious vaccine to New Spain."

The viceroy's smile was smug. "You might have spared yourself the trouble, sir. I myself brought the vaccine to these dominions months ago."

From upstairs came a soft voice. How rare a woman's voice had become to my ears! "Love? Who is it?"

"No one of importance," he called back, twisting the knife in the wound of our director's pride.

The children had commenced whining that they were hungry, that they were tired.

"These are your charges, señor. We shall leave them here for you to see to. Meanwhile, we, members of His Majesty's expedition, shall sleep on the streets."

Surely, he was not serious! My face must have betrayed my fear and disbelief. The children, who always took their cue from me, commenced sobbing.

Before too long, the mistress of the house made her way downstairs. She seemed quite shocked to find nineteen children in her parlor, all claiming to be her husband's charges. "How so?" she questioned the viceroy, who by now was in quite a temper at the uproar brought to his door at this ungodly hour by an arrogant doctor!

Finally, a servant was sent to fetch one of the city councilors to escort us to the residence that was to house us during our stay. "I must advise you that owing to the fact that we had not heard of your impending arrival, the repairs to the building have not been completed," the viceroy warned. And with that, he gathered his robes around him, his wife by the arm, and left the room.

We waited until the councilor had arrived with many apologies. He

corroborated the viceroy's claim. No word had been received about our arrival today. No doubt the courier whom Don Francisco had commissioned
to deliver our missive had dropped it off at the wrong office. Probably, our
director's letter was slowly making its way up the hierarchy.

We loaded the children back into their carriages and wended our way
back down the streets we had come. We traveled some distance. The noise
of our caravan brought people to their doors to see what army was afoot,
what trouble was brewing. Soon, I could tell by the bumpy, narrowed
streets and the foul smell in the air that we had entered the poorer environs of the city. In the morning we would find ourselves surrounded by little shacks and shanties and by several tanning factories; it was their refuse
that gave the air that sordid, raw smell.

We broke into that locked house—the city councilor could not find his
key—only to discover, as the viceroy had warned, that the place was under repair, full of dust and tools, and completely unfurnished. We slept
upon the hard floors, the boys and I, too tired to care. But all night, Don
Francisco's footsteps paced the halls, waiting for morning in order to call
again on the viceroy and lodge a formal complaint in the king's name.

I thought of going out there and urging him to get some rest. But I was
beyond trying to save our director from his worst enemy, himself.

NEW SPAIN—*DEPARTURE FROM* MEXICO CITY: *Who can bear to look
upon these youngsters and not weep for their terror, not feel their pitiful sorrow?*

*What is it they want, these frightened children, clinging to that sad woman,
who turns her face away to hide her tears? They are at the door of a dark and
damp building that dares to call itself the* Royal Hospicio. *See, on the other
side of the door, the young denizens of the place, sitting down at long tables
to bowls of greasy soup thickened with cornmeal. See their tricks, the hair
pullings and furtive punches, the small cruelties of the abused who become
abusers. See how the newcomers plead with the woman not to abandon them
here.*

We spent a little over a month in the capital, and I had to amend my
judgment of our director. He had an even bigger enemy than himself—the
viceroy. At every turn, Viceroy Iturrigaray impeded the progress of our expedition. He had stolen the glory of introducing the vaccine to his viceroy-

alty himself, but our director's presence qualified the achievement by raising questions.

Was the vaccine his doctors had propagated indeed potent?

Was wholesale vaccination the best way to proceed?

Was a system of juntas being instituted that could safeguard the territory against future smallpox epidemics?

I am sure the viceroy felt as if he had triumphed in a battle only to have
the enemy he believed he had slaughtered rise up to interrogate him.

Don Francisco paid with his own funds to print up broadsides announcing his vaccination sessions. But no carriers came forward, only the orphans from the Royal Hospicio and two dozen Indian babies wrenched
from their panicked mothers—a horrid scene I will never forget. When
several of the orphans died soon after being vaccinated, the viceroy set up
a commission of doctors to investigate our director's methods.

Finally, Don Francisco admitted defeat and decided to head for Puebla
and outlying villages. Before leaving, he petitioned the viceroy to pay us
our salaries and to arrange for the transport of the expedition to the
Philippines.

"We must leave as soon as possible for Manila," our director insisted.
"I have already written you several missives on this matter, sir. May I remind you, that you are ignoring not my humble person, but your king!"

"The only ship out to Manila is the galleon that leaves in January," the
viceroy countered. He had troops and friars ahead of us to send. He was
not sure that the January galleon would have room enough for forty or so
men and children.

"Very well, then, sir," Don Francisco countered. "We shall stay in New
Spain vaccinating until you have provided us passage to our next destination, as the proclamation orders you to do. May I remind you, too, that this
will be at your expense."

The proclamation stated that point clearly. The viceroy had no further
recourse. I think that was when he decided that he must rid himself of this
annoying expedition and its irritating director the sooner the better. Passage was arranged on the next Manila galleon. Too bad that January was
still five months away!

During those months, our director asked me to continue with the expedition on its journey through the provinces. My little boys were to be entrusted to the Royal Hospicio. Even so, I did not want to leave the environs of Mexico City until I could be sure the boys would be well taken care of. But I had yet to be paid. Viceroy Iturrigaray was in charge of the treasury funds in New Spain. Needless to say, he was not forthcoming.

But it was not just necessity that compelled me to continue with our expedition. We were now half the number we had been upon setting out from La Coruña. And New Spain, as I soon discovered, was a huge place. I could not desert our director now when he was most in need of my help.

Before we left the capital city, I said good-bye to the boys at the Royal Hospicio. It was a depressing place, especially the lower floor reserved for boys. The girls had the lighter, airier accommodations upstairs. But these were to be temporary quarters only, the viceroy had assured me. The boys would soon be placed in families. They were penisulares, the king's charges, there should be no problem.

"I will be back very, very soon!" I promised them. "I am just finishing my work here with Don Francisco."

"No!" They had already spent several weeks in the Royal Hospicio. Even the orlop deck of the *María Pita* on a stormy night was better than this horrid place among strangers. My boys clung to me and would not let go.

"Listen," I gathered them around me, my heart in my throat. "Remember those stories I told you?"

They nodded, sniffling, bottom lips quivering.

"They can come true. I will help you. But you must put in your part. You must be good, leave off swearing, do as your teachers tell you."

I held them with my gaze, and they seem tranquilized. But I knew their faith would last as long as I was by them.

I slipped away as they were eating their supper, busy with their bowls, guarding their fare from the bigger boys. But once outside the door, I wept so mightily that Don Ángel grew concerned. Don Francisco was summoned, but I refused the sedative he prepared. I wanted to feel the full measure of my culpability and despair. Later in the provinces I would hear the story of La Llorona, a crazed mother who drowned her children in the river to avenge their father's abandonment. No sooner had she realized what she had done, she repented and was condemned to spend eternity weeping for them.

"It is one of their superstitions," the finer ladies of those towns would say, embarrassed by the crude beliefs of their Indian maids. But I knew that it was no invention of theirs. Even after I had run out of tears, I could hear her cries in my ears. Nothing would stop her sorrow, except the knowledge that her children—and were they not all our children?—had been spared.

*NEW SPAIN—PUEBLA DE LOS ÁNGELES, QUERÉTARO, CELAYA, GUANA-JUATO, LEÓN, ZACATECAS, DURANGO, FRESNILLO, SOMBRERETE: These must be sketches for a larger work, studies of misery discarded as being too miserable or later used for the murals of a church, our Lord healing the sick; our Lord turning the water of tears into the wine of laughter; our Lord dispensing loaves to the numberless, hungry poor.*

*But this is not Our Lord with his long, sad face and his head aglow. This man is older, his gray hair tied back with a dirty ribbon, his shirtsleeves rolled up. He is ministering to the long lines of Indians and Creoles who have come to this village clinic to receive the smallpox salvation their king has sent them.*

*Beside him, weak and thin, a not very alluring Magdalene, a woman assists him, her hands a blur as if to suggest the many tasks she is performing. She seems intent on her ministry, as how can she not be? Behold the masses that will be saved future suffering! But there are tears in her eyes, a puddle at her feet.*

We set out on what would prove to be an exhausting tour of the provinces. At night, I slept fitfully, thinking now of my lieutenant, now of my boys whom I had abandoned to a place that resembled nothing more than a dungeon. This last was the biggest thorn in that crown of worries that seemed to dig at my temples as night descended.

I suppose the misery I soon began to see as we traveled away from the prosperous towns and cities somewhat mitigated the Royal Hospicio's deficits. This was need as I had not experienced so far. In our earlier stops in Tenerife, San Juan, Caracas, Havana, even Mexico City, I had been shielded, lodged with my twenty or so youngsters in a convent or a comfortable, well-appointed house. But now I was putting my hand on the very pulse of human misery. Don Francisco had been correct in the dismal picture he had painted during our first interview in La Coruña. Here was desolation to sear the soul, hundreds and thousands of miserable human beings, Indians and mestizos most of them, who lived without any hope at all. How could the world be ordered in this way?

Should smallpox break out, these were the very multitudes that would be most afflicted. I doubt these poor souls understood how the vaccine worked, but perhaps they felt some tender influence. A fleeting glimpse of love as Don Ángel cleansed their arms, as Don Francisco spoke to them calmly about the procedure, as I held them with my eyes. *We are here with you, brothers and sisters, you are not alone.*

Fifty-three days we traveled in the outlying provinces, setting up juntas that would vaccinate fifteen new carriers every ten days, a rotation that would ensure continuance of the vaccine for each new generation. Between sessions our director rode out to local ranchos to inspect sick cows. How wonderful it would be if the cowpox could be found on this very soil and so ensure a native supply of vaccine from here on out!

At each stop the local authorities provided us with carriers to the next village. It was my task to care for them, though by now I did a little of everything that was needed. I also looked after our growing pool of future carriers to the Philippines—twenty-six in all, Don Francisco had estimated. Most of these boys came from families who released them to Don Francisco on the strength of a plea by a local dignitary or church official. For some reason we could not find enough orphan carriers among these poorest of villages. Perhaps it was as Juana had remarked in Puerto Rico, all the poor had were their children, whom they were not willing to abandon.

As I had my boys. Just the thought was enough to bring on my tears.

PUEBLA DE LOS ÁNGELES: *This could be a deathbed scene: a gaunt, ill-looking lady lies propped up on pillows, a man, no doubt a doctor (we have seen him before), taking her pulse. All about her, hung like draperies from the walls of her chamber, are the scenes of her life like the stations of the cross, her girlhood, terminating in a bad illness; her young womanhood in what looks like a hospital and then, an orphanage. On and on, so small are these cameos we might almost miss them.*

*No window has been opened, no lantern lit, so where is the light coming from? Above, as if through the porthole of a ship or a hole in heaven, we see another woman, as yet unborn, peering down upon this scene. She seems intent on knowing the fate of the woman who lies ignorant of a future sister. Or perhaps this looming soul needs only a tint of crimson, a touch of gold, a look of hope to carry back into her own canvases we may someday soon be reviewing.*

In late December, we returned to Puebla after our exhausting tour of the provinces. The bishop generously lodged us in his own Episcopal palace. That very night, I collapsed in bed with a high fever. Perhaps knowing that my work was over, my body allowed itself the rest it sorely needed after weeks of travel and work. Indeed, we were all in need of a respite. Our director decided we would spend Christmas in Puebla before continuing to Mexico City.

As I lay in bed, I had time to think about the future. Lieutenant Pozo had said he would be back within the new year. But the news reached us while we were in Puebla that war had broken out with Great Britain. Spanish ships were being commandeered into the Armada. Would the lieutenant still be able to return as he had promised? Where would I settle in the meanwhile? Already, word came from Mexico, several of my boys had been adopted by Creole families. Perhaps the ones still left in the Royal Hospicio could be transferred to Puebla, where we could await the return of the lieutenant together.

I had no doubts that the boys would be welcomed in this hospitable city. While I had been traveling with Don Francisco, I had left Benito in the care of the bishop. Upon my return, I saw how good the interval had been for my son. He had grown an inch, I was sure of it, and looked stout and strong. But it was more than his health, he seemed happy in this warm and welcoming place. Bishop Gonzales was quite taken with the boy's intelligence and spoke of a possible future in the church or in some other worthy profession. "Perhaps you would like to be a doctor like our benevolent Don Francisco?" the bishop quizzed him.

The boy shook his head. He wanted to be a big, fat bishop like the bishop.

"Hush!" I scolded, but Bishop Gonzales laughed his booming laugh. "Out of the mouths of babes," he reminded me. "We should all have such a one around to keep us honest," he added. I was not sure a child's presence was any guarantee of self-knowledge. After all, I had been graced with hundreds of orphans and I still had difficulty seeing the speck in my own eye, even though many a child had pointed it out to me.

"So, Doña Isabel, you must consider settling here," Bishop Gonzales persisted, as if he sensed the plan I had been making as I lay in bed too weak to join him and Benito in the festivities of the season. In spite of the war, a blessed child was being born again in the Bethlehem of our souls and his arrival had to be celebrated.

The day after Christmas, our director announced that we would be departing the following morning. He could not have been surprised to hear that I was not well enough to travel, for I had been absent from all the gatherings of the last few days. But I don't think our director understood illness as a reason to keep from fulfilling one's mission. He himself was ill with the dysentery, and had been for the last six months, and still he had vaccinated over sixty thousand souls in America, found cowpox in the valleys near Durango and Valladolid, and set up a network of juntas of vaccination. He was ready for the next challenge.

He did not know that challenge would now be me.

When he entered the sickroom, I could see from the shock on his face that he was surprised to see me in such altered condition. We had all been so caught up in our work, and he particularly, he had lost sight of his own health and of the health of those around him.

"Your hard work has taken all your strength, Doña Isabel. I feel I am to blame. I pushed you too hard."

He himself looked thin and haggard. Perhaps he should also stay several weeks here in the city of the angels and rest. But our director was eager to proceed to Mexico City and continue on his way. "This man is not to be trusted, Doña Isabel," Don Francisco explained. "The sooner I complete my duties here, the better."

Hearing him say so, I felt afraid for my boys should anything happen to me. "Please promise me, Don Francisco, that you will see to it that the boys receive their promised legacy."

"You have my word, Doña Isabel. To be sure, they will all soon find new homes."

"And Benito," I worried. "Lieutenant Pozo has made arrangements to return." Don Francisco's look was that of a suspicion confirmed. "He would take in the boy, I am sure of it."

"I see," Don Francisco studied me a long moment. It must have seemed incredible to him that this scarred skeleton might command the heart of a lover. "But I see no reason for you to be making plans for your demise. In fact, I forbid it! A whole half world awaits us. We have much work still to do."

"We?" I questioned. A year ago the promise of our mission together had brought me out of an old life to this new one. But my work was over. Soon, the viceroy would grant me the five hundred pesos due me for the year I had served the expedition. With that sum, I could settle down in this city of angels with my Benito and whatever boys still needed a home and await the return of the kind lieutenant. I remembered Juana's prediction in Puerto Rico. I would have a happy life. I was ready to claim it.

"We cannot go on without you!" Don Francisco's voice had taken on a pleading tone. His face wore a worried look. "But we shall talk of this on our way to Mexico City. We will delay our return for a few more days until you are back on your feet again."

"You are the angel of our expedition," Don Francisco added in parting. At the door, he raised a hand in farewell. "Do not desert us, Isabel!"

I did not promise him anything, but I could feel myself sinking into feverish dreams, giving in as I always had to him.

# 7

The first few moments happen so quickly, Alma feels as if she's caught in a current that suddenly sweeps her off her feet and carries her wherever it is going. She is dragged across the porch by two, three, could be four playground-bully-type guys who have run out of the clinic. "¡Por favor! Don't!" she cries out, as if she can make them stop, as if she has any power now that she has surrendered herself to this force.

Once inside, she is shoved so hard she falls on the floor of what seems to be the clinic's waiting room: aqua blue plastic chairs bolted in place, several potted plants, a poster announcing that AIDS can happen to anyone.

This could be a free clinic in Vermont. But it isn't. Lined around the walls are four or five men with kerchiefs or ski masks covering their faces. The ski masks are ones that Richard brought down. The bag of clothes from the secondhand shop had been full of ski masks and baseball caps. Alma had questioned who in the tropics was going to need a ski mask. "They can roll up the bottom part and use them as caps," Richard had argued, demonstrating. "It gets chilly in the mountains." *Mad River Glen, Killington, Stowe*—how strange the names of these winter resorts seem on the heads of armed men.

Alma knows nothing about firearms—all she has ever seen up close are Richard's shotgun and the sheriff's little gun that looked like a toy poking out of his holster. But these men are holding serious-looking guns. Briefly, it crosses Alma's mind that these might be the bad elements Don Jacobo talked about.

She is about to repeat again that she is not armed, but the one with a jaunty red bandanna covering the bottom half of his face is screaming, "Check her out!"

Oddly, it's not the gun he aims at her as much as his high-pitch scream that scares Alma, and for a moment, she loses heart. What the hell did she think she was going to accomplish throwing herself in the hands of these thugs?

Meanwhile, the man guarding Richard has pulled him back inside and is yelling at him to shut his fucking mouth. And Richard, what is Richard saying? She can't make it out with all the screaming, some scolding about why she had to go do something so stupid and almost get herself killed.

One of the ski-masked men comes from the ranks and yanks Alma to her feet. He starts patting her down roughly. They must think she's some sort of suicide bomber, coming in with explosives to blow them all up. Maybe the general who is not a general is right, and these young men have been watching too much cable TV.

There is nothing to discover on her person—she has long since dropped the coffee cup she had in her hand, which she carried into the compound with her, not thinking to leave it behind. But then everything happened so quickly. Until the last moment, she had no idea that she was going to jump over those sandbags. Some vague notion had seized her that she might make a difference. Maybe she could listen to their stories, offer to write them up, send them to a publisher, and bring a protective cordon of readers to their cause. You'd think she'd been the one who was watching too much cable TV or reading the printed equivalent, best-selling inspirational memoirs and manuals.

Now Alma wishes she had planned ahead, stuffed the pockets of her light jacket with her jewelry—though she doubts she'd get far in this company with a charm bracelet or her high school graduation ring—brought along a toothbrush, sleeping pills, her bag of trail mix.

Her frisker pulls out the PowerBar she carried on the trip down in case she got hungry on the plane as well as her journal and what she had forgotten was in her pocket—Starr's cell phone she'd taken off the crate in their bedroom this morning in case she decided to make that phone call to the sheriff.

"It's a cell phone," she explains because the frisker is staring down at the little gadget, forehead creased, as if he suspects it might be a grenade. Any moment now, he'll hurl it out the back window and blow up one of the dormitorios where the imprisoned patients have begun calling out again that they are hungry.

"And cigarettes?" the red-bandanna guy asks her. "Where are our cigarettes?"

She wants to answer him, especially with that gun he keeps jabbing in the air at her. But she has no idea what he is talking about. "What cigarettes?" And then, of course, she remembers the deal Camacho told them about last night—the kidnappers had wanted cigarettes, meals, visas in exchange for releasing the women. Haven't they already gotten those cigarettes? They can't be that dumb, releasing the women before they had some part of the bargain in their hands.

This is how the idea blooms in her mind.

"I'm the journalist," she explains. She can almost feel a wave of calm come over the group, with one exception, Richard, whose eyes are boring into her, wondering what she is up to. She dare not look over at him for fear she will betray herself.

"A journalist?" The guy isn't totally convinced. "For what paper?"

"*El noticiero*, but I write for American papers, too."

Masked as they are, Alma can tell they are happy to know they have gotten the widespread attention they wanted. "What's your name?" The red bandanna seems to be the one doubting Thomas.

Mariana, Alma almost says, but stops herself. Mariana is attractive. The newspaper is probably savvy, prints the journalist's picture by her column. Not even by a long stretch can Alma pass herself off as the honey-skinned, thirty-something, black-haired celebrity. "Isabel," she tells him, hoping he is not a detail man who will ask for a last name that won't match up with whatever Isabel— if there is even an Isabel writing for *El noticiero.*

"Isabel," he repeats the name, looking her over with narrowed eyes, as if assessing the probability of Alma being an Isabel who is a journalist from *El noticiero* as well as an American paper. But there is convincing proof: the journal, the entries thankfully in English, so he can't read it and realize this is a private journal in which Alma talks about her feelings, her shock about Helen, her phone call with Lavinia, her saga novel that never got written, her buried antidepressants. But what seems to end all disbelief is the cell phone, which he must assume she uses to call in her columns to the newspapers. If he asks for further proof, Alma will just phone Tera and dictate a manifesto.

"I'd like to interview you," she addresses the guy with the red bandanna, as he seems to be doing most of the shouting and bossing around. "Readers want to know what it is you want—"

"We told them what we want!" the guy snaps back.

"Remember," Alma reminds him, her heart beating so loudly she is sure it is drowning out her voice, "you spoke with officials. I need the story direct from you."

"Okay," he says the word in English. "Okay." He lets his gun fall to his side. "Take him out back," he orders the young man handling Richard.

"Un momento." Richard holds his ground. Alma beams him a look that pleads with him not to blow her cover. He beams back: *I'm going to kill you when this is over!* But he goes along, no doubt thinking Alma is part of some elaborate plot cooked up by the army with the help of U.S. advisers. "I want to ask about my wife," he says in Spanish. "It is easier for me in English."

He is not exactly given permission to speak in English, but on the other hand he is not shoved away. Alma speaks up in a flat, matter-of-fact voice as if the information she is communicating is nothing to her. "Your wife is well. She wanted to be by your side. She was told that she would be eating leftover turkey with you in a few days. She did not call your sons so as not to alarm them. She says she loves you and to just go along—"

"Ya!" the red bandanna is getting nervous at this much talk he doesn't understand. Richard is shoved down a hallway that seems to lead out onto a patio where the rest of the staff is being held. She can hear talking and movement from back there, a little radio with the overinflated voice of a DJ announcing the next bachata, then, of course, the voices of the patients calling out from their dormitorios.

"The first thing to tell the world," the red bandanna tells her after his young comrades have taken up their posts at the windows, and he and Alma have sat down in two of the plastic chairs, the cell phone in the empty chair between them; the PowerBar seems to have been confiscated. "The first thing to tell them is that we are sick of being utilized. They come with their empty promises and build this fucking jodida clinic and bring in all the pájaros and putas so we all get sick, millones de dólares, to test their drugs and our children die because they cannot get medicina for a little fever that would cost us una fortuna to buy!"

Alma writes hurriedly, trying to keep up with what he is saying, to give a credible performance as a journalist. He is not very eloquent: *fucking fags and cunts*. If this is the best the group can do for a spokesperson, they are not going to get the following they need. But through the broken sentences and curses, Alma sees the little spark of human yearning. How can she blame him? She remembers telling Richard on their first date when he had explained what it was he did, consultancy for development projects in the triage nations of the world, that if she had been born one of the poor in her own homeland she would have had blood on her hands by now.

He had seemed startled to hear her say something so fierce. "But what would that accomplish?"

"Nothing," she had agreed. "But I'd kill, I would, if that's what it took to feed my children."

He had raised his brows and said nothing. Well, there goes a second date, she thought to herself. But she couldn't let it go. This periodic homeland rage that would crop up out of nowhere, even though she had been in the United States almost forty years, this feeling that her own luckiness was off the backs of other people, not because her family had been exploiters but because the pool of the lucky was so small in that poor little place that God forgot. In the United States there was a larger pool of luck, and the overspill trickled down: extra toilet paper in the stalls, soup kitchens, social service programs, sliding scales, legal aid, free clinics, adjunct teaching posts and arts enrichment grants so that people like Tera, like Helen, like Alma before she lucked out with her novels and marriage to Richard managed to scrape by.

The young man seems to have run out of things to say. He is looking her over again as if he is reconsidering this whole interview idea, not sure it isn't some delay tactic. He wants his visa. Fuck the double-crossing town and its ass-kissing mayor. He gestures toward the village beyond the windows. "They get a little solar panel and a hole in which to shit with a zinc roof over their heads and they are as happy as little pigs."

A few of the young men at their posts turn around to show their approval to their comandante. It must be a joke, worthy of repetition. "Happy as little pigs," he addresses them, laughing. "Jacobo's little pigs."

"So you are not representing the community, just yourselves?" Alma wonders out loud. She hopes it doesn't sound like a critique of his authority. It does seem like a question she should address to everyone, not just this jumpy guy, who seems to be the brawn, if not the brains of the operation.

"It is not just for us," one of the young boys speaks up. His mask is from Killington, a chilling name, given the situation. His voice is vehement. Maybe he doesn't find the joke so funny. "If we go to the United States with our visas, it is to help our families."

Alma doesn't have the heart to point out that Jacobo's group sells their souls for solar panels and latrines with zinc roofs, the comandante's group for visas, cigarettes, an interview with a journalist. In fact, she is glad they have a price. Otherwise what? Suicide bombers and plane hijackers? Desperation videos? A bloodbath?

"Does your group have a name?"

"We don't need a name!" The red kerchief's temper is tinder, and the wrong word a match. "Fuck having a name! So they can hunt us down. We're nobodies, nadies, the fucked-over and forgotten. Put that down." He points toward her journal.

Obediently, Alma writes down *nobodies, nadies, fucked-over, forgotten* and holds up her journal as if to prove she has done his bidding. He reads it over, nodding.

"But won't you need names for your papers and visas?" Alma points out, trying to sound helpful. Maybe they will realize their demands are so implausible, the best deal they can strike is shortened prison sentences in return for turning themselves in and turning over all their hostages unharmed.

"They can make up whatever papers they want!" the young man states angrily. Alma can't help thinking of the general in the car, how he thought the americanos were genios, who could cure leukemia, make cell phones that work wherever on earth they wandered.

"We ask for these visas because we have no other opportunity," the Killington ski-mask guy explains.

"But we will return!" The young man in the black kerchief who was guarding Richard has reentered the room. He has a thing or two to say to the journalist. "Con tu permiso," he defers to the comandante, who is, after all, the one being interviewed.

"Of course, of course," the red bandanna agrees in a gush that reminds Alma of that old line, "The lady doth protest too much." "We are all brothers," he adds, for Alma's benefit. He nods at her journal. She should write that down.

"We will come back," the black kerchief asserts. It's hard to tell his age with a kerchief covering half his face, but she'd guess him to be in his twenties, pale-skinned, with dark, sad eyes and thick, curly black hair. "We will infect them with our questions!"

Alma's heart quickens. She had been feeling sorry for this misguided group of kids, like watching her chosen candidate be stupid in a televised debate. She had hoped to feel solidarity with them, but their name-calling spokesman had made them sound like thugs, back-woods bigots, out for themselves only. Now the poet has arrived, and she feels a different kind of sorry: sorry for herself because she is not, nor could she ever be, one of them—she knows too much, wouldn't for the world give up her lucky life with Richard in Vermont—which leaves her on the side without poetry, without a redeeming story. "What would those questions be?" she asks the black kerchief. "The ones you would come back and infect them with?" Strange word, *infectar*, but he picked it, not her.

"What would be those questions?" the black-kerchief man repeats, looking around the room as if inviting the others to answer. But they all look back at him waiting, even the red bandanna, whose right foot, propped on his left knee, is shaking impatiently. How did he get to be the leader?

"The questions are very simple. Why do we go hungry? Why do our people die of curable diseases? What is it that has excluded us? What is it that has isolated us?"

His voice is impassioned, throaty, as if he were on the point of tears. Were it not that here in this place, cunning qualifies any genuine feel-ing, Alma would do a Patty Hearst, throw down her journal and ditch Starr's cell phone, and say, I am with you, compañeros! But she is fifty, frightened, eager to get her husband out and return to Vermont where she feels they can at least live simply, doing minimal harm.

"Can I write that down as your . . . statement." *Statement* doesn't sound right. But Alma doesn't know the word in Spanish, or come to think of it in English, for that glimmering of hope she sees underlying all his statements.

"Is this our statement?" the black-kerchief poet asks, again looking around the room at his companions, then narrowing in on the seated leader with the shaking foot. By his tone, Alma is almost sure he means this as a rhetorical question.

But the red-bandanna leader takes up the question. "Our statement is that we want an opportunity to be a human being." His black-kerchief comrade nods deeply as if their leader has said something brilliant. "You can put that in your book," the red bandanna adds with a touch of pride.

As Alma writes, the black-kerchief poet watches her with such awed, primitive attention that she is almost 100 percent sure he doesn't know how to read or write his own name. No wonder the other guy is the leader. "Is there anything else?" she asks, trying to include the red bandanna with a quick glance, but it is obvious she is asking the poet to continue.

"Everything we want my friend said, y ya. We can say too much. We don't have a platform like the politicians that come here every time there is an election. We don't stand for something that can be argued or taught in a book in a school. What we stand for is not an opinion, it is an intuition."

Why? Alma wants to ask him. Why with such a soulful, beautiful message that would mobilize anybody who has a heart in this world, why did he do something so stupid, take over a clinic without a real plan, get mixed up with this leader who has dumbed down their discontent to a plea for visas? If he had only gotten hooked up with Richard instead of the red-bandanna guy. But then HI was in bed with Swan, and Richard was hanging out with Bienvenido and Starr and reps from whatever aid agencies divvy up the help at this end. This guy's hope couldn't get through so many goodwill handlers.

The red-bandanna leader bolts out of his chair. He seems to have grown impatient with all the talking. Where are their visas, their cigarettes, their breakfast and coffee? He paces back and forth, everyone watching him. "Didn't they receive our demands?" he asks Alma, as if she should know. After all, sending a journalist was on the list and here she is.

Alma shrugs. "I think they did. With the women, right?"

Another round of pacing, back, forth, the length of the room. When he catches the young boys watching him, he gestures with his chin for them to look to their posts. Then he gestures toward Alma's notebook. "We'll write them down this time. Our demands."

In a heartbeat, Alma goes from journalist to amanuensis. TO THE

AUTORIDADES: WHAT WE DEMAND. U.S. visas are at the top. Cigarettes. Then meals: each meal delivered, one patient released; the staff and the rest of the patients will be freed after visas are in hand, safe conduct out guaranteed. Forgotten is the demand that Swan's drug-testing clinic be removed from the village, replaced by a health clinic for locals. Fuck the villagers, let those double-crossers get AIDS if they want to.

From time to time as they have been talking, there have been calls from the patients in the dormitories. Now there is an outcry, the loudest one yet. Someone has fainted. They need immediate medical attention.

"Shut those fuckers up!" the red bandanna shouts down the hall. Moments later, someone on the back patio fires what must be some warning shots in the air because after a long pause, the outcry starts back up again.

"It is that they are hungry," his black-kerchief comrade speaks up. He seems to be the only one willing to risk stating the obvious.

The red bandanna turns on him, a furious look on his face. "*They're* hungry?" he asks incredulously. "I'm hungry. They're hungry." He points to all the boys. "Is everybody hungry?" he asks, his voice almost a scream, and to a one, they all nod, yes, coño, of course they're hungry!

Alma gazes up at the large clock above the desk on which a funky, old-style phone sits, same vintage as Tera's wall mount. It is almost ten. All those big pots of plátanos she saw boiling in the mayor's house must have been for the soldiers. The time for breakfast has come and gone. Are Camacho and Jim Larsen and crew going to starve them out of their siege? Is that the plan? Don't starving desperadoes shoot innocent people, especially americanos whose country has denied them visas?

"The women last night said they would send food," the black-kerchief guy reminds them. "What hour is it?" he adds, as if there might still be time for miracles.

Alma wonders why he doesn't just look up at the clock. She remembers Richard's saying that he was glad he had brought down digital watches. Nobody knew how to tell time on a clock with hands.

The red bandanna is wearing a wristwatch. Alma wonders if he got it from Richard's duffel bag of gifts. "Nine zero seven," he announces. He seems pleased to be able to provide the exact time. Thanks to technology they can all know the very hour to the minute that they are starving. "That clock is wrong," he adds, pointing at it with his gun. And then, without warning, as if in fury at its error, he shoots it off the wall. There is a burst of gunfire, plaster and metal pieces flying. Alma drops to the floor, in shock. Around the room, everyone scrambles for cover.

A moment later, realizing where the gunfire came from, his comrades curse their leader softly for el susto he has given them. But none of the curses seem particularly fierce. They are probably impressed by his show of violence. Another reason he is the leader, he can tell both kinds of time and shoot the kind he doesn't agree with.

The black-kerchief poet is the only one who seems to have expected this outburst, no cowering or covering his head, no curses or admonition that the leader save ammunition. Instead, he looks dolefully at the hole in the wall, as if it he regrets ever having asked what time it is.

In the silence that follows this blast, they hear the patients again in the dormitorio.

The kerchief poet gestures for the red bandanna to come over to a corner to talk. Even with their backs to her, Alma can guess they are again disagreeing about the patients. She wonders if the poet is arguing for letting them go, even before any food provisions are delivered. These are sick men and women. Not fags, not cunts. Human beings. Intuition says they shouldn't be used as pawns. But after a while the poet falls silent, subdued, seemingly convinced. Perhaps he realizes that poetry has never gotten them anything. It needs the muscle of power. That is why he defers to the red bandanna. Their leader is the only one who can read, tell time on a clock with hands, check out that what Alma writes down is, word for word, their demands.

By midday, it looks like that power muscle is going to have to be flexed. No food has been delivered. The list of demands Alma wrote down earlier has been sent out and no reply has been returned. The leader dictates a second message that if food is not received by six in the afternoon, "we will begin to take action on the patients." Alma looks up as if to check that he means what he says.

"Write it down!" he screams when he sees her hesitate, the same high-pitch scream that so scared her when he first cried out that she should be frisked. Maybe Alma guessed wrong; maybe the leader doesn't know how to write down his own demands. Maybe she should embed some message. *Send food. These guys are not fooling around!* Her hand is trembling so much she worries that Jim and Emerson and Camacho won't be able to read her writing.

When she finishes, the red bandanna grabs her notebook, reads over what she has written, then tears the page, folds it, calls through the windows for a boy to be sent in. A little kid no more than five or six runs up to the porch and takes the note back. This time he returns with a reply.

The authorities will send in food once *all* the patients have been released. They will then give the captors until noon the next day to release the rest of the hostages.

Why are they starting with the patients? Alma wonders. Why not start with Richard and Alma, now that she has joined him? All lives are valuable, so the general said, but given the presence of Jim Larsen and the embassy boys, shouldn't the American lives be more valuable than others?

Maybe their strategy is to begin with the neediest, a strategy Alma would wholeheartedly approve if she were not part of the competing group of valuable lives that should go first. She has gathered from comments the young boys make while the leader is in the john or visiting the back patio that the patients have faucets and, therefore, water in their dormitories, but they have not eaten since Thursday's takeover. The captors and staff ate the last of the food in the Centro last night, cooked by the women before they were released with the promise that they would return with food this morning. Now this new development. Food only after the release of all the patients.

And no word on the visa demand. The amnesty demand. Not even a fucking box of Marlboros.

The red kerchief is furious. It's as if their voices make no sound. Their words mean nothing. He steps into the small bathroom and brings out a handful of toilet paper, wipes his boots on it. The brown smear could fool anyone. "Tell them," he tells the boy waiting on the porch, "this is what I think of their reply. Mierda! Mierda! We mean what we say. This is not a story. We will see what happens by tomorrow noon."

Since this morning when she was dragged inside the clinic, Alma has felt a low-grade fear like a pilot light that burns sometimes more brightly than other times. After all, it's unnerving to be surrounded by masked faces and firearms. But after hanging out for hours with them in the front room, she has started to agree with Don Jacobo, these are not criminals, they're kids, adolescents, most of them; they have to be listened to, to be talked to in the right tone of voice; to be given one of those golden eggs of hope. But their leader is a loose cannon, and led by him, this standoff could end in violence. Alma's fear kicks up a notch, a visceral fear, in the pit of her stomach, rumbling with panic.

She wonders if it puzzles the red bandanna at all that the only demand that has been granted so far is the one for a journalist to tell the world their story. All morning, on and off, he has made comments, expounding on libertad y justicia, dignidad y democracia, the clichés he has no doubt heard from politicians on election years. Mostly, he grows more and more irritable, kicking at one of the boys dozing at his window post, shoving another one back who is headed for the bathroom twice in an hour. Another of the world's bullies with his little army of fodder foot soldiers—don't they see through him?

In fact, Alma detects a growing tension among the young companions. From time to time, they exchange looks, increasingly worried. They have been led to this moment by a leader who hasn't thought through the details, meals, cigarettes, visas. They are beginning to wonder what will become of them.

At least he hasn't started picking on Alma yet. Hasn't asked her when she is going to phone in her interview to the papers. So far he believes her story. But she has been kept in the front room, away from Richard and the clinic staff on the back patio. As if she has to be at the ready, by his side, like a weapon. The writer who will tell the world their story that is not a story. Such a simple plot: teenage boys in ski-resort masks and cowboy bandannas asking for a chance to be human beings.

BY LATE AFTERNOON, the waiting room is hot, the only breeze is coming in from the hallway that leads to the back patio. The heat and lethargy and hunger are getting to everyone. When the leader is out of the room, Alma asks permission to use the bathroom, more out of hope that she might see Richard than out of need. No one bothers to escort her; the boys just point down the hallway. On her way, Alma peeks in an open door and is surprised to see the leader alone, his bandanna lifted like a woman's kerchief over his hair. He is sitting on an examining table, eating her PowerBar.

She hurries away. No telling what he'd do if he knows Alma has gotten a glimpse of his unmasked face.

In the bathroom, she looks around. On the back of the door hangs a poster of an attractive couple, in hot embrace, the copy urging everyone to use condoms even with a partner of confianza. The sink is tiny, the bar of soap a sliver, the medicine cabinet empty. In the mirror, Alma's face is pale, sweaty. The shower stall door is open, the floor still wet. Someone has taken a recent shower. Probably the leader, who seems to get all the goodies. A damp towel hangs from a hook.

Maybe she can leave Richard a note here. Her journal and pen are in her pocket. She could scribble something directly on the poster, but where to make sure Richard sees it? A balloon coming out of the woman's mouth? Right below the couple, by the words *partner of confianza*? Before Alma can think through the details, one of the young guardia has come back to retrieve her.

She feels like weeping as she sits back down at what has become her post, the chair she took this morning to interview the leader. How interminable this day has been! The hardest part has been her isolation from Richard. She needs to lay eyes on him, to touch his hands and face, to renew her flagging faith that everything will come out all right in the end. When it comes to being a doubting Thomas, she's just as bad as the red bandanna.

She wishes she could expose him to his minions. How can they trust a leader who hordes the last bit of food for himself? "Have any of you seen that candy bar I had in my pocket?" she asks, hoping to arouse a spark of suspicion. The boys perk up, eagerly search around. But the bar has vanished.

Maybe your leader would know where it is? she almost asks. But just then, as if sensing what's on her mind, he strides in, his red bandanna back in place, no doubt hiding a Cheshire grin on his face.

WHEN STARR'S CELL PHONE rings, Alma jumps, shocked at its nearby sound. There it sits on the chair beside her where she laid it down during their interview this morning.

Alma lets it ring because not only does she not know if she is allowed to answer it, but she is unsure what button to press even though Starr walked her through the easy-as-pie instructions last night before going to bed. She will give herself away as an impostor, not knowing how to answer her own cell phone—the one professional prop that seemed to convince her disbeliever.

"Answer it," he orders her. "You can tell them what we have been telling you." He must think the call is from the authorities, and the fact that they're using a high-tech cell phone rather than the mayor's five-year-old means they're ready to meet his demands.

Alma squints trying to read the small print on the teensy buttons. Finally, she presses the right button, because when she holds the nearly weightless phone to her ear, a big, booming voice is saying howdy at the other end. It's Daddy and he wants to know how his little girl's doing. Why the hell hasn't she called him today?

"This is . . . a friend, Mr. Bell. Starr is fine."

Her captor obviously feels uneasy hearing her speak English. He prods her with his gun. Just feeling that pressure on her arm makes Alma's hand begin to shake. What if it goes off? What if he shoots her by mistake? "What do you want me to say?" she whispers frantically. "It's a personal call."

"Hang up!"

That's easier said than done. What button to push with her fingers trembling like crazy? In a panic, Alma returns the little phone to the chair beside her. She can hear daddy's far-off voice demanding an explanation.

The thunderous explosion sends Alma flying away from her chair, sure she has been shot. She finds herself on the floor, covering her face, feeling an ache in her leg as if she has pulled a muscle. She lies still, waiting for a shocking burst of pain, afraid to move, lest she find out the limb she is trying to move is no longer attached to her body.

Slowly, Alma collects herself. Air floods her lungs. She has not been shot but her left leg has been struck by a flying scrap of plastic which has cut a nasty flap of skin off her thigh. It has begun to bleed. She hopes it is one of those cuts that looks worse than it is. "I'm hurt," she moans, not daring to complain too loudly. No telling what this crazy guy might do. First, he shoots the clock, now the cell phone, Alma is probably next. Not three feet away, the chair that held the cell phone has been demolished, the phone a scattering of springs and teensy pieces of metal, one of them, Alma now sees, has cut her right fore-arm, also bleeding.

"What are you doing?" The young poet has run in from the back with a drawn gun. Before she even sees him, she can tell from his voice that he has removed his kerchief. No doubt he thought troops were storming the front door and came running without bothering to cover himself. Now he is just eyeing the red-bandanna guy with a super-pissed-off look on his face. Only incidentally does he seem to notice Alma, wailing it must be in fear of her own spilled blood for nothing really is hurting that much. "You shot her?" he confronts the leader, who looks a little sheepish about wounding a journalist without meaning to.

In a moment, he recovers his bravado, drunk on the error he has set going that can only end badly, he is beginning to sense. He raises his gun toward his questioner, furious to be found making a mistake. "No, I didn't shoot her. Though I should. Shoot her, shoot you."

"Put that thing down, Bolo," a voice from behind urges him. It's one of the older boys at the windows. "We've got enough problems with guardia all around us."

Bolo, Alma is thinking. She doesn't remember seeing that name on Camacho's list. One of the bad elements. She tells herself to remember that name, in case of what? Will she even be able to continue carrying off her role as journalist? She looks around and spots her notebook lying across the room. The pen is nowhere in sight.

The red bandanna seems to spend an eternity reconsidering whether to put his gun away. "Okay," he finally says, again using the word as if it were a Spanish word. He not only puts his gun down, but like a teenager whose dignity has been wounded by being shown up in front of strangers, he stomps out of the room. Her defender now comes to kneel by Alma's side. He looks even younger with his nose and mouth uncovered. A mobile, sensitive face. "Let's see the leg," he says, and over his shoulder he tells one of the young men to go get la doctora from the back patio.

This is how Alma, who is not a journalist, but goes by the name of Isabel, ends up being a patient of la doctora Heidi Castillo, assisted by el doctor Cheché Pellerano, in the small examining room off the hall where she caught sight of the leader eating her PowerBar. Alma is not sure of the diagnosis, as it takes her a while to figure out that the two doctors are telling the young men one thing and her another. "It is a bad cut," they pronounce, then later in a whisper, assure her that all the wound needs is a cleaning and bandaging. "We need to take her to a hospital for some stitches," la doctora asserts, seconded by el doctor. Understandably, the two doctors are devising a way to get out from under the cross fire that is sure to come between the armed guardia and these stupid kids. Why shouldn't each one try to save his or her individual, valuable life? They have been stuck here for three days already. They want to go home to their families, for whom no doubt they were making this sacrificio of working at a remote clinic for what is probably a pretty good salary.

"I'm not leaving without Richard," Alma tells the two doctors. "El americano from the green center," she adds, because they don't seem to know what Richard she is talking about.

They both look perplexed, especially la doctora Heidi, who seems to be about Alma's age, a long-faced woman with beautiful, liquid eyes that moisten up readily—a good professional feature, Alma can't help thinking. La doctora has been told there is a wounded journalist in the front room. But Alma seems somehow connected to el americano, whose casual approach to everything is what has caused all this trouble in the first place. Before Richard, there used to be round-the-clock armed guards patrolling the Centro. But he, and la americanita, who must be Starr, changed all that. That's what left them wide open to these local gangsters who have grown desperate and killed the hen that would have laid enough golden eggs for everyone.

La doctora asks the young guard and el doctor Pellerano if they would step just outside the examining room while she dresses la señora's wound. The boy guard hesitates a moment, but he is still a boy, just starting to feel enough confidence to slip his hand under his girlfriend's blouse and touch her breasts. His modesty is still stronger than his cunning. Out he goes, with Dr. Pellerano, keeping the door slightly ajar por si acaso.

As soon as they are alone, la doctora tells Alma point-blank, "We have to get you out of here."

"But I don't want to go without my husband." Alma confesses all. The doctora's face softens. She has been in love herself, knows how a woman might cleave to a good man. "Is Richard doing all right?" Alma has seen him only briefly this morning but has heard his voice in the hallway all day long.

"He is feeling well," la doctora answers briskly, back to business. "Only a disturbance in his stomach," she adds, dismissively. So that's it. He has been going to the john. And here Alma thought he'd been unsuccessfully trying to talk his way to the front room so he could beam her an eyeful of scolding and a smile of tender concern.

"There is something muy urgente to discuss," the doctora whispers, looking over her shoulder at the slightly opened door. As she cleans up Alma's leg, dabbing at it, la doctora explains that a plan is in place. Last night, she sent word with one of the women who cook, a person of total confianza. The hostages are all on the back porch—seven in all, now eight with Alma. Once it is dark, the guardia can slip in the back entrance to the Centro. Under the cover of darkness, the guardia can easily approach from the rear, overpower the two or three back-porch guards, rescue the hostages, and then storm the front waiting room where the captors tend to congregate at night with their leader, listening to the radio and watching the small cable television.

Clean and easy. No one gets hurt.

"They get TV up here?" Richard never told her that.

Solar panels, a dish. La doctora waves away Alma's question. Time is short. Soon the boy guard's suspicion will overwhelm his modesty. As she bandages up the leg, la doctora goes over the exodus plan. What a mastermind, Alma can't help thinking. La doctora Heidi Castillo should be working for the military. Whatever happened to the Hippocratic oath? But la doctora is trying to save lives, a clean and easy plan, in which no one is going to get hurt if they follow her instructions.

"But we have to get you out of here," la doctora goes on quickly. Either Alma has to be out of the compound—that's why they've been pushing so hard to have her evacuated—or out of this examining room. "So you can be with us on the back porch when the rescue comes."

Suddenly, it seems awfully inviting to leave this place. To rest in the mayor's house and await a reunion later tonight with Richard. "Either way," she tells the doctora, too embarrassed to come out and say that she'd like to leave now but with Richard, who is arguably sick himself. The rest of the hostages can wait for their rescue operation that la doctora has worked out for tonight.

"If we ask for you to be evacuated . . ." La doctora's voice trails off, as she works out the options in her head. Alma can guess. If their request for her evacuation is refused again, as it was in the beginning, then the captors might not let Alma go hang out on the back porch in her critical condition.

So the plan is set. "We must get you to the back porch. I will say that I have cleaned the wound, and it is much more superficial than I thought, no stitches required. That you are faint because you are closed up in here without air. Okay?" She, too, uses the English word. Alma wonders if *okay* is now a global word, a bit of Esperanto from that bright land of promise where everything is okay, which is why so many people around the world want visas to go to the United States.

"Okay," Alma agrees. But as the doctora turns to call the two men back in, Alma wants to be sure, "No one's going to get hurt, right?"

La doctora looks sadly over at Alma. Her eyes moisten up. "You think I want to risk anybody's life here?" She has thought up a plan that will not violate the Hippocratic oath, a maneuver in which everyone goes home, or behind bars, unharmed.

WHILE LA DOCTORA NEGOTIATES with the leader over letting Alma join the back porch hostages, Alma lies on the examining table, trying to make out what is being discussed in the front room.

She closes her eyes, and her young guard must think that she has fallen asleep because he yanks off his ski mask—it is so hot in this windowless room. But when he notices her eyes flickering closed after she opened them only to realize she shouldn't have, he quickly pulls the mask back over his head. "Don't bother," Alma tells him. "The women gave out all the names last night."

This seems to convince him because he pulls off his mask again. A cowlick of black hair stands up at the back of his head. He can't be a day older than sixteen. He might not even have a girlfriend. "One of them is my mother," he confesses a moment later.

He is in trouble any way he cuts it. "Are they going to give us visas?" he wants to know.

"I don't know," Alma tells him, although of course she knows: they are not going to get visas; they are not going to get jobs with the green center; they might not even get a meal from the autoridades. The brief window of hope is now closed if it was ever open for these young fellows.

"Maybe if you give up now, you could get a pardon," she suggests. The young ones especially, maybe Richard and Emerson can plead their case. They're kids; they should be given a second chance to make something of themselves. But Alma knows damn well how their story will end. This is a place without first chances to begin with, which is why these kids got desperate in the first place.

A phone has begun to ring. For a second, Alma thinks she has dreamed up the shooting of Starr's cell phone. But no, it's that old, funky phone in the front office. There is a scurry back and forth in the hallway beyond her door. She thinks she hears Richard talking to someone in English.

"What will they do to us?" the boy persists. His young face is worried. Maybe he isn't even sixteen. Maybe like the Killington ski-mask boy, he wants a visa so he can go to the United States, earn good money, and win back the good graces of his mother and family.

"If I were you, I'd surrender *now*," Alma says, trying to keep the urgency out of her voice so as not to give the plan away. "You might get a better deal. Use your time of punishment to study, go to school when you get out." She wishes he could read. She'd give him the autobiography of Malcolm X, explain how this black guy at the bottom of the American heap memorized the dictionary in prison, became a great leader. She brings up Abraham Lincoln, who was born in a log casita, no bigger than where this boy probably lives with his mother and half dozen siblings. Alma makes Lincoln sound like a poor Midwestern campesino, president only recently. The point is not to trick the boy but to give him some narrative of hope, a piece of string he can take hold of to make his way out of this hellhole labyrinth.

"Are you in pain, señora?" the young boy asks because suddenly Alma's eyes are moist, like la doctora's eyes, with tears.

Yes, she could tell him, but not from the cut on my thigh. But from this blind alley history keeps taking you to. And here you are again, and there is not a thing I can do for you. She thinks of Walter or Frank, the collusive look he gave her. Fat chance these kids are going to get off as easy as she wants them to.

"You can become a lawyer, a doctor. There are all kinds of organizations that give money. My husband and I will help you. Once you know how to read and write, many doors will open," Alma goes on; she can't stop herself from imagining a way out for him because this is the way it has to begin, the story that is not a story, that might just happen if she gets him believing it can really happen to him.


THE RED-BANDANNA LEADER is reluctant at first to let Alma join the other hostages—after all, the two doctors originally made it sound like Alma's leg was so bad, it might even require amputation. He doesn't want her life on his head. Alma is relieved to hear this. The bully with the bad temper might have a workable heart after all.

Alma gives a convincing show of miraculous recovery, swinging her leg over the side of the table and taking a hop down, trying not to wince when her foot hits the floor.

"My leg is fine. But I do feel faint. I need air," she complains, clutching her chest. If this were an audition, she would lose the part for overacting. But the young man seems convinced. Women's ailments. He, too, can be hoodwinked by them.

"Okay," he tells her. She can go have her dinner with the others.

"Dinner?"

He laughs, a little throaty sound under his kerchief. It turns out that he has worked out a deal with the guardia, and food and cigarettes are on the way. In exchange, he has agreed to release all the women prisoners *after*—he is getting more savvy—their side of the bargain is in their hands. Alma is somewhat surprised that he has agreed to this compromise, but she can tell by the way he swaggers as he tells her that he considers this a victory, the beginning of negotiations that will ultimately get them amnesty, if not their visas. Even he is beginning to scale down his golden dream for the future.

As ALMA LIMPS ONTO the back patio, she is surprised to see that it has grown dark. A dim light has been turned on. Bugs and moths beat their wings against it. Everyone looks milky, spectral, but there is a feeling of palpable hope among the hostages.

Richard cannot contain himself. He rushes forward to find out how her leg is doing. He had gotten a curt report from la doctora. His wife, who calls herself Isabel and pretends to be a journalist, has a superficial cut on her right thigh and a bruise on her forearm. Nothing serious. Of course, she is okay.

"I am okay," Alma tells him. In fact, she's probably doing a lot better than he is. His unshaven face is drawn, his thin hair uncombed. There's such a forlorn, orphaned look about him. He is wearing his windbreaker, zipped up against the cooler night air, a present she bought him out of a catalog that turned out to be on the pinkish side of maroon, but still he stoically wore it in Vermont. Here, who cares? Seeing him, Alma's eyes fill up. Their vulnerable, valuable lives seem all the more valuable, vulnerable. "I hear from la doctora your stomach's acting up."

"No big deal." He waves away her concern. Of course, it's never a big deal with Richard. Probably not a big deal to be held hostage for three days by a bunch of desperate guys with guns. *It's okay*, he had said, *just a little ice,* as they skidded over the side of the mountain.

She touches his hand. *Rescue is on the way*, her eyes tell him. *We will soon be out of here.*

*I know.* He smiles back at her. *We will be saved.*

One of the guards comes over and jerks his head for los americanos to move into the roofed patio area where the staff are sitting on benches, waiting for deliverance. La doctora gives her a collusive nod: *Good. You are here.* El doctor Cheché smiles, expansive with the freedom that is coming. "Señora, how are you feeling?" As for the rest of the hostages, there are two women and two men, all of them wearing lab coats, their names emblazoned over their hearts. The introductions are brief, telegrammatic, as the guards get nervous when the hostages talk too much among themselves. Mostly, eye contact. Soulful and deep eye contact. Alma is sure they all know the plan. *We are in this together,* their eyes say. *We must be prepared; we must stay out of harm's way when the guardia come. By tomorrow at this hour, we will be celebrating our freedom. We, the lucky ones.*

The look goes around from one to the other. Alma feels a pang that it stops there, that they cannot include her boy guard whose mother, if he makes it home by tomorrow night, will give him hell. The Killington ski mask who wants to go to the United States and send dollars home to his family. The black kerchief who should learn to read—he would love Neruda's poetry. He could write his own book some day, a saga such as Alma and her ilk could never write in a million years. A story that is not a story, but a song to break hard hearts and put them back together again, beyond the ken of all the king's men.

The word comes from the front room that dinner bags and cigarillos have been received. The black kerchief and a ski mask from Stowe come out the back door to open up the female dormitorio and release the women. The outdoor lights have been turned on, a strange glow suddenly illuminates the wilderness. The crickets go still. Far off, Alma hears village sounds. A baby crying again, a dog barking. Some woman is laughing. Laughing! There is still laughter in this world, oh heavenly sound!

The door of the female dormitorio is thrown open. The guards shout for the women to evacuate. But no one steps out. Alma remembers an article she once read about how animals will grow so used to captivity, they won't run out even when the door of their cage is left wide open.

The young men shout again for the women to walk calmly toward the front gate. A brave soul peeks out. Her dark figure emerges, followed by another, and another, and soon there is a stampede of women, some alone, some hand in hand, some riding piggyback on others' backs, all of them running toward the opened front gate, crying, *We are sick! Please don't hurt us! Have mercy on us!*

Minutes later, a couple of guards come down the hall from the front of the clinic, their arms full of paper bags. The two boys on duty rush in to get their dinner. "Stay seated," one of the *guardia* instructs the hostages. "You will each get a bag."

"You hungry?" Alma asks Richard. She has felt weak-kneed and headachy from lack of food. Richard shakes his head. He doesn't feel much like eating.

"You should eat, though," she fusses. A brief look of annoyance passes over his face. Even in this godforsaken place, how easily they can slip into their little domestic riffs. Soon they will be bickering. You forgot to pick up garlic. Whose turn is it to do the dishes?

While they wait for the next round of bags to come from the front room, Richard tells Alma that she has gotten some calls on the clinic phone. "They were in English, so the guys had me go and take a message. You left the clinic number on Claudine's answering machine? Anyhow, the sheriff's been trying to find you."

"Did you tell him I'm indisposed?" She smiles grimly at how reachable technology has made everyone. Here they are, hostages on a remote mountaintop, under a cloudy night sky, with just a sliver of a moon showing like a last slice of a pie no one has room for, and a small-town Vermont sheriff is trying to reach her. Maybe soon she'll get a call from Hannah, reminding Alma they have made a deal with Helen's God. *Both men back in our arms, unharmed.* Alma has kept her side of the bargain. Maybe all will be well, at least for her and Richard, Mickey and Hannah.

"I guess the whole town's been quarantined. Some crazy story about some Hannah woman who claims she and her husband let loose a monkey pox virus. I couldn't understand it all. But I told them where you were, except I said you were shot in the leg and a hostage . . ."

So now she might be carrying monkey pox, infecting everyone

around her! This is totally insane! Alma begins to tell Richard the story of Thanksgiving Day, but the young guard who is handing out dinners comes over and thrusts a bag at each of them. "Silencio! Eat your dinner." She unwraps hers: a big bulky hamburger, probably from the McDonald's she noticed on the highway as they turned up the mountain. Alma is famished—she hasn't eaten all day. She looks around, hoping to trade hers for an Egg McMuffin. But everyone gets the same meal, a big Quarter Pounder, a Coke, a candy bar, a box of Marlboros. At first, she tries to eat around the meat, nibbling the soggy, white bun, but she ends up devouring the greasy patty. So much for her vegetarian principles. It is delicious.

A little later, they are allowed to spread blankets on the floor of the patio and get some rest. The hostages work silently, moving the benches to the side, all probably thinking the same thing, stack them securely out of the way of the storming guardia. By now the outdoor lights are off. The little radio is turned down so low that Alma wonders how the guards can hear it at all.

Alma lies beside Richard, face to face in the dark. She wants to find out what else the sheriff had to say about this monkey pox scare, what if she's harboring some deadly disease (but that's absurd—Hannah has pulled this trick before!), if they all get saved for nothing, but a fierce "Shhhh" comes from the two young guards made nervous by her whispering. They have taken off their masks in the dark and sit one on each end of a bench, leaning against the back wall, tired, dreaming of home perhaps. One of them burps often, without apology or seeming embarrassment.

The rest of the young men are inside, smoking their cigarettes, planning tomorrow's strategy with their leader. Periodically, Alma lifts her head slightly to check out where the guards are, and as she does she notices others doing the same. They are all waiting and waiting on this night that seems to go on and on. Perhaps the deal is off, now that the captors are negotiating, and the guardia will not come after all.

Alma struggles to stay awake, but in spite of her fear and anticipation she dozes off. She is with Isabel on the way to Manila on a huge galleon, about six times the size of the *María Pita*, four hundred souls on board. But instead of the promised accommodations, the boys are consigned to sleep on the floor of the powder magazine, tossed around with the pitch and roll of the ship. Don Francisco confronts the captain but it is as hopeless as trying to bargain with the red bandanna. Nothing happens. As weeks pass, the director's condition worsens, a bloody dysentery that might end his life midjourney. Isabel despairs for him, for herself, for the twenty-six young lives entrusted to her care.

In her dream, Alma looks down upon the weary Isabel, wishing she could offer some comfort, a whisper of hope, a glance that says, *You are not alone. We are here together.*

Some time later, she wakes up, feeling Richard stir. It's his stomach, the worse for the dinner he ate. Could it be Alma has infected him with monkey pox? Of course not; he was sick before she got here. It could be the island's version of Montezuma's revenge; Richard is never careful with the water, readily eats street food. But by now his system should be used to the local flora and fauna. Most probably, it's just nerves—though Richard would never admit it. Being a hostage three full days can work havoc on a first-world stomach.

He has to go to el sanitario. Carefully, he makes his way over the sleeping hostages, who are probably not sleeping at all, and calls softly to the guards. It takes a minute for them to wake up. Sleepily, they gesture for Richard to go on his own. Alma watches him disappear down that dimly lit tunnel.

She resists the pull of sleep, waiting for Richard to return, for his body to curl sweetly around her own, as if they were back in Vermont, as if their lives had not taken this dive into error and happenstance. She listens to the noises of the night. One of the guards is snoring; the wind is in the trees, a hushing, rushing sound, the beginning of a storm, maybe. It is chilly. Richard was right: ski masks would prove useful on such nights, but who would ever have thought they would come to the use they came to.

She thinks she hears Richard now, coming back to his place beside her, but it is a dark figure, which turns into two, three, a dozen dark figures, some of whom have overpowered the two captors, one of whom takes her hand as another takes another hostage's hand; each dark guardian seems to know which one he is to rescue. Meanwhile, a host of brother shadows are rushing into the Centro, as swiftly, unquestioningly, the hostages are being run out of the back patio, out of harm's way, for this is how luck works, happening to some and not to others, this oh-not-so-blind selection, which Alma is trying to alter, begging her own rescuer to go back, to tell the others that her husband is in the bathroom, that they mustn't mistake him for one of the captors. But before she can convince him, she hears thunder, lightning, a great burst of gunfire, a storm of rain and shooting men, that she will never forget for as long as she lives, for as hard as she tries to forgive them.

# VII

WHAT A HURRIED DEPARTURE we had from New Spain!
We arrived in Mexico City from the provinces the first week in January. In less than a month, we had the equipages of twenty-six boys to assemble, as well as our own. And this would not be a short journey hither and yon. Since only two ships set sail for Manila each year, the queue was long (troops, friars, silver to transport in order to buy and bring back silk, ivory, spices). It might well be a year before we would return to Acapulco.

Before I left Puebla, I sat down with little Benito. I explained to him that I was going on a long journey; that soon, very soon, Lieutenant Pozo, the tall, kind mate of the *María Pita*—Did he remember him? Of course, he did. The one who stammered and was so strict? That very one. This lieutenant would be back probably before I was. They should wait for me here in the city of the angels.

I anticipated a repeat of the anguished parting scene in Mexico City when I had left my boys in the hospicio. But Benito listened quietly, his face attentive, his eyes serene. "Have a safe journey, Mother," he wished me, and when I held him with my eyes, because I needed more, he asked, "May I go play now with the boys?" The seminary was next door, the school Benito would attend as soon as he was old enough to sit on a school chair and his feet touch the floor.

"Yes, my love," I said, holding him too tight. This is motherhood, I

thought, love and loss bound so tightly together, it is impossible to separate them.

I felt him pull away before I was ready to let him go.

WE HAD ASSEMBLED in the custom house in Acapulco, ready to
depart when Don Francisco was handed a letter; the seal of the viceroyalty was unmistakable. For a moment, I thought, the man has come
around! Now that we are leaving, he can wish us godspeed.

Our director was shaking his head with disbelief and disgust. "Listen,
Doña Isabel, to the gratitude we get."

> You should take with you all your equipment and expedition members and
> return to Europe directly from the islands. You must not come back here
> as your services are no longer needed. If you should return after this warn-
> ing, be advised that you do so at your own expense.

My heart sank. "But I must return. My child . . ." My voice broke. I
could not continue. The pressure of the preparations of the last few weeks
had worn down my self-control. I could not bear this last injunction. How
could I *not* return? I had twenty-six boys in my care to bring back from
Manila, a son left behind in Puebla de los Ángeles, and a dozen more in
the Royal Hospicio to worry after until homes were found for them.

"Pay him no mind, Doña Isabel." Don Francisco led me gently by the elbow to the outside galería. We stood under a projecting roof and watched
as stevedores and porters loaded up cargo in boats rowed out to the
*Magallanes*, too large a nao to come in to the bay. The loading had been going on all week. The ship would hold about five hundred of us. Even that
frightened me, my nerves were so frayed. "I have written to His Majesty
with my report." Don Francisco held up his own letter. "The man's behavior will not go unpunished, trust me, Doña Isabel."

I had to, for I had already cast my lot with Don Francisco. And surely
the viceroy knew my plans. He had paid me a part of my salary, which I
had left behind with the kind Bishop Gonzales for my Benito. The remain-
der would be paid to me when I returned with the twenty-six boys upon
concluding our mission.

"Surely he knows we are coming back?" I asked Don Francisco.

"Surely he knows you are," our director replied. It did not strike me until later that our director had not exactly answered my question.

THE *MAGALLANES* WAS A small city afloat on an endless sea. Its large size made it much steadier than the *María Pita*. My seasickness was mild and passed quickly for the weather was fair and the breezes propitious. Much of our time was spent on deck. Every day, it seemed I saw new faces. Friars, soldiers, merchants, and—yes!—women, about fifty of us, all told. Most were the wives of officials returning to their homes or setting out to join their distant husbands. Many brought maids, native girls from New Spain, or for those returning, from the islands themselves. These I especially studied in order to acquaint myself with the natives I would soon be meeting. Small-boned, pretty girls, with copper skin and shiny hair the color of ebony.

The wives were certainly curious about me. I was *not* married to our director? *None* of these boys were my sons? A *smallpox* expedition? (At this, they edged away.) Our director, hearing that panic was mounting among the passengers, decided to give a talk one evening about our mission. After that, the ladies were more kindly disposed toward me and the children. But, oh my, twenty-six boys! How could I manage them all without a maid to help me?

How could I manage? Barely! All of my new boys were between the ages of four and six, with only one older boy of fourteen, Josef Dolores, who proved to be a great help to me. They were much more demanding to care for than my Coruña boys, as I had not raised them myself, so I did not have that deep understanding that comes with helping nurture their natures.

Knowing that the trip was long and wearying, Don Francisco had paid top price for the best accommodations. A few days out, he grew alarmed at the poor quality of our fare—the boys had been served only lentils and meat so rotted that hungry as they were, they cast it aside, which at least made the rats happy. Yes, rats! The boys had been stowed in a small storage area where the magazine powder was kept. The captain was certainly not keeping his part of the agreement.

"How is it possible?" Don Francisco shook his head in disbelief. "How can a man trick us in this way when he knows we are embarked on a beneficent mission?"

"Surely there has been a misunderstanding." Don Ángel always sought to think well of everybody. "Perhaps the captain needs only a gentle reminder."

But our director was not one to tactfully wait and present our case calmly to Captain Ángel Crespo. In a trick of fate that proved most ironic, our captain had the very same name as our own Ángel Crespo. But it was as if the Lord had created two versions of the same human being, then decided to keep both and no doubt love them both equally, a lesson to all of us prodigal sons and daughters. And it might have been a fruitful lesson had we not been at sea, with eight more weeks to go, and our health and well-being dependent on the least angelic of these two Ángel Crespos.

The captain assured Don Francisco he would look into the matter. But our second week out, the boys were still sleeping in the magazine and their food was as close to inedible as possible. Even the rats were turning away from it, biting the boys instead. Don Francisco began to worry about other infections and plagues. Seven more weeks under these conditions, and not just the vaccine but our boy carriers, too, were in danger of being lost before we arrived in the Philippines.

I could not bear the thought of losing one more child to this expedition. I fretted and fussed over my boys. At night I could not sleep thinking of little Tomás, Orlando, Juan Antonio. Amid the slap of waves on the hull, the groans and snores from other berths, I heard their voices calling to me.

Some nights in the throes of these nightmarish imaginings, when I feared that I would scream and wake all the women in my partition, I felt an invisible hand on my forehead soothing away my fears; a voice crooned in my ears. *Everything will turn out well, trust me.*

Those nights I slept, my scarred face wet with tears.

AMONG THE WOMEN ON board was a lady about my age who had been traveling the better part of a year. Señorita Margarita Martínez had set out from Cádiz, landed in Veracruz, crossed overland to Acapulco by mule, and was now en route to the Philippines to join her brother, the captain of the militia in Manila. "You must call me Margarita," she insisted. I was glad for the liberty. Señorita Margarita sounded too much like a silly girl in a comedy.

Margarita had a lovely "little cabin" with a "little bunk" and a "little desk," and enough room to hang a hammock for the "little maid" she had brought with her from Mexico. She had to keep her eye on the pretty girl. She had already lost two maids to America. The first refused to get back on board after a stop in Havana, so petrified was she of the sea. The other had run off with one of the crew she had *befriended* on the crossing. "A little tart!" Margarita attached the diminutive to everything. It was a way for her to make the world doll size and safer, so I came to believe.

She offered to show me her cabin, and it was almost as nice (and twice as large) as her description. Indeed it reminded me of the mate's cabin on the *María Pita*. Was he on his way back to meet me? I wondered. Or had his ship been intercepted by the British? If he did manage to make it through enemy lines, would he be angry that I had not waited for him? In the letter I had left with Bishop Gonzales, I had explained that I needed to see this expedition through to the end. That I would be back. That he should forgive me.

"So where is your little nest, Isabelita?" Margarita was eager to see it. What else was there for a fine lady to do on board besides embroider and read and visit with other ladies? And though I was not a fine lady, I was connected with six gentlemen, one of them, Francisco Pastor, a bachelor and quite handsome. As for me, busy as I was with twenty-six boys to care for, I was lonely for another woman's companionship.

One afternoon, while the boys learned to tie knots on deck with the crew, I invited her down below. Yes, we were two decks down from her, in the steerage in curtained bunks; mine, thankfully, was in a section partitioned for women servants. "But I thought yours was a *royal* expedition?" The señorita was visibly disappointed.

"Indeed we are, not to mention that our director paid a *royal* price for our transport. You should see where the captain put my boys." I doubted that Margarita would go to the forward end of the ship, where a lady must never go.

"May I ask . . ." She hesitated. It was not mannerly to probe, but hers was a polite way to ask a question without asking it.

"Five hundred pesos!" She was shocked. We were paying over double her passage and receiving much worse fare!

I knew if I told our director this, he would surely strangle the captain in his sleep. So I kept my counsel. But a ship, as I should have known from my time on the *María Pita,* is a sieve of gossip. Our director soon found out that we had been grossly overcharged and were being insultingly underserved.

By the end of the second week, Don Francisco had had enough. He burst into the captain's quarters, demanding immediate restitution of the funds we had been overcharged. But Captain Crespo had dealt with mutiny and piracy and kept a number of loaded firearms within reach. He drew a revolver and threatened Don Francisco with the justice of the high seas should he dare to raise trouble again. Our director was forced to bear his grievances in silence until we reached our destination and charges could be lodged with Governor Aguilar in Manila.

February turned to March and March to April. The year would be half over before we arrived! But our crossing proved to be safe and expeditious. The vaccine was kept alive by the grace of God and by our own resourcefulness. The captain had forbidden the smallpox carriers any contact with the other passengers. We were forced to bed the two boys in question with the others in the magazine. With the jostling of the ship, the sleeping boys rolled into each other, and seven were vaccinated at once.

From then on, we took the two carriers aft, when the captain wasn't looking. Somehow we managed our ruse, despite the fact that there seemed to be no way to keep secrets on a ship. Perhaps our captain, with his eagle eye out for the problematic director, did not notice the gentle rectoress hurrying midship to her quarters with her red cape bulging around her.

AFTER MONTHS AT SEA, the sight of a desert island would have been wonderful! How much more so to behold these enchanting islands. In the distance we made out mountains, so richly green, they seemed vibrant, living beings; the air smelled fragrant like spices; the light looked like diamonds tossed on that turquoise bay. Dozens of natives rowed out in their canoes to greet us, short, copper-colored men and, I soon realized, young girls dressed in loose garments, the fabric so sheer, I could see their dark nipples through it. What lively intelligence lit up their faces! Their gaiety was remarkable. Why the least thing made them laugh!

"We have landed in the blessed isles," Pastor observed. He could not get enough of waving at the native girls giggling in their small boats.

As was his habit, Don Francisco had written ahead to Governor Aguilar, but again there was no welcome waiting for us. True, we had disembarked at the first opportunity, for Don Francisco did not want to spend one added moment on the same ship as the despicable captain.

"I've gotten so that I hate the sound of my own name," our Don Ángel muttered. It was the first time I had heard the kind soul exclaim bitterly against anyone.

"Perhaps you will find someone willing to give over his name to you," Pastor remarked. Margarita had related a curious bit of lore that her brother had written to her. Certain natives exchanged names as a sign of friendship.

When it seemed no one would appear at the wharf to greet us, our director hired several carriages for the ride to the governor's palace inside the walled city. There we were informed that we had just missed Governor Aguilar, who had gone to the docks to greet the newly arrived galleon.

Sometimes it took all my patience to bear with our impatient director.

Thirty-three bone-weary, sun-browned, thin travelers climbed back into their carriages and headed for the docks to receive their welcome.

THAT MISTIMED GREETING PROVED to be a prelude of things to come. Not that Governor Aguilar was another mean-spirited viceroy out to thwart our expedition. But he was the governor of a distant colony that lay halfway around the globe from its mother country. Loyalty was paramount among the small group of peninsulares, surrounded as they were by a staggering number of savages. No doubt Governor Aguilar did not want to alienate the prosperous and powerful Spanish merchants who owned the *Magallanes*. And so, when informed of the captain's egregious charges, the governor did not respond with the warmth our director expected.

"This is a matter you must take up with the commander of the marine," Governor Aguilar explained. This commander was presently inspecting some island ports but would be back within a week or so.

"But you are his superior, are you not?" Don Francisco persisted. He had waited too long to now be told to wait some more.

"I must observe the laws and procedures that have been set up." The governor held firm to his resolve.

Our director was testy. His dysentery had worsened on board. Curiously, mine had vanished, as if duress were my cure. "I will lodge my complaint with His Majesty, and it shall include your name."

The governor's long face grew longer. Perspiration gleamed on his brow. Indeed we were all bathed in sweat. It was almost midday; the sun was directly overhead, the heat oppressive. I felt as if I was being cooked inside my petticoat, dress, bonnet, and cape. I half envied the native women I had seen. How innocently they bared their arms and hiked up their skirts midcalf, their feet bare, their hair in a topknot. How simply they seemed to live compared with the difficulties our expedition was always encountering!

As we stood on the dock and listened to the heartfelt reunions of passengers with their families (Margarita was weeping joyfully in the arms of her brother), I felt the desolation of our own arrival. How homesick I suddenly felt for Puebla and my little Benito.

If only our director had waited to begin complaining. I agreed with him on every count about the injustice of the captain's charges. But all twenty-six boys had made it safely to these shores, the vaccine was alive, and we had a great deal of work ahead of us. I suppose our director's total dedication to his mission made it difficult for him to accept any less from others. It was as if he wanted to rid the world not just of smallpox but of any smallness whatsoever.

Strange, then, that under his tutelage, I was learning an opposite lesson: goodness had to be coaxed into being, and change might well take centuries to unfold. How many strokes of a pen were not needed to fill a page with words, and dozens of those pages to tell a tale. (I should know!

All that writing in the book Don Francisco had given me, now leagues under the sea to protect him.)

After a tense moment of silence, the director informed the governor that vaccination sessions would begin tomorrow. "I will thank you to make an announcement to the populace." He gestured toward the assembled crowd.

But the governor had a different idea. Rather than beginning with public vaccinations, he wanted to proceed in a quiet, discreet manner. It seemed the bishop of Manila and other high church officials had heard that the vaccine might be dangerous. They had already informed Governor Aguilar that they would not be promoting it from their pulpits.

This was too much for our director. He turned on his heels and left the governor with his explanations in his mouth. From then on, as in Puerto Rico, it was a war of wills and a conversation through intermediaries and letters.

"Isabelita!" Margarita was before me with a tall, fair-haired duplicate of her own person, though much more comely in its male version. "This is my brother, Captain Martínez."

"Thank you for taking such good care of my sister," the brother said warmly. I felt sheepish receiving praise I did not really deserve.

Our director was rounding us all up into our carriages. No, we would not be needing the governor's escort to our accommodations. He bowed curtly to the señorita, who bravely plowed on with her manners and introduced him to her brother.

"Sir, if I can be of any help at all." The captain was stationed here with the militia and was at the royal expedition's service.

The director suddenly stopped in the midst of his stormy exit. It's as if he had suddenly sighted land after being lost at sea. Perhaps he was beginning to realize that we knew no one in this distant colony. We would need allies if we were to win this battle against the Spanish savages.

THE VERY NEXT DAY we commenced vaccinating in Manila. Captain Martínez and the dean of the cathedral had come to our aid. The accommodations Governor Aguilar had provided for us were deemed by our director "indecent" and "miserable" (a rather old building located near the Chinese Parian gate, an inferior and disease-infested part of town). Captain Martínez offered the house he had leased for his sister and himself, an invitation his sister warmly seconded. She was delighted to have my company, even if I came with twenty-six little ruffians in tow. There is something about being confined to a ship at sea that brings out the wildness in a little boy! Thankfully, the house had a large hall on the first floor with sliding wooden windows, ideal for a dormitory. Meanwhile, the dean offered his own rectory as a center for our vaccinations.

Our sessions proved to be enormously successful even without the governor's promotion or that of the bishop. Smallpox had killed so many on these islands, crowds would have come even if we had been offering powdered smallpox scabs to be inhaled by long, thin reeds, as we heard was done in nearby China. In fact, in the Visayan islands to the south, the warriors put down their arms against the Spanish in order to be vaccinated!

Finally, Governor Aguilar relented. He brought his own five children to the rectory, thus displaying to any naysayers that he trusted the vaccine. But he had already made an enemy of Don Francisco, whose disenchantment at our reception reopened a wound that now would not heal. All his struggles in Spain to organize and fund the expedition (I had been hearing bits and pieces of this story as we traveled together), the disenchantments in Puerto Rico and New Spain, the trickery of Viceroy Iturrigaray and the *Magallanes* captain, the lackluster reception by the governor here—it had all become too much to bear. Add to this his bloody dysentery and his age, fifty-one years; we all kept forgetting our director was not a young man! Weakened and weary, he collapsed in bed, and not all the teas or bleedings in the world seemed to be helping. The angel of death was at his side. I wondered if he would ask me to take down another dictation to Doña Josefa.

But he was too weak even to arrange his affairs. All that was left to do was pray for him. Meanwhile, we could not falter in our mission—that he had made clear to us all during our travels. Should anything happen to him, we must bear the standard forward to victory. I had always imagined our director falling to an attack by natives brandishing spears or drowned in a mighty tempest or hanged by evil pirates—all the overblown adventures I had read about in Doña Teresa's discarded *Gacetas*. But here he was brought down by dysentery and a bad temper!

He lay close to death—any day now . . . I braced myself. Dr. Gutiérrez, who had taken charge of our mission, reminded us that we must keep our promise. We had innumerable islands to visit (several hundred in all, we were told); numberless natives and hundreds of colonists to safeguard. But even with all the exceptions I had taken to our director, I prayed that God would not leave us an orphaned mission. We had come halfway across the world with our healing caravan of children. Don Francisco could not abandon us now in the wilderness. From ships docking at the port, we heard about the war raging with England. Many were dying at sea and at home. It seemed we were saving the world only so that it could be lost to violence and further adversity.

I prayed harder. But I had never had much faith in my prayers.

I VISITED HIM DAILY in an upstairs room of the rectory. He insisted on being there, above the bustle of our activity, comforted by knowing his mission was being carried out. Most days, he seemed far too ill to be cognizant that we were downstairs. I'd climb up at midday to look in on him, wishing there were more windows to throw open, fanning him with a fan made of palm fronds. We had arrived in the hot, dry season, which would peak in May. And this was only at the end of April!

Because he had found them comforting in the past, I told him my stories. How we would vanquish smallpox from the world, how his name would be known down the generations, how he would return home to a great welcome, how Doña Josefa would be waiting. His face softened, a smile touched his parched lips. I fanned him, and myself, more vigorously.

April turned to May and indeed the heat worsened, but our director rallied; or rather, I should say, he had good days and bad days, mostly the latter. On good days, he insisted on settling our affairs. Tantamount among them was his desire that I and the boys return on the very next galleon to New Spain.

"We will settle all this later when you are well," I suggested. But I was touched by his concern for my particular welfare.

No, our director insisted. We must depart, the sooner the better. With the war with England escalating, it might prove harder to secure passages. There was a galleon leaving for Acapulco in July. He would petition the governor for spaces for me and the boys as well as for funds to replace the clothing the boys and I would need; the daily wear at sea had made rags of the small wardrobe we had hurriedly assembled in our rush out of New Spain this past January.

I did not take the dictation—Don Ángel did—or I would have softened the strident tone our director assumed when addressing men who had failed him. The governor returned the letter with a sharp admonition that it be reduced to the decorous terms befitting his position as first magistrate of the islands. The admonition was addressed to "the consulting director."

"I am *the* director of the Royal Philanthropic Expedition of the Vaccine, not the *consulting* director," Don Francisco thundered back. After several exchanges, the governor finally replied that he would accommodate us on a galleon when room could be found at an economical fee.

"Don't read it to him," I advised when Don Ángel recounted the contents of the governor's letter.

Don Ángel looked at me as if disbelieving my advice. "Doña Isabel, how do you think I know what was in a letter *addressed* to the director unless he had ordered me to open and read it to him?"

Men are full of subterfuge; armies surprise and slaughter each other; kings are betrayed and beheaded by their ministers. But let one of my sex suggest that a secret be kept or a hard truth softened, and they lift their heads indignantly and speak of honor and integrity!

"Don Ángel," I said, looking directly back at him. "When you are about to vaccinate a screaming child, do you not soothe him and tell him it will not hurt, although you know very well that the tip of a lancet piercing the skin will be somewhat painful?"

Don Ángel's face colored at the criticism implied. The many disillusionments of our journey had worn away his perennial good nature. He seemed crankier, more likely to take offense. Perhaps with time, all angels turned into men. "Doña Isabel, don't you see, a child doesn't understand that I am trying to save his life."

"Precisely," I replied.

THE BOYS AND I did not leave in July with the returning galleon. It was packed full with soldiers and with silk and spices needed to pay for our expensive war with England and our subsidy to France. We would have to wait until the next galleon—hopefully before the year was out.

The boys were happy enough with our prolonged stay. Their homesickness had worn off. Margarita had begun a little school for them, but the weather was still so hot—the anticipated rains had not come—that most days she called off classes and let them play outside all day long. With their sunburnt skin and raggedy clothes, they might well have been native children. In fact, from a distance, I could not tell many of them apart from the sons and daughters of our servants.

There were so many servants! Captain Martínez had inherited those of his predecessor, the former captain of the militia, as well as those who had come with this residence he had leased. And since every servant brought along several relations and a half-dozen children, we had a small village to attend to our every need.

One inhabitant in particular had attached herself to me, a native woman, her face also pocked by smallpox, which might have accounted for her connection to me. Kalua, as she was called, spoke a little Spanish, but often reverted to her own strange language of Tagalog, so I was not sure I understood her story.

It seemed her mother and father had died of the smallpox as had her brothers and sisters. She had wandered in the jungle, feverish and ill, in search of help, but whenever she came upon a village, the inhabitants cried for her to turn away or else they fled in terror. Somehow, she had survived, and one day walked into a village already afflicted with the smallpox, so she was able to nurse the sick. There, she had settled, marrying, bearing two sons. . . . Here her story unraveled as if she did not want to say what had happened next. I guessed a brutal or indifferent man or perhaps she was a widow.

Kalua was grateful for the vaccination we had given her sons, as she had firsthand experience of the terrible ravages of this disease. Her boys were part of the large and noisy pack running wild in the back garden. On those days when she saw my energy flagging and my heart heavy, she took on the care of all the children. "You are my Nati," I told her.

"Nati?" she repeated.

"A very special friend," I explained to her.

More and more I had to leave the boys in her care. Pastor and Don Pedro Ortega had departed for other islands: Misamis, Zamboanga, Cebu, Mindanao—I loved the sound of their strange and sonorous names. They would be back when they were finished vaccinating and setting up vaccination juntas at the different missionary outposts—six months, a year. Meanwhile, in Manila, Dr. Gutiérrez was left with a reduced staff: Don Ángel Crespo, Don Antonio Pastor, and myself. I could not be spared.

Don Francisco was now convinced that the only way he would recover his health was to move to a kinder climate. The area around southern China, he had heard, had much more pleasant weather. In addition, the ancient healing arts practiced there might prevail where science had failed. Once his constitution was strong again, he would sail around the cape on a Portuguese vessel for home, vaccinating en route. I could see that this was a way he might fulfill the mission he had set out to accomplish: spreading the vaccine around the world, not just in our Spanish dominions.

I felt such a confusion of feelings. Don Francisco had brought us here, so he must take us back. But Viceroy Iturrigaray had practically forbidden him to return. I recalled our director's words in Acapulco; he had not included himself when he had assured me that I would return to New Spain. Had he been hatching this plan back then?

"Can't we go on with you, sir?" I wasn't asking to accompany him as much as I was hoping he would not abandon us.

"It will be better this way," he explained. Without a large retinue, he could move at his own pace, with less preoccupation and inconvenience.

As he spoke, the veins on his thin neck stood out with the effort of speech. His face was gaunt, his bones visible under the loose skin. How distressing to find in the basin by his bed bloody spittle and several teeth! He would not survive if he stayed, I could see that. But I doubted that he would survive even if he went away.

Don Francisco petitioned the governor—and this time Don Ángel asked that I take the dictation—to grant him a passport and four boy carriers to set sail for Macao. A ship bound for that island was presently at port. He pleaded his poor health and went on to add that glory would rebound to the governor in the court of King Carlos for promoting this extension of our mission which would bring new friends to Spain. Perhaps it was this desire to clear his good name, but for the first time, the governor replied promptly and agreeably to consider the petition granted. I can't help thinking that the little touches of courtesy and praise I added to Don Francisco's dictation helped bring about Governor Aguilar's change of attitude.

Don Francisco's impending departure filled me with dread. I felt as shipwrecked parties might feel watching their captain sail off in a small boat with half of the rescued supplies. The smallest things vexed me beyond reason. I don't know why. A great impediment to our success would soon be removed. For Don Francisco's belligerence had now become legend in Manila. Our mission in these islands was bound to succeed in Dr. Gutiérrez's able hands. Still, with our director's departure, everything would be diminished, like Margarita's reduction of the world by qualifying everything as "little." It was a necessary change, but there was nostalgia still in me for that grander measure that had propelled me out of my old life toward America.

None of the expedition members noticed my mood, busy as we all were with too much work. Margarita was sure it was my menses, gone awry after months of grueling travel. But Kalua seemed to understand it was something of the spirit that was affecting me. She made me teas as Juana had done in Puerto Rico and pinned an amulet on my dress. Sometimes she told stories, of which I understood very little. But just the sound of her voice pronouncing her musical language soothed me.

In her company, I felt transported. It was a state of mind more than a place, an intuition more than a certainty, a sense that the spark of faith must be kept alive, like our own vaccine through carriers, or we would fall prey to violence and inhumanity.

It was imagining that future that filled me with apprehension. I could not seem to make those imaginings stop, except when I immersed myself in work or sat back and listened to the servant woman talk.

• • •

SEPTEMBER 3, 1805! The day I had been dreading finally arrived, a cloudy Tuesday. I hoped the rain would hold off.

I dressed my boys in the remnants of their uniforms and asked Captain Martínez if he might round together a band of musicians. I had copied out a list of the boys who had accompanied us thus far on our mission; at the bottom of the list, I added my own name, a declaration of faith in the dream our director had struggled—and never was there a truer verb attached to an enterprise—to carry out.

Until I was writing them all down, I had not realized how many children had come through our hands! And these names were only a small part of the thousands who had carried the vaccine to far off regions beyond where we had stopped. I could not help thinking of Dr. Salvany and Dr. Grajales, Don Rafael Lozano, the gruff Don Basilio Bolaños still proceeding down the length of South America toward the viceroyalty of Río de la Plata with boys on loan from village to village. Salvation carried on the arms of so many children and in the imagination of a handful of individuals!

We lined up at the docks. From the roof of the Customs House, our lookout called down that Don Francisco's carriage was approaching. The band was ready to play and the boys to sing a hymn for the safe journey of our director. Just as we were poised to begin, we heard a rumble as if the rains we had been awaiting for weeks were finally coming. But no, it was the sound of carriage wheels, more and more of them descending from the walled city, hundreds of citizens showing up to say farewell to Don Francisco!

The governor now had several kind words to say about our mission. The bishop gave his blessing. The band played, we sang, the cannons boomed farewell. Three boys went ahead aboard the *Diligencia*—I wondered what had happened to the fourth carrier, since our director had requested that number. I was still worrying over the details of how it would go for Don Francisco.

He looked cadaverous: his clothes hung on him and his mouth seemed to have sunk into his face, for he had lost most of his teeth. This was not the elegant stranger who had appeared at the orphanage two years ago in La Coruña. I felt a wave of emotion sweep over me as our own Josef

Dolores read out the long list of names and handed the document to our director, who bowed his head, overcome by this unexpected homage.

Now it was time for good-byes. He stooped down and spoke to the boys, reminding them to mind me. When he was done, he had to be helped back on his feet by Don Ángel.

He spoke some last-minute instructions and then embraced his faithful colleagues who had been by his side since he set out from Madrid. He lifted a feeble hand in salute to the crowd. I half hoped I would be included in this general farewell. Should he address me personally, I could not vouch for the weakening dam of my self-control.

"Doña Isabel." He was before me. His hand was bony in my own. "We have come a long way. I would not feel at ease leaving these boys behind if it were not that they are in your care. And the others," he said, waving his arm in the air. Did he mean the three members of our expedition standing with our boys? Don Pedro Ortega and his nephew had not yet returned from their journey to the islands. Or perhaps he meant the boys left behind in the Royal Hospicio in Mexico City. "You will take care of all them?"

I could not trust my voice. I nodded. To the best of my ability, I thought. But I would not qualify his hope. He would need every bit of it to carry him home.

"And you will take care of yourself," he added. His voice was tremulous, an old man's voice. I lifted my eyes to him and the look that passed between us bound us forever in that place I had imagined as the servant woman told her stories. *We are not alone. We are here together.*

I watched the frail figure proceed down the length of the wharf and board the *Diligencia*. I will never see him again, I thought, as the boys and I waved our kerchiefs, though mostly, I used mine to catch my tears.

That night after the boys were in bed, that sense of dread returned. I suppose I had indulged my tears at the dock, and now my fears were getting the best of me. I paced the room, recalling Don Francisco's worries about our delayed return. Without our director fighting our battles would we ever get back to New Spain? The governor had yet to guarantee our passage or release the funds so I could begin preparing our equipage.

When would I see my Benito again? What if we found ourselves in the hands of another dishonest captain? What if our throats were cut at sea and our bodies thrown to the deep that tells no tales?

"Faith!" I told my flagging spirits, as I had once advised Don Francisco.

There was a knock on the door. The servant woman had seen my light and, thinking I was ill, had come to check on me. "No, no, I am fine," I assured her. But she read the weariness in my eyes and stayed under the guise of turning down my bed.

We could not converse much in the small vocabulary we shared. But she helped me off with my dress and insisted I sit down while she combed my hair. In the mirror, we looked at each other, two scarred faces glad for the other's company. Outside the rain that had threatened all day began to fall. Thinking of Don Francisco, I hoped it was a local squall.

"Kaluluwa." She uttered the strange name I had heard the other native servants call her, a name her Spanish masters and mistresses found difficult to remember and had shortened to Kalua. "It means—" She touched her breast above where her heart should be.

"Heart?" I asked, and then imitated the thumping organ.

She shook her head and made a gesture of something further, beyond the heart.

"Kaluluwa," I repeated as if saying the name over would enlighten me as to its meaning. Behind me, she smiled in the mirror. There was anticipation in her eyes. And then I remembered the story we had been told about natives exchanging names as a sign of friendship. "Isabel," I offered.

"Isabel?" she repeated, perplexed. She had thought my true name was Nati.

I laughed, realizing the earlier misunderstanding. "I'm Isabel," I said. Except that now I was also Kaluluwa, a name I later learned meant *soul* in Tagalog.

When she left, I lay in the dark, listening to the rain. Each time a fearsome thought entered my feverish brain, I felt that soothing touch on my forehead again. *Faith!* Perhaps, by year's end, I would be reunited with my Benito, wed to my lieutenant, sitting down to dinner together in the city of the angels.

# 8

For days, or is it hours, maybe years, Alma enters a strange time she cannot measure on a clock. It is the time grief keeps, which everybody wants to speed up for her, for themselves. But neither they, nor she, have any control of those hands that move at their own lugubrious pace, *A Wooden way / Regardless grown.*

Those lines by Emily Dickinson are ones that memory sends up, from a poem that Alma had to memorize in seventh grade. Her English teacher had assigned each student a poem to learn by heart, and this one fell to Alma. "After great pain, a formal feeling comes . . ." Great pain in seventh grade was a toothache, the taunts of bullies, harsh punishment by Mamasita, Papote's silences.

*A formal feeling? The Hour of Lead?*

"What is your poem about?" the teacher asked after each recitation.

"'After Great Pain' was written by Emily Dickinson, who was a great American poet, who was born . . ." Alma rattled on, hoping biography might supplant meaning.

"Very good, Alma. But can you tell us what the poem is about?"

Alma shook her head. She had no idea what this poem was about. Now she knows.

THE MINUTES AFTER THE siege are interminable, gun blasts shake the thin walls of Don Jacobo's house, knock his solar panel off the roof. Darkness descends upon them, though almost immediately, as if she had been waiting in the wings like an actress, Don Jacobo's wife walks in with a gas lamp. By its light Alma sees the worried look on Emerson's face as he reenters the room for the umpteenth time. He has been outside again, conferring with Jim Larsen, Walter, and Frank, who are all trying to get hold of Camacho on his radio. What the hell is going on? A rescue mission is not a massacre!

Nobody, it seems, can answer Alma's one question and its endless variations: *Where is Richard? Has he been found? Is he all right?* Alma looks around for Starr. Starr would know, Starr would tell her. But la americana has gone down the mountain to the Codetel phone trailer to make some phone calls. Probably Starr is calling Daddy after discovering her cell phone disappeared. Disappeared is right! Smashed to smithereens. Alma begins to shake with the terrible knowledge of what a bullet can do to a cell phone, much less a human being.

*Where is Richard?*

She can't sit still. Instead, she paces, limping back and forth across the narrow room. It's making her leg ache more, which is the point, except her old trick isn't working, of making something else hurt to keep her heart from breaking.

*Where is Richard?*

"That leg is going to get infected," Mariana worries. Why isn't she outside covering this story? Even if they were all ordered to stay indoors, isn't she a journalist?

"I don't care." Alma's voice is breathless, edged with panic. So what if her leg gets infected, takes longer to heal. She'll give it up if she can have Richard back. *Please, God, please, let him be all right*, Alma bargains, wringing her hands.

Mariana must think Alma is praying because she digs out a rosary from her ready overnight bag and drapes it over Alma's clenched hands. Later, all Alma will remember of the horrible moment when she hears the news is pulling the rosary apart and sending beads flying all over Don Jacobo's floor.

And the poem, Alma will remember the poem. She will not remember the time. *This is the Hour of Lead.* She will remember asking over and over, *Why?*

WHY A SIEGE? Why did sixty-plus members of a special security squad need to storm a little clinic in a tiny village in the middle of nowhere? Swan didn't order this. The U.S. embassy sent up two of its best negotiators to broker a peaceful release of hostages. Lord knows, HI wants to cut loose from the negative publicity. And the villagers—they never imagined this would happen. Originally, they were all behind the kids—well, all but Don Jacobo and a few of his cronies. They, too, wanted a clinic for their sick; they, too, wanted water they could drink, jobs that paid a decent wage; they did not want a clinic full of prostitutes and pimps spreading AIDS germs all over their village.

But they saw that the way to get these things, according to el americano and la señorita Starr, was to be patient, to work through the new Centro, to learn how to take care of the hens that lay golden eggs. The science of AIDS was explained to them. There was no harm with this clinic. In fact, this clinic's programs would do good things for the villagers and the surrounding area.

It was the young people who were not convinced, the young people who began holding meetings with radical elements from other villages, who in turn brought in weapons, drugs, money, bitterness. The young people took over the clinic and Centro to speed up the golden process, to hold Swan and the americanos to their promises.

But never in a thousand years did anyone expect this showdown. Those boys would have walked out of the clinic with their hands in the air if they'd known this bloodbath was coming.

But somebody somewhere, maybe Camacho, maybe the general who is not a general, is poised on the edge of a promotion, on the eve of announcing his candidacy for presidency. A career is made out of the right moves at such critical moments, setting an example of what must be done with terrorists, sending the world a signal. No matter that these kids were kids, like kids everywhere with an axe to grind, incited by desperation and misinformation, led by a bully, who is ironically the only captive to survive the siege unharmed. Everyone else is wounded or dead or has fled into the rain that begins to fall steadily at dawn.

HOURS LATER, OR MAYBE minutes that feel like hours, Emerson puts his arm around Alma's waist. "We're going to head out now," he says quietly. His face is somber, his voice hushed. "Van's waiting," he adds, probably because Alma is looking at him as if he has just said something crazy.

She lets herself be led as far as the front door, as if she has to see what Emerson's talking about to make any sense of what he is saying. The van has been pulled up to the door, wipers going. Now Alma will get to ride with the top dogs, Jim Larsen and crew, the noble widow who so loved her husband she jumped over a barricade to spend his last hours with him. Her crazy deed now spun into a romantic, tragic story.

Alma balks at the sight of the van. She is not ready to go, not just yet. "I want to see him."

"Richard is being transported out, Alma." Emerson's voice has taken on a creepy, intoned quality, like that of an undertaker. "You'll get to see him first thing in the capital. The funeral home—"

"No!" Alma cries out. "I want to see him now!" She feels like a two-year-old, throwing a tantrum in the mayor's house. "I'm not going till I see him." She is sobbing, but not the kind of female sobbing that means she is breaking down, ready to be helped to the next moment of her life without Richard. She is serious. Let them arrange another siege, if they want to, storm Don Jacobo's house, shoot her down, one more casualty to add to their body count.

"Alma, please, I know you're upset."

"I am not upset!" Alma cries out. Then, in a calmer voice, so they can't dismiss her, the bereft wife who needs a sedative, she adds, "I'm not leaving till I see him."

Emerson glances over at Jim, who steps outside. A moment later, he returns, nods. "Out back."

Out the back door under an umbrella that suddenly blooms above her, Alma follows the guardia who seems in charge of the after-siege operations. Emerson's arm is again around her waist, or so she thinks, but a moment later when the arm releases her so that they can each go single file past the sandbags that have been heaped to either side of the narrow gate, Alma is surprised to look up and find that it's Jim Larsen by her side.

"We never gave these orders. I want you to know that, Mrs. Huebner."

"I don't care." She turns on him. "I told you those guys were going to bomb. You didn't believe me." The more she says, the angrier she is. "I don't want you with me," she cries. "I want to see Richard alone! Please!" Her furious command becomes a plea.

He lets her go. In the days to come, which might be years, or hours, minutes, who knows, Alma will discover that her terrible grief scares people. They will give her whatever she says she wants. Mostly, to be left alone, and not be left alone. For everything, she will have a yes and no. It's not that she doesn't know what she wants. Alma knows precisely what she wants, but no one in the world can give her that.

INSIDE THE CLINIC, men in oily-looking, black gear—they look like divers—are sorting out the dead. It is an eerie scene, a gray, rainy light filtering in through the windows. Some accessory lights have been set up on tripods, as if this scene is being filmed. Alma hears a motor going, the generator.

The dead are laid out like kindergarten children on mats for their nap. When Alma enters, the crew is tagging the bodies for transport. Most of the men are wearing masks, which strikes Alma as strange. The dead are newly dead. They can't smell yet. Maybe these men are masked in solidarity. Inside their body bags, the dead have just been divested of their ski masks and bandannas.

Or perhaps these men, like the dead boys, are afraid of AIDS. They are packing up bodies that might be contaminated. There is blood everywhere, a dark spill so resembling the reddish mud on her shoes that Alma at first thinks the death crew's boots are muddy. But this is blood, precious blood—the boys', Richard's—which they are afraid might infect them.

The guardia who is her guide gives out his order. La señora wants to see the americano. Nobody here thinks this is strange, she notes, not the way Emerson and Jim reacted as if Alma had voiced some crazed, grief-stricken request. It makes perfect sense. The wife wants to see her husband. Maybe she wants to remove a ring or some other personal effect that might get "lost" in the transit.

One of the men lifts his mask. He summons her, raising his hand, palm up, the fingers scooping her toward him. As Alma follows down the hall, she is filled with a terrible nostalgia. Just hours ago, which might be minutes or days or years, she walked down this very hall to the back patio. Just hours ago, she saw Richard enter the dark tunnel to the john. If only she had called him back in time, he would now be with her, riding down to the capital in the embassy van.

She will drive herself crazy if she does this! She has to get it through her head that this is not a story. She cannot revise the past; she cannot make a deal with Helen's or anybody else's God.

Alma enters an examining room—maybe the same one in which she lay just hours ago. It's hard to tell, one examining room is probably so much like another. The overflow of the dead have been laid out on the floor, except for one, lying on the examining table in meaningless hierarchy. The cleanup guy works the zipper down on this bag and pulls back the flap. Alma's whole body begins to shake with grief, a huge wave that will surely carry her away. *As Freezing persons, recollect the Snow— / First—Chill—then Stupor—then the letting go—*

When she looks down, she is so ready for Richard's face that she wonders if maybe in death people become someone else. Stony and pale beneath the hand she has automatically extended to stroke Richard's face is the black-kerchief poet, except he is no longer wearing his kerchief. His thick hair looks matted down, wet, as if the rain beating on the zinc roof has somehow leaked through. But, no, it's blood, still liquid, still running! Alma pulls her hand back. "This is not my husband," she wails. "This is not Richard."

The guardia in charge is full of apologies to Alma and furious at his underling for making such a mistake to further upset the grieving señora.

"Don't worry about it," Alma stops him. "It doesn't matter. I just want to see my husband." Tears come to her eyes. Her husband. He was wearing a pinkish windbreaker, she wants to say. Alma looks around the room, as if she will be able to spot him inside one of those dark, ominous bags.

Meanwhile, the underling has begun unzipping and zipping body bags, looking for the señora's husband. A wild, joyous thought enters Alma's head. Maybe the reports were wrong! Maybe Richard is alive, maybe he crouched behind the door of the john, under the poster of the lovers, waiting out the shoot-out. Maybe they will go home, sit down to leftover turkey with his three sons, and Richard will regale them all with his lucky story.

But this is a story that is not a story. A moment later, when the relieved worker pulls back the zippered flap, it is Richard.

ALMA EXPLAINS TO THE guardia who is her guide that she is not going to leave her husband's side. She will ride down to the capital with Richard and the other dead in the back of the military truck, if need be. The guardia summons Mr. Larsen, but no one can talk Alma out of her peevish grief. Richard is carried by two of the cleanup crew toward the waiting van. Jim and Alma step inside the mayor's house to say their good-byes.

But Starr has just come back from her phone calling with some bad news. "We're going to have to stay here in quarantine till we get the okay." She shoots Alma a dark look, eyes narrowed. "Why didn't you tell us you might be infected with monkey pox?"

This can't be happening, Alma thinks. Was it only a couple of months ago, or years, that she got that AIDS phone call from Hannah, the same day she saw that trespasser on their property who turned out to be Mickey? Alma had thought she had gone crazy, entered a strange twilight zone of the bruised and broken. But it's not her; it's the world that has gone mad. This story that is not a story in whose craziness she is trapped.

As best she can, Alma explains what happened back in Vermont. It wasn't till the flight down when she read the short news piece in Emerson's paper that she even knew about Mickey's suspicious denial. Then someone called the clinic yesterday afternoon—was it only yesterday? Richard had been the one to take it, so Alma can't even say if it was Claudine, the sheriff, maybe even Tera.

"I called the embassy to let them know so they should start getting stuff in order." Starr is avoiding Alma's eyes. Probably, she's referring to some death certificate paperwork she doesn't want to mention in front of Alma. "They'd gotten this strange call from a sheriff in Vermont. And one from Daddy, too." Now she does look at Alma. "Did you take my cell phone with you? Daddy says somebody answered and there was all this whispering and shouting and then the line went dead."

Alma explains, though the more she talks, the more she thinks she sounds like she's stark raving mad.

"Well, poor Daddy, you can imagine, he called everybody."

Alma can imagine who all *everybody* is. People with connections and money. VIPs who will save his golden child, airlift her out, if necessary. A cherished life, protected by the bubble of power. Hers around Richard was only a bubble of love, not good enough.

"Anyhow, we're all going to have to be quarantined here in the village until we get the word." Thanks a lot, her tone says.

"How long is this going to go on for?" Jim asks, looking at his watch. Days? Weeks? He is a busy man.

"They've sealed off the old woman's house and they should know soon. Some disease-control specialists have been flown in. Meanwhile, the embassy's going to send up some cell phones we can use, cots, supplies. A forensic guy is coming up." Again she avoids Alma's eyes. "We're to sit tight."

"We've been a lot of places," Emerson reminds Starr. "The airplane, all those people."

"Tell me about it," Starr says. Her tone, if not her look, implicates

Alma. "It's going to be a real mess tracking down this virus if the guy's wife's telling the truth."

"She's not," Alma finds herself saying. How can she be so sure? She saw the syringe in Mickey's hand. What was it filled with? "I can't be 100 percent sure," she adds, since everyone is looking at her now with true suspicion. "It's just that this guy and his wife are not all there." She tells them how Mickey's wife, Hannah, claimed to have AIDS and called up a whole bunch of people, saying she'd slept with their husbands. When she was taken into custody and tested, it turned out she did not have AIDS, she wasn't even HIV-positive. "They're talking in metaphors. They call themselves ethical terrorists."

"*Ethical* terrorists?" Starr makes a face as if she has just tasted the words and they are putrid. "Unethical, if you ask me!"

"Most terrorists claim they're being ethical," Walter or Frank observes. This could be a book-club discussion in Vermont. Some nonfiction book on current events they are all reading in order to indulge the one or two men in the group who are tired of novels. "But I agree with you." Walter or Frank nods at Starr. "Inexcusable."

"People get desperate," Alma offers. Since when has she turned into Mickey and Hannah's defender? "And if you want to know what's inexcusable it's what the army did here." She looks from one to the other, her eyes fierce, daring them to contradict her.

Even when they meet her gaze, after a moment, they look down at their muddy shoes. Have any of them noticed how much the red mud they've tracked into the mayor's house looks like blood?

Only Starr holds her gaze. "Those guys *were* armed, you know," she begins. But Emerson shoots her a glance, stopping her. Be kind to the widow who just lost her husband to this mess. Go along with everything she says.

"I tried to talk to them," Starr says a moment later. "I thought they understood." She dissolves into tears. "I'm sorry, Alma."

"So am I," Alma returns angrily, but soon, she, too, is crying. She lets herself be held in the young woman's arms, thinking they will never be Richard's arms. There is no solace here. Still, she rests for the moment, as if catching her breath for the long climb out of hell that will go on for months, days, years.

A moment later, she feels Starr stiffening, and then tactfully but decidedly pulling away. That's right, Alma thinks. She might have monkey pox. And even if Hannah is bluffing again, even if Alma is totally clean of any and all deadly viruses, she has been infected with a sorrow that will leave her scarred and changed. But she is also carrying a living story inside her, an antibody to the destruction she has seen, an intuition, like the poet said, which must survive beyond her grief.

UNTIL THE CRAZY QUARANTINE is lifted, they are trapped, living and dead, in this village.

As a possible carrier, Alma is given a mask to wear. It is the same hospital-blue color as those of the cleanup crew, probably where it came from. Of course, if she is indeed infected, the harm has already been done. Still, these are the recommendations sent up by the Departamento de Salud, Oficina de Emergencia. Alma complies—it seems somehow fitting that she, too, wear this grim disguise.

Alma hears Starr and Jim Larsen and the embassy guys in Don Jacobo's front room, discussing how best to approach the sensitive issue of having Alma sleep alone in one of the little houses in the Centro. "She shouldn't be left alone," Emerson weighs in.

"Don't sweat it," she tells him, surprising the group with her back-door entrance. Her voice sounds weird, muffled by a mask, sent back into her own lungs, as if she were speaking to herself. How could the boys stand wearing ski masks made of wool in the heat of the day, for hours on end?

Alma would just as soon sleep alone in the two-room casita Richard shared with Bienvenido. Her utensils, her bowl and cup, are also kept separate. When she gets too close, she can feel her fellow Americans tense in self-defense. But Don Jacobo and his family either don't understand or don't care if Alma is carrying germs. They think of her as one more AIDS patient. Besides, what more can be done to their devastated corner of the world?

Every household is mourning a son or a nephew or godson or novio. The cowlick boy whose mother was the persona de confianza with whom la doctora Heidi sent her instructions for a siege in which no one would get hurt, the Killington ski-mask boy who wanted to support his family, the black-kerchief poet whose novia loved to hear him talk his fiery talk—there will not be enough room in the little village cemetery to hold so many dead, not enough room in the heart to mourn this inhuman loss.

All through the day, Alma hears wailing coming from one or another house. An angry crowd shows up at Don Jacobo's door, ready to burn it down. *Why? Why?* they cry out, echoing and amplifying Alma's grief, like a Greek chorus. Why did the autoridades not give these boys a chance? They were mere muchachos. Boys who had let their mothers go free even before they got their cigarettes and food, boys who would have been satisfied with a pool table, a training program that might lead to a job that might lead to some money in their pockets, the keys to a pasola, una ropita decente to throw on their backs for a parranda on a Saturday night. It was only when pressed against the wall that they started acting tough, asking for crazy things, visas and such.

"I told them all of this," Don Jacobo puts in.

But the villagers don't want his excuses. Their grief is huge and furious. Beside it, Alma's individual grief feels manageable. Maybe she will move here and finish the work Richard set out to do. Maybe if she changes everything in her life, it won't feel so weird that Richard isn't around. In the months to come, Alma will catch herself at this game of trying to dodge her grief, to lose it, to diminish it. But nothing works, except for minutes at a time, when she leaves herself behind and joins Isabel as she recrosses the wide Pacific, returning with her boys to Mexico after two years away, her health compromised, her faith diminishing. Maybe it is a trick, but who cares, it works, this story that becomes Alma's lifeline, this thread of hope she picks up in a dark time. Something important in that story, which can't be left behind.

What does it mean not to lose faith with what is grand?

But these are thoughts that will accost her later. In the early-morning hours in the empty bed. Nights when she comes home and the house is dark. Times when she picks up the ringing phone and it is not Richard.

The crowd moves on from the mayor's house to the clinic. Alma joins them. They are mostly women, many of them mothers of the dead boys. At first, they were told that their sons were criminal elements. They did not have any rights even in death. But now that the dead are quarantined with the living, the bodies have to be cleaned up and buried quickly, before they become another health hazard. This is the tropics, after all. Richard, too, will have to be buried for now, the remains exhumed later and taken back to the States.

*Remains, exhumed.* Alma can't bear to hear Richard spoken of in this way! Briefly, Richard will be buried in her birth land, a last embrace from a country he loved. He would have liked that, she thinks, though almost immediately she rejects the pat, posthumous thought. Richard would want to be alive, as would the dozen dead boys. No getting around that simple fact.

The guards let the women through the Centro gates, up the walk, into the clinic. Each one finds her dead. Richard has been returned to the examining room, placed on the table, the poet transferred to the floor. A young woman kneels beside him—a lover, a sister?—wiping his face with a cloth. When the women begin saying a rosary, Alma cannot pray with them. She cannot save Richard, she cannot save anyone. Compassion flows from this terrible knowledge.

She finds her way out to the back patio where hours ago . . . Gently, she pulls herself back from that edge. She has to outlive these terrible moments, step by hopeless step. She cannot let loss have the last word. Was it Richard who said, in one of his rare moments of grand philosophizing, or it could be Alma read it in one of those photocopied articles Tera loves to send her, annoyingly highlighted and commented upon in the margins: something about how you can't live entirely for your own time, how you have to imagine a story bigger than your own story, than the sum of your parts?

The rain has let up. A wind is blowing. The night will turn cold. Just ahead, there are lights on in the dormitorios, which shouldn't surprise Alma. Of course, like everyone else, the patients are under quarantine. Inside the women's dormitorio, la doctora Heidi is checking blood pressures, dispensing medicines.

La doctora stops her work when she catches sight of Alma just outside the door. She would like to express her sentimientos to the wife of the dead americano. Her hand is at her heart, her eyes fill. She is in pain over the violence that was never a part of the original plan. "The soldiers are saying the boys opened fire. They had to defend themselves by firing back."

Alma shakes her head. She doesn't want to hear their excuses, the stories that will be used to explain the deaths of a dozen boys and her husband. She doesn't want vengeance, but she won't shut up either. Swan, Camacho, whoever gave the orders, whoever helped create this desperate situation, must be held to account. *We will infect them with our questions*, as the black-kerchief poet said. Tera, dear Tera, will know where to begin, who to call.

"Will you come in, please?" La doctora has noticed Alma is holding her arms, shivering.

"I shouldn't." Alma points to her mask. The patients are vulnerable. The last thing they need is exposure to monkey pox.

The doctora has heard about the scare, but it is beyond her realm of comprehension. Why would anyone willingly spread an illness and cause more suffering in the world?

Why would anyone take a simple plan of rescue and turn it into a bloodbath? Alma could ask her. But la doctora has enough grief on her hands right now.

"I have to continue," she excuses herself. Her patients have been many days without any treatment. They cannot be abandoned. In the men's dormitorio, Dr. Cheché is attending to the men.

But instead of moving back inside, la doctora waits at the door as if for Alma's permission to go on with her lucky life, helping unlucky people.

Over her shoulder, Alma can see the thin, worried faces of women
and girls. They look back at her with a cleaving look that reminds her
of the hostages, the look they all gave each other, a look of fear, a look
of hope. A look that aches for a look back. *I am with you. We are here
together.* It makes her feel uncomfortable, this naked need. She turns
to go. But the look will follow her from now on, eyes that will peer out
at her in the dark, Richard's eyes, the poet's eyes, infecting her with
their questions, needing her hope.

Back in the clinic, Alma finds that the women are camping out by
their dead. She gets two of the younger ones to help her put Richard
on the floor where she struggles to take off his pinkish windbreaker.
*You don't have to be a good sport anymore,* she tells him in one of the
many conversations she will have with him in her head from now on.
The inner lining is stained with his blood. It's already dry. Alma
closes her eyes to keep her tears to herself. This will be her first
night without him, then a second, a third . . . The beginning of so
many good-byes.

In a while the guardia come and evacuate the place.

That night in Richard's bunk bed that still smells of him, Alma will
not be able to sleep, not after two Ambiens, not after roaming the little house and finding Emerson asleep on a mat in the front room. She
will enter the little bathroom and burst into tears at the sight of the
glowing toilet seat. She will bring the lid down and sit in the dark, her
leg hurting, her head aching, and wonder how she can stand to go on.
And because she hasn't a clue, she will cast about for an answer that
is not an answer. How could Isabel bear the disappointment of seeing all the hard work of the expedition unraveling as revolutions over-
ran the Americas and destroyed the vaccination juntas and the vaccine
was again lost? How could she live with the burden of knowing that
the stories of hope she had told the boys were just that, stories that
were just stories?

"Alma?" It's Emerson at the door. "Are you all right?"

"I'm okay," she sobs.

This is how you do it, Alma thinks. You stand up because someone
needs to use the john. You turn your light on and try to read, then turn

it off, and pull yourself from the edge, from the eyes you keep seeing in the dark. You tell yourself a story—Isabel's returning to Puebla, to Benito, waiting for her lieutenant—until you fall into a drugged sleep.

You keep going for as long as it takes, years, months, weeks.

*The stiff Heart questions was it He that bore, / And Yesterday or Centuries before?*

THE VERY NEXT DAY, the forensic guy issues his certificates. The bodies are released. The list of the dead makes its way to Don Jacobo's house; the names are legal names, so they don't match the earlier list with the nicknames the locals knew these young men by. Not one of the dead is over age twenty-five. It turns out two are still at large, but the ringleader, Francisco Villanueva, known as Bolo, is in custody.

How did he manage to escape the bullets indiscriminately sprayed into the front room? How did he and his buddies get arms? Why did he stage this suicide takeover? As far as Alma can gather, Bolo is not talking. They will probably break him with torture and then execute whatever is left of him. Poor guy. It probably would have been luckier for him to die in the bloodbath, after all.

"They're just scapegoating him," Alma tells the little group of los americanos, as they are collectively known now in the village. The group is spending its quarantine together at the mayor's house. Alma is in and out of the house, in and out of their discussions. The masked woman. "Why pin everything on this one guy?"

"He's been in trouble before." Walter or Frank happens to know for a fact. "This isn't the first time."

Of course not. Unlike the others, Bolo learned to read and write; he got out and looked around and saw enough to tell him he hadn't been dealt the best hand. A chance to be a human being, the lucky kind.

"No one's going to scapegoat anybody," Walter or Frank asserts.

Right, Alma thinks, just like nobody was going to bomb anything. One good thing about wearing a mask, no one can see her mouth twisting, the scorn she momentarily heaps upon them.

"He's the only one left to help now." Alma can't let it go. "He and the patients. I hope Swan's not going to desert them," she addresses Jim straight on. "I mean, you can't just walk out on them."

"Swan will honor its agreement," Jim speaks up quickly, publicly. "We're committed to the patients until virological failure. And the Centro, we'll have to decide where to go from here . . . if it makes sense . . ." Jim sighs. This fiasco has been his first and it will probably be his last. At the head office, his replacement is already being discussed.

"It makes sense." Emerson has been out in the rain, checking on the hundreds of trees planted, the tiny saplings in the nursery ready for the new terraces Richard and Bienvenido's crew had just completed. It'd be a shame to let the project die now.

She looks over at Emerson, and for the first time since this nightmare started he meets her eye. Alma might have to remind him every step of the way, but Emerson is not going to bail out. One bad thing about her mask, he can't see Alma smile for the first time since the nightmare started and the last time in a while.

THE BURIALS START THAT very evening, and since the cemetery lies just outside the village, the corteges go by Don Jacobo's house, past the Centro, visible to every eye, audible to every ear. Starr and Mariana try to distract Alma, as if her mind were not already a tangle of distractions, punctuated by awful moments. One of the worst has to be when the cell phones arrive from the embassy, in a shipment of supplies left at the roadblock at the edge of town. Alma calls her stepsons. The connections are terrible. Both Ben and David are out; Alma can't bear to leave a message on their machines, so she hangs up.

Because it is still early on the West Coast, she manages to get Sam, half asleep. "What time is it?" he asks, his voice groggy.

Alma is grateful for this brief stall before the awful moment that is coming. She remembers the black-kerchief poet's asking for the time, Bolo's proudly announcing the hour, to the minute, then shooting the clock. Alma tells Sam the time in their two time zones, and then she tells him the news she can't make sound any less shocking than it is.

"You can't be serious?" Sam says. He is totally awake now.

Alma wishes she could spare him, one more orphan in the world. "Oh, Sam, I'm sorry."

But Sam seems impervious to the news. He just talked to his father on Monday. They were making plans to meet in that week between Christmas and New Year's. Sam would fly down to Florida, meet up with Alma and his dad. Sam goes on, detail by painful detail, as if to prove Alma wrong. How can a father who was making holiday plans a few days ago not be around anymore?

Alma has to agree with him. It's inconceivable. "But it's true, Sam, Richard is dead. He got caught in the cross fire during a siege." Keep it simple. There will be plenty of time later to infect everyone she knows with her questions.

A wrenching silence follows. And then, as if released from their cage of denial, a half-dozen questions fly out, so fast, one after another, Alma can't keep up with them. "What *siege*? Dad didn't say anything about a siege. Why was there a siege? Look, I'm coming down. How do I get there? I mean, where do I fly to?" He is moving around. Opening a door, turning on a faucet. He must be on a portable. A woman's voice is asking him something. A woman in Sam's life! And here she'd been telling Richard for years that Sam was gay. The good looks, the swift clothes, the privacy around his personal life. So Sam has a girlfriend. A bit of news Alma would have wanted to share with Richard. There will be so many of these moments, and that will be how time heals. In months that will turn into years, Alma's life will be filled with so many stories Richard will never hear. She will be living some other life than the one that stopped hours ago here.

"The thing about coming, Sam, is I don't really know if you'll be able to see your father." She explains about the quarantine. How they all have to wait. How Richard has to be buried temporarily. At one point when she breaks down, telling her story, Emerson comes forward. Does Alma want for him to talk to Sam? She shakes her head. Sam doesn't need one more stranger between him and his dead father. Alma explains how Richard had always said he wanted to be cremated.

Maybe if the quarantine gets lifted soon, the boys can come down and see their father and then they can have him cremated here and take his ashes back.

"I don't want his fucking ashes," Sam sobs.

When Alma hangs up, she feels what bomber pilots must feel, returning from a mission, having dropped off their deadly cargo. They can't let themselves imagine the suffering they have just sowed, the woman still up tending to a sick child, the lovers in bed, the father washing his hands, ready to eat a late supper, the people caught in the middle. They must shut off that knowledge or how else can they go on living?

BY WEEK'S END, they get the all clear. The guys from the Centers for Disease Control found no evidence of monkey pox or any other deadly virus in the Marshall residence or in Michael and Hannah McMullen's pickup. What happens next? Hannah, and maybe Mickey, will probably get convicted, terrorist threats being a serious federal crime these days. Or maybe they'll be deemed too crazy to stand trial and be locked up in the state hospital at Waterbury instead. Meanwhile, the mad world gets off scot-free, Alma can't help thinking bitterly.

Everyone is relieved. Jim Larsen, Emerson, Starr, Starr's daddy who has flown in and is waiting in the capital to take her home. Alma, too, is glad to get off the mountain. Now she can go back to a life that will never be all clear again. Her clean windshield is gone. Like Helen coming through her stroke to die of terminal cancer a few weeks after Alma finally gets back to Vermont.

Out of guilt or a sense of responsibility, Emerson can't do enough for her. When the boys arrive at the Las Américas Airport, Emerson goes out with her. She spots them coming through Immigration. Their first time in her country and probably their last. Why would they ever come back? And Richard so wanted them to fall in love with this place! To come volunteer for a week while he was on site. But the gene for personal passions does not get passed on by blood. *Not an opinion, but an intuition.* How to pass on that intuition? Alma wonders. Only by story, if at all.

As she watches from the glass partition, Alma realizes she is looking at her stepsons with a new intensity, trying to find traces of Richard. They are built like their father, slender and not too tall, though they seem tall here, surrounded by the shorter Dominicans. How bereft they all look, glancing around as if they are lost in this place of color and noisy crowds and oppressively bright sunlight.

Watching them, Alma is reminded of her wedding day, ten going on eleven years ago. They were just boys—Sam was only twelve, for heaven's sake—all of them trying to be happy for their father's new life, which is now over.

Interestingly, Sam is the only one to bring his girlfriend with him. Soraya Guzmán. A Latina, must be, maybe Mexican, maybe Ecuadorian, hard to pin down. "I was born here, I mean, the States," she answers when Alma asks where she is from. You know, the brown skin, the last name of Guzmán.

Fair enough, Alma thinks. A strong, no-nonsense woman, just what Sam needs right now. Of the three sons, Sam is the one who has given Alma the hardest time, fiercely loyal to the past—the true, original family, his father's second marriage being an aberration, his violent death proof of this error. And yet, over time, Sam will be the son who stays in touch. David and Ben, both friendly, tolerant sorts, will disappear from her life except for occasional communications.

But all three will keep their promise: next summer on Snake Mountain.

# VIII

**Summer 1810**

"Doña Isabel, a visitor from Spain!" Benito was calling out.

My heart leapt with joy. After six long years of sacrifice and waiting, I was to be rewarded, after all. Lieutenant Pozo had come back to keep his solemn promise!

I was in bed that morning, a bad morning, of which there were many since my return from the Philippines. I had held off my own home-coming to go, village by village, returning my charges: six from Valladolid, returning five; five from Guadalajara, all accounted for; one from Queré-taro; six from Zacatecas; five from Fresnillo, returning four; two from Sombrerete; one from León.

My work completed, Viceroy Iturrigaray had granted me permission to settle in the city of the angels with my son, allotting me a stipend until I regained my health. Of course, what I hoped was that the lieutenant would be waiting for me and the stipend would prove unnecessary, though helpful. But no word had come from Lieutenant Pozo during my absence. So began the long wait — six years since our parting in Veracruz! — which this morning, as I heard my son's summons, I was convinced would end with gladness.

"Doña Isabel!" Benito kept calling from the front room. He knew better than to yell like that. It seemed I was back in La Coruña, unable to curb the wildness of my little boys as they stampeded down the hallways, an-nouncing the arrival of Doña Teresa. When we returned from Manila, a letter from Nati had been waiting for me, written the year before. Our benefactress had taken ill with a catarrh and died; Nati's own sons had been pressed into the navy; one son had been wounded at Trafalagar; a grandson had been born.

"I will be there presently," I called from my back room. Quickly, I dressed and brushed my hair. In the glass, I appraised myself. How would I look after a six years' absence? Far too thin, gray in my dark hair. But the sun and sea and the years themselves had been kind to me, just as Don Francisco had promised. The fresh air had invigorated my skin, so that the marks were less disfiguring. Or perhaps I had learned to live with my pocked face at last.

Don Francisco and his promises . . . Some of them had come true, I thought as I slipped on my shoes. We had gotten news even before we left Manila that he had made it back to Spain. The only one of us to return! He had been received by the king—when we still had our king, honored at the court. But then Spain had been overrun by the French and our king had gone into exile; the world across the ocean had crumbled.

I could hear Benito chattering in the front room, a boy of about eleven now. Strange, the boy was usually more of an observer than a talker. When questioned, he often took moments to consider before replying. Although in many ways he had thrived under the bishop's direction and advanced in his studies, my long absence had hurt him. It seemed at first the boy had asked constantly after me. Then, abruptly, his questions had stopped. After my return, though I earnestly petitioned him and sometimes punished him, he would no longer call me mother. Not that there was any disrespect in his address. He used *usted* and always preceded my name with *doña*. I might have saved thousands upon thousands from the smallpox, but I had failed him. Was it possible to act in this world, I wondered, without hurting someone?

"Doña Isabel works with cures," I heard the boy saying. "She nurses the sick when she feels well herself. Mostly, she's sick, though. She has a weak heart, and some days she has to stay in bed all day long."

I hurried my steps. By the time I could greet my suitor, my son would have driven him away.

"Good day," I said, entering the room. My first glimpse of the lieutenant, I thought: he is no longer as tall as I remember him.

Don Francisco!

I reeled with surprise and shock and seemed to be about to prove my son's pronouncements by fainting on the spot. Our local doctor had indeed diagnosed a weak heart and advised that I guard against anything that might excite me. How to keep life at bay in order to go on living?

Don Francisco came forward and led me to a chair. "I never thought I would see you again," I confessed. How had he made it out? Of course, I was thinking, if an older man could get through enemy lines, why not a younger lieutenant?

"I was lucky," Don Francisco was explaining. He had fled from Madrid when the French invaded, following the Junta Suprema to Seville and, when Seville fell, to Cádiz. It was this very junta, the only legitimate authority while Napoleon had our king in chains, that had authorized him to come to New Spain. He was on his way to the capital and had stopped in Puebla to say hello to his old friend, Bishop Gonzales. What a surprise to hear that Doña Isabel and her son were living across the courtyard in the old porter's cottage!

"I see you have made a home here." Don Francisco gestured with a sweep of his hand, a gesture more suited to the court than to this humble house at the entrance of the Episcopal palace. He was not as ill or old as when I had last seen him in Manila. He must have gotten new teeth. And his face was fuller. He had begun wearing a wig—I believe it was a wig. Perhaps he had lost his hair?

"You look well," I noted. "How brave of you to come see after us."

He bowed, acknowledging my compliment. "What have we to lose but our lives, which are not ours to keep anyway?" he observed. He went on to detail his losses. His home in Madrid had been sacked; the Botanical Gardens with all his specimens from Canton and Macao had been overrun; the Royal Biblioteca with the Spanish-Chinese dictionary he had donated and hundreds of prints of medicinal plants were now part of Bonaparte's booty. His wife had died.

This last piece of news came at the end of such a long litany, I almost missed it in the outpouring of his story. Poor Doña Josefa, to have awaited her husband for three years, only to leave the life they might have shared! "I am sorry to hear of your loss," I intoned in consolation.

"The invasion, the destruction of our home . . . She never did want to leave Madrid." He had refused the chair I offered him. His was a brief visit. He was eager to reach the capital, to ascertain the disturbing rumors circulating in Spain. The colonies were in rebellion. The vaccination juntas were falling apart. The vaccine itself was dying out. He looked around, suddenly anxious to combat this encroaching disaster. I saw the plainness of our home through his eyes—the bare walls but for a simple crucifix, the benches stacked by the door for our patients. The old porter's cottage had become our vaccination center here in Puebla. Benito and I had been granted the rooms in back. Bishop Gonzales had been kind.

As we spoke, the boy had been intently studying our visitor. He had heard about the lieutenant who would return and become his father. Was this the man? If so, why didn't I throw my arms around him? Why didn't I usher the boy forward to meet him?

"Benito, you remember Don Francisco?"

The boy thought a moment before nodding, probably sensing that was the polite answer I wanted him to give. But Benito had last seen the director five and a half years ago. Only vaguely did he recall the expedition, the Atlantic crossing, the wonderful time he had had in Havana with the Romay brothers.

"Of course, he remembers the adventure of his life!" Don Francisco laughed. "And the other boys?"

I told him about the Coruña boys, four remaining in the new Escuela Patriótica, moved over from the Royal Hospicio. The Mexican boys had been returned. All but two, who had died on the journey home.

Don Francisco's face darkened. "I wondered that I had not heard from Gutiérrez."

What use was it sending reports to Spain when so few ships were getting through? Upon our return from the Philippines, Viceroy Iturrigaray had ordered us to remain in New Spain until a peace had been reached. He had been generous, which had surprised me, granting me a pension and permission to live in Puebla, paying the other members in the capital a stipend while they waited to return home. Either he had received an admonishment from the court after Don Francisco's return and before the court itself fell or our poor treatment earlier had been on account of the director's temper.

I tried to explain our present circumstances, but I could see Don Francisco thought he had come back to the country he had left five and a half years ago. Now plots were rife to free ourselves before Spain fought off the French invaders and beat us back into subjection. "We are ourselves in revolution," I ventured. "You will see when you get to the capital," I added. "Dr. Gutiérrez and your nephews and Don Ángel Crespo . . . they will tell you—"

"I noted you did not include Don Pedro Ortega. Is he not in the capital?"

"Don Pedro died in Manila." The same fevers that had almost killed Don Francisco. "He fell ill while he was vaccinating with your nephew in the islands."

"And Gutiérrez didn't recall him?"

The case was building against our substitute director. How to bank these fires before they raged into a temper? Don Francisco would need all his tact if he was to survive in today's Mexico. I could see the years had not softened his character.

"Everything was done for him. He died peacefully in my arms." In spite of the time that had elapsed since that day, my eyes filled with tears. Don Pedro had left behind a widow, two sons. He had saved so many lives. A whole world made better by his sacrifice. But his wife had lost a husband and his two boys a father. No one in the world could make that up to them, not that anyone would try.

Except Don Francisco. I had forgotten that about him. His ferocity for justice made him at times pigheaded but it also made him our champion. The forgotten, the downtrodden, the helpless, and powerless—he would not desert us. He would be the one to try. "We must be sure his wife gets his pension." Don Francisco took up the fallen man's cause. "All the more reason why Gutiérrez should have notified me."

His mind was already set against his old friend whom he had left in charge when he departed from Manila. The pigheaded, vain man was back. This is what I found so tiring about him, I remembered. One adored and detested him in the same breath. There was no middle ground.

He did not stay long—he had many leagues to go before darkness fell. But he would be back through Puebla on his way back to Spain when he was finished. He promised to look in on the boys at Escuela Patriótica and bring me news of those adopted by families. As for how long it might take him to rebuild the vaccination juntas and restore the vaccine to New Spain, that was anybody's guess. He had alluded to the fact that he was also trying to win the hearts of the colonists back to their mother country.

Don Francisco had never taken his challenges in small portions. In that respect also, he was still the same.

"Doña Isabel, it has done my heart good to see you again," he said warmly, pressing my hand in farewell.

Benito and I watched from our door as our visitor mounted the carriage that was waiting for him by the bishop's house. "That's not him," the boy concluded.

"No," I murmured. Another disappointment for the boy, or so I thought.

"We will be fine, Mamá." He patted my back as if I were the child.

*Mamá!* I tried not to show too much pleasure. Change would come in its own time and in the smallest increments. Hadn't I said so once to Don Francisco?

And sometimes it would not come at all. It was finally clear to me that the lieutenant would not be coming back. That the life I now had was to be my life, with Benito for a time.

IN THE YEAR FOLLOWING Don Francisco's visit, we were all caught up in the revolution that swept through the countryside. North of us, in Dolores, Father Hidalgo rang his church bells, calling his poor parishioners to defend themselves against the oppressive rule of the Spaniards. Eighty thousand marched on the capital, cutting throats and burning fields along the way, a trail of blood and death that terrified even those sympathetic to their cause from joining the rebels.

What could be expected of these desperate souls? I had been up north with Don Francisco when we toured the provinces vaccinating. I had seen the mines and the horrid conditions under which so many lived. But I had to be careful what I said in Puebla in defense of Father Hidalgo's cause, for the bishop as well as our town officials were all fierce royalists. Instead of the Virgin of Guadalupe, whom the rebels had embraced as their own, we were to pray to the Spanish Lady of los Remedios. It had come to this, fighting over our virgencitas.

I, too, was a Spaniard, as was my son. But I admit I was glad that having come at such a young age and having spent so many years in Puebla, Benito no longer sounded like a Galleguito. If the rebels came through town, it was I who would have to be careful. Attached as we were to the bishop who had approved the excommunication of that monster Hidalgo, we might well be struck down by his furious rabble.

I worried over my boys in the capital, the ones still interned in the Escuela Patriótica. If the rebel army stormed the city, surely they would not strike down children . . . Of course, the older boys were now in their teens. They might well be pressed into action by either side. My poor children had loaned their bodies to bring salvation to mankind. Had they saved the world for this?

With travelers headed north, I sent several letters to Don Ángel Crespo, who still resided in Mexico City. How were they all faring? Was the city under siege? If so, he and the others were welcomed to join me and bring our boys from Escuela Patrótica. I heard back in bits and pieces. The inhabitants of the capital were awaiting the horrible siege . . . And then after several weeks of silence, another letter. Father Hidalgo had withdrawn his forces. He would not invade Mexico City and cause more bloodshed. The populace had not turned out to support him. He would not impose his rule over them.

I breathed easier. The monster priest was not a monster, after all. Perhaps he would look kindly on the fearless doctor who had headed into the eye of the storm to preserve the vaccine that was in danger of being lost. Don Ángel explained that weeks before the siege, against everyone's advice, our old director had traveled north into rebel territory. Two months had passed, and still no one had heard from Don Francisco.

Living next door to the bishop was like living next door to the hospital at La Coruña. As much news as it was possible to receive during these unsettled times found its way to the Episcopate. The rebels had taken Valladolid. They had set up their stronghold in Guadalajara.

It was several months before we next heard of Don Francisco. It seems he had become involved in a battle of a different kind. In the midst of war, he was trying to revive his vaccination centers! When the several provincial officials refused to help him, preoccupied as they were with fighting the insurgents, Don Francisco accused them of being rebels. These indignant officials had filed a suit against him for defamation of their good name. But Dr. Balmis had failed to appear in court. It seemed he was still in the provinces, trying to save the vaccine, dispensing his translation of Moreau, as if there were no war going on but his very own.

## SUMMER 1811

Don Francisco did keep his promise. A year after his surprise visit, he stopped by on his way to Veracruz where he would board a ship to Spain. He was leaving the embattled colony. There was nothing more he could do. The revolutionary struggles had destroyed the whole system of juntas he had established. Here and there, in isolated locales, the cowpox vaccine was still alive. But soon, unless something was done, it would die out. A whole new generation would be born without protection against the next onslaught of the smallpox. "Mark my words, Doña Isabel, mark my words!" He paced, incapable of sitting still as if the thought itself were after him.

As he spoke, I noted how lean and spent he looked again. The wig was gone; the vigorous bearing, the gallant gestures. True, he was not as bodily ill as when we had parted in Manila. But now there was a haunted look about him. Perhaps the rumors were right: Don Francisco had gone mad with his salvation scheme.

To spare him further agitation, I did not tell him that we had lost the vaccine here in Puebla. The vaccinated had not been returning so that the cowpox fluid could be harvested for the next round. The countryside was too dangerous. The perpetuating system Don Francisco had devised was breaking down.

"All our efforts wasted." He seemed to be at the point of breaking down himself.

I felt the familiar pain in my side. My heart could not bear up under his disappointment as well as mine. "But we might still reconstruct what has been lost," I sought to reassure him.

Don Francisco shook his head. "There is no money for the centers. No organization, no method. And there has not been a change"—he tapped his temple—"of attitude. Of realizing that this is not an extravagance."

"Surely in the capital?" With such a large populace, it seemed there could always be available carriers at hand. Although his nephews had left for Spain, Dr. Gutiérrez and Don Ángel Crespo were still there and could at the very least maintain a central junta where we could all repair.

At the mention of Dr. Gutiérrez's name, Don Francisco's vigor returned in an outpouring of grievance. The man had not proven himself worthy of the charge the director had placed on him. Did I not know that the scoundrel had gambled Don Pedro Ortega's wages, the patrimony of two orphan children? He had also appropriated funds due to Don Francisco's nephews. I was shocked. It did not sound like the Dr. Gutiérrez I had known, so correct in all his doings.

"But at least on that front, justice will be served," Don Francisco continued after a fit of pacing. It seemed he had started a suit against his old colleague. I recalled that other suit against the director himself. The charges had finally been dropped, his accusers convinced that the doctor was indeed a madman.

But I was not at all convinced that our director was crazed. Or perhaps he had been so from the start, believing against all odds that the world could be saved from smallpox. How mad the scheme now seemed! But had it not been for him, even the possibility of doing what he had done would not have been sown in history. That is the way I wanted to think of it. Of all we had sacrificed in the name of his mission.

It was closing on the noon hour. Don Francisco had arrived on a mount with a guide, who waited by their pack mules to renew their journey. But I insisted they must eat something before departing. As we were sitting down, Benito hurried in from the seminary next door. He had heard that there was a vagabond at our cottage. He stayed on, either out of courtesy to my guest or protectiveness of his mother, listening eagerly to Don Francisco's stories of his time in the rebel territories. He had arrived at Valladolid, only to be caught in the middle of the fighting. While trying to arrange his passage out, he learned that the doctor for the royalist forces had gone over to the insurgent side. Rather than desert his loyal countrymen, he had enlisted to take care of their wounded.

"Did you meet Father Hidalgo?" Benito had been taken with the stories of the rebel priest. One day he had come home with a copy of a pamphlet, which I burned in the cookstove. Hidalgo was proclaiming the abolition of tribute, abolition of slavery, distribution of land to the landless! The man was a monster, but from time to time some of his pronouncements sounded like those of Jesus in the Gospels Benito was studying.

Don Francisco shook his head. "At first, I thought only to take care of our own," he continued with his story. "But then the wounded began coming in, and I could not tell them apart, rebel from royalist." Don Francisco's eyes seemed to be viewing those boys once again. "I was tending to one youngster, whose shattered arm would have to come off. Our commander hurried over and ordered me to move on. 'Don't you see?' he said. 'This soldier is a Creole rebel.' 'Sir,' I replied, 'this is a human being, and I am a doctor under oath to save lives.'"

I felt a surge of pride in him. At that moment, I forgave him all his smallness and arrogance. He had a spark of goodness that shone bright from time to time. I had followed him to this new world, which was proving as full of savagery as the old one. As much in need of his light, which I now saw reflected in the tears in my son's eyes.

It was only after Don Francisco left us that I wondered about his standoff with the royalist commander. They had almost come to blows, Don Francisco confided. He had omitted telling us whether he had saved the young rebel's life or whether, while the two men argued, the boy had died.

**SUMMER 1830**

Don Francisco's prediction turned out to be true.

This was years later, after our wars of independence were finally over. Across the seas, the Spanish king had been returned to his throne. I had heard of Don Francisco's death in Madrid in the winter of 1819. In his last years, it seemed he received more titles than that first string he had recited to me years ago in La Coruña. He had been decorated for his loyalty to His Majesty and for his extraordinary mission. His house had been restored to him. Dr. Jenner himself had praised the expedition as one of the most noble philanthropic enterprises in the annals of history. Don Francisco had gone on to propose the creation of a post, inspector of vaccination, which he had volunteered to be the first to fill. I was glad for him. Somehow, he had regained his faith that his work had not been in vain.

All this news I heard from Don Ángel Crespo, who had remained in the capital city, his wife finally joining him. Dr. Gutiérrez had also stayed, fighting in court, and finally clearing his name of all our director's allegations. In fact, Dr. Gutiérrez was now an important man in our new nation, a dean and director of the Hospital of San Andrés.

My own Benito had grown up, a quiet man, a mystery to me, this son I had not conceived but had loved with all my heart. The good bishop had steered him into the priesthood, though Benito had refused a post in the Puebla episcopate, preferring the smaller parishes in far-off settlements. His first assignment had been in Mitla, then north to Carácuaro, finally settling in Chilpancingo. I followed him in all his moves, though I was ready to rest, an old woman, as I would often protest. "You have been an old woman for a long time, Mamá," Father Benito noted. *Father* Benito, I teased him back.

He was right. In spite of my poor health and my weak heart, I seemed to be hardy in my frailty. "The good Lord is saving you for something," Benito would joke on days when I took to bed with that knife blade in my left side. But the worried look in his eyes recalled the terrified boy clinging to the post outside the orphanage door in La Coruña.

Somehow, wherever we moved, word got out that I could cure. The poor flocked to see me. The rich had their doctors. Not that we had that many rich in Mitla or Carácuaro or Chilpancingo.

The day I saw the angry eruption on the face and arms of a young child, my heart sank, remembering Don Francisco's prediction. Immediately, I quarantined the mother and her small children, but soon there were others in her village stricken with the viruela. Panic was spreading, especially when word came back from the capital and northern cities that the precious vaccine seemed to have run out everywhere.

It was then I remembered how Don Francisco had discovered cowpox in cows, years back, during our tour of the provinces. Don Ángel had been along on these scouting journeys; he would know where to go. Benito tried to dissuade me. Don Francisco's claim had never been proven. Then, too, most of the old ranches had been burned, the cattle slaughtered, during our many independence battles.

But my mind was made up. I would go visit Don Ángel, and together we would apply to Dr. Gutiérrez, who was in the position to know important, wealthy people who might fund such an expedition. I confess I also hoped to see my now grown boys. Perhaps I knew that I was nearing my time to depart this earth.

"Mamá, you are not of an age—"

"I have been an old woman for a long time," I quoted him.

And so I undertook the long journey north. *Long!* I had to smile. A mere league compared to all I had wandered. We traveled on mules, my Benito joining me at the last minute. It was my first time back in the capital since we had become our very own nation. Spain no longer ruled us, though it was hard to tell the difference. The poor were still so poor. Perhaps a little less desperate, temporarily, because of hope.

We found the small house on the street I knew only from his letters. Don Ángel and I both wept to see each other once again on this side of the grave. His wife served us a refresco of lemons that reminded me of Don Francisco's medicine against the scurvy. She kept nodding at her husband's stories, as if hearing them so often she was convinced that she had been along on all his adventures.

Soon enough, we were talking of the smallpox emergency. Outbreaks were occurring all over Mexico. It would take at least a month before we could get the vaccine from Caracas, where we had heard the juntas were still functioning. And even then, the vaccine might not be active upon arrival. Meanwhile hundreds, thousands of children would die, and many more be afflicted.

"There is a more immediate solution." I reminded Don Ángel of how he and Don Francisco had discovered cowpox in the valleys near Durango and Valladolid. "Don't you think we could find the cowpox again there?"

"We?" My former colleague regarded me with a playful look. "Your eyes must be as bad as mine, Doña Isabel. Can't you see, I am an old man?"

"But perhaps we can get some young ones to help us." Our boys from La Coruña were grown men by now. And out in the provinces we could enlist our former carriers who had traveled to the Philippines. No doubt they would want to ensure their sacrifice had not been in vain.

"You are still living in a dream world." Don Ángel was shaking his head.

"No, Don Ángel, I am living in this very real, distressing world, and I am having desperately to dream in order to go on living."

"That is the truth." Don Ángel nodded. His wife hesitated and then nodded as well.

Don Ángel agreed that such an expedition was worth a try. But trying to enlist Dr. Gutiérrez would be a mistake. "Even the mention of the word *expedition* turns that man the color of that clay pot." He shook his head sadly. "I don't know why Don Francisco turned on his old friend. As if we didn't have enough enemies already."

We were quiet a moment, thinking of our old leader.

But if not Dr. Gutiérrez, who else could we apply to here in this capital city? Don Ángel's lined brow grew even more furrowed. My dear friend *had* gotten old! His shoulders were stooped; his hand shook stirring sugar in his coffee; his white hair was so thin that his scalp was plainly visible. But those kind eyes were still familiar, two orbs of now cloudy light. Soon, too soon we would be leaving this world, a world we had meant to improve before putting into the hands of the young who had already replaced us.

"I have it!" Don Ángel's exclamation made us all jump.

"Ángel!" his wife scolded him, her hand above her heart. "You frightened our guests," she added, unable to complain on her own behalf.

"I have a plan, I have a plan!" Don Ángel announced in that same voice of discovery as our sailors when they sighted land. "Ladies, please ready yourselves for an outing."

But it was already late afternoon, his wife fretted. Benito and I must be tired after all our traveling. She was not dressed for visiting. At the very least she needed to know if she must wear a bonnet or a veil, slippers or boots for walking down the Alameda paseo.

My old friend refused to disclose where we were going. It would be a surprise. Old as he was, he might have known that such kinds of surprises take their toll on an aged heart! Mine was beating away, as if it belonged inside a much younger woman.

Don Ángel hired a carriage, consulting quietly with the driver as to where he was to take us. We drove by the old viceroy palace, recalling that late-night arrival over two decades ago with nineteen weary boys. Oh my, but the viceroy's wife had looked apoplectic at hearing these were all her husband's *charges*! The Royal Hospicio was still standing, grim-looking and noisy with new orphans; across the street, the newer Escuela Patriótica was becoming shabby itself. Don Ángel would not stop to inquire about my boys. He was as intent on his mission as our director had once been about his expedition. Tomorrow there would be plenty of time to go visiting.

We drove as far as our first house in the city, now no longer in the outskirts, but part of the city itself. The old tanning factories were gone; handsome, white houses now lined the wide street, giving the impression of suspicion with iron grilles at the windows and liveried guards at the gates.

"Here!" Don Ángel called out to our coachman.

We had stopped in front of a house as elegant as its neighbors. A servant came to the gate. "Please tell Don Francisco that he has some visitors. Don Ángel Crespo, he knows who I am."

Don Francisco! Could it be that the report of Don Francisco's death had been an error, and our director was living in our midst, a prosperous old man?

"Perhaps we should wait in the coach, Mamá," Benito suggested. So many surprises might be too much for me. But my weak heart was going strong.

Before I had made it to the door on my son's arm, a gentleman was bounding down the stairs, two steps at a time.

"Doña Isabel!" He seemed to know me. He was tall and stout, the buttons straining on his satin waistcoat. When I went to give him my hand, he threw his arms around me, then dared me to guess whom he might be.

My bully Francisco!

"You will be burned as a witch if word gets out, Doña Isabel!" He laughed. The future I had foretold had come to be, with some slight differences. He was not a prosperous merchant, but he had studied hard, gone to the university, become a lawyer, been appointed to the city council, signed his name to city ordinances.

"Love?" A honey-skinned, pleasant-looking woman had followed him down the stairs.

"Come meet these old friends." Francisco reached out a hand possessively to her. "This lovely lady, my Estela, deigned to marry a poor Gachupín bastard—"

"What language for a son of King Carlos IV! That is what the document says," she explained, smiling at us. "The document we showed my father before Francisco asked for my hand in marriage." That must have been some years back, for down the stairs came as many sons as might compete with Dr. Romay's family! We must stay for a refreshment. We must stay for dinner. We must let their carriage take us home. Francisco bullied us into visiting.

Benito seemed to have grown even more bashful before his old companion. Next to the plump and prosperous lawyer, he looked shabby in his dusty, brown robes and patched sandals. Perhaps he felt that he had failed to live up to being royal progeny. But my son soon regained his self-possession. His presence was in demand, as the little boys tugged at his hands to come see the outdoor chapel that was filling with roosting doves at this hour.

Don Ángel lost no time in asking our Francisco if he could have a word with him. The two men went off to the library—my Francisco had a library! I had owned only two books in my life, both given to me by Don Francisco. One was still in my possession in my old sea chest at home in Chilpancingo; the other lay at the bottom of the sea somewhere off the coast of Puerto Rico. What worry had led me to take such a drastic measure? Some desire to protect Don Francisco's reputation by destroying any evidence to the contrary? Or a desire to protect myself from painful memories that the years would kindly erase but that paper would remember forever? Who could tell? It all now seemed so long ago.

While Don Ángel and Francisco conferred and Benito visited the cooing chapel, we ladies chatted in a parlor that recalled Doña Teresa's old receiving room in the orphanage in La Coruña. The chairs here, however, were quite comfortable.

When the two men returned, I did not have to ask what agreement they had come to. Don Ángel winked at me. Our Francisco was grinning, his chest puffed out as if readying itself for some future medal.

"My dear, meet the new deliverer of Mexico!" Francisco laughed at the baffled look on his wife's face. "We are going to find cowpox in the provinces! I myself will accompany the expedition!" His wife was full of questions, which he promised to answer later. "Anything to repay your kindnesses," he said, smiling fondly at me.

I shook my head at the undeserved praise. If only this man knew how hard I had struggled to love the boy he had once been.

We returned late to Don Ángel's house, after quite a struggle to extricate ourselves from Don Francisco and Doña Estela's insistent hospitality. Couldn't we stay longer? Shouldn't we spend the night? They had plenty of rooms. The streets were full of thieves and scoundrels at this hour. But we arrived back in the small, cozy house, without incident, our guardian Francisco having accompanied us himself in his very own carriage. The long day was finally done. Never did sleep come as easily as that night.

It was early morning, the light seeping in through the unglazed window. I awoke with that familiar pain in my chest as if one of my boys' arrows that had once struck the steward had hit its mark. The steward! What had become of that unpleasant man? Someone no doubt had loved him, wed him, borne him children.

And my lieutenant? Had he perished on a burning ship, routed by the British? Had he survived to enlist in fighting the French invader? Or perhaps he was back, bounding down the stairs in a vest that was getting to be too tight for his well-fed belly?

I saw his tall figure so clearly, that for a moment, I thought, I was back on the *María Pita*. Faces and memories flooded into my mind. We were all together again, dressed in our elegant uniforms, the boys and I, boys who were now men. Soon, soon, we would set out for the north. I imagined the reunions with my Mexican boys, the discovery of cowpox in the valleys, the new juntas we would set up. It was not so much that I was believing this story, as I was running as fast as I could from the doubts pursuing me. And as I ran, I realized that I, too, was a carrier, along with my boys, carrying this story, which would surely die, unless it took hold in a future life.

This Summer on Snake Mountain

It has to be the hottest day of the summer. There are so many mosquitoes. Impossible to have the requisite mourning attitude with these dive-bombing pests flying around. Luckily, Emerson thought of bringing Off!, which he lavishes on anyone who offers himself or herself up to his spray can. He has already endured Tera's lecture on aerosols. And Tera has endured dozens of righteous bites, as if she isn't already red-faced enough with the climb. It would just be Alma's luck to lose her best friend before the double service is out.

Double service because she can't make everyone climb Snake Mountain twice. And except for Mickey and Hannah, everyone who is mourning Helen would come with Alma when she scatters some of Richard's ashes on this mountaintop. It was one of his favorite places. On a clear day, you can get a God's-eye view of the whole Champlain valley. *Hello?* he'd call up, hand at his mouth. *Are you there, God?* "He's out," Richard would conclude after several echoes back. "Busy with the trouble spots."

It's taken a lot of talking to get Mickey and Hannah released for the day. The judge questioned why there couldn't be a service in the state hospital chapel, after which Helen's ashes could be dispersed by friends. But finally, permission was granted, thanks to hospice and Emerson, who, Alma is discovering, treats Vermont like a third-world country whose laws can be got around if you know how to bargain. More likely, the judge, an old-timer who knew Helen, doesn't want to disappoint her even posthumously. So Helen's last wish is granted, a summer scattering of her ashes on Snake Mountain.

Mickey and Hannah come from Waterbury, looking for all the world like an old hippie couple hiking a muggy trail. They are both wearing rolled-up bandannas around their foreheads as sweatbands and carrying water bottles with their names printed in Magic Marker on the sides. A hint of institutional provenance.

When she first saw them climbing out of the van, Alma felt a pang. *Your man for mine, both in our arms, unharmed.* Unlucky Hannah got to be the lucky one.

Accompanying them are two overweight, puffing deputy sheriffs in plainclothes with little firearms tucked in holsters. They have picked up the two inmates at the state hospital and will drive them back once this cockamamie ceremony is over.

David and Ben and Sam are here. This time, they have all brought their partners, as they call their girlfriends. Sam and Soraya will drive up to Quebec tomorrow in Alma's car for four days, leaving her Richard's pickup to use while they're gone. David and Jess, Ben and Molly will hang around for a week, seeing childhood friends, sorting through boxes of their father's things, which Alma has piled up in the basement, making little dashes downstairs with another box of heartbreak whenever she feels brave enough. And then David and Ben will disappear from Alma's life, until she next hears from them, calls announcing their weddings, David's to Jess, and Ben's to Franny, two girlfriends down from Molly. But for now they are here, an indulgence to Alma, as she well knows.

All three boys and Alma had a ceremony last December on the property. They scattered Richard's ashes in the back field, near the spot where Alma once buried her antidepressants. Just this morning, they went out there again and placed the simple granite stone that has taken the stonecutter far too long to finish, a rectangle, the size of a shoe box, flat on the ground. The marker seems terse, but given Richard's message-machine habits, it suits him: RICHARD HUEBNER, his dates, then BELOVED. When she sells the house at the end of the sum-

mer and rents a condo closer to Tera, Alma will take the stone and the
tiny satchel of Richard's ashes that will be scattered with hers when
the time comes. She will place the stone on her desk, disrespectfully
using it as a trivet for her coffee cup, a place to set a vase of flowers,
a worry-bead-type object whose letters she will absently trace when
she sits at her desk writing down the story of Isabel, with whom she
will not lose faith.

Alma has also gone ahead and ordered a stone for Helen, and she
has asked the hospice team to ask Mickey where they might place it.
Helen's local church already had a service for her in January, and today the young minister, Reverend Don, and his wife, Linda, are along
on the hike. Alma supposes there will be at least a Lord's Prayer at
some point during the informal service. She will bow her head and feel
wistful. Helen's God is with Helen now. She will miss him.

Most nights when she wakes up in the middle of the night, Alma
strains, listening for any whisper, any dim communication from the
other side. *Hello? Are you there, Richard?* Nothing. Just the eyes that
look out at her in the dark and that Alma is learning to close with
promises and with Ambien. She has to get sleep, she has to get strong.
She is going back to the mountain project once the story of Isabel
is done. *We will come back; we will infect them with our questions.*

"How's Bolo?" she asks Emerson, who comes by regularly to see her.
"How're the patients?"

"The patients are okay. That doctora Heidi is terrific."

Hmm. Alma wonders if Emerson is hitting on la doctora. He has
gone down several times a month to check in on the Centro, which
Bienvenido is now directing. The clinic has been moved to the capital
and the vaccine trial is still continuing. Bolo is awaiting trial. Emerson
is helping by paying a good lawyer.

"You're a good guy, Emerson," she tells him the night before the hike
to Snake Mountain. They've gone up to Burlington together to pick up
Sam and Soraya at the airport, catching a bite at a nearby cafe. David
and Ben and girlfriends will probably be at the house by the time they
get back, having driven up from the city in a rented car.

Emerson looks down at his dish, a vegetable soup Alma talked him into ordering. The cafe does mostly soups, sandwiches, no booze. He feels responsible, Alma knows he does, though she has told him that he's not to blame and is only as responsible as any of them are at how desperate so many people in the world are. She is grateful for his help, coming at critical moments. She remembers the time he showed up at her door, her first day back full time at her house. She'd been down in the basement trying to hook up the water softener, using her little spiral notebook of instructions. She'd messed up, and there was water softener salt all over the basement. She'd sat down on the spare sack of softener and wept, self-indulgently wishing there was an entry in the spiral notebook for doing yourself in. Upstairs, she heard steps on the porch, pounding at the door. Oh no, Mickey! she had thought, wondering where to hide herself. That's when she realized: even without Richard, she wants to live, to write a book, to fall in love again, to learn to work the water softener.

"You don't have to finish it," she tells Emerson about the soup. A pall has come over them. Any moment now, Alma will burst into tears and Emerson, who specializes in trouble spots around the world, will not know what to say to her.

He checks his watch now, lifts a hand for the waitress to bring the check. He is afraid of her grief, most everyone is, except Helen, when she was alive, and Tera. Her stepsons have heard her blubbering on the phone so many times, including this time about the Snake Mountain plans. They cough and clear their throats, and soon most of their communications with Alma are through e-mails.

But here they are together on the mountaintop one last time. One advantage of climbing Snake Mountain on this tropical day: they've got the place to themselves. Alma's leg has healed, a faint purple scar she calls her fault line. Some days she feels a jab of pain at the spot, as she does now, maybe from the long hike, maybe from the imminence of a good-bye she is still not yet ready to say.

David and Claudine thank everyone for coming, then outline the service. Anyone who wants can say something about Helen or Richard, read a poem, tell an anecdote. The gathering will conclude with a prayer from Reverend Don, then the scattering of ashes.

David kicks off the stories. A funny memory, about his dad climbing Snake Mountain, calling out Hello! So the act preceded Alma, the details a little cleaned up, either because Richard might not have wanted to sound disturbingly disbelieving in front of his young boys or because one of those kids, now grown up, knows a minister is in their midst and he better keep his story passably Christian.

Stories abound. Claudine has several funny Helen escapades. Mickey in a kind of slow drawl—Alma wonders what medication he might be on—tells about the time Helen came to visit him when he was living in Guam. Alma had no idea. Helen in Guam! Except she got on the wrong plane. Ended up in Manila. Is he making this up? Alma looks over at him, and for a moment their eyes lock. They are Helen's eyes in his face, just as from Sam's face Richard's eyes stare back at her.

It's disconcerting seeing these vague traces of the people she loves in the people she fears or feels unsure about. How will Mickey turn out? she wonders, remembering how much Helen worried about what would become of her troubled son. Those last weeks in which Helen outlived Richard, Alma came down every day from Tera's to visit her. Alma still could not stand being in her own house, deluged with memories. Helen could tell something was wrong, and so Alma had told her. Helen's eyes had filled with tears. "Come here by me," she had said, patting a spot beside her on the hospital bed. And Alma had come and bowed her head into the old woman's shoulder, and together they had wept.

When Helen slipped into her coma, Alma sat by, waiting numbly for this next important departure. Occasionally, she had wet one of the little pink sponges the nurse had left in a glass and put it to the old woman's lips. The parched, toothless mouth would open and suck heartily. It was odd to feel that tug, that pull of reflex, that lusty will to live even in this comatose old woman. *Helen*, Alma whispered from time to time, *I love you, I'm here.* And a few times, to indulge Helen, to indulge herself, she told her old friend, *Say hello to Richard.*

Several times, especially as the wave of stories begins to die down, Alma thinks of speaking up. She has several anecdotes ready and a love poem she'd once written for Richard. But each time her heart, if not her mind, goes blank. Why did she think this was a good idea? Beyond in the haze, she can see the neat, husbanded little plots of land, the earth's horizon, curved and turning toward the south, where her family came from, where she lost Richard, where the world grows poorer and sicker. What can she say about these two beloved people in the face of that bigger vision?

Again that feeling wells up in her, an intuition, as the black-kerchief poet called it, and with it that story she has held on to for so long it is now the quivering little needle of her moral compass.

"Anyone else?" David, of course, is remembering that this was Alma's idea. Surely, she has something to say. His voice is tentative, gentle—that father gene did get passed on. But Alma has nothing to say or, rather, has a whole story to tell them, the story of Isabel, of how some people, real people, have kept faith no matter what, how she wishes that for all of them. But it feels as if the moment she says so, she will be closing down this baffling world with a homily soaked in her tears. Better let the reverend take it from here.

"Okay then, let's bow our heads in prayer," Reverend Don says, as if reading her mind.

After a handheld Our Father, the ashes are passed around. Two urns make the rounds. Alma wonders whose is Richard's? Helen's? She fills her hands, one fistful from each one. When the urns have gone full circle, the group lines up at the edge of the stony outcrop.

Alma feels as if she should make a wish, like blowing out candles, like seeing the first star in the sky. But she has entered a world where wishing would only return her to grief. She has to make a bigger leap, into a story that is not just a story, her own and not her own. Richard and Helen, Isabel and Balmis, the black-kerchief poet, Benito—they are inside her now, wanting her faith, needing her hope. So this is how the dead live on.

No one says, Now! but after the first person flings a handful, the others follow. There is no wind today, another good thing about it being hot, becalmed. The ashes fly out from all their hands—*floating on faith, floating on love*—blessing the ground.

# Further Reading and Acknowledgments

THIS NOVEL COULD NOT have been written without the immeasurable help and support of so many generous and special people.

First and foremost, my deepest appreciation to Catherine Mark, scientific editor at the CNB in Madrid, helper par excellence, for sending e-mails with needed details, dates, and oodles of encouragement. This trusting soul loaned a perfect stranger books from her ample Balmis collection, which books crossed the Atlantic twice, once here and then back. Her own translation of Gonzalo Díaz de Yraola's *The Spanish Royal Philanthropic Expedition: The Round-the-World Voyage of the Smallpox Vaccine, 1803–1810* (*La vuelta al mundo de la expedición de la vacuna, 1803–1810*), a facsimile of a 1948 edition (repr. Madrid: Instituto de Historia, Consejo Superior de Investigaciones Científicas, 2003), along with Michael Smith's *The "Real Expedición Marítima de la Vacuna" in New Spain and Guatemala*, Transactions of the American Philosophical Society, n.s. 64, pt. 1, (Philadelphia, 1974), are the two most thorough studies of the Balmis expedition in English. Also helpful are articles by John Z. Bowers, "The Odyssey of Smallpox Vaccination," *Bulletin of the History of Medicine* 55 (1981), 17–33; Sherbourne F. Cook, "Francisco Xavier Balmis and the Introduction of Vaccination in Latin America," *Bulletin of the History of Medicine* 11 (1942): 543–60 and 12 (1942): 70–101; as well as various articles by José Rigau-Pérez, who specializes in the Puerto Rican fiasco.

Special thanks also to Professor Ricardo Guerrero, whom I had the good fortune to meet as I was touring Galicia, for his gift of Gonzalo Díaz de Yraola's book, which led me to befriend its translator, Catherine Mark. To other Balmis aficionados in Spain, including Manuel Prada and José Luís Barona, who kindly answered my queries, and José Tuells, whose book is listed below, muchas gracias and many thanks. Also my thanks to Tom Colvin for information concerning Mexican and Philippine portions of the journey.

Closer to home in my own stomping grounds of Middlebury, Vermont, many thanks to Rachel Manning of Middlebury College's Interlibrary Loan Department, who brings the world's treasures here for us to study. To her and to Joy Pile and the wonderful staff at this library, I owe my deepest appreciation and gratitude. To the incomparable Paul Monod, professor of history, for his good humor and patience with all my tireless questions. And to John Quinn, for his legal help with my troublemakers.

Also to the extraordinary nurses of Addison County Home Health & Hospice and to Dr. Chris Nunnink, for taking the time to help me. To M. H., and her family, for blessing me with your precious time and friendship!

Many thanks to Brian Simpson, editor of *Johns Hopkins Public Health Magazine*, and Suzanne Fogt, then working at the Sustainable Enterprise Program, World Resources Institute, for their help on current world epidemics, biological terrorism, and on the increasingly desperate situation of so many of the world's poor. Jessica Hagedorn and Luis Francia kindly added to my knowledge of late-colonial Philippine history and lore; Liliana Valenzuela stepped in with Mexican history expertise.

As for making my novel seaworthy (all sea lingo and wind direction errors are mine), I want to thank the intrepid Joan Druett, whose wonderful books on sailing, most especially, *Hen Frigates* (New York: Simon & Schuster, 1998), acquainted this landlubber with a watery world she knew nothing about. To Brian Andrews and Deidre O'Regan, who loaned me books and arranged for me to go aboard the *Spirit of Massachusetts* and experience seasickness firsthand: many thanks. And to Herb and Shayna Loeffler, whom I met aboard the *Spirit*, for answering any number of tedious questions on board and later by phone and e-mail, thank you both.

I owe a special thanks to Dr. Ellen Koenig, for educating me about the AIDS crisis in the Dominican Republic. Her clinic in the capital is far and away the best treatment center for AIDS in the country. I want briefly to acknowledge her work here. At a time when very few Dominican physicians dared sully their practices by treating those with this "pariah" disease, Dr. Koenig, then a comfortable American woman in her forties married to a Dominican businessman, decided to earn a medical degree in order to tend to those in such dire need. Thank you and your assistant, Dr. Carlos Adon, for taking time out to accompany me to other needy clinics and for persevering in running a first-rate care facility for AIDS patients in the Dominican Republic. There are Isabels afoot in this world! It is an honor and a privilege to know you.

In commemoration of the recent Balmis bicentennial, several books have been published in the last few years, all of them in Spanish: two by Susana Ramírez, who probably knows more than anyone about the smallpox expedition and has been writing for years on the subject: *La salud del imperio: La real expedición filantrópica de la vacuna* (Madrid: Fundación Jorge Juan, Ediciones Doce Calles, 2002) and, along with coauthor José Tuells, *Balmis et variola* (Valencia: Generalitat Valenciana, Conselleria de Sanitat, 2003); Emilio Balaguer Perigüell and Rosa Ballester Añón's *En el nombre de los niños: La Real Expedición Filantrópica de la Vacuna* (1803–1806) (Monografías de la Asociación Española de Pediatría, 2003; electronic book available at http://www.aeped.es/balmis/libro.balmis.htm); Juan Carlos Herrera Hermosilla's *El sueño ilustrado: Biografía de Francisco Javier de Balmis* (Ediciones Paracelso, s.l., 2003). Earlier studies include the aforementioned Díaz de Yraola's book as well as Francisco Fernandez del Castillo's *Los viajes de Don Francisco Xavier de Balmis* (Mexico: Galas de Mexico, S.A., 1960). There is also a wonderful booklet put out by the Alicante Rotary Club/Fundación Dr. Balmis, *Balmis y los héroes de la vacuna: Expedición Filantrópica a América y Filipinas, 1803*. In addition, a new anthology of articles by Balmis experts from around the world, edited by Susana Ramírez, *La Real Expedición Filantrópica de la Vacuna: Doscientos años de lucha contra la viruela*, will soon be available from Consejo Superior de Investigaciones Científicas in Madrid, Spain.

The novel's Isabel chapters follow closely the trajectory and main events of the royal expedition. But the creation of character and circumstance based on these historical personages is my own invention. Isabel, under several surnames, was indeed the rectoress of the orphanage in La Coruña and was the only woman to accompany the expedition. Her adopted son, Benito, was one of the original twenty-two carriers. Only twenty-one are named in the official documents, thus the license to invent Orlando. Isabel did go on to the Philippines with the twenty-six Mexican boys, returning two years later to Mexico, and settling down finally with Benito in Puebla de los Ángeles, the City of the Angels.

In addition to Isabel's original twenty-two carriers, hundreds of children, slaves, military recruits, and other adults donated their arms to the cause. Without their contribution the chain of vaccinations would have been broken.

Thanks are also due to my dear editor, Shannon Ravenel, who fortunately is not at all like Alma's editor and whose faith in the journey of discovery that every novel entails kept me going on stormy days when my faith was tempest-tossed and my craft lost at sea. And to my feisty agent and faithful friend, Susan Bergholz, who—ditto—is thankfully not at all like the Lavinia in these pages, my gratitude for making it possible for me to do my work, for never losing faith.

Virgencita de la Altagracia, gracias for so many blessings, not least among them the opportunity to learn from and befriend the special people named and appreciated in these acknowledgments.

# BOYS FROM LA CORUÑA, SPAIN, TO PUERTO RICO
## (VIA CANARY ISLANDS)

Pascual Aniceto (age 3)

Cándido (age 7)

Clemente (age 6)

José Jorge Nicolás de los Dolores (age 5)

Vicente Ferrer (age 7)

Francisco Antonio (age 9)

Juan Francisco (age 9)

Francisco Florencio (age 5)

Jacinto (age 6)

José (age 3)

Juan Antonio (age 5)

Gerónimo María (age 7)

José Manuel María (age 6)

Manuel María (age 5)

Martín (age 5)

Tomás Melitón (age 5)

Domingo Naya (age 6)

Andrés Naya (age 8)

Vicente María Sale y Bellido (age 5)

Benito Vélez

Antonio Veredia (age 7)

Unknown boy

# MEXICAN BOYS TO MANILA, PHILIPPINES

Juan Nepomuceno Forrescano (age 6)

Juan José Santa María (age 5)

Josef Antonio Marmolejo (age 5)

Josef Silverio Ortiz (age 5)

Laureano Reyes (age 6)

Josef María Lorechaga (age 5 )

Josef Agapito Yllán (age 5)

Josef Feliciano Gómez (age 6)

Josef Lino Velázquez (age 5)

Josef Mauricio Macías (age 5)

Josef Ignacio Nájera (age 5)

Josef María Ursula (age 5)

Teófilo Romero (age 6)

Félix Barraza (age 5)

Josef Mariano Portillo (age 6)

Martín Marqués (age 4)

Josef Antonio Salazar (age 5)

Pedro Nolasco Mesa (age 5)

Josef Dolores Moreno (age 14)

Juan Amador Castañeda (age 6)

Josef Felipe Osorio Moreno (age 6)

Josef Francisco (age 6)

Josef Catalino Rivera (age 6)

Buenaventura Safiro (age 4)

Josef Teodoro Olivas (age 5)

Guillermo Toledo Pino (age 5)